Silent Walls, Speaking Stones

A Novel

Nishi Chawla

First printing, November 2025
Library of Congress Control Number: *pending*
ISBN 978-1-965784-28-0 Hardback
ISBN 978-1-965784-29-7 Paperback

Cover Art, Design & Typography by **Kurt Lovelace**
Cover *Bauhaus Dessau* **Alfarn** by Céline Hurka, Elia Preuss,
Flavia Zimbardi, Hidetaka Yamasaki, and Luca Pellegrini.
Body & Chapter Titles set in **No 9T**
Headers in **Jenson** by Robert Slimbach
Flourishes set in Emigre Foundry **Dalliance**, by Frank Heine
Emigre Foundry **ZeitGuys**, by Bob Aufuldish, Eric Donelan
Typefaces licensed Adobe, Linotype, & URW GmbH

PierianSpringsPress.Com
PIERIAN SPRINGS PRESS, INC
30 N GOULD ST, STE 25398
SHERIDAN, WYOMING 82801-6317

"Is there a space where both worlds can coexist within me, or must I forever choose one to silence the other?"

"For every crumbled stone, I dream of planting a seed; for every shattered belief, I envision a place where faiths can coexist without fear of collapse."

Contents

Chapter 1 | 1
Chapter 2 | 19
Chapter 3 | 39
Chapter 4 | 61
Chapter 5 | 77
Chapter 6 | 95
Chapter 7 | 115
Chapter 8 | 135
Chapter 9 | 153
Chapter 10 | 171
Chapter 11 | 187
Chapter 12 | 203
Chapter 13 | 223
Chapter 14 | 243
Chapter 15 | 263
Chapter 16 | 279
Chapter 17 | 291
Chapter 18 | 307
Chapter 19 | 325
Chapter 20 | 343
Chapter 21 | 359
Chapter 22 | 383
Epilogue | 397

ABOUT THE AUTHOR | 411

Silent Walls, Speaking Stones

1

In Ayodhya and in its troubled soils—where gods have walked and empires have crumbled into dust—I was born on December 6, 1992. I am Saanvi Trivedi, a child of two faiths, bearing the ancestral weight of my birth city carved by devotion and division alike. My Muslim mother carried her faith like a whispered *ayah* of the Qur'an, soft and steadfast beneath her breath. My Hindu father moved through life with Ram's name etched into the rhythm of his own. Their love was forged in the fires of defiance and noncompliance—an intimate rebellion against inherited boundaries and the invisible fences drawn by tradition. It was a quiet subversion of cultural expectations and religious conformity, daring to imagine a life beyond the communal lines that have long scarred this ancient city into wounds of difference. Now, as I stand by the banks of the Sarayu river, on this hallowed ground where temples and mosques rise like rival prayers and have whispered contempt to each other, I ask myself: Is there a space where both worlds can coexist within me, or must I forever choose one to silence the other? Can both truths live within me without demanding the exile of the other? Or must I silence one faith to give voice to the other?

Growing up in Ayodhya, a city where history is not just a story but a living, breathing entity, has meant that I was always acutely aware of the legacy of split faith that has defined my no-identity. And to confuse further this sense of no-identity, this hyphenated Hindu-Muslim lack of clear identity, is the knowledge that my family has carried within it the history of not just one, but two generations of interfaith unions. That is to say, and to further complicate my sense of my split and divided identity, this hyphenated existence of being neither fully Hindu nor Muslim, is the knowledge that my family's long history is woven not from just one, but from two and maybe more, generations of serial interfaith unions. Entangling my already splintered self is the inherited history of layered hybridity, where each generation has deepened this liminal identity, a lineage not cleanly claimed by either tradition, yet shaped by both. Each generation adds another layer to this blurred line, this bordered identity, where faith and devotion and heritage have intertwined, leaving me adrift in a space where neither faith fully claims me, yet both shape who I am. My grandparents, my parents, and now as I stand here on the banks of the Sarayu river—represent the ambiguous generations born from the intricate weaving of Hindu and Muslim lives. With each passing generation, the burden felt increasingly weighty, a palpable heaviness that has pressed down on our collective consciousness. It was as if the complexities of our hyphenated identity, woven from threads of Hindu and Muslim heritage, have accumulated like dust on a forgotten shelf and almost obscured the muted colors of our convoluted and blended lineage. Each generation had inherited, not the peace and joy of interfaith union, but the baggage of nameless struggles, the unspoken fears, and the silent and unwritten expectations that came with them. The weight of history, intertwined with the intricate trajectory of love and conflict, seems to grow more intricate and suffocating, challenging our very essence and leaving us to grapple with the shadows of our ancestors' choices. I wrestle with my identity at some moments and let go in others. My own mother, her mother and my grandmother before her, had straddled the challenges of worlds that had often seemed irreconcilable. The question of my fluid identity has, as a result, become more complex and even more questionable. I, Saanvi, can only bear the weight of that knowledge that I belong nowhere.

As I grew older, I began to realize that the question I had been asking was not just about Ayodhya, but about myself. Could I, the only child of a Hindu father and a Muslim mother, truly belong to both worlds? Or would I always have to choose? My father raised me with a strong Hindu identity, teaching me the traditions, prayers, and rituals that he hoped would shape my own worldview. For him, there was no ambiguity. I was a Hindu and followed a lineage he held deeply in his heart. Of course, he was aware of the complex family dynamic that my mother's Muslim faith had embedded in me. Although he, Ramesh, and my mother, Yasmin Khan, always chose their own individual paths, it was partly because Yasmin refused to convert, and also out of a quiet respect for each other's beliefs. That gave me the rare gift of freedom, allowing me to witness both faiths closely. I was shaped by two worlds, each rich with its own philosophy and unspoken truths. My father's Hinduism was a landscape of devotion and tradition while my mother's Islam whispered a quieter, more introspective faith. In the spaces between, I wandered, not bound by one but exploring both, never pressured to choose by my parents, who, despite their differences, always nurtured my right to find my own path. But I suspect that my father's so-called freedom wasn't just a gift; his passion for his political career, his fear of rebelling against his own family, and God knows what other unspoken fears may have also played their part in giving me the space to explore. Perhaps this 'freedom' was less about liberality and more about his own careful maneuvering, avoiding the confrontation he feared. It so turned out that I had the chance to experience two worlds, rich with distinct practices and philosophies, providing a unique foundation for my own journey and my own personal identity. Though divided by faith, my parents offered me unwavering love. They never forced me to choose. They had allowed me to explore both faiths, to find my own spiritual path. But as I entered adolescence, the subtle freedom I had once enjoyed began to erode, and the pressure to choose became more pronounced, casting a shadow over the tranquility I had once known. My friends, my teachers, even strangers in the street, would sometimes ask me pointblank: Are you Hindu or Muslim? I would sometimes feel embarrassed by the question. At first, I had tried to brush off the question, to pretend that it didn't matter. But the truth was that it did matter. It mattered to the people around me, and it mattered to me. I began to feel as though I were living a double life. At home, I wore the mantle of the dutiful daughter with practiced grace—responsible, restrained, and bound by a loyalty I never dared to question. The first twelve years of my life unfolded in my father's household, where Diwali was observed with quiet reverence, flickering lamps casting long shadows on the walls of our silences. Then came the shift, a boarding school nestled in the hush of the Himalayas. And sometimes, when my mother, Yasmin, gently asked my father, I would mark

Eid in her modest home, just the three of us—she, my always silent grandmother Amina Khan, and I—drawing warmth from ritual, memory, and a grief we never named, as my mother recited verses from the Quran in a voice both tremulous and steady, as though stitching torn histories together. Outside the home and in my boarding school, I felt like a stranger in both worlds and in my dual existence.

It was during this time that I began to seek out answers in the sacred texts of both faiths. I tried to read the Quran and the Bhagavad Gita, searching for some kind of common ground, some place where both worlds could meet. But the more I read, the more confused I became. For every passage that spoke of love and unity, there was another that spoke of division and difference.

Now, as I stand on this sacred ground where temples and mosques once whispered in hostility to each other and in contiguous silence, I ask: Is there a space where both worlds can coexist within me, or must I forever choose one to silence the other? Ayodhya as a city has not changed much since my childhood. The streets are still filled with the sounds of chanting and prayer, the air still thick with the scent of incense and the call to prayer. But the divisions run deeper now, the wounds more visible. As I walk through the streets of Ayodhya, I think about the legacy my parents have left me. They chose physical passion and love over division, and sought unity over the shadows of fear, defying the boundaries that sought to keep them apart. But in doing so, they also left me with a question that I have yet to answer. My parents have bequeathed me with a question that lingers in the air like an unanswered prayer: Can two faiths, two worlds, truly coexist within one person?

Ayodhya, a city revered in both Hindu and Islamic traditions, holds within its ancient walls the stories of gods and emperors, the ebb and flow of faith and politics, and the continuous struggle for a normative identity. According to established Hindu belief, the city is the birthplace of Lord Rama, an incarnation of the divine. Its streets echo with tales of epic battles from the *Ramayana*, a cornerstone of Hindu mythology. Temples dot the landscape, standing as monuments to devotion and a reminder of the countless generations that have walked these sacred paths in search of spiritual fulfillment.

And yet, the history of Ayodhya is not solely defined by its pronounced Hindu heritage and its Hindu population. I well know that over the centuries, Muslims have also made their mark on this ancient city. It is said that with the arrival of the Mughal Empire in the sixteenth century, a wave of cultural and architectural transformation had swept through the land. Amidst the fervor of devotion, mosques and elegant Islamic structures began to rise, their intricate designs adding another layer to the city's complex identity. I imagine the artisans and craftsmen of that era, pouring their souls into the stone and marble, creating a legacy that still resonates in the hearts of those like me who have walked these streets. As I wander through the winding streets of Ayodhya, I can almost feel the echoes of history whispering around me. The Babri Masjid, built by Emperor Babur, and struck down the day I was born, was once a significant landmark in Ayodhya. The blending of diverse religious veins and cultures has created a unique historical narrative in Ayodhya, where the sacredness of both Hindu and Muslim traditions coexists. The stories of these two communities intertwine, shaping a landscape rich in both spiritual significance and cultural complexity. Even the Jains, with their reverence for all living beings, have long held a place in this city, their temples whispering tales of non-violence and compassion. I have sometimes seen Jain monks in their simple white robes, walking barefoot through the narrow lanes of Ayodhya with a serenity that feels almost elemental. Their presence—quiet, ascetic, unselfconscious—seems to recall an older rhythm of the city, one that predates its political tumult. Few remember that Ayodhya is not only the birthplace of Lord Rama but also of Rishabhanatha, the first Tirthankara of the Jains, and four others who followed. For centuries, Jain pilgrims have come here to honor that sacred lineage. In the stillness of these monks, I sense an echo of that other Ayodhya—less spoken of, yet equally rooted in the soil.

And then, there are the faint but enduring traces of Buddhism—an ancient faith that once shaped the intellectual and spiritual contours of this land. I often imagine the measured pace of monks moving through early morning light, their thoughts attuned not to doctrine, but to silence and inner clarity. Perhaps they once paused by the Sarayu's edge—not to worship, but to observe, to listen, to let the river mirror their own impermanence. In Ayodhya's layered textures—its weathered walls, its mingled tongues—I have come to understand that spirituality resists definition. It is not fixed, but refracted through memory, culture, and the quiet urgencies of the self. Whether in a whispered invocation, a slow procession, or the hush of solitary reflection, I begin to sense not difference, but kinship—a kind of human consonance that dissolves the illusion of division.

Ayodhya's history is also marred by deep conflict. In the sixteenth century, after the Mughal Emperor Babur had built the Babri Masjid, the mosque would become a flashpoint for deep religious tension in the years to come. The mosque's construction was both a testimony to Islamic faith and a source of contention among Hindus who believed it was built on the ruins of a temple dedicated to Lord Rama. This belief sowed the seeds of division that would fester for centuries, culminating in the tragic events when the mosque was demolished by a frenzied mob on the day that I was born. The aftermath was a violent eruption of communal riots, a heartbreaking reminder of how faith can fracture relationships, families, and communities.

As I navigate these historical layers, I am struck by the realization that my divided identity makes me stand out even more profoundly in a world often eager to categorize and segregate. The inheritances I carry from my parents are not just spiritual, but lived, etched into the fabric of our fractured togetherness. Their love was never loud; it endured quietly, in defiance of the partitions that others insisted should separate them. My mother, Yasmin, has often spoken of the anchoring stillness she finds in prayer. I have watched her perform namaz with the calm of someone who understands silence as strength. During Ramadan, she would invite me, gently but persistently, to witness the grace of *iftar*—where restraint gives way to shared nourishment. Compassion and community were not abstract ideals to her; they were a discipline. My father, Ramesh, moved through devotion differently. He taught me that belief is not passive. He believed in festivals not as rituals, but as collective affirmations of presence and joy. His voice would soften when speaking of the *diyas* lit at Diwali, or the sacred murmur of mantras before dawn. He believed faith must step out into the world and shape it gently, not thunder over it. Between them, I learned that faith is not a fortress, but a bridge—precarious, yes, but necessary.

And yet, this is not how the world perceives it. I find myself perplexed when others struggle to accept my dual faith and identity, as if the love and teachings of my parents are somehow insufficient to bridge the chasm that divides us. In a world that often demands clear-cut definitions, my existence feels like a contradiction to many. I have faced whispered judgments and disapproving glances almost as if I should wear my mother's hijab during Ramadan, only to be met with confusion when I refuse to light *diyas* on Diwali. To some folks, my mixed identity is a source of discomfort, a reminder of the complexities they would rather ignore or gloss over. Their anxiety seems overshadowed by a desire for clean lines, for singularity, for either this or that, leaving me questioning my place in a society that favors boundaries over bridges. It weighs heavily on my heart that I am expected to choose one path over another when both have shaped my spirit. I long for a world where my unique blend of faiths and intertwined beliefs could be understood and accepted instead of scrutinized, where the essence of my upbringing could bridge gaps rather than widen them. Sometimes I imagine gathering people into a space where food and faith do not compete, but quietly recognize one another. Yet, the reality remains that my identity is often reduced to a point of contention rather than stay a cornerstone of my strength. I grapple with the reality that is my two faced life, as it were.

If I had grown up in a city like Mumbai—or perhaps somewhere in the West—my identity might not have felt so fraught. In those sprawling, supposedly modern cities, diversity is not just tolerated but paraded, even if imperfectly. Perhaps, my identity would have been better accepted. People of different faiths, accents, and ancestries move through shared spaces, weaving their lives into something that at least aspires to inclusiveness. In such places, my dual heritage might not have been scrutinized or treated as contradiction. It might have been seen for what it is: a composite truth, both fragile and resilient, held together by memory and hope. In such spaces, my dual faith might not be a point of contention but rather a reflection of the melting pot that many tout as their defining feature. The modern world's mantra of inclusivity would likely embrace my experience as part of the chimera called multiculturalism, where my duality could be seen as an asset rather than a liability.

In these modern, so-called secular towns, where Hindu temples and mosques share the skyline, where festivals from both faiths light up the streets in a display of togetherness, perhaps my identity would not raise an eyebrow. There are sights and smells and sounds that make these spaces feel alive. Perhaps, I would have felt less alone than in my own hometown of Ayodhya. I picture myself walking those streets, my footsteps tapping over stones worn smooth by centuries of shared history. The smell of marigolds lingers in the air during Hindu festivals, mingling harmoniously with the enticing aroma of *biryanis* and *kebabs* sold at stalls during Eid. It may be a façade, but at least, there is a display, a gesture towards coexistence. The streets echo with laughter and music—Bollywood hits played during Diwali celebrations alongside the solemn, rhythmic calls to prayer during Ramadan. Perhaps in these places where *diyas* glow alongside crescent moon decorations, and children of all faiths chase one another through clouds of Holi color, my identity would not be questioned. I imagine myself walking through such streets, the stones beneath my feet smoothened by centuries of coexistence, and catch snippets of conversations in Hindi, Urdu, and even English. These imagined towns shimmer with an almost utopian glow, yet they are grounded in the mundane reality of chai stalls, bustling markets, and the cacophony of honking cars and vendors calling out their wares. In their diversity, these towns embody a quiet rebellion against division, a reminder of what is possible when people choose connection over conflict. Amid the din, there's a certain quiet, a kind of unspoken defiance against fracture. Even if this coexistence is sometimes more performance than reality, the gesture itself matters. It creates the possibility of something finer, more whole. In these towns, diversity is not a slogan but a daily negotiation, messy and unfinished. People would see me here as simply another person navigating the complexity of faith, like the many others who partake in the traditions of multiple communities without the harsh judgments that I sometimes face in less progressive spaces. And in that, perhaps, I would have found room to simply be.

In the West, where the ideals of freedom and self-expression reign, my dual faith is an example of the modern, hybrid identity that defines a new generation of individuals who resist simple categorization. They admire my ability to navigate multiple worlds, viewing my upbringing as a testament to the power of pluralism and tolerance. It seems performative and somewhat unanalyzed sometimes, but then.... Deep down, even in these cities that pride themselves on openness, I know there would still be questions—questions of curiosity rather than judgment, perhaps, but questions nonetheless. They would ask how I reconcile the different worlds within me, how I navigate the competing demands of two religions, two cultures. And still, I would find myself explaining, still offering glimpses into the quiet beauty and layered complexity of my existence. In the end, even in these places that seem more accepting, I would face the same challenge of translating my dual identity in a way that resonates with others, making them see it not as a puzzle, but as a story of love, of coexistence, and of faith.

Would it be easier? Perhaps. Would it be less complicated? I doubt it. For wherever I go, there will always be those who prefer the comfort and certainty of one path over the uncertainty of two, who fear the ambiguity of standing in two worlds at once. They prefer boundaries—clean, unmuddied—over the effort it takes to build a bridge. But maybe, just maybe, in these more modern cities, I would find a few more souls who understand the beauty of walking two roads at once, who understand what it means to hold contradictions without apology. For them, and for me, walking two roads is not a burden but a quiet kind of strength—a way of weaving together histories, faiths, and selves. The journey becomes the bridge, and wholeness lies not in choosing, but in embracing the fullness of all that I am.

Growing up between their two worlds, I would never have felt so divided. I would not have felt the need to bear the stamp of any single faith. And I have progressively come to understand that I do not need rituals, prayers, and the daily practices of any one religion to understand the world around me. I only feel distressed when I encounter a different world—a world that seems to find my dual identity perplexing, even unsettling. I am only uncomfortable with the weight of whispered judgments, the stares, the uncomfortable silences that fill rooms when I introduce myself. At times, I've noticed people shift, their eyes darting away, as if afraid to see the fluidity of my beliefs. To them, I am a contradiction, often a living paradox they don't know how to place or categorize. Their eyes widen, and I can feel the walls in their minds rise, cold and silent, whenever they see me engage with both sides of my heritage. My very existence, it seems, challenges their need for singularity, for neat divisions that offer the comfort of simplicity. There are moments when I wish I could share the ease with which I carry both faiths, each enriching my world and giving it depth, my acceptance of living with two faiths that shape my world and fill it with meaning. But when I try, my words often meet resistance, the discomfort evident as they change the subject or offer tight smiles, as if uneasy with the reminder that faith, like life, can be many things at once.

I grapple with the isolation that this sometimes brings—the feeling that my identity is seen as a complication, a point of contention rather than a bridge. There is a quiet ache in explaining myself that feels as instinctive as heartbeat, as undeniable as dawn breaking over the ancient stones of Ayodhya. It weighs on my heart that I am asked, implicitly or explicitly, to choose one path over the other, as if my upbringing is somehow at odds with the world's need for certainty. To embrace one faith fully, in their eyes, is to erase the other—and yet, both are woven into my soul, threads of a single cloth that I cannot and do not wish to separate.

My parents, as if sensing the weight I carry, had always told me separately and in their own unique ways, that I am the living bridge between worlds that others struggle to unite. I cling to this, to the memory of their quiet strength, whenever I feel the scrutiny that surrounds me. I feel my identity splinter under the weight of others' expectations, and I wonder if the world will ever allow me to be whole. In rare, unguarded moments, I catch glimpses of a quiet beauty, a gentle assurance that my path may not be one of conformity but of quiet defiance—an invitation for others to see that truth rests not in dissolving differences, but in honoring them. Ayodhya, with its centuries layered in faith and fracture, its echoes of gods and saints, warriors and pilgrims, becomes a mirror of my own spirit—a landscape of contrasts, beauty and scars intertwined, holding within it the fragile potential for reconciliation, if only one dared to seek it.

And so, in the fading glow of twilight, as the evening *aarti* hums in the background and the waters of the Sarayu ripple like molten copper, I find myself drawn to the edge of the river. The temple bells chime in rhythmic succession, their sound mingling with the faint call of the *muezzin* from a nearby mosque. For a fleeting moment, the cacophony of Ayodhya's discordant histories melds into a harmony that feels like a whisper of possibility.

This river, which carries the weight of millennia, also carries the weight of my father's voice—not in words, but in the pauses, in the spaces where meaning hangs heavy. Ramesh Trivedi, the retired college lecturer turned political crusader who built his career upholding ideals of unity, now seems to be a man battling shadows he refuses to name. I remember the intensity of his gaze at breakfast one morning, the way his knuckles turned white as he gripped the newspaper. It carried yet another inflammatory headline: "Ayodhya's Wounds, Still Bleeding." He didn't speak. He rarely does when it comes to the town that made and could unmake him. But I have come to recognize the way his silence burns. I can never forget the afternoon when my paternal grandfather had pulled his only child, his son, Ramesh Trivedi aside, his fingers tight around his shoulder, and said to him: "Politics is a dance, Ramesh. You will learn to step in rhythm with it, or you will be swept away." He had taken the lesson to heart. As a young man, Ramesh had watched his lawyer father navigate the churning waters of Ayodhya's political landscape with the precision of a seasoned dancer. He had watched him become a figure to be feared, respected, and, when necessary, adored. But there was always a tension beneath the surface, a weight that pulled at Ramesh's chest when he looked at his father's stern face, when he saw the way his eyes darted nervously when old friends came to visit.

For as long as I can remember, my father's public persona has been one of unshakable convictions, whether it was in his teaching career or his political one. Yet, in private, there are cracks. As a child, I once wandered into his study and saw him staring at an old photograph. It was of a woman I quite recognized, her eyes brimming with a quiet sadness. When I asked him to show me the photo again, he snapped the album shut and told me to go play outside. But that fleeting glimpse of vulnerability left its mark on me. It was the first time I sensed that my father's strength was a carefully constructed illusion, one that hid a lifetime of compromise and loss.

Over the years, as my father's career had taken off, so did the silences in our home. I saw my father become someone else, someone consumed by the very apparatus he had built. But I cannot quite shake the feeling that, at the heart of it all, my father had never truly let go. His abiding and deep love for my mother, Yasmin Khan, the hidden affair and marriage—was it the thing that had shaped the man my father had become? I could sense how my father, Ramesh Trivedi, would always feel the weight of his own decisions. Should he continue to walk the path his own father, Shyam Trivedi, had laid before him? Should he pretend the past never existed, or should he carve his own path—one not bound by the invisible threads of a secret long buried? Ayodhya, he knew, was never just a city. It was a mirror to his own soul. The more he looked at it, the more it reflected back his own contradictions, his own longing to be free from the burdens his father had placed upon him. Yet, in his heart, he knew this was the place where his fate would be decided. The city's streets—etched with the echoes of history, the cries of devotion, and the silent wounds of a love he had always sustained—became the very stage upon which my father's drama would unfold. And in that act, Ramesh was not just a bystander. He was a part of the performance, unwilling or unable to break free.

His wife, Yasmin Khan, had never been part of their family's story, her presence obscured by the political machinery my father had built. Yet, in the quiet moments when my father thought no one was watching, I had seen the tenderness in his eyes, almost like a photograph surfacing from a forgotten album. Those were the stolen moments, small glimpses of a love that had never seen the light of day but would always be there for Yasmin, the woman who would always hold my father's heart, the woman who never fit the mold of my father's political circle. In my childhood, I had wondered about the whispers surrounding my mother who we visited every weekend, the woman whose absence would always loom over our house, our Trivedi mansion. Yasmin Khan was not a name often spoken aloud; it was a name uttered only in hushed tones, when my father was not present, when the walls seemed to lean in and listen. That was before I understood the full cost of my father's political ambitions, before he himself knew the price of loyalty in a world so tangled in lies. My mother, Yasmin, will remain an enigma I've never been allowed to fully understand. I was taken away from her as an infant, and have only known her through weekends together and mostly fleeting encounters. She writes in flowing, poetic Urdu, her words laden with longing and regret. She sometimes feels like a shadow in my life, as much a part of my story as the land of Ayodhya itself—ever-present yet always just out of reach, though my heart tells me she is still very close to me.

Tonight, as the moon rises over the ghats, its pale

light illuminating the steps worn smooth by centuries of footsteps, I think of her. I think of the sacrifices she made and the price she paid for loving a man who loved her as much in return, but who could never quite give her the life she deserved. Their story, like the story of Ayodhya, is one of irreconcilable differences. Yet, within the cracks of their fragile and complicated relationship, there exists a truth that neither of them can deny: that love, like faith, is not meant to erase differences but to hold them with tenderness and respect.

The air is thick with the smell of dust and promise. The city of Ayodhya has always been a place of paradoxes: sacred yet turbulent, ancient yet alive with the fire of modern politics. For generations, the city had cradled the mythic and the mundane in equal measure, both sanctifying its streets and staining them. I have grown up in its shadows, a child molded by the very contradictions the city exhaled. As a child, I had believed that life was as simple as the stories I was told, stories of gods and kings, of heroes and villains. But as I grew up, the layers of complexity have become impossible to ignore. My father, a politician whose name is now known in every corner of the city, has made sure to grapple with and understand the game of appearances. To appear unwavering in conviction, even when one's soul is bent and broken. To smile even when the heart is bruised, and to keep secrets closer than one's own skin.

I dip my fingers into the river's cool waters and close my eyes, letting the weight of the day slip away. The voices of pilgrims blend with the distant chants of monks, creating a symphony that feels both timeless and ephemeral. In this moment, I feel a strange sense of clarity. Ayodhya's wounds may be deep, but they are not beyond healing. The same is true of my own family.

When I open my eyes, the world feels sharper, more

vivid. The stars above seem to burn brighter, as if urging me to take the first step toward reconciliation—not with my mother or my father, but with myself. I stand and begin to walk along the riverbank, the sound of my footsteps mingling with the gentle lapping of the water. Each step feels like a declaration, a silent promise to seek the truth, no matter how uncomfortable or painful it may be.

Ayodhya is not just a place. It is a state of being, a reminder that within every conflict lies the potential for change and transformation. As I make my way back toward the heart of the town, where the streets throb with life and the air is thick with the smells of incense and hope, I know that my journey is only beginning.

The first few chapters of my life have been written in the language of division and silence. But tonight, under the watchful gaze of the moon, I resolve to write the next few in the language of strength and connection. And so, with Ayodhya as my witness, I step into the unknown, ready to embrace the contradictions that define me and the land I call home. But what, after all, is identity? Is it the name we are given or the one we choose to claim? Is it the language of our ancestors or the silence we carry inside? Can the truth of who we are to be found in bloodlines, borders, or belief? Or does it shift, like memory, like myth, with each telling? Whose version of the truth holds sway? What happens when identity is fractured—by history, by exile, by love? And if we wear many selves, which one will survive the telling? Where, then, does the truth truly lie? In the facts we inherit, or in the fictions we make of them. Is the divine diminished when we choose to see it only through one lens, one God, one story?

2

In the ancient city of Ayodhya—where gods once walked, where empires rose and crumbled into dust— I, Saanvi, took my first breath. A child born of two faiths, two worlds long at odds, I carry within me not only the blood of my parents but the burden of a history etched into the very soil of this land. From the beginning, I carried more than just a name. I carried inheritance. A daughter of two faiths, of two histories never allowed to rest side by side, I came into the world already marked— by love, by conflict, by the uneasy lineage of devotion and defiance. Ayodhya is no ordinary city. It is a force, a memory made visible in crumbling facades. It is not merely a setting. It holds its stories in stone and dust, stories that refuse to fade. Every wall, every path remembers what it has witnessed—devotion, division, violence. It breathes through its stones, murmurs through its shrines, and remembers every wound of division. In the fragile union of my mother and father, I was shaped, tempered and forged by reverence and rebellion, sanctity and sorrow. A child not just of love, but of contradiction. Is there a space within me vast enough to hold both truths? Is there a language in which both halves of me can speak without being erased? Can I be whole without forever being pulled between what was and what cannot be? Or am I destined, like this city, to remain divided—forever caught between the echo of a question and the silence of an answer? I ask: Is there a space where both worlds can coexist within me, or must I forever choose one to silence the other? Must I choose? Or is there still a space where both worlds—faiths, histories, bloodlines—might live together, not in harmony perhaps, but in honest, uneasy coexistence?

My mother, Yasmin Khan's water broke on that fatal day in 1992. On the morning of December 6, 1992, the sky over Ayodhya was a peculiar shade of steel-grey, as though it too sensed the weight of the events that were about to unfold. The air was tense, saturated with the anticipation of something monumental, a silence that felt unnatural for the time of day. My mother had felt this heaviness deep in her bones as she stood in her small kitchen, clutching her swollen belly, the blue flame of the gas stove flickering beneath a somewhat battered pot, casting her face in a soft, wavering glow. Her breath came in shallow gasps, and her fingers shook as she absently rubbed the curve of her abdomen. The baby was restless today, as if sensing the world outside would be different from the one it had known in the womb.

The distant roar of voices reached her ears, growing louder by the minute. First, it was a low hum, but soon it swelled into a cacophony of anger, fervor, and zeal. Men, thousands of them, had gathered outside the Babri Masjid, chanting slogans, their fists raised in the air as though trying to tear down the very sky above them. My mother could hear the thud of feet, the shrieks of war cries, a sound so alien to her that she could hardly comprehend it. The walls of the mosque trembled under the weight of their noise. Inside her home, a few miles from the site, my mother, Yasmin Khan, felt the tremors. She put a hand on her belly again, a soft attempt to soothe the agitation within. But it wasn't the baby's agitation she should have been concerned about. It was her own body. As the men outside prepared to destroy a piece of history, her body prepared to bring new life into the world. Her water broke with the sound of a thousand shattering pieces. She gasped, clutching the edge of the kitchen counter as the warm liquid pooled at her feet, mixing with the dust and the faint smudges of oil that streaked the worn kitchen floor. A great wave of pain swept through her, and her legs nearly gave out under the weight of it. She called out, but her voice was drowned by the escalating riot outside, where men in saffron scarves wielded iron rods and hammers, shouting praises to Lord Rama, proclaiming their desire to reclaim the land that, according to them, had always belonged to their god. The Babri Masjid stood like an ancient sentinel, towering over the chaos, dark and foreboding, the minarets slicing through the air. A centuries-old monument, its walls had seen the passage of time, the changing of empires, and the evolution of faith. But today, it would witness something far more tragic: its own demise.

Yasmin Khan, my mother, staggered to the door, hoping to catch the attention of a neighbor, anyone who could help her in her time of need. But the streets were deserted, as though the entire world had converged on the mosque. Only the cries of the crowd filled the air, rising higher and higher like a poisonous fog. The mob surged forward, their faces flushed with fervor, their eyes blazing with conviction. This was no longer a protest; it had transformed into something primal, something violent. The mosque trembled again, this time more violently, as the first strike landed on its exterior. An iron rod crashed against one of the ancient stones, sending shards of it flying through the air like shrapnel. The crowd erupted in cheers, a sound so deafening that it seemed to shake the very earth. Yasmin Khan felt another sharp contraction, and she screamed. Her voice was lost in the din. She clutched her belly, sinking to the floor as the pain tore through her. The baby was coming, and there was no one there to help her. Her husband had left her that Sunday morning, after spending the night with her, seemingly unaware of the chaos that would soon consume the town. He had promised to return before noon, but it was already past the hour. The sun was high in the sky, casting long shadows on the walls of the modest home. Outside, the destruction continued. One by one, the mob tore into the walls of the mosque, their hammers crashing against the stone like a relentless tide. Each blow seemed to reverberate through the air, as if the very soul of the structure was crying out in agony. The intricate carvings on the walls, the delicate arabesques that had stood the test of time, were soon to be obliterated. Dust and debris clouded the air, choking those who stood too close, but no one cared. They were driven by a force far more powerful than reason: faith.

Yasmin Khan's breathing grew shallow, her vision blurring as the pain intensified. The baby was close. She could feel it pushing, demanding to be brought into this world, a world that seemed intent on tearing itself apart. She crawled across the floor, her fingers scraping against the rough concrete as she pulled herself toward the small cot in the corner of the room. She had no strength left to cry out. All she could do was pray in silence, her lips moving in whispered supplication.

"Allah, protect my child," she murmured, her voice barely audible even to herself.

As if in answer to her prayer, there was a sudden lull

in the chaos outside. The mob paused, their attention momentarily diverted by something unseen. For a brief moment, the world held its breath. Then, with a collective roar, the men surged forward once more, this time with a single, unified goal: to bring the entire structure down. A great cheer went up as one of the minarets crumbled, collapsing into a heap of rubble and dust. It was as if the heavens themselves were weeping, for the dust that rose into the air seemed to blot out the sun, casting the entire town into a twilight of destruction.

Yasmin Khan could barely see through the haze of pain and exhaustion, but she knew the time had come. Her own mother, Amina Khan, silent for years since the tragic loss of her son, moved with a quiet, trembling urgency as she tried to support her daughter through the labor. Her hands, worn and trembling, fumbled as she attempted to prepare a space, smoothing blankets and fetching water, gestures both tender and unsteady. She hadn't spoken a word since that day of terrible grief when she had lost her son, her voice swallowed by a silence so profound it seemed to seep into her bones, weighing her movements. Now, as Yasmin went into labor, her eyes – widened in silent desperation—spoke the words her voice could not. Yasmin could scarcely see her mother through the mist of pain that blurred her vision, her world shrinking to a foggy blur of motion and shallow breaths. Each wave of pain came with a shuddering intensity, but she felt the presence of her mother close, fumbling but determined, as if Amina's silence might be redeemed in these acts of care. Yet Amina was adrift in the silence she had dwelled in for so long; her hands, unsure, trembled over the shallow bowl of water, her fingers failing her in these moments where skill and strength were so urgently needed. Amina could not even bring herself to step outside to call for neighbors or assistance. The weight of years of unspoken sorrow held her in place, silent and helpless, an anchor in a storm.

As Yasmin Khan lay on the hard, cold floor of her home, her body wracked with pain, the shouts and clamor from the riot outside filled the air, drowning out her cries. She felt utterly alone in that moment, the intensity of her contractions making her weak and desperate. The noise outside seemed to grow more distant, like a faint echo as the pressure of childbirth overtook all her senses. Her hands grasped at the floor, her fingernails digging into the cracks between the tiles, but there was no one near to offer a comforting hand. She could barely catch her breath.

But then, through the thick haze of her pain, she heard a voice. A familiar voice, muffled at first, then clearer—a neighbor, Fatima, who lived just across the narrow alley. Fatima had heard Yasmin's scream, distant but distinct above the tumult of the street, and had rushed over despite the danger lurking outside. As she banged on the door, Yasmin's strength wavered, but she managed to call out for help, her voice weak and strained.

"Yasmin! Open the door!" Fatima shouted from outside, her voice a lifeline in the maelstrom. The pounding on the door grew louder as Yasmin fumbled to find the strength to move, but her body was too weak, too consumed by the agony of labor. Fatima, sensing the urgency, didn't wait for an answer. She called to a few of the other neighborhood women who had been sheltering in their homes, terrified of the violence erupting on the streets. Despite their fear, two other women, Razia and Shireen, joined her, and together they forced the door open even as Amina also tried from inside, flooding Yasmin's small home with a whiff of air and the presence of help.

"Yasmin, we are here," Fatima said, rushing to her

side. Her weathered hands were gentle but sure as they pressed against Yasmin's damp forehead, brushing aside the hair plastered to her skin by sweat. Fatima, a widow with four children of her own, had seen births before, though never under such dangerous circumstances. Her heart pounded with fear for the riots outside, but her focus was entirely on the woman in front of her, fighting to bring a new life into the world.

"The baby is coming," Yasmin managed to gasp, her voice barely above a whisper. Her body trembled with the effort of each breath, and she clung to Fatima's arm like it was the only thing tethering her to the earth.

Razia quickly grabbed a few old pillows from a nearby shelf and laid them under Yasmin's head, trying to make her as comfortable as possible. Meanwhile, Shireen ran to fetch water, her footsteps swift and purposeful as she returned with a metal bowl of warm water she'd managed to heat on Yasmin's small stove.

"We need the *dai*," Fatima said urgently, glancing over her shoulder at Razia. A midwife, a *dai*, was essential in these moments, especially when there were complications with the birth. They all knew of Khadija, the trusted *dai* in the neighborhood, but with the riots outside, calling her over seemed dangerous. Still, there was no choice. This was not something they could handle on their own.

"I'll go," Razia said without hesitation, despite the terror in her eyes. She pulled her *burqa* tightly around her, the black fabric swathing her in a veil of quiet resolve, bracing herself for the chaos she would have to navigate outside. She was gone in an instant, leaving the small, dimly lit room behind. Inside, the air was heavy with tension. Yasmin's breathing grew more labored as her contractions became stronger and more frequent. Each wave of pain seemed to last an eternity, crashing over her like the violent sounds of destruction outside. But she held on, gripping Fatima's hand tightly.

"It's going to be okay, Yasmin," Fatima said, though the uncertainty in her voice was clear. She glanced at Shireen, who was nervously fidgeting, tearing pieces of clean cloth into strips to prepare for the delivery. The moments stretched on, and the room was thick with anticipation. Yasmin's body was on fire, her muscles trembling with the strain, her thoughts consumed by fear for her baby. Would the child be born into a world so cruel? Would it even survive this night?

Then, the door swung open again, and Razia burst in, followed by Khadija, the *dai*, who moved with the swift, sure movements of a woman who had seen countless births in her lifetime. Khadija was old, her face lined with deep wrinkles, her eyes sharp and focused beneath the faded fabric of her shawl. She carried a bag of supplies slung over her shoulder, and though the riot outside had left her breathless, her hands were steady as she approached Yasmin.

"Allah's mercy is with us," Khadija said quietly, placing a reassuring hand on Yasmin's swollen belly. "We will bring this child into the world, no matter what is happening outside."

Yasmin's tears flowed freely now, a mix of pain and relief. Khadija knelt beside her, instructing Fatima and Shireen on what they needed to do. They moved with precision, cleaning Yasmin's legs, laying down more cloths to absorb the inevitable blood, and fetching whatever tools Khadija needed.

"You are strong, Yasmin," Khadija murmured. "You've not done this before, but you can do it."

Yasmin nodded weakly. She longed for my father, Ramesh, to be by her side; yet, she knew he could not be there. This felt unlike anything she had faced before—

more frightening, more urgent, as if the world itself were collapsing around her. The faint sounds of the mob breaking through the mosque's walls still filtered through the air, but Khadija blocked it all out, focused only on the task at hand. Time became a blur. The walls of the house seemed to shrink, the air growing thick with the mingling of prayer, urgency, and the scent of labor. Yasmin's body moved through the motions, pushing and breathing as Khadija guided her through each contraction. Fatima wiped Yasmin's brow, murmuring encouragement in her ear, while Shireen held her hand tightly, as if willing her strength through the connection of their palms.

Then, after what felt like hours of pushing and straining, the baby crowned. Yasmin let out a deep, primal cry as Khadija gave the final instructions. In one fluid, practiced motion, the *dai* caught me, the newborn child as I slipped out from my mother, Yasmin's body and into the world. For a brief moment, everything went silent. The cries from outside, the shouts of the rioters, all seemed to fade as the women in the room held their collective breath. With one final, desperate push, my mother, Yasmin Khan had brought her child into the world. My baby cry was soft at first, a feeble wail that barely rose above the din outside. But then it grew louder, more insistent, as if protesting the very nature of the world it had been born into.

Then, I let out a wail—a strong, fierce cry that seemed to echo in the small room, a sound that cut through the tension like a knife. Khadija smiled for the first time that day, lifting me, the baby up so that Yasmin could see her child. I was a girl, small but healthy, my tiny hands already reaching for something unseen, my skin flushed with the heat of birth.

"A daughter," Khadija said softly, handing the child

to Yasmin, who took her in trembling arms. My baby cries filled the room, louder than the sounds of destruction outside, as if protesting the chaos I had been born into. Yasmin wept as she cradled her daughter, kissing her forehead, feeling the warmth of her new life against her chest. The fear and the pain that had gripped her heart for hours melted away in that moment, replaced by an overwhelming sense of love and gratitude. This was her child, her Saanvi, born into a world torn apart by hate but delivered in love.

As the women around her quietly cleaned up, tending to Yasmin and to me, the newborn, Khadija stepped outside for a moment. The streets were still, but in the distance, the Babri Masjid was no more. The mosque had fallen, its domes reduced to rubble, its walls a crumbled memory. The air was heavy with dust, the sky darkened by smoke, and yet, in the small home behind her, a new life had begun. Khadija closed her eyes and whispered a prayer under her breath, for the child, for the mother, and for the broken world outside. Inside, my mother, Yasmin whispered Saanvi's name, kissing the tiny fingers of her daughter, her heart filled with both sorrow and hope. She would tell Saanvi one day about this moment—the day her mother's water broke and the Babri Masjid came down, and how she had been born amidst the destruction, a light in the darkness.

I, Saanvi's first breath was taken amidst the rubble of a crumbling mosque and the shattered hopes of a nation. As my mother held me close, tears streaming down her face, the world outside continued to burn. The Babri Masjid had fallen, reduced to a pile of rubble and ash. The men who had destroyed it stood triumphant, their fists raised to the sky in victory, but their triumph was hollow. For in their quest to reclaim their god's land, they had lost something far more precious: their humanity.

The dust settled slowly, blanketing the town like a shroud. The mosque was gone, but its spirit lingered, a haunting presence that would remain in the hearts and minds of those who had witnessed its destruction. And amid it all, in a small, unremarkable house, a new life had begun. I, Saanvi, born in the shadow of destruction, would carry with me the weight of that day for the rest of my life.

Yasmin's silent mother, Amina, watched her daughter cradle the newborn child in her arms, her own heart heavy with a secret she had carried for decades. The Babri Masjid, now reduced to ruins, had been a symbol of faith, of identity, of belonging. But Amina knew that faith could be as fragile as the stones that had once held the mosque together. She had been born into a Hindu family, a secret she had not shared for years. And now, as she watched the dust settle over Ayodhya, she felt the weight of that truth pressing down on her.

When Yasmin asked how to honor her child's birth in such a moment of grief, Amina's voice broke, the ghost of her Hindu childhood surfacing after years of silence. "Burn the dead," she whispered to herself, remembering the fires of her ancestors, the flames that once carried the souls of the dead to their final resting place. She had long buried those memories beneath layers of her adopted faith, but today, as the mosque crumbled, so too did the walls she had built around her past. They were Muslim. And Muslims did not burn their dead.

In the quiet aftermath, as the streets of Ayodhya lay covered in ash and stone, Amina found herself alone in her grief, a woman caught between two worlds, two faiths, and a lifetime of secrets. Quietly and with deliberate intention, she opened her Godrej cupboard that had remained untouched for years. Inside, hidden behind old blankets and forgotten trinkets, were the idols of Hindu gods she had once worshipped as a child. They were covered in dust, much like the rubble of the Babri Masjid, relics of a past she could never fully leave behind.

As I, Saanvi, grew up, Amina watched her granddaughter with a quiet reverence, knowing that in this child, born on the day of destruction, there was a possibility of reconciliation, a chance to bridge the divide that had torn her country—and her heart—apart. But that day in 1992, as the Babri Masjid came down and the cries of the rioters filled the air, all Amina could do was weep for the world her granddaughter had been born into—a world fractured by faith, but still, somehow, filled with the fragile hope of new life.

As the years passed, the events of December 6, 1992, would be etched into the annals of history, a scar on the soul of a divided and fractured nation. But for my mother, Yasmin, that day would forever be remembered not as a day of violence and hatred, but as the day her daughter was born, a day of life amidst death, of hope amidst despair. It was a wound on the spirit of its people —a day when Ayodhya, usually resonant with the hum of prayers and temple bells, was instead filled with the harsh, metallic clangor of hammers on stone, a discord that seemed to reverberate through the very soul of India. But for Yasmin, it would be remembered differently, not as the day of the fall of the Babri Masjid, but as the day her daughter took her first breath—a slender thread of life woven amidst the cacophony of destruction. It was a day of quiet, a paradox she would hold within her, its essence tied to life rather than to violence.

The Babri Masjid, an enduring structure of pale sandstone, had stood for nearly five centuries, a stoic witness to the ebb and flow of empires. Built in 1528 by Mir Baqi, a general of the first Mughal emperor, Babur, it had long occupied a precarious space in India's collective memory. To some, it was a symbol of conquest, its minarets shadowing the birthplace of Lord Rama. To others, it was simply a mosque, a house of prayer and peace. But on this day, it was reduced to a battlefield of identity, a testament to how history is less a timeline and more a weapon.

The dawn of December 6, 1992, had arrived with an unseasonal chill. Even the winds, it seemed, hesitated, unsure whether to bring renewal or ruin. Ayodhya lay under a brooding sky, its ancient temples shrouded in the fog of predestined turmoil. This city, once steeped in mythology and sanctity, stood as a battleground, not of warriors with swords, but of ideologies sharpened over decades. It was the day I, Saani Trivedi, would take my first breath, as I repeat and remind myself—oblivious to the upheaval unfurling in the heart of my birthplace. I often wonder: was my wail, sharp and piercing in the delivery room of the district hospital, lost in the crescendo of slogans echoing from the *kar sevaks*? Or did it intermingle, a tiny, unnoticed vibration within a seismic roar that would reverberate across the nation?

It wasn't a spontaneous uprising, though that was how it was later painted by many. Behind the demolition lay years of carefully scripted narratives and manufactured outrage, helmed by leaders of the Hindu Party and affiliates of the Sangh Parivar. The political rise of Mr Krishna, his Rath Yatra of 1990 carving its flaming trajectory through the heart of India, was as much a spectacle as it was a harbinger of what was to come. Mounted atop a chariot-like vehicle, Mr Krishna had invoked tales of Ram Rajya while stoking a more divisive fervor. His rally cries were simple but potent: reclaim the birthplace of Ram. That December morning, over a hundred and fifty thousand *kar sevaks* or volunteers, assembled before the mosque, their saffron-clad forms a sea of determination. Many carried pickaxes, iron rods, ropes, tools not of devotion but of destruction. A few Hindu leaders who were later identified, exhorted the crowd with fiery speeches, their words igniting a fever pitch of zeal and kindling the fervor into an unstoppable blaze. *"Ram Lalla hum aayenge, mandir wahin banayenge!"* The chant reached a frenzied crescendo as the first hammer struck the ancient walls. The crowds were ignited by speeches ablaze with conviction, their voices fanning the embers of collective zeal.

When the first dome fell, a cloud of dust and disbelief rose into the winter air. The Babri Masjid crumbled and ultimately collapsed, not in silence but amidst roaring cries of "Jai Shri Ram," as though the bricks themselves yielded to divine will. Outside the mosque, the crowd was relentless, each blow on the structure carried a finality that seemed to split the very fabric of time. The stones, carved and worn by centuries, fell one by one, each thud resonating through the town with a sense of finality, each sound like the beat of a funeral drum marking the end of an era. The Babri Masjid had stood through monsoons and droughts, had been part of the land like the river, like the hills that cradled the town, but now it was a symbol undone by human hands. The act was swift and brutal, executed over hours, yet built on decades of simmering tensions. By noon, the masjid was no more. In its place lay rubble, a grim metaphor for the fractured idea of secular India. It seemed like history had been undone from the outside in.

I picture my mother, Yasmin Khan, cradling me, her face pale, her heart torn. Raised a Muslim, she had quietly married my father, Ramesh Trivedi in a Hindu temple, unknown and against the tide of social expectation. For her, the destruction of the mosque was not merely the loss of a structure but the collapse of a fragile ideal, the coexistence they embodied in their union. The news of the demolition broke like a dam, flooding every corner of the country. Front pages of newspapers carried screaming headlines the next morning: *"Babri Masjid Brought Down: Communal Tensions Soar;" "A Dark Day in Indian Democracy;" "Mandir Politics Claims Its Prize."* Television channels, still in their infancy, looped grainy footage of *kar sevaks* atop the mosque, wielding hammers with manic resolve. *Doordarshan* was still the primary broadcaster, and private television was just beginning to merge around the year of my birth. Zee had barely been launched two months before the demolition. Political commentators and editorialists described the event and its aftermath as a deliberate desecration of India's secular fabric, while others heralded it as a "rectification" of historical wrongs. The international press was less ambiguous, condemning the act as religious vandalism. Governments around the world issued statements of concern. But within India, the reactions were sharply polarized. In towns like Ayodhya, crackers burst in celebration; in cities like Mumbai and Delhi, Muslim homes were set ablaze. In the days that followed, riots erupted across the nation. The death toll climbed into the thousands, with entire neighborhoods reduced to ash. A judicial inquiry was launched, but justice, like the Babri Masjid, seemed an impossible reconstruction.

My father must have, of course, found himself trapped between duty and romantic love and consequent despair. "This is not about Rama," he had said in a rare moment of intellectual candor and honesty to my mother. "This is about power. And we have failed to stop it." His words must have hung heavily in the room, mingling with the faint antiseptic smells from my mother's bedside. Why he was not by my mother on that fateful Sunday is something I cannot ever rationalize. What call of familial duty had made him return to his parents' home, is somewhat blurred. As dawn had broken over Ayodhya on that day of reckoning, the air had already carried a peculiar tension, a silence sharpened by unspoken foreboding. Yasmin, cocooned in the dimness of her room, felt a shift within her—a tightening, a sense of inevitability that was not just her labor but the echo of something greater stirring outside. News had drifted in fragments over recent days: crowds gathering, emotions swelling, and an impatience that grew feverish as men chanted outside, their voices rising in waves that carried through the narrow streets. From her window, she had glimpsed figures moving with purpose, a grim procession filling the town's ancient arteries, swelling towards the disputed site like a flood, unyielding and resolute. For Yasmin, that day was a blur of sweat and pain, of sharp breaths and fractured moments as her labor had advanced with a rhythm that had felt both intimate and epic. Her own struggles, entwined with the faint roar from outside, had brought a strange dissonance—her body ushering in life while, beyond the walls of her home, crowds seething with fury, were driven by a need for destruction that seemed almost primeval.

Her mother, Amina, her face pale and tense, had hovered beside her, unable to voice the fears that hung in the room. Amina's silence, usually a cloak of quiet grief, had felt like a forewarning, an acknowledgment of forces too great, too terrible to name. Yasmin had clenched her mother's hand, the pain drawing her attention inward, even as the distant cries of protest had broken and risen again, reverberating like a violent pulse.

Beyond our house, the streets of Ayodhya had been awash with a fervor that felt both ancient and immediate, men driven by a sense of destiny that they believed justified the power in their hands. The Babri Masjid, a structure that had stood for centuries, was now just a few meters from their reaching grasp, its stones bearing witness to a history too convoluted to separate myth from memory. But none of that mattered to the crowd—each crack of a hammer, each shove against the ancient walls, became a statement of belief, an offering of sorts in a struggle that had transcended words.

The sky was a pale, washed-out blue by midday, and from where Yasmin lay, her view was limited to the small square of sky visible through her window. She focused on that piece of open space, using it as her anchor against the waves of pain that came like the relentless, driving tide. She wished desperately for Ramesh, who had gone to observe the gathering with a wary eye, his heart torn between the sentiments of his community and the quiet, steadfast love he held for his wife and the child they had awaited. Though they never spoke of it, she sensed his turmoil—a man of faith witnessing the rupture of that very faith, split down the middle by blood and bone. Yasmin's cries had mingled with the shouts from outside as her labor had reached its peak, her body pushed to its limits. With each contraction, it had felt as if her life force mingled with the ground beneath her, her own blood and sweat binding her, in that moment, to Ayodhya, a town marked by an uneasy, fragile coexistence that was now breaking under the weight of fervor and fire. The city, her city, was transforming, reshaped by an intensity that would not cease until all was rubble and dust. In those final moments, as Yasmin's pain surged into a realm beyond the physical, her senses sharpened to a haunting clarity. She felt her mother's hand—cool and steady—resting gently against her fevered brow. The room around her dissolved into shadows, heavy with the thick smell of incense entwined with the metallic sting of blood. Outside her fragile sanctuary, the distant roar of destruction ebbed and faded, swallowed by the narrowing tunnel of her awareness, until all that remained was the steady rhythm of her own breath, drawing her inward, deeper and deeper into silence. And then, in a moment as swift and timeless as a heartbeat, the child came into the world, her cries breaking through the room like a small but potent symbol of life.

Amina wept silently, her shoulders shaking as she held her granddaughter, pressing the tiny bundle close, as if her very soul poured out in those quiet, reverent tears. Yasmin, exhausted and spent, felt an odd sense of peace amidst the tumult outside. Her daughter's cries were a fragile reminder of life's endurance, a quiet affirmation of something pure that persisted despite the shadows cast over the city. In that moment, Yasmin understood that her child's birth, this beginning, was a silent defiance against the forces tearing the town apart. Outside, the final blow to the Babri Masjid landed with a resounding crash, the stone crumbling, a symbol reduced to dust. But within her home, Yasmin held her daughter close, the warmth of new life radiating against her chest, a reminder that hope, fragile yet unwavering, had also been born on that day.

The years would pass, and the memory of December 6, 1992, would come to mark a scar on the nation's soul, a day invoked in whispers and debates, in prayers and bitter reproach. For the world, it was the day Ayodhya lost something irreplaceable. But for Yasmin, it was a day of quiet resistance, a day that held a seed of hope, something beyond the reach of destruction. Her daughter, born amidst the violence, would carry the paradox within her—a life entwined with a day of despair, a reminder that even amidst ruin, something beautiful could emerge, if only one dared to believe in it.

As for me, I have carried the weight of being born on this day for years, as though my life was inextricably linked to this moment of rupture. I have often wondered: could my first breath ever atone for the collective sigh of anguish that rose from the rubble of Babri? Or was I born to plant a seed of hope? Perhaps the soil beneath my cradle bore witness to both destruction and creation, a paradox of history that shaped my very existence. It feels as if the cries from that day seem to echo in my bones, whispering questions that refuse to fade, demanding that I uncover their meaning, demanding that I choose a side: Am I a child of despair or a harbinger of healing? But what if my purpose is not to choose, but to reconcile? To bind together fragments of the past into a future that remembers, but does not bleed? I sometimes do believe that the purpose of my life lies not in choosing sides, but in bridging them, binding together fragments of the past into a future that remembers, but no longer festers. For every crumbled stone, I dream of planting a seed; for every shattered belief, I envision a place where faiths can coexist without fear of collapse.

3

Ayodhya, an ancient city steeped in myth and history, served as both the cradle and crucible of my father Ramesh Trivedi's political aspirations. Born to a distinguished lawyer, he inherited not only a legacy of intellect and eloquence but also the weight of expectations. His ambitions were fiercely his own, distinct and unyielding. As he moved through Ayodhya's charged streets, where faith and power blurred into one another, his life revealed itself as a quiet battleground of contradictions. His secret marriage to my mother, Yasmin Khan, a union defying societal norms, bore both the marks of deep love and quiet heartbreak, surviving in ways that defied logic and convention. His political journey unfolded with an uncanny parallel to the tensions in his personal life, each reflecting the other's struggles and quiet persistence. At the time of my birth, Ayodhya stood at the crossroads of its destiny, its political and religious landscape becoming a battleground for conflicting ideologies. Born into a world where faith and ambition are inseparable, only Ayodhya, fraught with the complex interweaving of religion and politics, could set the stage for his political dreams.

My father, Ramesh Trivedi, was born into a prominent Hindu family in Ayodhya, the only son of Shyam Trivedi, a distinguished lawyer who built the Trivedi Mansion, stone by stone, with quiet resolve and unyielding ambition. Shyam Trivedi's sharp intellect and steely perseverance earned him not only a thriving practice but also the deep respect of the community. The mansion, rising gracefully against the changing skyline of Ayodhya, stood as a living monument to his toil and triumph, a structure that seemed to breathe with the spirit of his hard-earned success. Within the wide halls and verandah flooded with light, Ramesh grew up amid unspoken expectations and the steady, insistent rhythm of his father's relentless drive. Even as a boy, he sensed the fine threads of justice and ambition weaving through his father's world, a world where integrity was non-negotiable and every victory was born of discipline. These were the values Shyam Trivedi etched into the very foundation of his home; a legacy he hoped his son would one day carry forward.

While other children in the neighborhood played carefree games, my father found himself drawn to the discussions that swirled around him, conversations about governance, justice, and the socio-political climate of their beloved Ayodhya. The city, steeped in ancient history and religious significance, was a fertile ground from which my father's aspirations to become a political leader sprang forth. Ayodhya's streets, layered with history and belief, shaped my father's vision for change— not just for himself, but for the people he felt bound to serve. His path was far from straightforward; marked by ambition, personal loss, and an unyielding drive to realize a future he believed in.

How my mother, Yasmin Khan, came into my father's life remains a mystery to me. Their union was not something easily explained, as if it had emerged from a realm beyond comprehension, formed by forces that defied the everyday logic of our world. To me, it was almost as though a temple had somehow nestled itself within the sacred space of a mosque, two sanctuaries entwining in a fusion so intimate, so profound, that they seemed to consume one another in the act of becoming one. For my mother, Yasmin, and my father, Ramesh, their love was both an act of creation and one of quiet destruction. They were raised in faiths with distinct philosophies, surrounded by rituals and rhythms that had nurtured their separate identities from birth. Yet something in each of them recognized a kindred spirit, a hunger, perhaps, that transcended the known boundaries of their worlds. When they came together, it was as if they crossed into sacred territory that neither faith could entirely hold or sanctify. They existed in that shadowed, mythic space between temple and mosque—a space that was neither and yet somehow both, a union shaped by two powerful forces that could not help but change one another in the act of merging.

It was almost as if a temple suckled at and gained access inside the body of a mosque, and the twain destroyed each other in making love to each other.

My mother, Yasmin's first trip to Lucknow, was supposed to be a family affair, an ordinary pilgrimage to the city of nawabs and kebabs, of exquisite *chikan* embroidery and bustling bazaars. She had grown up hearing tales of Lucknow's charm, her father's voice weaving stories of the grand *Imambaras*, the regal Chowk, and the narrow lanes lined with fragrance-laden attar shops. But nothing had prepared her for the city's ancient rhythms that echo through its streets like the breath of time itself, for the intensity of life that crowded its streets and flowed like the Gomti River in gentle, meandering currents. It was on one such afternoon, beneath the blazing September sun, that Yasmin first saw Ramesh. She stood by a tea stall near the Residency, gazing at the ruins—weathered, unbowed, and steeped in silence—when a sudden, inexplicable awareness washed over her. It was an uncanny feeling that made her turn around just in time to see him stepping off his motorbike, dusting off his kurta as if he were brushing away the city's grit to reveal the essence of himself. He didn't notice her right away, but Yasmin's gaze lingered. There was something about him, an intensity to his movements, a look of quiet resolve mingled with the unguarded curiosity of a man unafraid to consume in the world around him.

And then, as if orchestrated by fate, he looked up. Their eyes met, and the world stilled for a brief, breathless moment. Yasmin felt a strange sensation blooming in her chest, a mixture of anticipation and calm, as if her life had somehow found its axis in that gaze. Ramesh, too, seemed struck. His eyes softened, taking in her delicate, windswept hair and the gentle curve of her lips, which held the faintest trace of a smile. He felt, in that instant, as though he had been waiting for her all his life without ever realizing it.

They exchanged shy smiles, then looked away, embarrassed by the intensity of their mutual awareness. But the universe had other plans. A gust of wind rattled the tea stall's flimsy roof, sending an errant paper cup flying towards her, and in the instinctive chaos of a smile and surprise, Ramesh reached out, his fingers brushing hers as he steadied the cup in her hands. It was a small gesture, yet Yasmin felt the warmth of his touch spread through her as if she had held a flame. In that moment, the stranger standing before her was no longer just another face in the crowded streets of Lucknow. He was, inexplicably, someone she felt she had always known.

They struck up a conversation, initially formal and restrained, as strangers do. She learned that he, like her, was from Ayodhya, a college lecturer by profession, though currently in Lucknow on a political errand—one he described with casual dismissiveness, as if politics were not the compass of his life but merely a pastime. Yasmin, in turn, shared that she was visiting Lucknow with her friend, her voice laced with the slightest hint of restraint, cautious of revealing too much. After all, she was a Muslim girl from a conservative family, and here she was, standing alone, without her burqa, with a stranger who spoke with a voice as steady as the flow of the river and as warm as the sun on her skin.

But as the minutes turned into hours, they found themselves walking together through the bustling streets, losing themselves in the labyrinthine lanes of the Chowk, Yasmin gesturing animatedly as she explained the stories her father had told her of Lucknow city's historic splendor in her childhood, and Ramesh listening intently, captivated by the way her eyes sparkled with each word. She noticed the slight furrow in his brow when he was deep in thought, the way his laughter, though infrequent, was a sound so rich it felt like a gift each time he allowed it to escape. They lingered at an old bookshop, sifting through dusty volumes of Ghalib's poetry, and something about those verses of love and longing seemed to speak directly to them, as if they were not just two people meeting by chance but characters in a story that had been written long before they were born. Yasmin's fingers brushed against a fragile page as she recited a couplet, her voice soft and lilting, and Ramesh, mesmerized, found himself wondering how it was possible for someone to bring such tenderness to words he had heard countless times before.

As dusk approached, they wandered towards the riverfront, where the fading light cast a golden glow over the Gomti water, and the sounds of the city softened to a gentle hum. It was there, in the warm embrace of twilight, that Yasmin felt a truth settle within her—she had fallen in love. It was an absurd thought, a reckless one, even, but there it was, shimmering in her heart like a fragile, iridescent wing. And somehow, she knew that Ramesh felt the same. The silence between them was as intimate as a whispered confession, each moment a quiet affirmation of the connection they shared.

Yet, even as she allowed herself to savor the joy, a sliver of apprehension crept in. She got to know that Ramesh was Hindu; his family, his world, were bound by traditions and beliefs that stood in stark contrast to her own. Her mind flickered to the stories she had heard, of young lovers torn apart by the uncompromising walls of faith and family. But when she looked at Ramesh, those worries faded into shadows. Here, in this moment, they were simply two souls who had found each other in the crowded chaos of life. As the evening drew to a close, Ramesh took her hand, his fingers tentative yet resolute, and she felt a rush of certainty that this connection, this love, was worth any risk. They exchanged details, promising to meet again in Ayodhya, though neither of them spoke of the challenges that lay ahead. It was as if voicing them would somehow make them real, intruding on the delicate, perfect beauty of their newfound love.

That night, my mother, Yasmin lay awake in her room, her heart a riot of emotions—joy, fear, hope, and a fierce, unyielding desire to be with the man who had, in a single afternoon, transformed her world. She knew the path ahead would be far from easy, that society's scrutiny and their families' expectations would hang over them like a sword. But for now, she clung to the memory of that chance encounter, to the warmth of Ramesh's touch and the depth of his gaze, and she allowed herself to dream. In the months that followed, their love blossomed in secret meetings, stolen glances, and whispered conversations in Ayodhya. They were bound by something larger than themselves, a force that transcended the boundaries of religion and tradition. And though they both knew the road ahead was perilous, Yasmin and Ramesh held on to the hope that, somehow, their love would find a way to survive.

The serendipity of their meeting and the instant, almost fated, connection they shared in their chance encounter in Lucknow sealed them in unexpected ways. Deep down and in their first chance meeting, they had known that they were for each other, and that their fates had to accept each other. The thought of seeing Ramesh again, of crossing paths in their own city, stirred something restless in my mother's heart. Weeks had passed since their first encounter in Lucknow, but his voice, his laughter, and the warmth of his gaze lingered in her memory like a secret she carried everywhere. Ayodhya was quieter than Lucknow, yet there was an intensity in the air that felt alive, humming with centuries of devotion and unspoken stories. Yasmin could feel the city's gaze upon her as she walked its streets, an insider treading reverently on soil soaked in history and faith. When she reached the small *chai* shop in Faizabad where they had agreed to meet again back in their hometown, her heart fluttered with nervous anticipation. My father, Ramesh was already waiting, leaning against a column with a calm, yet unmistakable energy about him. When he saw her with her *hijab*, a smile spread across his face—so sudden, so radiant—that

Yasmin's breath caught in her throat. She walked towards him, her footsteps quickening as he stood to greet her. For a moment, they simply looked at each other, letting the world around them dissolve into a blur. Then, with a quiet, unspoken understanding, he took her hand, guiding her away from the bustling street.

They walked through the winding alleys of Ayodhya, a part of Faizabad district then, neither speaking, yet every glance and touch conveying the words they dared not say aloud. Ramesh led her to a secluded spot by the river-bank, where the sun dipped low over the water, casting golden hues that softened the edges of the world around them. It was a quiet, hidden corner where the gentle lapping of the Sarayu River filled the silence, and the weight of the city's history seemed to recede, allowing them a moment of privacy. As they sat on the grass, Yasmin felt the warmth of Ramesh's shoulder against hers, and an almost unbearable tension settled between them. She could feel his gaze on her, and when she looked up, their eyes met, locking in an exchange that held all the longing and unsaid confessions they had carried since their last meeting. His hand reached up, tracing the curve of her cheek with a tenderness that left her breathless. Slowly, hesitantly, his fingers moved under her *hijab*, finding their way to her hair, cradling her face as he leaned closer. Their lips met in a kiss that was gentle at first, filled with the careful restraint of two people who had longed for this moment but feared breaking its fragile beauty. But as the seconds passed, restraint gave way to physical need, and their kiss deepened, the world around them dissolving into a blur of sensation. Yasmin felt herself melt into him, every nerve alive with the fire of his touch, his smell, the solid warmth of his body pressed against hers. Yasmin had forgotten the secret and complicated history of her own mother's life.

Without breaking their kiss, Ramesh guided her to lie back on the grass, his movements slow and deliberate, as though savoring each second. Yasmin felt the cool earth beneath her, grounding her even as she was swept away by the force of her desire. His hands roamed her body with a reverence that made her heart ache, his touch mapping every curve, every contour as if he were memorizing her. She felt her own hands slipping beneath his shirt, tracing the lines of muscles that flexed beneath her fingers, pulling him closer, needing him as she had never needed anyone before. Hidden beneath a moored boat's canvas along the ghat, they made love in silence, their bodies moving with the slow rhythm of the river, as ancient and inevitable as desire. Even with the weight of risk in a watchful, conservative town, they found each other beneath the dimming sky, their bodies moving with a quiet urgency, a rhythm as natural as the river's flow. In that brief, forbidden union, it felt as if time had stilled— and for a heartbeat, they belonged only to each other, untouched by history, unburdened by faith. Yasmin lost herself in him, in the feel of his skin against hers, in the quiet gasps and whispered endearments that escaped their lips. Time ceased to exist; there was only the warmth of his breath on her neck, the press of his hands on her hips, the intense, overwhelming connection that bound them together in that moment. For her, it was a moment both defiant and sacred, where love felt truer than law, and her body no longer a site of boundaries, but of belonging. When they finally lay entwined in each other's arms, the sky had deepened into twilight, the first stars beginning to glimmer overhead. Yasmin rested her head against his chest, listening to the steady beat of his heart, a sound that felt like a promise, a reminder that they had found each other in a world that often felt vast and indifferent. They stayed like that for a while, neither speaking, savoring the quiet intimacy of simply being together.

As the night descended, reality crept back in, and Yasmin felt a pang of fear settle in her heart. She knew their love was a fragile thing, something that could shatter under the weight of expectation and scrutiny. Ramesh's world was bound by tradition and family honor, a world that might never accept her, a Muslim woman, as part of it. She remembered her own mother, silent and silenced, waiting back home. Yet, despite the uncertainty, she couldn't bring herself to regret this moment, to wish for anything other than the way his arms tightened around her, as if to shield her from the world. Ramesh seemed to sense her unease. He lifted her chin, his eyes searching hers with a look of quiet determination. "We'll find a way," he whispered, his voice filled with a conviction that made her want to believe. "No matter what, Yasmin, I'll fight for us."

She nodded, feeling the weight of his promise settle over her, filling her with a hope she hadn't dared to acknowledge. They shared one last lingering kiss, sealing a silent vow between them, a promise that they would hold onto this love, no matter how uncertain the path ahead might be. When they finally parted, Yasmin felt as if a piece of her heart had been left behind with him, buried in the soft earth by the riverbank, where they had shared the most intimate moment of their lives. She knew the road ahead would be fraught with challenges, that their love would be tested by forces beyond their control. But as she walked away, glancing back to see Ramesh watching her with a look of quiet yearning, she felt a renewed strength within her—a determination to fight for this love, to defy the expectations that sought to keep them apart. In that moment, beneath a sky scattered with stars, Yasmin knew her heart belonged to Ramesh. Whatever the future might bring, they would carry this night within them. Whatever lay ahead, their time spent together would remain etched in both of them —a fragile, defiant memory of love found across forbidden lines, against all the odds their faiths had set.

The love between Ramesh and Yasmin was a force that grew like wildfire, a flame that burned brighter with every stolen moment they shared. For them, desire was not merely a flicker of attraction; it was a living, breathing creature, an unrelenting hunger that drove them to seek each other out with an intensity that defied reason. Yasmin's small, humble home, tucked away in a narrow lane, became their sanctuary, a secret haven where the world's prejudices and expectations faded away. Her mother, Amina, once spirited and outspoken, now lived in a silence that seemed to deepen whenever Ramesh entered the house. She knew of his visits, of course, but she stayed in the back room, her presence like a shadow that loomed just beyond their line of sight. And yet, even Amina's silence and maybe her disapproval, could not douse the fire between them. Her home was nestled in the labyrinthine lanes of *Katra Mohalla* neighborhood where the air was thick with the smell of *kebabs* sizzling in small roadside stalls, mingling with the distant echo of the *azan*. The house itself was unassuming, a modest single-story structure with faded green shutters that creaked in the wind and a small courtyard enclosed by crumbling walls. In the evenings, the courtyard would come alive with the soft golden glow of a solitary lantern, its light spilling onto the bougainvillea vines climbing the brickwork. Here, she would sit, writing verses or sewing with quiet precision, her gaze often drifting to the narrow lane beyond the gate, waiting for him. Inside, the house was sparse but warm, with walls adorned with black-and-white photographs of a time long past, and shelves lined with books, poetry by Ghalib, history texts, and a few well-thumbed novels. A brass hookah stood in the corner, a relic from her father's time, though it had long since fallen silent. The lane outside seemed to be always bustling, with children playing cricket with makeshift bats, vendors calling out the prices of their wares, and old men in white kurtas discussing politics and the fate of their community. Yet, her home remained a quiet sanctuary, a place where he could step out of the blinding glare of his public persona and simply be a man in love.

In the dim light of Yasmin's modest bedroom, their passion became an unbreakable ritual. Every time Ramesh walked through the door, she would feel a thrill course through her, a visceral recognition that stirred her body before she even laid eyes on him. Their initial glances were charged with unspoken longing, the air between them crackling with the anticipation of touch. As soon as he was close enough, her hands would reach for him, tracing the planes of his shoulders, the hard line of his jaw, pulling him toward her with a fierce urgency that brooked no hesitation. Their love was not gentle, nor was it quiet. It was a whirlwind of need, a tempest that filled the small room with the sound of their breaths, the press of skin against skin, the rhythm of bodies moving in desperate harmony. Yasmin felt Ramesh's hands on her, his touch both tender and possessive, as though he sought to claim her, to imprint his essence onto her soul. Her fingers would sink into his back, clutching him as if she feared he might vanish, as if by holding him closer, she could make the world outside disappear.

Each time they came together, they discovered new

depths to their passion, new ways to communicate the love they could not always voice aloud. Ramesh was attentive, his lips and hands worshipping every inch of her, learning her responses, coaxing sighs and whispers from her lips. And Yasmin responded in kind, her body arching beneath him, surrendering to the waves of desire that crashed over her, filling her with a sense of completeness she had never known. Yasmin and Ramesh's love was like a river that had broken free from its banks, surging wildly and unapologetically. Each encounter between them felt like an uncontainable wave crashing upon the shore, a raw, almost primal connection that swept them up in its force, leaving them helpless in the grip of their mutual desire.

Every time they came together in my mother, Yasmin's small bedroom, the rest of the world faded away, its constraints and expectations falling silent before the symphony of their bodies. They moved together with a fierce, relentless rhythm, as though they were racing against time itself, seizing each stolen moment as if it might be their last. Their breaths mingled, heavy and uneven, filling the air with the sound of longing finally fulfilled, of restraint giving way to surrender. Ramesh's hands explored every inch of her, his touch both tender and possessive, like an artist tracing the curves of his most cherished creation. Yasmin responded to him with an intensity that bordered on abandon, her fingers gripping his shoulders, pulling him closer, urging him to lose himself in her completely. She felt him respond, felt the urgency in his movements, the way he seemed to press deeper, as if he could merge their souls along with their bodies. And when he would finally enter her, they would both gasp, a shared breath that held all the weight of their longing. Their bodies met like river and shore, inevitable, rhythmic, aching with the weight of what could never be named aloud. Yasmin's voice rose, soft at first, a breathing whisper of his name that grew louder as she felt herself surrender to the waves of pleasure that consumed her. She clung to him, her nails digging into his back, her moans filling the room, a testament to the unbridled desire they could no longer contain. It was a union born of opposites, graceful and raw, holy and profane, almost consecrated and cursed, almost like a prayer and a provocation.

Ramesh matched her intensity, his own groans blending with hers, his voice a low, guttural sound that seemed to resonate from the very core of him. They moved together, caught up in the throes of a passion that was as fierce as it was tender, as wild as it was devoted. Each thrust, each movement was an act of defiance against the world that sought to keep them apart, a reaffirmation of the love they refused to let go. In those moments, there was nothing but the two of them, wrapped in each other's arms, their bodies entwined, their voices mingling in a symphony of pleasure and love. When they made love, they were utterly present, lost in each other in a way that felt sacred, as though they were stepping into a realm that existed beyond time and judgment. And yet, there was a wildness to it, too, a feverish urgency, as if they understood that each moment was a gift that could be stolen away by the world at any time. Their lovemaking was a rebellion, a defiance of the boundaries that sought to keep them apart, an act of devotion that transcended the constraints of their different faiths and backgrounds.

In the mornings, when Ramesh would slip out before the sun rose, Yasmin would lie in her bed, her skin tingling with the memory of his touch, her heart aching with a longing that refused to be sated. She would listen to the sounds of her mother stirring in the next room, her footsteps slow and deliberate, as if she moved under the weight of unspoken sorrows. Yasmin knew that her mother disapproved, that she saw her daughter's love for Ramesh as a betrayal, an abandonment of her own father's faith. And yet, Yasmin could not let him go. He was her sanctuary, her escape, her joy. On the days when they could not meet, when duty or circumstance kept them apart, Yasmin would feel his absence like a physical pain, a hollow ache that gnawed at her from within. She would sit by the window, watching the street below, hoping to catch a glimpse of him even if only from afar. And when they finally reunited, the intensity of their longing would explode, drawing them into each other with a fierceness that left no room for hesitation. In those stolen moments, lit only by the hush of the night, Yasmin and Ramesh shed everything but longing, their bodies answering to a rhythm no faith could forbid. They knew the risks, knew that their love was a fragile, forbidden thing, but they also knew that it was worth every sacrifice, every consequence. For as long as they had each other, they had everything. In those quiet hours, they were neither Hindu nor Muslim, but just two people risking everything for something fragile and unnamed. It was a quiet rebellion that glowed where no light of religion was meant to live.

Through sheer coincidence though, my father, Ramesh, also found himself drawn into politics just as he was falling in love with my mother, Yasmin. To him, it felt like fate pulling him in two directions that were, in some strange way, bound by a shared intensity. By day, he was swept into the fervor of Ayodhya's political landscape, navigating a world where words and ideals held the power to move entire communities. By night, he would lose himself in the quiet sanctuary of her presence, their passionate lovemaking an intimate rebellion against the rules that governed his waking hours. In her small, dimly lit room, he would let go of the fiery rhetoric and bold speeches that defined him in public, surrendering to a softer, unspoken language between them. He craved the hungered simplicity of those moments, where every kiss was an affirmation, every bodily touch a satiation. Ramesh had set out to change his career trajectory from college teaching to becoming a politician instead. He had always envisioned himself as a leader of some sort. There was a restlessness within him, a need to push against the boundaries of the life he'd known. When he was younger, he had often listened to stories of India's independence struggle, tales of leaders who had carved a path for future generations. As he grew older, he became drawn to those who spoke of a new kind of freedom, one where justice and equality could thrive, even in a land as divided as ours. He started attending gatherings in Ayodhya, where men spoke about the possibilities of change, about rebuilding a society where every voice could be heard. At first, he was a quiet observer, listening from the back of crowded rooms. But as he became more engaged, his voice grew bolder, finding confidence in the ideas he had once only dared to think. He began speaking at these gatherings, his natural eloquence resonating with those who longed for a leader who could both understand and inspire them. He spoke of the importance of education, of the need for a society where children of all faiths could learn together, free from the prejudices that had divided their elders. His speeches were fiery, but his words carried a softness as well, a hope that hinted at the possibility of unity, of a future built on mutual respect.

And his love for my mother, Yasmin was balanced on a blade's edge, tender, fleeting, and never safe in daylight. They were two souls wandering in a broken world, each searching for a place of belonging. Their love lived in shadows, always there, and never meant to be seen. Ramesh would slip into her home under cover of night, leaving behind the mantle of public responsibility that had begun to shape him. In those hours, he shed the weight of his growing ambitions, immersing himself in the quiet intimacy they shared. It was a contrast that defined his life—by day, he was the young leader, the voice of a new Ayodhya; by night, he was simply a man in love, driven by a desire that he couldn't explain, a need that transcended the politics that had begun to consume him.

His love for Yasmin and his passion for politics were intertwined, each feeding something within him that had long been dormant. He began to see his political work as an extension of his love for her, a way to build a world where they might exist freely, unbound by the religious divisions that defined their society. He spoke of communal harmony not as a distant ideal but as a tangible reality he wanted to bring to life for her, for them. The people of Ayodhya sensed this fire within him, a conviction that was both personal and universal. His words moved them, not because they were grand or polished, but because they carried a truth that was rare in the world of politics—a truth rooted in love and hope, in the belief that change was possible. Ramesh's speeches grew more impassioned as his love for Yasmin deepened. He talked about Ayodhya as a place of shared history, a city that had once been a symbol of coexistence. He spoke of the need to revive that spirit, to remind people of the unity that lay buried beneath decades of division. His words struck a chord with the youth, who were tired of the old conflicts, eager for a future where they wouldn't be forced to choose sides. They began to gather around him, drawn to his vision of an Ayodhya where every faith had a place, where each community could thrive.

In time, Ramesh became an embodiment of hope for Ayodhya's youth, a voice that echoed their frustrations as well as their dreams. He was no longer just a young man with a vision; he was a leader, a figure who could speak for those who felt voiceless. Yet, as his influence grew, so did the tension in his life. He was living in two worlds that didn't easily coexist, a public life defined by ideals and a private life bound by secrecy. Every weekend, he would return to Yasmin's home, slipping through the shadows, knowing that their love was a risk that could unravel everything he was building for his future political career. Their love was a rebellion, an act of defiance in a world that demanded conformity. Ramesh knew that the same people who cheered his speeches would likely turn against him if they knew about Yasmin. Yet, he couldn't walk away from her. In her arms, in their almost animalistic lovemaking, he found a solace that his public life couldn't offer, a peace that balanced the tumult of his days. She became his sanctuary, the quiet center that held him steady as he navigated the complexities of politics and ambition. The nights he spent with her were a balm to his spirit, a reminder of why he fought for change. In those moments, he was no longer the leader, the speaker, the symbol of a new Ayodhya. He was simply a man in love, driven by a need that defied the rules of his world. Yasmin understood this side of him, the vulnerable heart beneath the passionate speeches. She saw the man he hid from the world, the man who dreamed of a life where love didn't come with consequences.

As his public life continued to grow, the pressure began to mount. His success brought him into the orbit of more powerful figures, men who saw Ayodhya not as a city of hope but as a battleground for their ambitions. They spoke of unity, but their words were hollow, their vision rooted in division rather than reconciliation.

Ramesh found himself torn between the ideals he had fought for and the reality of the political landscape he was entering. He saw how easily ideals could be twisted, how quickly a message of hope could be used to justify acts of exclusion. He held on to his vision, clinging to the belief that he could bring about real change. His love for Yasmin gave him strength, a reminder of the world he wanted to construct. In her eyes, he saw a reflection of the city he dreamed of, a place where love could transcend the barriers of faith and tradition. Her presence was a quiet affirmation that his dreams were not foolish, that his fight was worth the cost. His involvement in politics and his love for Yasmin were two halves of a whole, each fueling his desire to create a world where their love could exist without fear. He became a man divided, yet united by a singular vision—a vision of an Ayodhya where love and faith could coexist, where the quiet sanctuary of his love for Yasmin could one day be a reality for all. His natural charisma and eloquence quickly set him apart, drawing people to his cause. Politics to him wasn't merely about governance; it was about the potential to enact real change. Inspired by leaders of the past and present, he started to engage with local youth organizations, voicing his thoughts on the importance of education, communal harmony, and social justice. He became known for his impassioned speeches that ignited a spark of hope among the youth of Ayodhya.

However, his political aspirations were not without their challenges. As he delved deeper into the political landscape of Ayodhya, he found himself ensnared in the complex web of religion and politics that defined the region. Ayodhya, revered as the birthplace of Lord Rama, was a symbol of Hindu pride; yet it was also a flashpoint for communal tensions. My father grappled with this duality; he understood that while he sought to uplift his community, he had to navigate the precarious balance between faith and politics. In his pursuit of political power, my father recognized that his relationship with my mother, Yasmin Khan, would be considered a threat. When he broached it with her, she was hesitant about converting to Hinduism to solidify her place beside him, aligning herself with his family's values and his burgeoning political image. As my father's political ambitions grew, so too did his recognition that her faith would impact his political career. My father, Ramesh, who had harbored dreams of a seamless family narrative that could endear him to both traditionalists and modernists in Ayodhya, knew that his political ambitions could be perceptibly jeopardized. In the world of Indian politics he was venturing into, her very existence in his life was a liability. In Ayodhya, where old loyalties and communal lines ran deep, the revelation that a rising Hindu politician had a Muslim girlfriend or wife could spell disaster for my father's carefully crafted public image. A Muslim woman at his side, even in the quietest, most concealed corners of his life, was an unspoken threat to his ambitions. It would have been seen not as a symbol of love or unity but as a scandalous flaw, a betrayal of cultural expectations that could have fractured his supporters' trust. People would have questioned his values, his loyalty to the cause he claimed to champion. A woman like her in his life wasn't just a risk; she was a wedge that could splinter his chances, a shadow that could mar his future. My father knew that one whisper, one slip, and it would all come crashing down—the accusations of divided loyalties, the whispers that he might be too 'compromised' to represent his community fully. And so, their love lived in shadows, their meetings held in the secrecy of her humble home, as he tried to balance the unforgiving weight of public expectation with the quiet, unyielding truth of his heart.

And yet, he could not look beyond the madness he felt for my mother. Her world, tucked away in the shadows of *Katra Mohalla,* became his escape, a fragile haven where the weight of his newly minted public life would dissolve into the quiet murmur of her voice and the steady rhythm of her presence. In those moments, they were neither Hindu nor Muslim—only two human beings, stripped of history and name, bound not by ritual but by the ache of loving. They defied every headline, every rallying cry, every invisible line etched into their city's soil. Their love was not sanctioned by scripture or state. It was a quiet insurrection, tender and treasonous all at once. Their love, unmarked by *sindoor* or *nikah*, was a quiet rebellion, tender and treasonous all at once. It had no language but touch, no banner but the shadows that swallowed them whole. Perhaps, my father felt that it could not last. Perhaps, my mother did too. But in that narrow room, with the ceiling fan spinning above and the world reduced to the hush between heartbeats, they built a fleeting sanctuary. Not from God, but from human beings speaking and communicating in God's name.

4

I was only three, too young to understand what I was witnessing, but old enough to feel the weight of it, the intensity of the scene unfolding before me. The memory is fragmented, but vivid in its emotions—the warmth of the room, the quiet and the silence of the world outside, the way everything seemed to hold its breath, suspended in that brief, primal moment. The air was thick with something unspoken, something that buzzed through the walls and settled deep within the floorboards. I was hidden in the shadows, peering out from the edge of the door, barely tall enough to see over the threshold, my tiny body stiff with a mixture of curiosity and confusion on the night I saw them. It wasn't the words or the gestures I understood, but the energy in the room. It was something that filled every corner, thick with the smell of human need, of longing that transcended logic or reason. My father, Ramesh, the man I knew as my protector in everyday life, was no longer the figure who stood tall in front of me with quiet authority. He was someone else entirely, someone softer, more vulnerable, yet charged with energy I couldn't name.

Yasmin, my mother, was the quiet center of this energy. Her presence, so steady, so sure, held him in place, as if they were two forces of nature that had always been drawn together, always meant to converge. I didn't understand love or intimacy, not in any intellectual way, but I could sense that this moment was a world of its own, something that existed outside the bounds of everything I had been taught to believe.

Their bodies moved together with a rhythm I couldn't comprehend, but their energy spoke louder than any words. There was something intense in the way they connected, something so powerful that it seemed to vibrate the air around them. I could feel it in my bones, a deep, unsettled sensation in my chest. It wasn't fear, but something else, something primal, like witnessing the raw power of nature itself. The silence of the room was broken only by the soft rustle of sheets, the faint sounds of their breathing.

I stayed frozen in place, unable to move, unsure of what I was witnessing but unable to look away. I wasn't meant to be there—of that much, I was certain. But there was a part of me that knew, even then, that what I saw was a world I wasn't supposed to understand, and yet it was impossible to turn away from it. They were both so unaware of my presence, so lost in their own world, that they might as well have been the only two people alive.

The sensation of being an invisible observer, a silent witness to something far beyond my comprehension, settled deep in my bones. I remember the way the light in the room shifted, the way shadows danced across the walls, painting the scene in hues of gold and dark blue. Time seemed to slow, stretching each moment into something timeless. I could hear my own heartbeat in my ears, the thudding in my chest, and it matched theirs in some strange way, a rhythm I didn't know existed. And then, in a way that only children can sense, I understood that this was not just about bodies. It was about something else, something deeper, more ineffable. It was as though their very souls had collided in a way that left the world around them waiting for something to happen, something monumental, though I didn't know what it was.

My father's face was softened, his expression one I had never seen before—open, vulnerable, stripped of the masks he wore in the world outside. Yasmin, too, had a look on her face that was foreign to me—something close to surrender, but also strength. It was a look of acceptance, of being fully seen in a way that was intimate and yet unspoken. I don't know how long I stood there, hidden, watching them, until the moment passed, until they both became aware of their surroundings again, of the world outside their little sanctuary. I left quietly, retreating to the safety of my room, the soft click of the door behind me as if the world had snapped back into place. But the image of what I had seen lingered. It was a ghost that followed me for years, something I couldn't put into words, but that was with me, tugging at the edges of my consciousness.

As I grew older, I tried to make sense of that night, of what I had witnessed. It became a puzzle I couldn't quite solve. It was a moment I didn't fully understand at three, but one that imprinted itself on me—on my soul, maybe, long before I had the words to articulate what it was. The confusion of that night never fully left me. I would see my father and my mother in the light of day, and they would seem like two separate figures—my father, the politician, the man who stood on the edge of power, and Yasmin, the mother with whom I would come to spend some time on weekends and who would then nurture me with quiet strength in her own modest house. But in the quiet recesses of my mind, I knew there was more, something hidden in the spaces between their words, between their silences, between their lives. I began to understand that their love, if you could call it that, was something complex, something that could not be labeled or defined in conventional terms. It was not a simple thing, not something that could be easily explained or broken down into pieces. It was messy, tangled, and full of contradictions. It was the kind of love that existed in the shadows, never fully seen by the world, never fully acknowledged, but always there, always just beneath the surface.

For a long time, I couldn't reconcile the two worlds I saw—the one where my father was the political man, the man who commanded respect, and the one where he was someone else entirely, drawn to Yasmin in a way that defied reason. I realized that I would never fully understand the complexities of their relationship, nor would I ever be able to fully comprehend the depth of what I had witnessed that night. But the memory of it shaped me, shaped the way I saw love and connection, and left me with questions that I would carry with me into adulthood.

As I grew up, I learned that the things we witness as children are often the things that shape us the most. The things we don't fully understand, the things we can't articulate, are the things that stay with us the longest. And for me, that night, that primal scene became a shadow that lingered in the corners of my mind, unresolved, but deeply etched into my being. I knew that despite the physical distance and the seeming separation that defined their lives, the bond between my father, Ramesh, and my mother, Yasmin Khan, could never break. It was a connection that neither time nor circumstance could sever, one that thrummed beneath the surface, quietly enduring in the shadows of their lives. Though he had taken me from her after my birth, it was clear that something deeper than parental duty or legal rights was at play between them. For years, they maintained an intimate, clandestine relationship that was as much about the weight of shared history as it was about something more profound, an unspoken yearning that neither could extinguish, even as they lived separate lives.

Ramesh, my father, was a man driven by ambition, his eyes constantly set on the next step, the next rung in the political ladder. His world was full of speeches, handshakes, and the carefully constructed narratives that he wove around his public persona. But in the silence of the night, away from the eyes of the world, he was a different man. Yasmin was his tether to something more real, more visceral. The politics, the career, even the expectations of his family—all of that was distant when she was near. There was a quiet, secret place where they met—an unspoken pact between them, a space where the complexities of religion, culture, and family dynamics faded into the background. I had always sensed the passion they held for each other, even as a child, although I never had the words for it then. Yasmin, in her quiet grace, occupied a place in his heart that was not easily extended or shared with others. Their relationship was not something that could be explained in simple terms—it was layered, complicated by the choices they had made and the life they had built separately. But there was no denying that something bound them together, even if it was a bond forged in the silence of unspoken promises. They would meet in the dead of night, when the world outside had quieted down and the shadows of the house seemed to stretch longer, more welcoming. Ramesh would come to her in moments of stillness, when the weight of the day had lifted, when the demands of his political world had receded, even if only for a few hours. Their meetings were never grand, never announced. They were quiet affairs, often carried out in whispered words and tentative touches, as though both were aware of the fragility of the moment. Yet, there was a passion there that couldn't be extinguished by time or separation.

Yasmin never asked for anything more than this, it seemed. She didn't ask him to leave his world behind, to abandon his ambitions for the sake of a life with her. Instead, their moments together were brief, but they were always full of an intensity that seemed to be more about the memory of a love lost than the present moment. They didn't need grand gestures. What mattered was the unspoken understanding they shared, the quiet, intimate connection that passed between them like a current of electricity. In these moments, there were no barriers between them—no religion, no family expectations, no cultural divides. Just the raw, human need to connect, to be seen, to be understood. Yasmin was his refuge, the one person who could see beyond the political figure, beyond the family man, and into the soul of the person he was when he was with her. And in turn, she sought his presence, the kind of connection that only he could give her, despite the choices they both had made. It was a love that existed outside the boundaries of what the world expected from them. They were complete in themselves and never sought to marry anyone else. They were not reckless ever. Their love was deep, an undercurrent that flowed through the gaps in their lives, feeding off the history they had shared, the things they had lost, and the things they had never been able to fully relinquish. When they were together, it was as if the world outside ceased to exist. There were no political careers to protect, no family to navigate around. There was only the moment— the slow, careful touch of hands, the quiet murmur of words exchanged in the darkness. It was as if, in those moments, they were allowed to breathe without the weight of the world pressing down on them.

But even in this stolen intimacy, there were always boundaries. Ramesh's fear of the consequences loomed over them both, an unspoken but ever-present reality. He knew the risks of being seen with her, knew the power his family had to destroy what little they had built. Yasmin, too, had her own quiet fears, a sense that no matter how much they loved each other, they could never truly be together in the way she might have dreamed. There was too much at stake, too many forces working against them, too many people who would never accept their union. Yet, in those moments when they were together, they existed in a world of their own—a world that was created by the force of their emotions, by the memory of their shared history. It was a history marked by passion and loss, by choices made in the heat of youth and the calm of later years, by a love that had never fully extinguished but had merely been tempered by time. Ramesh would leave her in the early hours of the morning, just as quietly as he had arrived, slipping out into the world he had created for himself. And Yasmin would watch him go, her heart heavy with the knowledge that this was all they could have—these brief, stolen moments that were as much about the past as they were about the present. Yet, there was a part of her that could never let go of him, a part that would always carry the memory of what they had shared, even when he was no longer there to hold her.

I grew up in the shadow of their love, never fully understanding its complexity, never fully aware of the depth of what they had shared. I saw them as two separate figures in my life—my father, the politician, the man who had taken me from my mother and raised me with a sense of duty, and my mother, Yasmin, who loved me with a quiet devotion that I could never fully appreciate until much later. But in the spaces between them, there was something more—a connection that could not be easily explained, a bond that defied logic and reason, that defied everything they had chosen for themselves. Now, as I look back, I realize that their love was never truly about the physicality of their meetings, nor was it solely about the unfulfilled promises of a life that never came to be. It was about the quiet power of what they shared, something deeper than passion or politics, something that remained constant despite the world around them. It was a love that endured, not because it was perfect, but because it was theirs, fragile, imperfect, and yet unmistakably real. These were the complex boundaries of their love.

Ramesh, my father, never married my mother, Yasmin, in the way one would expect, not in the grand ceremonies that are often associated with traditional unions. There were no elaborate rituals in a family home with loud chants, feasts, and guests who came from both sides of the family to witness the union of two lives. In the eyes of the world, it was not a marriage—at least not by societal standards—but for my parents, it was an understanding, a deep connection that surpassed all conventions. He had told me once when I was curious about the nature of their relationship, that he had taken Yasmin to a small, lesser-known temple in Ayodhya. It was a place away from the bustling crowds and political pressures, nestled between narrow alleys, where the air was thick with the scent of incense, flowers, and the gentle hum of reverence. Ayodhya, with its history woven into the very fabric of India's religious conflicts, was the backdrop to their quiet union, a place both sacred and fraught with contradictions, where religion and politics clashed and converged. For my father, it was the perfect place for something so deeply personal, a union that defied the religious walls between them.

The temple, where my father took Yasmin, was not one of the grand, well-known structures. It stood like a forgotten relic in the labyrinth of narrow streets, a humble abode that seemed to resist the flood of pilgrims that often swarmed to the more famous temples. There was an old banyan tree in the courtyard, its roots curling around the stones, and the temple's stone walls were weathered, covered in a blanket of moss. The air inside the temple was thick with centuries of devotion, the smell of burning ghee and incense rising to the heavens. It was a place where time seemed to stand still, where the sounds of the outside world were muffled by the stillness inside. It was here, in this place of quiet holiness, that Ramesh chose to bring Yasmin, not for an ostentatious ceremony, but for a quiet vow, one that neither demanded attention nor approval from anyone but themselves. I remember him describing the place to me, his voice quiet, reverential even as he spoke of it, as if the memory held an almost sacred weight to him. The temple had a serenity about it, a peace that he said felt like an ancient understanding between the land, the gods, and the people who dared to seek truth outside the boundaries of prescribed rituals. It was not large, but the walls were adorned with the intricate carvings of gods and goddesses, their faces serene and their hands frozen in eternal poses of blessing and grace. There was a statue of Lord Vishnu near the altar, a symbol of preservation and protection, and nearby, a small shrine to Lord Shiva, the destroyer and the transformer, representing the divine forces that shaped the world. To Ramesh, this was an apt space for a union that defied the norms, one that blended faiths and cultures in a way that was truly his own. Ramesh had taken Yasmin to the temple in the early morning, when the air was still cool and the world around them was waking up. The streets were empty, save for a few early risers, and there was a quiet stillness in the air. My father had made no grand preparations. He wasn't one to announce such things to the world—he was a man of actions more than words. All he had told Yasmin was that he wanted to take her somewhere sacred, a place that would be their own, where they could share a vow in the most intimate way possible.

When they entered the temple, a priest, old, bent, but with eyes that seemed to hold centuries of wisdom, was already waiting for them. The priest had no questions, no judgments. He did not ask for an explanation of why a Hindu man had brought a Muslim woman to be wed in a temple that, in the context of religion, was not supposed to accept such a union. The priest simply nodded in acknowledgment and went about his work. In that moment, there were no barriers, no differences between them. The priest did not need to ask if Yasmin was a true believer of the Hindu faith; he did not ask her to renounce her Muslim faith or adopt the Hindu rituals of worship. He simply performed the rituals, knowing that what they shared—this quiet love—was as sacred as any vow spoken in the presence of a hundred gods.

The priest began with the ancient chants, his voice slow and steady, reciting the traditional mantras that bound two people in marriage. His hands moved over the fire, the flame dancing in the brass vessel, as he offered prayers to the gods for the couple's well-being. Yasmin stood quietly beside my father, her eyes cast downward, a slight flush coloring her cheeks. Ramesh, too, was quiet— his usual political fervor and boldness tempered in the presence of this sacred space. His hand was on Yasmin's, not possessively, but as if holding her was the most natural thing in the world, as if the weight of their connection was enough to speak louder than any words ever could.

The priest continued with the ritual, taking a pinch of red powder, *kumkum*, and asked Ramesh to place it on Yasmin's *maang*, the parting of her hair, as was the custom in a Hindu marriage. The red powder, symbolizing the blessing of the goddess, was an ancient gesture, a sign of devotion, a mark of belonging. He did this not to change Yasmin, not to erase her Muslim identity, but as a symbol of her place in my father's heart, and in that moment, in his world, where they both stood together. It was a simple, intimate act—a gesture that had been repeated countless times before, yet for Ramesh and Yasmin, it held its own meaning. It was their act of defiance against the divisions between them, a quiet rebellion that spoke of love that refused to be confined by the walls of religion.

The priest then tied a sacred thread around their wrists, a bond of protection and unity. It wasn't the traditional sacred thread that would be tied between the bride and groom in a usual Hindu ceremony, but a simple string, symbolizing the promise they made to each other. The string was tied in a knot, one that neither time nor circumstance could undo. They exchanged no vows in words, but their eyes spoke volumes. Yasmin, for the briefest of moments, seemed to look beyond the priest, beyond the temple, into the world outside. She was in this moment, and yet, she was suspended somewhere between her faith and the world my father had built for her. Ramesh's gaze, too, was fixed on her, a silent promise. When the ritual was complete, the priest gave a final blessing, one of prosperity and happiness, of long life and good fortune. His voice was deep and reverent, carrying the weight of centuries of tradition as it filled the temple, reaching its echoes into the corners where dust settled on forgotten carvings. The room was silent except for the occasional flutter of a bird outside and the faint smell of incense hanging in the air.

They left quietly, walking side by side, the weight of what they had done settling between them like a shared secret. For the world, they were not married—not in the way that people expected, not in the way that society demanded. But for them, in that moment, in that quiet temple, they were bound by something much stronger than any ceremony or tradition could offer. Their union was a testament to the fact that love, real love, transcends all boundaries, all labels, and that true connection is never something that can be defined by religion, race, or culture. It was a bond that would live on, quietly, beneath the surface, in the spaces where no one could see it. Despite her staunch attachment to her faith, there was a part of Ramesh that was undeniably drawn to Yasmin. Her presence, the very air around her, seemed to hold a magnetic pull he couldn't escape. The physical satisfaction that their nightly lovemaking offered was undeniable, but it was the connection, the silent understanding between them, that lingered long after. In her, Ramesh found someone who saw him not just as a politician, not just as a son of a respected family, but as a man who craved something deeper—a partner who could hold the weight of his soul without demanding anything in return. She didn't need him to perform or prove anything. She accepted him with the quiet grace of someone who knew that some things were never meant to be changed.

But what lay at the heart of Ramesh's refusal to let the world know that he had married Yasmin? It wasn't just about love; it was about everything else. His fear of the repercussions that would come from such a decision weighed heavily on him. He was aware of the strict expectations his family had of him, especially in terms of his choice of wife. The weight of cultural expectations was heavy, and the scrutiny that would come with marrying a Muslim woman would have been intense. The political world he inhabited did not leave room for such vulnerabilities, not if he wanted to keep climbing. It was also my father, Ramesh's choice, a decision rooted in practicality, fear, and the invisible forces that shaped his life. To understand why he never acknowledged his marriage to the world, it's necessary to peel away the layers of his personality and examine the subtle forces that played out between him and my mother over the years. His life was one where everything had its place, his political ambitions, his societal standing, and his deep-rooted convictions about family and tradition. But in his relationship with Yasmin, the traditional rules were bent and broken. His marriage to my mother was a line he had crossed and yet refused to cross as a social act. Ramesh was, by all appearances, a man content with fulfilling his physical and emotional needs with Yasmin, though he kept the relationship tucked away in a shadowed corner of his life, where it existed only for the moments when he could steal away from the weight of his public obligations. To him, marriage was more than a bond between two people. It was not a public statement nor a declaration to the world, and he was never ready to make such a declaration. The political landscape he navigated every day demanded a kind of clarity, a precision of identity that he couldn't allow himself to lose, not even for the woman he still sought with such intensity. My mother, Yasmin's faith, could only add layers to this tension. From the time my father's family came to take me away after my birth, a deep quiet descended between them. Yet, despite their separation, the emotional connection remained as strong as ever. Ramesh and Yasmin had crossed paths in their youth, drawn together by the sheer force of their attraction to one another. That attraction, once kindled, could never be fully extinguished. They were like two parallel rivers, flowing alongside each other, unable to merge but never completely drifting apart either.

Their relationship, as secret as it was, was also marked by a strange kind of fulfillment. There was never any talk about the future, no mention of what could be or what should have been. Instead, what existed between them was a silent, steady recognition that the here and now was all they could claim. Ramesh's visits to Yasmin were always brief, stolen moments in the quiet hours of the night, when the rest of the world slept and his public life paused for a moment. The world outside didn't matter when he was with her. In those precious hours, there was no political ambition, no family pressure, no expectations—just them, together, as they had once been. Their union was a connection that defied all reason, all logic, and all the barriers life had placed in their way. Ramesh never needed Yasmin in the traditional sense of a wife. She was not a companion in the way that society expected her to be, and he was not the husband who would promise her the world. What they shared was different. It was a quiet, intimate arrangement—a kind of emotional parallel to the worlds they occupied. He didn't need to announce his relationship with her to the world, and she never pushed him to. Their bond existed outside the realm of tradition, of public recognition, and yet it was real. For all his outward stoicism, Ramesh found something in Yasmin that he couldn't find in anyone else: a space where his vulnerabilities were safe, where his choices didn't define him, and where love didn't come with the weight of expectation.

And Yasmin, for her part, never demanded more than what Ramesh was willing to give. She was a woman who had lived a life of quiet strength, understanding that the world often placed constraints on what a woman could ask for, especially a woman in her position. She loved Ramesh in a way that transcended the notion of possession. What mattered to her wasn't the title of a wife—it was the deep and abiding connection they shared, no matter how fleeting. She knew that in him, there was a man who could never be fully hers in the way she might have hoped, but she was willing to accept that reality. She had learned long ago that love, in its purest form, was not always about ownership or societal validation. It was about the moments they could share, and those moments were enough. For years, they continued with this arrangement, fulfilling the physical desires and emotional needs that neither had fully realized could be fulfilled by anyone else. The complexity of their bond only deepened over time. Ramesh would return to his life as a political figure, a father to me, a son to his family, always the man who carried the weight of expectations. But when the night fell, when the world slept, he would seek out Yasmin, and for a few hours, he would be the man who could let go of his public persona, who could simply be himself, not a politician, not a son, but just a man with the woman he had never fully let go of.

For Yasmin, these moments were not merely about physical satisfaction. They were about connection, about the quiet understanding between them that transcended the years they had spent apart. She knew that their love, however imperfect, was real. She had learned that love was not always about the ideal or the perfect, but about the space between the moments, the shared silences, and the acceptance of one another, flaws and all.

5

My mother, Yasmin Khan, was born in 1966 into a devout Muslim family in Ayodhya, when India, still freshly independent, was beginning to define itself beyond the long shadow of British rule. Ayodhya, ancient and fiercely alive, seemed a reflection of that uncertain awakening: a city where myth and memory tangled in narrow lanes, where history echoed like the lingering notes of a sitar played at dusk.

Her family lived in a compact brick house tucked deep within the Muslim quarter. Its walls, once a vibrant blue, had faded with time, but the intricate motifs carved into the plaster remained, quiet guardians of heritage. Their neighborhood would always be alive with the sounds of vendors hawking fresh produce, the rhythmic clanging of metal from nearby workshops, and the melodic calls to prayer echoing from the mosque just a few blocks away. The *masjid* was more than just a physical structure situated near the bustling market of Ayodhya; it embodied the spirit of the community. With its tranquil courtyard and weathered Mughal arches, the mosque served as the heart of their lives. It was a gathering place where prayers resonated, celebrations unfolded, and laughter mingled with the aroma of communal meals, creating a sacred and social space.

As a child, Yasmin often accompanied her mother, Amina, on quiet morning walks to any of the mosques in the city: *Masjid Dorahikuan, Masjid Mali Mandir ke Bagal, Masjid Kaziyana Achchan ke Bagal, Masjid Imambara, Masjid Riyaz ke Bagal, Masjid Badar Paanjitola, Masjid Madaar Shah,* and *Masjid Tehribazar Jogiyon ki.* Though it was not customary for women to pray inside mosques in Ayodhya during those years, Yasmin and her mother would still visit, quietly and respectfully, often pausing in the shaded courtyards or standing just beyond the arched entrances. There were no designated spaces for women then, but on special days, especially during Ramzan or community gatherings, the atmosphere softened. The mosque became more than a place of worship; it became a shared cultural space where Yasmin, even as a child, sensed the warmth of belonging and the unspoken rhythms of faith. Of them all, she felt most drawn to *Masjid Tehribazar Jogiyon ki—* its history as curious as it was beautiful, said to have been built over two centuries ago by Hindu ascetics known as *Jogis.*

Draped in a simple but graceful headscarf, she would run her fingers along the cool stone walls, as if listening through her skin to the prayers that had echoed there for generations. The mosque's warm interior was a kaleidoscope of colors and textures, a blend of worn, colorful carpets underfoot, dust-mottled glass, and geometric designs etched with patient devotion into the plaster. The air was thick with the fragrance of rosewater and old incense. It was in this sacred hush that she first encountered the teachings of the Quran, verses murmured by her mother in a soft, almost hesitant tone, and reinforced by her more zealous father with reverence and unwavering discipline.

Ayodhya is a city of layered silences and sudden clangs. A few miles or so from the narrow lane of their house, the slender shikhara of the *Hanuman Garhi* temple pierced the sky, its sandstone ribs catching the sun like old memory. Vendors nearby sold garlands that smelled not sweet but acrid, heavy with wilted marigolds and the sharpness of turmeric dust. Temple bells would ring out in a wild rhythm, urgent, chaotic, while from the opposite lane, the *azaan* floated out from the mosque, its long, drawn syllables pressing gently against the heat. She often paused between the two sounds, uncertain which belonged more to her. My mother, Yasmin Khan, grew up in the embrace of these dual worlds, their histories intertwining yet often fraught with tension. In the nineteen sixties, conversations about faith and coexistence flickered through the markets like the flickering flames of the oil lamps that illuminated homes at dusk. Her own father, Adil Khan, a respected schoolteacher known for his unwavering integrity, often opened his home to host community gatherings hoping to foster a spirit of togetherness and dialogue. Yet, despite his efforts, families from Hindu faith seldom attended these gatherings, reflecting a wider divide in the community. These missed opportunities weighed heavily on him, as he believed that true progress could only be achieved through open hearts and minds engaging in meaningful conversations. Beneath his gestures for progressive discussions lay an undercurrent of unease, a reminder of the political struggles that had marked their lives, the remnants of colonialism still felt in the collective psyche of the community.

As a young girl, my mother, Yasmin Khan, used to lose herself in Ayodhya's narrow alleys—not out of mischief, but in quiet fascination. She once told me how she could recognize shopkeepers by the rhythms of their shouts. The man who sold turmeric always sang his prices, while the woman who sold lentils clapped twice before speaking. The bazaar had its own music. Steam rose from roadside *biryani* stalls, curling around heaps of custard apples and bitter gourds that looked, to her mind, like characters from stories yet to be told. Even as a child, she understood that the city wasn't just noisy; it was layered, like a prayer whispered under breath. She was alert not just to color and sound, but to the careful lines people didn't cross. She could name which alleys were safe for a girl with her name, and which stalls would go quiet when she passed. The market bustled, yes—women haggling over fruits, children flinging pebbles like prayers—but behind the music of daily life was an unspoken tension, brittle as dry tamarind pods. She loved the city, but even then, she knew love here came with conditions.

As she grew older, Yasmin Khan became somewhat aware of the delicate balance her family maintained in a city revered for its sacred sites, yet also marked by deep-seated divisions. She would sometimes feel the weight of her city, the religious traditions and rituals that had shaped her life. She could also sense the longing for acceptance in a world that demanded allegiance to one faith or another. Her town's delicate façade of unity often masked the conflicts that simmered just below the surface. It would challenge and undermine her own and her older brother, Aarif Khan's understanding of belonging.

My mother, Yasmin Khan, studied at Ayodhya Model School in the 1970s, a modest institution tucked behind a crumbling post office, its colonial bones showing in cracked cornices and window frames forever stuck half-open. The fans wheezed more than spun, and the marigolds in the courtyard bloomed unevenly, one corner always bald from boys sneaking through at lunch. The school spoke often of communal harmony, pinning slogans beside the chalkboards, but Yasmin noticed that when trouble stirred outside the school walls, certain classmates grew quiet or absent. She still loved those mornings, standing beside her Sikh and Jain friends during the anthem, but even as a child, she sensed that unity was more performance than fact, an anthem more than a reality. In her classroom, Yasmin sat beside her best friend Aditi, whose laugh sometimes drew the teacher's eye before either girl could hush it. They traded not just secrets, but misunderstandings too. Aditi once brought Yasmin a box of homemade *laddoos* during Ramadan, only to learn that fasting meant waiting, not feasting. Yasmin was captivated by Aditi's stories of Diwali nights aglow with firelight, the air smelling of sweets and alive with colors from intricate rangolis. Yet, more than the floor patterns, what lingered was the quiet emptiness in her mother's eyes when Eid came around. There was something cloaked in her gestures, a story Yasmin sensed but never dared to ask about. Yasmin told me that her own mother would become somewhat melancholic at the turn of these religious festivals. It was almost as if she was hiding something. What Yasmin remembered most was her mother turning silent, almost withdrawn, her smile stretching too carefully, as if stitched over something frayed. There was always a moment, right before guests arrived, when Yasmin would find her standing alone in the kitchen, one hand resting on the counter, as if steadying herself against a memory she refused to share.

The teachers at Ayodhya Model School believed in discipline, but there was room, just enough, for imagination. Mr. Sharma, the principal, often veered off the text-book, inviting the older students to argue over dates and dynasties, to think about whose stories got preserved and whose were erased. My mother, Yasmin, was especially drawn to those sessions on Ayodhya's layered past, the rulers and saints, yes, but also the weavers and fakirs who had left quieter marks. It was there that she first understood history not just as memory, but as something that could be contested.

Outside the classroom, she found herself drawn to the stage. At the annual cultural fest, she'd perform short plays—some comic, some political—her voice steady even when the audience erupted in laughter. Her best performances, she said, were with classmates she barely spoke to during the day, their connection forging in rehearsals after school under the neem tree. Holi brought color, yes, but also complexity—some parents frowned at interfaith frolic, others looked away. Winter meant sports day. Yasmin once won a race with her shoe flying off halfway down the track. Her friends teased her about it for weeks.

But even as she laughed, Yasmin sensed a shadow. The whispers had begun—about the old mosque, about rightful claims, about who belonged and who didn't. Discussions at school stayed civil, but the air at home grew heavy with unsaid things. No one spoke of a Muslim aunt's marriage to a Hindu man. No one mentioned the conversions. But shadows crept in. Conversations grew cautious. Whispers about the Babri Masjid, abandoned but not forgotten, began to circulate. Some older students parroted their parents' talk; others stayed silent. Yasmin listened. She watched. She carried it all inside, the silences louder than the words. She yearned for a version of Ayodhya where faith didn't require hiding.

My mother, Yasmin Khan, was still young when her

world tilted irreversibly, on the day her older brother, Aarif, died. Until then, Ayodhya in the early 1980s had throbbed with life for her. Its narrow gullies echoed with the cries of vendors selling fragrant marigolds, hot *samosas*, and glass bangles. The air was a mingling of incense, turmeric, and the sweet call of the *muezzin* blending, sometimes uneasily, with temple bells. Yasmin had always sensed something brittle beneath the surface, like the stillness before a storm. But in those days, joy still felt possible. Of course, she was aware of the grounds shifting slowly as well, beneath the colorful façade, and the simmering tensions that lurked like the heat of the midday sun that was always unyielding and oppressive. But they were happy until Aarif suddenly died. Her older brother, Aarif had been the sun around which Yasmin's family, and their world and modest home, had orbited. With his wild curls and disarming, almost infectious smile, he had an effortless charm that drew people to him. Aarif made friends as effortlessly as he breathed. His laughter, his teasing, and his irreverent brilliance, were unmistakable aspects of his personality. And then, on a harsh summer afternoon, everything stilled. One moment she was in the courtyard tying her braid; the next, the air had changed, as if the sun itself recoiled. Her brother was gone. And nothing could fill the silence he left behind. Yasmin Khan could never have anticipated how swiftly her world would fracture.

That morning in Ayodhya unfolded with its usual cadence—the clang of hand-pulled rickshaws, the hiss of boiling milk at the tea stall, the smell of fried *pakoras* curling into the air.

Aarif rose early to complete a paper on Urdu verse, Faiz's poetry open beside him like a conversation unfinished. He had a quiet intensity about him in the mornings, as if the world's noise had not yet caught up. He loved mornings like these, when the world felt orderly, the chaos still held at bay. But the city was shifting. With a major Hindu festival approaching, saffron flags had begun to flutter with a strange new urgency. Loudspeakers tied to trees played devotional songs on loop, louder than in previous years, less about celebration, more about presence. Devotional *bhajans* resounded through the streets, more fervent and unrelenting than in years past. Posters with bold, inflammatory slogans clung to the walls like warnings, with pointed intensity. Local politicians, eager to stoke their constituencies, had made fiery speeches in the weeks leading up to the festival, subtly urging their supporters to assert dominance in the disputed area. In the weeks before, speeches had grown sharper, crowds larger, and Yasmin remembered sensing, though not yet understanding, the friction that crackled just beneath the surface.

Aarif couldn't have known that the path he took home that day would intersect with more than just a procession. It would brush the live wire of something far older, and far more dangerous. That day, Aarif chose a different route home, nothing dramatic, just a shortcut to make up for time. He didn't know that a procession would swell into his path, or that a raised voice could splinter a gathering into panic. He didn't see it coming. None of them did.

The unrest began with a Hindu religious procession. It was not an uncommon sight in the city. The procession wound its way into a predominantly Muslim neighborhood, a labyrinth of narrow alleys and densely packed homes. The residents, already wary, watched from their windows as saffron-clad men chanted slogans. It began innocuously—some children playing cricket stopped to gawk at the spectacle. Then came the loudspeakers. The devotional music, laced with political undertones, boomed through the neighborhood, rattling window-panes and fraying nerves.

The scuffle began near the local mosque. A group of Muslim shopkeepers, irritated by the blaring volume, stepped forward to request that it be lowered. Words were exchanged, tempers flared, and the situation escalated with alarming speed. What started as a verbal argument turned into a physical altercation when one of the shopkeepers shoved a marcher. Within minutes, the narrow alley became a battleground. Stones were hurled, shops shuttered in panic, and bystanders scattered.

Aarif, then only nineteen, was on his way home from college. He had taken a detour through this neighborhood, hoping to avoid the larger, busier streets. As he rounded the corner, he found himself in the thick of chaos. He saw the mob before he heard it—a seething mass of bodies, shouting and shoving, with stones flying like projectiles. Aarif froze, unsure whether to retreat or forge ahead.

A young man in a saffron scarf lunged forward from the mob, swinging an iron rod like a weapon forged in hatred. His scream tore through the air, guttural and raw, a sound that silenced even the chaos behind him. Aarif raised his hands in a gesture of surrender, trying to convey that he was not involved. But the man in saffron, blinded by fury and the mob's momentum, had swung the rod with brutal force. His rage, cold and deliberate, had assumed the terrifying calm of someone who knew exactly what he wanted to destroy. The rod connected with Aarif's temple, sending him crashing into the ground. Blood pooled beneath his head, mingling with the dust of the street. Aarif's heart raced as he caught the glint of the trident and the screech of hatred piercing the air, a horrifying sound that would have reverberated in his being before he was hit hard. Those who witnessed gasped, a collective breath held in disbelief. Time seemed to stretch, the world around him blurring into an indistinct haze as he lay bleeding to death. When the sickening thud echoed through the street, Aarif felt his soul tear apart. Aarif's body crumpled like a rag doll; his laughter silenced forever. Chaos erupted and intensified in the melee. People screamed, some wept, and others stood frozen, caught between shock and the instinct to flee.

For a moment, the chaos paused. Even mobs, wild and untamed, can sometimes sense when a line has been crossed. But the moment was fleeting. Someone shouted, "Move him!" and two older men from the neighborhood rushed forward to lift Aarif's limp body. They carried him through the maze of alleys, away from the clamor, finally laying him down on the verandah of his family home.

Amina, Aarif's mother, was the first to see him. She had been preparing his favorite dish, *keema paratha*, when the commotion outside drew her attention. When she saw her son, her heart seized. The pot slipped from her hands, spilling hot oil across the floor, but she didn't notice. She rushed to Aarif, her hands trembling as she tried to shake him awake. The sight of his bloodied face, his half-closed eyes, and the stillness of his body shattered her.

Neighbors gathered quickly, some murmuring prayers, others offering hollow words of comfort and condolence. Someone ran to fetch Adil. When Adil arrived, his usually composed demeanor crumbled. He sank to his knees beside Aarif's body, his face a mask of anguish. He ran his fingers through his son's hair, now matted with blood, and whispered his name over and over as if willing him to respond.

My mother told me how her world had narrowed, her

vision focused solely on her brother lying lifeless on the front porch, blood pooling beneath him like a dark stain on the world. The mob mentality took over as the news spread like wildfire. The Muslim men from the neighborhood, faces twisted in anguish and rage, surged toward the possible killer or killers. Everyone had watched in horror as a torrent of fury and grief had swept through them. Their voices rose to a deafening crescendo, a primal roar that echoed through the streets, calling for justice. They shouted, "Murderer!" their fists clenched, eyes blazing with the fire of a community wronged. Yasmin had stood rooted to the spot, her heart pounding in her chest, caught between her desire to bring her brother back to life and the chaotic fury that enveloped her. The iron rod had been transformed into a symbol of the gory violence that lurked just beneath the surface of their lives. Several potential Hindu killers, terrified and bewildered, became targets as the mob descended upon them, fueled by grief, anger, and a thirst for vengeance. In those moments, my mother, Yasmin, had felt her grief morph into a maelstrom of emotions, of anger, despair, and confusion. The lines between right and wrong blurred as she watched the scene unfold. Her Muslim community, bound by their shared pain, was on the brink of destruction. Yasmin could only clutch her hands together, feeling the warmth of her brother's absence envelop her like a suffocating blanket.

As the family sat in shock, the larger implications of Aarif's death began to ripple through the community. Word spread quickly. By evening, the narrow lanes were filled with mourners. The men sat silently in the courtyard, their expressions heavy with grief and anger. The women gathered indoors, their low wails echoing like a lament for the city itself.

Adil Khan's transformation began that night. Something in him had snapped. He had always been a man of principle, known for his even temperament and refusal to be drawn into communal disputes. But as he stared at his son's lifeless body, something inside him changed forever. Aarif's death was not just a personal loss; it became a symbol of the systemic neglect and oppression faced by Muslims in India. He thought of the numerous incidents of communal violence that had gone unpunished, the promises of justice that had never materialized, and the political rhetoric that seemed designed to divide rather than unite.

The days that followed were a blur of rituals and unrest. Outside the family's immediate grief, the city simmered. The news of Aarif's death became a rallying cry for the Muslim community, who saw it as yet another example of their vulnerability. Protests erupted, demanding justice for Aarif and an end to the escalating communal violence. But the Hindu community, bolstered by local political leaders, framed the incident as a defensive act, claiming that the procession had been provoked. The truth was lost in the cacophony of accusations and counter-accusations.

For Adil, the aftermath was a study in betrayal. The police, instead of investigating Aarif's death, filed charges against Muslim residents for "instigating violence." The local media painted Aarif as a bystander caught in the crossfire, a narrative that, while technically true, stripped his death of its larger significance. No one spoke of the mob, the iron rod, or the systemic failures that had allowed such violence to become commonplace.

Amidst the chaos, Amina clung to her faith, praying for strength and justice. But Adil grew increasingly bitter. He began attending community meetings, speaking out against the systemic inequalities that had taken his son's life. His voice, once measured and calm, now carried an edge of anger. He spoke of Aarif not just as a victim but as a martyr, a symbol of the price minorities paid in a country that promised equality but delivered little. The city, meanwhile, edged closer to an inferno. The Babri Masjid-Ram Janmabhoomi dispute, reignited by the violence, became a flashpoint. Politicians on both sides used Aarif's death to further their agendas, turning a family's tragedy into a political tool. Adil watched in despair as his son's memory was co-opted by people who cared nothing for his life. Days later, as the city began to recover from the riots, the pain of Aarif's loss remained raw. His room, untouched since that fateful day, became a shrine of sorts. His books, his clothes, even the pen he had left on his desk, were preserved as if he might return at any moment. Amina would often sit in the room, her fingers tracing the spines of his books, her tears falling silently onto the pages.

Days turned into a complete blur as the aftermath of Aarif's death consumed the family. The funeral preparations were a cacophony of muted whispers and muffled sobs. Yasmin felt as if she were moving through a dream, a ghost among the living. The air in their home was thick with incense, curling in lazy spirals through every room and mingling with the bitter tang of sorrow. Relatives filled the small space, their faces etched with grief, their voices low and hushed. Amid the mournful atmosphere, Yasmin's mother, Amina, always calm and stoic, began to crumble. The loss of her son had completely shattered her. In a moment of vulnerability, she started pleading to her husband, Adil Khan, who was equally engulfed with grief and the pain of losing his son. Along with a brother's loss, Yasmin had become aware of the dark secret that had been buried deep within her own mother's heart. "Aarif. Aarif," she whispered, her voice trembling and shaking. She soon started growling and howling with grief, "I cannot bury him, Adil. I must cremate him. Adil. Adil." The air grew taut with disbelief, as if waiting to snap. Grief had unraveled her, fraying the edges of her sanity, leaving her adrift in a sea of despair. She had gone daft, to be sure, and had lost her mind in her grief, caught between tradition and the haunting truth of a mother's request. In their Muslim family, cremation was an unthinkable act, a violation of everything they had held sacred. "*Ammi*, we can't," Yasmin protested, her voice cracking under the weight of her emotions. "It's not right." Tears streamed down her mother's face as she clutched Yasmin's hands tightly. "You don't understand. I was born Hindu. I cannot let him be buried. It's against everything I believe." The revelation hung in the air like a specter, darkening their grief. Yasmin's world tilted, and the foundations of her identity began to crumble.

Driven by an insatiable need to understand, Yasmin found herself rummaging through the house, seeking solace among the shadows. In the dim light of her mother's room, she stumbled upon her mother's Godrej cupboard, its metal surface worn and faded. As she opened it, her breath caught in her throat. Inside lay a collection of Hindu idols, dust-covered and forgotten, each one a relic of a life her mother had chosen to forget. Confusion reigned in Yasmin's heart as she grappled with her mother's past. In the quiet moments between sobs, she began to see the fractures in their lives. The idols of Hindu gods hidden away in her mother's cupboard whispered of a childhood long buried, a life left behind in the dust of denial. The complexity of her family's identity had twisted and turned in her mind, as she had felt the heavy weight of the generations before her.

Yasmin's heart raced as she held the idols in her hands, their painted faces staring back at her with a mixture of compassion and understanding. How could her mother have hidden this? How could she have abandoned a part of herself so completely? The clash of identities surged within Yasmin, battling for dominance. She felt betrayed, not just by her mother but by the very fabric of her existence. Days turned into nights, and the weight of Aarif's death clung to Yasmin like a shroud. The community gathered to mourn, their voices mingling in a somber chorus that reverberated through the streets of Ayodhya. Yasmin felt the collective grief envelop her, binding her to a legacy of pain that spanned generations. Yet, amidst the mourning, a sense of anger simmered beneath the surface. How could her mother have kept this secret? How could she have lived in the shadows of her past?

In a moment of seeming daring and with deep sadness, Yasmin confronted her mother, the hidden idols still fresh in her mind. "Why did you hide it from me that you were born Hindu, *ammi*?" she asked gently but firmly and despite the weight of Aarif's death hanging over them. "All these years, you've kept this part of yourself buried and a secret from me and our Aarif? He's gone, and he went without knowing what you are?" Her mother, Amina, aged and weary, met her gaze with a mixture of regret and sorrow. "Does it matter? I thought I could protect you. Does it matter anymore?" she said softly. "I thought I could protect myself. But in doing so, I lost a part of me, of my own self, that I can never reclaim." She burst into tears again. The words hung in the air, a painful reminder of the choices made and the lives lived in silence. Amina sat silently, her face pale and drawn. She knew the moment she had feared for so long had finally arrived. There was no more hiding. She could no longer keep her two worlds separate. The sad confrontation of her past would become a cathartic release for both women. Yasmin's anger and hurt slowly morphed into understanding as she looked at her mother, Amina.

She imagined her mother's Hindu childhood unfolding in the margins—in early mornings thick with woodsmoke and the rustle of saris, in the metallic clang of prayer bells drifting from a neighbor's courtyard. She pictured her not as a girl draped in ritual, but watching from doorways, mimicking mudras in secret, fingers trembling with borrowed divinity. Not festivals, but textures: the oily press of turmeric-stained fingertips, the sting of neem on the tongue, the quiet humiliation of not knowing a *mantra* fully, mouthing the syllables anyway. Hers was not a loud faith, but a quiet choreography of belonging and exclusion—learned through glances, gestures, silences. She imagined her mother's Hindu faith, not through rituals or festival days, but in the quieter, more forbidden hours: the hush of a temple procession winding past her street, the muffled drumbeats under her skin, her eyes drawn to the painted faces of gods she wasn't meant to see. Not reverence, but recognition—brief, electric—held her there, as though the air itself might answer back. The night was thick with an unspoken tension, and Yasmin could feel the burden of her mother's secrets closing in, like the walls of the small room they sat in. Her hands trembled as she grasped her cup of tea, the rim shaking just slightly enough to ripple the surface of the liquid inside. It had been years since Yasmin had asked her mother anything about her past. And tonight she had finally learned the truth. Yasmin's mother had been living with her secret for decades, and had no relationship left with her own family. It was a secret that had weighed on her heart and soul since the day she had decided to marry Adil Khan, Yasmin's father, and convert to Islam. She had been born Uma, a devout Hindu woman raised in a conservative family in the heart of Ayodhya. Marrying a Muslim man and embracing Islam had been more than just an expression of love; it was a quiet defiance against tradition, a bold step into a world her family never imagined for her. It had come with consequences that she had carried like an invisible burden for decades.

"Tell me, *ammi*," Yasmin's voice trembled with unspoken grief as she asked her mother: "Why did you never tell us about your family, not even to your own children? Why did you keep who you were before you met *abbu* a secret from us?" Tears streamed down her cheeks, a raw ache for her deceased brother mingling with a longing for the stories left untold. Each word felt heavy with loss, as if unraveling her mother's silence could somehow bring her brother back to her. The question hung in the air, both a demand and a plea. Yasmin had always known that there was a part of her mother's life that she had kept hidden. And though her *ammi* had been a loving mother, Yasmin always sensed a profound sadness that had never truly left her. Despite Amina's unwavering love and devotion as a mother, Yasmin could feel a deep-seated sadness lingering in her eyes, a quiet ache that surfaced in the moments of silence between them, as if every smile was underpinned by the weight of unshared memories and unspoken grief.

Amina's eyes darted around the room, avoiding her daughter's gaze. She sighed heavily and her throat felt tight, as if words had been trapped there for decades, locked behind bars she had built herself. It was time to set them free, but she feared what would happen once she did. Amina had been a young and happy soul when she had met Adil, a charming and intellectual young man who had also lived in Ayodhya. Their first meeting had been purely accidental when Amina had been visiting the local library where she bumped into him near the history section. What began as a polite exchange of words had soon blossomed into an intense, hour-long conversation that meandered through history, politics, and the world far beyond Ayodhya. Despite their vastly different backgrounds, an unspoken connection simmered between them, undeniable and impossible to ignore. Their polite exchange of words had turned into a full conversation that lasted over an hour, discussing history, politics, and the world beyond Ayodhya. They came from different worlds, but there was an undeniable connection that neither could ignore. Adil was respectful, kind, and open-minded, but he was also Muslim—a fact that Amina was aware would be met with disapproval by her Hindu family and community. Yet, over the next few months, their meetings became more frequent, and their bond grew stronger. Adil was not like the men she had known; he respected her intellect, encouraged her independence, and admired her strength. But love, she knew, would not be enough to bridge the gap between their worlds. The thought of introducing Adil to her family filled her with dread. She could already imagine the harsh words, the anger, the shame her parents would feel. Hindu and Muslim marriages were considered a betrayal by both communities in her small town, a sin that would bring dishonor to both families. Despite this, she found herself standing at a crossroads.

6

For as long as she could remember, Uma had gone to the *Kanak Bhawan* Temple to seek clarity within the sanctuary. Bathed in the soft golden glow of the oil lamps that lined its grand entrance, the temple looked every bit like the "Palace of Gold" it was known as—a place where the sacred stories of Lord Rama and Sita came alive. The air was always thick there, in the Hindu abode, with the scent of jasmine and marigold garlands, the rhythmic chanting of bhajans echoing in the background like a balm for troubled souls. Under the temple's towering domes, she had once knelt as a child, praying to her gods with a heart full of devotion. But that one night, as she stood before the stone-carved idol of Sita, her mind was a tumultuous sea, offering no comfort, no familiar answers. The peace that had always been so readily available in this sacred space now eluded her. All she could think of was Adil—his warmth, the way his laughter could pierce through her insecurities, the tenderness in his eyes that made her feel truly seen. She had argued with herself for days, her mind churning in silence. Could she really step away from the world that had formed her? The rhythms of ritual, the cadence of prayers spoken in chorus, the festivals that returned through the years like seasons—all had once seemed inevitable. Now, they felt like a skin she wasn't sure she still lived in. Here, in the heart of Ayodhya, in this temple built in reverence to Lord Rama, the very ground seemed steeped in her heritage. She had always believed her path was already set —solid as the stone steps she now stood upon. And yet, with Adil, everything felt different. The weight of tradition, once so comforting, now seemed stifling. He had never pressured her to change, never mocked her beliefs. In him, she saw not a different faith but a shared future— a life built on love, on the kind of respect that transcended boundaries of religion and custom. Could she leave behind her gods for him? Or perhaps, more frightening, was the realization that she wasn't leaving them behind at all—but that love itself might be a different kind of worship. A tremor ran through her fingers as she clasped them together in prayer, searching for the words she had always known by heart. But that pivotal night, they felt foreign on her tongue. Could love and faith coexist? Could she merge the two worlds that had so far seemed destined to remain separate? The silence around her only deepened as her thoughts continued to swirl. Could she truly leave behind everything she had ever known for a man who practiced a different faith? For days, she had wrestled with her conscience. She had grown up steeped in the rituals and traditions of Hinduism. She had performed pujas with her family, had fasted for their gods, and believed in the teachings of her ancestors. And yet, with Adil, she saw the possibility of a new life—one built not on rigid customs but on love and mutual respect.

Beneath the watchful eyes of Lord Rama, Uma made her decision—one that would change the course of her life forever. The quiet murmur of prayers drifted through the temple, but inside her, there was only the storm of her thoughts. She had come here seeking clarity, as she always had. Yet now, the solace she once found in the flicker of oil lamps and the sacred murti of Ram and Sita eluded her. The faces of her gods seemed distant; their eternal smiles as unreachable as the stars that hung heavy in the sky above Ayodhya. Could they sense her turmoil? Uma had weighed this choice for weeks, each moment gnawing at her sense of duty, her heart torn between two worlds. She knew it with unwavering clarity —she would marry Adil. He was the one person who saw her as more than just the sum of her traditions, more than the obedient daughter who recited ancient prayers by rote. With Adil, she had found laughter, a partnership that felt like breathing in fresh air after a lifetime of suffocating inside her family's expectations. But there was a price, and it came not in the form of gold or ritual but in something far more complex: her identity. Adil had never pressured her. He loved her as she was, never once asking her to change her faith. And yet, Uma understood the unspoken expectations. His family, steeped in their own customs and traditions, would only accept her if she converted to Islam. The weight of that knowledge pressed on her like the heavy air before a monsoon, laden with unspoken fears and invisible barriers. She had spoken to Adil about it at length, his reassurances like soft whispers in the wind, promising her that they would find a way. But the reality was clearer to her now than ever. Without conversion, their union would be a constant battle, a relentless push against a tide too strong to resist. In her heart, Uma knew the conversion would be more symbolic than spiritual. Could she really sever the bond she had nurtured with her gods? Could she erase the quiet rhythm of her childhood—the smell of incense, her mother's fingers guiding her over the flickering flame? And what of the gods she had whispered to in the dark, the ones who had never asked her to choose? Those memories were woven into her very soul, as much a part of her as the blood in her veins.

To convert was not just to change a name or a faith, but to leave behind a world where she had once found meaning. And yet, she had already made up her mind. When she would kneel at the mosque, she would become Amina, a name that would mark her rebirth into a new life, but not an abandonment of her old one. Amina and Uma could coexist, even if no one else understood it.

Her marriage to Adil was a small, private affair, held under the cool marble arches of the mosque. The ceremony had been simple—just the two of them, Adil's close family, and a few friends. As the Imam blessed their union, Amina tried to silence the ache that tugged at her chest. Her family's absence loomed over her like a shadow. Her father had not even considered attending. The moment he learned of her intention to marry a Muslim, he had closed the door to her heart with a finality that shook her to her core and left her reeling. "You are dead to us," he had said, his voice cold, his eyes holding none of the warmth she had once sought in him.

"Here? On Ram Janam Bhoomi? In Ayodhya, the birthplace of our Lord Rama?" His voice cracked with disbelief, rising like a wave before crashing into anger. "Such betrayal! Here, in this sacred land where dharma was born? You dare to forsake your ancestors and your gods for him? For this man who worships differently? What have you become, Uma?" His words had cut through her like shards of glass, leaving her raw and bleeding inside. Her mother had stood beside him, eyes red from days of weeping, her mouth sealed in silence. The heartbreak was etched into the deep lines on her face, but she had spoken no words of comfort. Uma, now Amina, could almost hear her mother's prayers, whispered to the deities in her absence, pleading for her daughter's return, for her redemption. But the door had closed. The finality of her father's disowning left her untethered from the past. All she could cling to now was the future—a future with Adil, where love and respect would forge a new path. And yet, standing beside him under the mosque's archways, she couldn't help but feel that, like the name she had taken, her life was now divided—two names, two identities, two hearts, forever separate.

On her wedding day, Uma wore a simple white sari. It draped around her awkwardly, unfamiliar and foreign, a stark contrast to the vibrant red she had always dreamed of wearing as a Hindu bride. White was not the color of celebration, of life—it was the color of mourning for Hindus. The irony wasn't lost on her, and as she stood in the small, dimly lit mosque, she couldn't help but feel like she was mourning a part of herself. The verses of the *Nikah* drifted through the room like incense—measured, serene, ancient. The imam's voice was calm and steady, but inside her, a storm raged: memories colliding, doubts rising like smoke, and a silence that screamed louder than any vow. Each word seemed to pull her further from the life she had once known, a life steeped in rituals and prayers that now felt distant, like a half-remembered dream. The *Shahada*—the Islamic profession of faith— trembled on her lips as she repeated it, her voice low and hesitant. The words came easily enough, but her heart felt like it was somewhere else, clinging to memories of the past. As the ceremony continued, her thoughts drifted to her family—her father's cold, unforgiving words, her mother's tear-streaked face. They should have been here. She should have been surrounded by the familiar faces of her childhood, by the warmth of her own Hindu community. Instead, she stood here, feeling like a stranger in her own skin. Guilt unfurled inside her like a dark flower, its roots digging deep into her heart. She tried to push it away, smiling at Adil as he glanced at her with those eyes full of love and hope. But the smile felt thin, fragile, as though it might shatter if she let her thoughts linger too long on what she had left behind. Had she betrayed her family? Her faith? Herself? As Uma recited the *Shahada*, guilt surged through her like a slow-burning fire, spreading quietly, consuming parts of her she thought she could keep safe. It started as a whisper, an unease she thought she could brush aside. But as the imam's words filled the air, that whisper grew louder, until it echoed in every corner of her mind, impossible to ignore.

She had told herself that this was love, that Adil's kindness, his unwavering support, and their shared dreams were enough to justify the changes she was making. But standing here, beneath the gaze of a god she didn't know, in a house of worship that felt so foreign, she had felt a profound sense of loss. It was as if the threads that had once bound her to her family, to her Hindu faith, to her very identity, were being severed one by one. A part of her clung stubbornly to the rituals she had grown up with—the familiar smell of incense wafting through her family's small temple at home, the rhythmic chants of the priests that always brought her a sense of peace. She could still hear her mother's voice, soft yet insistent, guiding her through each prayer, reminding her of the gods they worshiped, the traditions they honored. Now, those prayers seemed distant, unreachable, as though she had crossed a line she could never return from. And yet here she was, standing in a mosque, a new identity draped over her like this stark white sari. She couldn't help but feel she had betrayed her family's trust, had abandoned their faith for the love of a man who, though dear to her, could never fully understand the weight of her sacrifice. She had grown up in the shadow of the gods—of Lord Rama and of Lord Krishna, of the many faces of the divine that had shaped her worldview. But today, in this sacred space, she felt their absence acutely, as if they had turned their backs on her. Her father's voice echoed in her mind: *You are dead to us.* The words stung as if they were freshly spoken. Uma had always prided herself on being dutiful, on honoring the teachings passed down to her, and yet, in choosing Adil, she had done the unthinkable. She had broken the delicate thread that connected her to her lineage, and no matter how much she loved him, she could not shake the feeling that she had chosen wrongly—that she had, in a sense, betrayed a deeper part of herself, something sacred and untouchable. The *imam* finished the recitation, and suddenly, it was done. She was no longer Uma. She was Amina now, a new name for a new life. But as she looked down at the simple white sari draped over her body, she wondered if this new life would ever truly feel like her own. Her new name, Amina, felt foreign on her tongue, as though it didn't quite belong to her. It was a name her heart had yet to embrace, a name that stood between her and the woman she once was. Would this guilt be her constant companion now? Would it grow with each prayer left unsaid, each festival uncelebrated, each visit to her family denied? Even as she smiled at Adil, the guilt gnawed at her insides, sinking deeper, like a wound that wouldn't heal. And with that guilt came a terrible uncertainty. She had thought that love would be enough, that Adil's love could make her forget the ties she had severed. But standing there, beneath the weight of her new identity, she realized that love alone might not be enough to fill the void her choice had created. Could she truly live with this guilt? Or would it swallow her whole?

Amina had converted to Islam in name, but her soul had not followed. In the privacy of her heart, the rituals of her Hindu upbringing remained as constant as the air she breathed. Every night, after Adil had gone to bed, she would tiptoe to the old Godrej cupboard, her movements slow and deliberate, as though any sound could give away her hidden devotion. There, buried beneath layers of her new life—folded head scarves and old books—she kept small idols of Lord Rama, of Lord Krishna and Ganesha, concealed like a secret too precious to share. The soft glow of the oil lamp she lit secretly, bathed the idol in a tender light, and in that moment, Amina allowed herself to be the woman she used to be. She would fold her hands in prayer, her lips whispering the names of the gods she had grown up with, the gods who had once filled her life with color and comfort. The familiar warmth of devotion would rise within her, offering a peace that nothing else could. Here, in the dark corners of her home, she was Uma again, not Amina. Here, she was her father's daughter, not Adil's wife. But that peace was fleeting, always tainted by the weight of secrecy. Each night, as she extinguished the flame and returned the idol to its hiding place, guilt clawed at her chest. She was living two lives, divided between the woman Adil Khan believed her to be and the woman she truly was. By day, she played her role well—the dutiful Muslim wife, gracious and loving. She prepared for Ramadan, learned the prayers, and immersed herself in the customs of Adil's faith, performing them with an outward devotion that masked her inner turmoil. But by night, she returned to her roots, to the gods of her childhood, the gods who still held her heart captive. The duality of her existence began to eat away at her, a slow erosion of the self she had once known so well. When she prayed alongside Adil, she couldn't help but feel like a stranger in her own skin, mouthing words that didn't carry the same weight as the mantras she had learned as a child. She had traded one set of rituals for another, but the exchange felt hollow, as though she had lost something irreplaceable in the process. Every time she knelt before her hidden idols, she was reminded of the price she had paid. Her father's disownment, her mother's tear-filled silence, the absence of her family at her wedding—it all hung over her like a shadow. And yet, despite the pain, she couldn't let go. The act of lighting the lamp, of offering her silent prayers, tethered her to the past in a way that nothing else could. It was the only part of her former life that remained, the only part of herself that hadn't been consumed by the choice she had made.

Yet, even in this sacred ritual, there was no escape from the guilt that came with it. She knew that Adil loved her, that he would never demand more from her than what she could give. But how could he understand? How could he comprehend the depth of her connection to a faith she could never fully leave behind? She was not simply converting for him. She was tearing herself in two, and the weight of that division pressed down on her more each day. She was bound by love to a man who saw her as Amina, but her heart beat to the rhythm of the woman she had been—Uma, the daughter of devout Hindus, the one who had once believed her path was set. The conflict inside her grew sharper with every passing day. As much as she tried to embrace her new life, the old one clung to her, refusing to be erased. Could she truly live like this, split between two worlds, two faiths? Or would the woman she had become eventually overshadow the one she had been? In the quiet darkness of her closet, in the faint flicker of a dying flame, Uma wondered how long she could keep up the pretense, how long before the weight of her secret would crush her beneath its burden. And each night, as she whispered her prayers to her Hindu Gods, to Rama and to Krishna, she wondered if she was asking for forgiveness —for betraying her family, her gods, or perhaps even herself.

Soon after their marriage, Amina gave birth to their first child, a son named Aarif. His arrival cracked something open in her, a joy so raw it made her ache. The house, once quiet, now hummed with his cries, his questions, his laughter that bounced off the chipped walls like sudden sunlight. She poured herself into motherhood, into the daily rhythm of lullabies and laundry, the smell of milk and talcum lingering in the room. Aarif was a curious and energetic child, his laughter echoing through their modest home, bringing light into even the most difficult of days.

At night, as she rocked Aarif to sleep, she sang to him, sometimes a gentle Urdu *nazm* her husband had taught her, other times an old Hindi bhajan her mother used to hum while grinding spices. The songs tumbled together, just as her two worlds did. She told herself this was harmony. That a child could be both. But inside her, a quiet unease curled up, a fear that this stitched-together world might someday fray. She tried to reassure herself that these dual identities could coexist, that she could raise Aarif in the Islamic tradition while still holding on to the memories of her own past. But deep down, she feared that this fragile balance might one day crumble. Amina's nightly ritual of lighting the small lamp in front of her hidden Hindu idols continued, though now it was done with more caution. With Aarif growing more curious by the day, she took extra care to ensure that her small shrine was well-hidden. She feared what it would mean if he, too young to understand, stumbled upon it and asked questions she wasn't ready to answer.

Motherhood had deepened her sense of duty, but it had also intensified her guilt. She was no longer just living a double life for herself—now, she was shaping the life of her son. Would Aarif, as he grew older, sense the distance in his mother's heart, divided between the traditions she shared with Adil and the ones she kept for herself? Would he resent her, as she feared he might one day, for not being fully honest about who she was? As Aarif learned his first words, Amina was struck by how naturally they came in Urdu, echoing the prayers and phrases Adil taught him. She smiled and encouraged him, yet each word also served as a reminder of the faith she had outwardly adopted but never fully embraced. While Adil beamed with pride at their son's growing understanding of Islam, Amina's heart remained heavy. She loved her son more than she had ever imagined possible, but she could not shake the feeling that she was betraying both him and herself by not being entirely true to the woman she had once been.

A few years later, their lives were further changed with the arrival of their daughter, Yasmin Khan, my mother. The arrival of the tiny, perfect girl filled Amina with joy so profound it almost overwhelmed her. In Yasmin, she found her new purpose endorsed again, a new identity beyond the roles she had already been playing—the loving wife, the converted Muslim woman, the hidden devotee of her old gods. Motherhood wrapped her in its warm embrace, and for a while, she allowed herself to believe that it could be enough to quiet the restlessness in her soul. She poured herself into caring for Yasmin, finding solace in the purity of the bond between them. In her son and her daughter's laughter and innocence, she saw the possibility of redemption, a chance to leave her conflicted past behind and be fully present in this new life she had chosen. But even as she rocked Aarif and Yasmin to sleep in the late hours of the night, the whispers of her old faith never truly left her. They lingered like a distant melody, soft but insistent, reminding her of the vows she had once made in temples, the promises that had bound her to her Hindu gods who had not forgotten her. And though she tried to silence those voices, they always returned when the world around her grew still.

Motherhood had brought Amina a new kind of happiness, but it had also deepened her guilt. The stakes were higher now, more complicated. She feared what Adil would think if he ever discovered the nightly rituals she had never abandoned, if he realized that the conversion she had undertaken was only in name, never in spirit. But even more, Amina feared what Aarif and Yasmin might think of her one day. What would her son and daughter feel if they uncovered the truth—that their mother had lived a lie, that she had carried a secret so heavy it sometimes made her breath catch in her chest? She imagined the questions Yasmin might ask when she was older, when she had grown beyond the simplicity of childhood. "*Ammi*, why did you keep this from me? Did you not believe in what you taught me? Who are you, really?" And Amina had no answers to those questions, only the knowledge that she had woven herself into a web of deceit, one that she had not known how to escape from once it began. She had crossed into this new life with Adil, leaving behind the colors, the Hindu prayers, the temple bells of her past. Now, those moments felt like stolen time, borrowed from a life that no longer belonged to her. Yet, those remnants of her former self clung to her like a second skin, impossible to shed.

Amina was not whole. She had become a woman split in two, constantly torn between the life she had chosen with Adil and the faith that had shaped her before she had even known him. The prayers she uttered in the quiet of the night brought her peace, but they also deepened her fear. Every time she folded her hands before Krishna, she was reminded of the precariousness of the life she had built, a life that could unravel and be disrupted with a single revelation. Each night, after Adil and Yasmin were sound asleep, she continued to slip out of bed, her steps careful and deliberate, as though the very walls of the house were listening. In the dark, she would light the small lamp in front of her hidden idols, her hands trembling with both devotion and fear. The flame danced in the dim space of the closet, casting flickering shadows across the face of the gods she had once worshipped openly, without shame. Each time she whispered her prayers to Krishna, she wondered how long she could keep up this facade, how long before the truth would demand to be revealed. The thought of Aarif and Yasmin, pure and innocent, seeing their mother as a woman divided, a woman caught between two faiths, was unbearable. Aarif and Yasmin were growing quickly, their curiosity blooming with each passing day, and Amina knew the questions would come sooner than later. There was no room for half-truths in motherhood, no place for the careful lies Amina had told herself and others. Aarif and Yasmin deserved a mother who was whole, a mother whose beliefs were clear and unwavering.

Aarif and Yasmin were Muslim, children of the faith that Amina had married into. She recited the *surahs* with Adil, her voice trailing just a beat behind his, mimicking the words with a child's innocent devotion, unaware of the tangled history that had brought her into being. Amina would watch her daughter, her heart swelling with pride and yet aching with a strange sadness. Yasmin seemed free from the burden of conflict, free from the pain of divided loyalties. Amina would watch her daughter, her heart swollen with pride and yet aching with quiet sorrow. And Amina longed for her to remain that way, untouched by the weight of her mother's choices. She knew that day would come, when Yasmin would look into her eyes and see the truth. And when that moment arrived, Amina could only hope that her daughter would understand. Understand that love, no matter how strong, could not always erase the past. Understand that faith was not something you could simply exchange like a garment, but something that lived deep within you, as much a part of you as your heartbeat. Understand that her mother had tried, in her own imperfect way, to be true to herself even as she walked between two worlds. Until then, Amina continued her nightly ritual, carrying the secret like a wound that had never quite healed. And each time she returned the idol to its hiding place, she wondered not if, but when the life she had built would collide with the truth she could no longer keep concealed.

As Aarif and Yasmin grew older, Amina found herself increasingly torn between two worlds. With each passing year, the boundaries of her identity blurred, creating a constant tug-of-war in her heart. She had married Adil, a devout Muslim, fully embracing the life they built together. In their modest home, the call to prayer resonated through the small rooms, and the teachings of the Quran were the foundation upon which they raised their family. Amina devoted herself to ensuring that Yasmin and Aarif would grow up immersed in the Islamic faith, honoring Adil's beliefs and traditions. She taught Aarif and Yasmin to pray, guiding their tiny hands in the motions of *salat*, her heart swelling with pride as she watched her son and daughter mimic her movements. Amina would kneel beside them, whispering the Urdu words, hoping that the beauty of the language would weave itself into her children's soul. Each Ramadan, she fasted alongside her children, sharing stories about the significance of the month and the lessons of empathy and gratitude that came with it. They would break their fasts together, the sweet dates a symbol of their devotion and the joy of community. In the quiet moments after dinner, Amina would watch her children as they played, their laughter filling the room. Yet, beneath her serene exterior, a profound yearning simmered. She had chosen to keep silent about her Hindu heritage, believing it was best for Yasmin and Aarif to grow up in a single faith, unburdened by the duality that had plagued her own life. Of course, it would have been easy for her to tell the simple truth about her being born a Hindu before she got married to their father.

But Amina had witnessed the struggles of living between two worlds, and she wanted to spare her children the same pain. She thought that by shielding them from her past, she was protecting them. The weight of her decision would often grow heavy with time. In the quiet of their narrow living room, where traces of cardamom and fried onions still clung to the air, Amina sometimes felt a heaviness stir—the weight of stories she had long buried. She longed to share with her children her Hindu heritage, especially the songs her mother had sung to her at night. On rare occasions, the festival of Diwali, the rangoli designs and the lights in the clay lamps, made her ache for the rituals that connected her to generations past. There was a part of her that she had wanted Yasmin and Aarif to experience—the joy of lighting *diyas* and bursting firecrackers, and to understand the significance of good triumphing over evil in the story of Rama and Sita. She would worry how Adil would react if she introduced her Hindu traditions into the house. Would he see it as a betrayal of his faith? Would he feel that she was diluting the Islamic teachings they cherished?

As the days turned into months, Amina observed her children's curiosity about the world around them. My mother, Yasmin began to ask questions that made Amina's heart race with both pride and fear. "Mama, why do we pray five times a day?" Yasmin would ask, her bright eyes filled with wonder. "What do those words mean?" Amina would respond with tenderness, explaining the significance of prayer in Islam, but inside, she wrestled with the desire to also share her own Hindu beliefs. There were evenings when she found herself sitting on the edge of Yasmin's bed, her daughter's innocent questions filling the silence. "Mama, are there other stories about God? Stories that you know?" Yasmin's inquiries tugged at Amina's heartstrings, reigniting the longing to share her heritage.

One night, as they nestled beneath a blanket, the soft glow of a bedside lamp illuminating their faces, Amina decided to share a story. "There's a beautiful tale about a prince named Rama and his wife Sita," she began, her voice barely above a whisper. She described the epic journey of love and righteousness that transcended time, each word igniting a flicker of nostalgia within her. Aarif listened intently, captivated by the narrative, his imagination painting vivid pictures of the forest, the brave warrior, and the challenges they faced. Yet, with every story Amina shared, a wave of guilt would wash over her. Was she betraying Adil? Was she introducing confusion into their children's lives? She couldn't shake the feeling that each time she mentioned her Hindu past, she risked creating a divide within her family.

The tension within her would sometimes suffocate her. Amina would often feel as if she were walking a tightrope, balancing the respect she held for Adil's faith with the longing to honor her own. The duality of her existence began to manifest in subtle ways. She noticed her children observing their friends' holiday decorations —colorful lights for Diwali and cheerful Christmas trees —and their eyes would sparkle with curiosity. Yasmin would often exclaim, "*Ammi*, Aditi has such beautiful lights outside her house! Why don't we have any?" Amina would smile, her heart heavy with the weight of unspoken memories. "Our lights are in our hearts, my love," she would reply, a smile masking her sorrow. But deep down, she wished she could show them the flickering diyas that had once brightened her childhood home.

One evening, as the family gathered for dinner, Amina felt a shift in the atmosphere. Adil had just returned from a community event, his enthusiasm palpable. He spoke passionately about an interfaith dialogue he had participated in, emphasizing the importance of understanding and respect among different cultures. Amina listened, her heart swollen with admiration for his commitment to fostering harmony. Yet, as Adil spoke, a thought gnawed at her—what if their conversations turned to the topic of heritage and identity? Would he accept her past as she had accepted his?

In the midst of the lively conversation, Yasmin piped up, her voice bright and innocent. "*Abbu*, can we have a Diwali party? I want to see the lights and sweets like the ones we saw at my friend's house!" Amina's heart sank. She felt the weight of Adil's gaze, sensing the sudden stillness in the room.

Adil's expression changed, a flicker of surprise crossing his features. "Diwali? But we celebrate Eid. Isn't that enough?" he replied, his tone reflecting genuine confusion.

Yasmin's eyes widened, sensing the tension. "But

ammi said it's a happy festival too! Can't we celebrate both?"

Amina felt her breath catch. Here was the moment she had dreaded, the crossroads of their lives. She looked at Yasmin, then at Adil, her heart racing as she sought the right words. "It is a beautiful festival, Adil," she interjected softly. "Just as Eid brings joy, so does Diwali. It's a celebration of light and hope. I think it would be wonderful for our family to share in both."

Adil frowned, his brow furrowing as he processed her words. "But how do we reconcile that, Amina? Our faith is different. I want our children to grow up with clarity in their beliefs."

Amina felt the ache of her heart deepen. "I understand, but I also believe that understanding different cultures can enrich their lives. It doesn't mean we abandon our faith; rather, we can embrace the beauty in diversity."

The silence that followed felt heavy, as if the air itself held its breath. Yasmin watched her parents, confusion clouding her features, her innocence caught in a struggle she couldn't comprehend.

Finally, as Adil spoke, his voice became steadier. "I appreciate your perspective, but we must also consider the values we want to instill in them. I don't want them to feel torn between two identities."

Amina nodded, recognizing the sincerity in his words, but also feeling a deep ache for the part of her that yearned to share the colors of her past. "I'm not asking for them to abandon their Islamic faith, Adil. I want them to grow up with a sense of unity, an understanding that embraces both our heritages."

The conversation stretched into the night, quiet, searching, unguarded. They spoke of belief, of identity, of what it meant to raise a child in a house where more than one God could be watching. Amina listened more than she spoke, but when she did, her voice carried fragments of a life she'd tried to forget: the sharp scent of camphor, her mother's voice rising in song, the small rituals that once steadied her. She didn't say everything. Some memories still hurt too much. But each word she offered felt like lifting a stone from a buried place, exposing the shape of who she had been before silence became her refuge.

The years had slipped by, and the weight of Amina's guilt had grown heavier with each passing day. She had distanced herself from her Hindu identity so deeply that she no longer recognized the woman she had once been. Yet, the guilt of abandoning her family and her faith haunted her, like a shadow she could never escape. She thought of her mother, wondering if she was still alive, wondering if her father had ever forgiven her in his heart. But Amina had never reached out. She had told herself it was better that way, that reopening old wounds would only cause more pain. In the silence of the night, she wept for the family she had lost and the religion she had forsaken. Her guilt was not only for what she had done but also for what she had failed to do—for never reconciling with her parents, for never explaining to Yasmin the complexity of her decision.

And now, with her son, Aarif gone, she was forced to speak the truth. "I didn't want you to grow up confused, Yasmin," Amina said softly. "I didn't want you to carry the burden of my choices. I married your father out of love, but I never truly let go of my past. I thought... I thought it was best for you to have a single faith, a single identity. I didn't want you to feel the conflict that I have felt for so long."

In her heart, she knew she could no longer compartmentalize her life into neat labels. Aarif's death had shattered the boundaries that had once defined her.

7

The burial ground in Ayodhya, a town layered with religious significance, where Aarif would rest, the *Qabristan*, or Muslim cemetery, is located on the outskirts of the city. The cemetery is an old one, bordered by towering *neem* and *peepal* trees that cast long shadows across the earth, especially during the golden hours of dawn and dusk. This quiet plot of land, often overlooked by the bustling activity of the town, serves as a serene, sacred space for Ayodhya's Muslim community, a place where stories of generations have found their final chapters. Entering *Qabristan* feels like stepping into a secluded world. The high walls enclose the graves, providing a sense of privacy and protection. The gate, an ornate yet weathered iron structure, stands as a solemn entrance, marked by a simple arch with the words '*Ya Allah*' inscribed above, invoking the mercy of God. As visitors pass through, there is a natural silence, a calm that invites quiet reflection. Stone pathways, uneven and dotted with patches of wild grass, weave through rows of graves marked by simple, unembellished headstones. The layout is humble and respectful, each grave facing Mecca, in accordance with Islamic tradition.

A gentle breeze rustles through the leaves of the surrounding trees, and sometimes the smell of incense from nearby homes drifts into the cemetery. Scattered among the older graves are the resting places of those who have recently departed, with headstones bearing freshly inscribed verses from the Quran, testifying to the community's continued devotion. The marble headstones vary in size and style, some small and unmarked, others with inscriptions in Urdu or Arabic, asking for peace for the departed in the afterlife. A small, shaded area near the entrance serves as a place where families gather to recite prayers. This area, with its worn and ancient stone benches and low wall, is where visitors often sit with prayer beads, murmuring *surahs* from the Quran, their voices low and reverent. The *imam*, an elderly man with a gentle demeanor, often stops by, offering comfort to the grieving, leading special prayers for those who request them. In the early morning light, *Qabristan* is a place of quiet beauty, with dewdrops clinging to the grass and birds beginning to sing. The sunlight filters through the tree branches, casting soft patterns on the graves below. This is a place where sorrow is palpable, but so is peace. It is a reminder of the cycle of life and death, of love and loss.

The news of Aarif's death had arrived on a calm afternoon, the skies deceptively blue, flooding Ayodhya's streets with an unforgiving light. The sun hung low, etching stark shadows as if the heavens themselves had been wounded. As Amina had seen the limp body of her son on their verandah, her breath caught, she had stumbled, bracing herself against the wall. Aarif, her precious son, full of life, had always been a constant reminder of the love and joy in her marriage with Adil. But in a single moment, that life was gone. The shock had rippled through their small family in irrevocable ways, each coping with grief through lenses colored by a world of memories and maternal instincts, Yasmin, torn between her love for her brother and the unexpected weight of his loss, struggled to reconcile the image of Aarif she held in her heart with the reality of his death. Adil Khan, the proud and devout Muslim, took refuge in his faith, praying through the night for his son's soul and seeking solace in rituals that felt both hollow and essential.

For Amina, the pain was unfathomable. Aarif was not merely her son; he was her firstborn, her confidante, a bridge between the worlds of her lost childhood that she had never spoken about to her children, and her life with Adil. She had raised him with the gentleness of a mother who saw pieces of her past in her child—moments of laughter, lost and buried memories, and a sacred tenderness that had been lost when she had married into a different faith. Aarif represented hope, a promise of continuity, a link to a future she had imagined as a young bride. She struggled with her grief alone, too heartbroken to share it with Adil or Yasmin. Amina fell into a deep silence, her grief vast and consuming, and never recovered from her loss. Her memories of Aarif would flood back, each more painful than the last. She remembered his first steps, the way he held her hand, his infectious laugh that echoed through their house. Each fragment of memory cut her deeply, a reminder of what she had lost. She felt as if her heart had shattered into pieces, each one jagged and irreparable. In spite of her sorrow, Amina clung to rituals, grounding herself in the familiar motions of preparing for Aarif's funeral. She meticulously ironed his burial shroud, her hands shaking with each fold, as she recited silent prayers that spanned both her Hindu upbringing and the Islamic faith she had embraced. She knew that Aarif's soul transcended the boundaries of faith, that her love for him was not bound by the religion he was born into. In her heart, she prayed that wherever he was, he was at peace.

Yasmin's grief was raw, bewildering, tinged with guilt and confusion as her world had become upturned. Aarif had been her older brother, her protector, the one who always understood her without needing words. They had shared secrets, laughed at jokes only they found funny, fought over trivial things only to make up moments later. Now, he was gone, and Yasmin was left to grapple with the void his absence created. As the days passed, Yasmin found herself unable to cry. She felt numb, as if a wall had gone up around her emotions, shielding her from the full weight of her loss. She went through the motions, attending the funeral, reciting the prayers, but her heart felt hollow. She was too young to understand the complexities of grief, too unprepared to cope with a loss so profound. She clung to her mother, seeking comfort in her presence, but even that felt inadequate. The world around her had changed irrevocably, and she felt lost, adrift in a sea of sadness.

At the time of the funeral, Adil tried to find some respite and solace in his faith. He tried to assure himself that everything happened according to Allah's will, that Aarif's death was part of a divine plan he could not understand but had to accept. He prayed fervently, seeking peace in the familiar rhythms of his faith. He recited verses from the Quran, asking Allah to forgive Aarif's sins and grant him a place in paradise. Yet, beneath his stoic exterior, Adil struggled with his own grief. Aarif had been his son, his pride and joy, a continuation of his legacy. He had dreams for Aarif, dreams that would now remain unfulfilled. He had wanted Aarif to grow up strong, to follow in his footsteps, to carry on the family's traditions and beliefs. Aarif's death left a void in his life, a void he filled with prayer and faith, but one that would never truly be healed. Despite the backdrop of religious differences, Adil was adamant about following Islamic burial rites, honoring Aarif's faith. Amina supported his decision, but deep down, she wished to include elements of her own heritage, a tribute to the duality that had marked Aarif's life.

On the day of the funeral, the air was thick with sorrow. Friends and family gathered at the cemetery, each person bearing their own memories of Aarif, their own private grief. Aarif's funeral was also attended by many who had never met him but felt compelled to stand in solidarity. Adil led the prayers, his voice steady but his heart heavy. He recited the *Janazah* prayer, asking for Allah's mercy and forgiveness for his son. Amina stood beside him, her head bowed, her hands clasped in silent prayer. Amina, feeling the weight of her heritage, quietly tied a small red thread—a symbol of protection in Hindu culture—around Aarif's wrist before he was laid to rest. It was a small, silent tribute, a way for her to honor her Hindu past and bid farewell to her son in a manner that felt deeply personal. The burial itself was conducted with utmost respect and adherence to Islamic customs. Aarif's body was washed and wrapped in a simple white shroud, a symbol of purity and humility in death. He was laid to rest with his head facing Mecca, a final act of devotion to the faith he was born into. As his body was lowered into the ground, Adil felt a resolve harden within him. He would no longer remain silent. His voice broke only once as he recited the words that would grant his son peace in the afterlife. The cemetery was quiet, save for the soft murmur of prayers and the occasional sound of birdsong. Amina, standing by Aarif's grave, felt a profound sense of loss, a grief that transcended words. She looked around at the people gathered, each person a reminder of the community Aarif had been a part of. The support they projected was small comfort, a reminder that Aarif had been cherished, that his life had left an indelible mark on the world.

Yasmin approached the grave, her heart heavy with sadness. She placed a single flower on the freshly turned earth, a final act of love for the brother she had lost. She whispered a quiet goodbye, her voice barely audible, but in that moment, her grief was raw, real, and profound. It was a farewell that transcended words, a moment of silent connection between siblings, a bond that death could never truly break.

In the days that followed Aarif's burial, Amina, Adil, and Yasmin moved through their grief as if caught in separate currents, each navigating the depth of loss in their own way. For Amina, the house felt unbearably quiet, the familiar laughter and footsteps of her son reduced to echoes that seemed to taunt her in the stillness. She would wake before dawn, the call to prayer drifting faintly from the nearby mosque, and sit alone in Aarif's room, her fingers tracing the grooves in his schoolbooks, the pencil marks he had made in the margins. She found herself singing softly under her breath, the lullabies her mother had sung to her in another time, another place. The same songs she had once sung to Aarif, who would lie still in her lap, his tiny hands reaching up to touch her face. Now, each note felt like a thread tethering her to him, each word a memory woven into her aching heart. Sometimes, she would light a small incense stick in front of his photograph, letting the scent fill the room, as if creating a bridge between this world and whatever place he had gone to. She wondered, only once or twice though, why no one from her own Hindu family had even tried to contact her or offer comfort, in the face of such a shattering loss.

For a few days, Adil sought refuge in the mosque, his forehead pressed to the cool stone in deep, silent prayer. After each supplication, he would close his eyes, whisper Aarif's name, and plead with Allah to grant his son peace in the afterlife, and to forgive any burdens he might have unknowingly borne. On the day of Aarif's death, he had knelt by his son's bed, whispering words from the Quran, his voice faltering as he asked Allah to welcome his boy among the blessed. Now, every evening, he performed extra *rak'ahs*, the prayers becoming a rhythm, a means of holding onto the belief that one day he would see his son again. When he returned home from the mosque, he would sit in silence, holding his *tasbih* beads, the rhythmic movement of his fingers through the beads offering a sliver of calm amid the turmoil inside him.

My mother, Yasmin Khan, young and grasping to understand a reality that had changed overnight, found herself slipping back into the fragments of their shared world. She would sit in their small courtyard, clutching Aarif's worn cricket bat, running her fingers over the wood's rough edges, each scrape and scratch a memory of his carefree laughter as he played. The bat still bore smudges of dirt from the last game they had played together, and Yasmin could almost hear his voice, teasing and playful, as he called her out for cheating. She clung to these quiet moments—the way his eyes sparkled when he laughed, the way he would nudge her shoulder, always teasing but always protective. She often cried herself to sleep, clutching his favorite sweater to her chest, the faintest scent of him still lingering. She didn't have the words to explain her grief, but she knew that his absence was a shadow that would follow her.

Each of them was suspended in their own cocoon of

memories and rituals, touching the empty spaces Aarif had left behind, feeling the sharp ache of his absence. Together and alone, they held onto the remnants of his presence in their own ways, piecing together their lives without him, their grief uniting them even as it set them apart. The burial had passed, but the ache lingered, settling like mist over their lives. Aarif's absence was a ghost in their home, haunting their thoughts, echoing in the stillness of evenings when the family would otherwise gather for tea and quiet chatter. Now, the cups sat untouched, the tea growing cold, as silence took its place at the table.

My mother, Yasmin, restless and sleepless, often found herself drawn back to the *Qabristan*. It was a place where her thoughts could unravel, where the weight of her loss seemed lighter amid the stillness of the graves. She would sit under the shadow of the *peepal* tree, its rustling leaves like whispered prayers. There, she would talk to Aarif, her words tumbling out in a stream of sorrow and love. She shared her fears, her guilt, her longing for his teasing laughter. "Why did you leave us, Aarif?" she whispered one evening, her voice cracking. "You promised you'd always be here."

For Yasmin, the *Qabristan* became a sanctuary where faith and memory converged. It was not the Muslim rituals of the burial, nor the Hindu symbolism of the red thread her mother had tied, but the simple act of presence that gave her solace. Sitting beside Aarif's grave, she felt connected to him, to the universe, and perhaps even to something beyond both faiths.

At home, Amina had taken to sitting by the window every evening, gazing out at the changing hues of the sky. In the quiet of twilight, she spoke softly, reciting prayers that blended the Hindu mantras of her childhood with the Islamic verses she had embraced after her marriage.

It was in these moments that Yasmin began to see her mother as a bridge between two worlds—a woman who had sacrificed much, yet carried her dual identity with quiet dignity.

Adil, however, remained rooted in his faith, seeking solace in the mosque. The imam, noticing his frequent presence, often paused to offer words of comfort. "Grief is a test, Adil bhai," he would say. "And through patience, Allah grants us strength." Adil nodded, absorbing the words, but they did little to quell the ache in his heart.

One evening, as the family gathered for dinner, the tension finally broke. Amina, her voice strained, said, "Adil, Aarif was more than his faith. He was a part of all of us. Shouldn't his memory reflect that?"

Adil looked up, his expression unreadable. "He was a Muslim, Amina. That is the faith he lived by, and it is the faith he rests in now."

"But he was also my son," Amina countered, her voice trembling. "A piece of me. Of my past, my family, my roots. Can't there be space for both?"

Yasmin watched them, torn between their perspectives. She saw her father's steadfast devotion as a source of strength, yet her mother's quiet insistence on honoring both sides of Aarif's heritage resonated deeply with her own inner struggles. That night, Yasmin lay awake, reflecting on her family's shared grief. She thought about the small rituals each of them clung to— her father's prayers, her mother's incense, her own whispered conversations at the *Qabristan*. Each was a way of keeping Aarif alive, of holding onto the love that bound them together. And yet, those very rituals also exposed the quiet divisions etched into their shared loss.

The next morning, Yasmin made a decision. She gathered her father's prayer mat and her mother's incense sticks and brought them to the *Qabristan*. There, she set them down beside Aarif's grave, creating a quiet, unspoken truce between the two traditions. "We're all here for you, Aarif," she said softly. "In our own ways."

As the weeks passed, the family began to find a fragile balance. Adil continued his prayers, but he no longer bristled at Amina's small acts of remembrance. Amina, meanwhile, withdrew further from her new reality, seeing it not as a source of conflict but as a reflection of what she had denied to herself after she had gotten married to Adil. In Ayodhya, the seasons turned, and the town's rhythms carried on as they always had. Yet for Yasmin, Amina, and Adil, life would never return to what it had been. Aarif's absence was a wound that would never fully heal, but in the quiet moments of shared memory, they found a way to move forward together.

Outside their home, Ayodhya moved to its own rhythm, drawn from memory, belief, and daily ritual. In the early 1970s, before the headlines, before the fractures, the town had been a quieter place. Narrow lanes wound through shaded neighborhoods, bazaars spilled over with vendors, and the Sarayu flowed past it all with an ancient indifference. In the years when Yasmin and Aarif were still children, the town was quieter, its future tensions still distant silhouettes on the horizon. Narrow lanes curved past homes shaded by bougainvillea, and bazaars rang with the calls of vendors selling chilies, jaggery, and ripe guavas. The smell of marigold garlands clung to temple gates, mixing with sandalwood smoke from roadside shops. Children chased rubber balls through courtyards; pilgrims walked barefoot to the ghats, their cotton robes rustling like dry leaves. The Sarayu flowed, unhurried and opaque, bearing the weight of centuries without complaint. From the trees came the shrill chatter of monkeys, while from rooftops, the *azan* mingled with the soft rise of *aarti* bells. In those years,

Ayodhya was still a place of shared silences—temples and mosques casting their shadows across the same courtyards, neighbors bound not by sameness but by proximity, kindness, and old stories. Grief, when it came, was absorbed quietly, tucked into gestures, folded into everyday rhythms, never demanding more space than the day allowed.

In the 1970s, Ayodhya remained a quiet, unassuming town nestled within the larger administrative district of Faizabad in Uttar Pradesh. Although geographically contiguous, Ayodhya and Faizabad held distinct identities shaped by their differing historical trajectories. Faizabad had once served as the glittering capital of the Nawabs of Awadh. Under Nawab Saadat Khan (Burhan-ul-Mulk) and his son Shuja-ud-Daula, Faizabad emerged as a center of political and cultural significance in the eighteenth century, replete with Mughal-inspired architecture, lush gardens, colonial-era cantonments, and wide roads shaded by ancient *neem* and *peepal* trees. It was only in the late 1700s, under Nawab Asaf-ud-Daula, that the capital was shifted to Lucknow, whose cosmopolitanism eventually eclipsed Faizabad's Nawabi charm.

Ayodhya, in contrast, was smaller and quieter, but steeped in religious symbolism and devotional life. It was revered by Hindus as the birthplace of Lord Rama, a sacred geography animated by temples, hermitages, *akharas*, and the serene flow of the Sarayu River. The rhythm of daily life was dictated by rituals, pilgrimages, and spiritual practices that had remained relatively unchanged for centuries.

In the 1970s, communal tensions around Ayodhya had not yet reached their later political crescendo, but subtle undercurrents were beginning to stir. The Babri Masjid, a 16th-century mosque built during the reign of the Mughal emperor Babur, still stood relatively undisturbed, though it had become the subject of quiet contestation in certain quarters. The Ram Janmabhoomi movement—calling for a temple to be built on what was believed to be the exact birthplace of Lord Rama—was in its early, murmuring stage, gaining traction through local organizations and regional politics, though not yet mainstreamed into national consciousness. The broader sociopolitical climate of the decade—marked by economic anxieties and the rising tide of identity politics —created a backdrop against which historical grievances and mythologies slowly gained political shape.

Thus, while Ayodhya and Faizabad coexisted in physical proximity, they represented different timelines—one shaped by secular power and Indo-Islamic grandeur; the other by sacred memory, myth, and religious resonance. The quietude of the 1970s, in hindsight, bore the echoes of deeper shifts that would profoundly alter the region's destiny in the decades to come.

In those years, Ayodhya had not yet been thrust into the national spotlight. Ayodhya was part of Faizabad district until 2018, when the district was officially renamed Ayodhya. In the 1970s, it was indeed considered a town within Faizabad district. It moved gently to its own cadence—pilgrims came and went, saints sat under banyan trees reciting *Ramcharitmanas*, and the narrow lanes echoed with the sounds of temple bells, conch shells, and the *azan* from neighborhood mosques. Sadhus in saffron robes mingled with local Muslim shopkeepers who sold brass utensils, sweets, and fabric dyed in earthy hues. People of both faiths lived side by side, their lives interwoven by centuries of cohabitation and shared festivals.

The town's streets were dusty, often crowded during the mornings when cows meandered and shop shutters creaked open. Bazaars brimmed with the smell of freshly fried *kachoris*, jasmine garlands, and incense. Tongas and bicycles jostled for space, and rickshaw-pullers knew the shortcuts between Faizabad's busier colonial buildings and Ayodhya's quieter, temple-filled heart. The pace of life was unhurried, marked by a deep respect for the past and a rhythm shaped by ritual, not politics.

At twilight, the ghats along the Sarayu shimmered under rows of flickering *diyas*, while children ran along the banks with carefree joy. Ayodhya, then, was not a place of contest—it was a town where mythology and daily life coexisted without dissonance, folded gently into the larger embrace of Faizabad's multicultural legacy.

As Amina, Adil, and Yasmin each walked the streets of Ayodhya, they were reminded of Aarif in every familiar sight: the corner where he had bought sweets, the fields where he had played cricket with his friends, the mosque where he had first learned to pray. Ayodhya, with all its stories and history, had become a living monument to their memories of Aarif, every street corner and narrow alley a reminder of a life now woven into the timelessness of the town itself.

The city of Ayodhya, known for its temples and tranquility, carried an unspoken burden. At its heart lay the Babri Masjid, its dome glinting under the harsh sun, a silent witness to centuries of devotion, conflict, and betrayal. Mir Baqi, one of Babur's trusted generals, had arrived in Ayodhya in 1528. The construction of the mosque was part of a broader effort to consolidate Mughal rule by embedding Islamic architecture into India's landscape. Allegedly built on the site of a Hindu temple commemorating Lord Rama's birthplace, the mosque had also been seen as a contested symbol of power and faith. While the Mughals sought to establish their dominance, local traditions and Hindu sentiments began to resist the transformation of their sacred geography.

For much of its history, the Babri Masjid stood as more than a religious structure. It was a shared space, where communities lived side by side, their interactions punctuated by moments of tension and camaraderie. However, colonial documentation from the British era revealed frequent clashes over religious practices. In 1859, the British administration had erected a fence, physically separating Hindu and Muslim worshippers. It was a precursor to the modern legal disputes. As the decades turned into centuries, Ayodhya evolved, but its wounds festered, growing more intricate and complicated. The town carried both a sacred as well as a contested spirit, where memories of gods and mortals intermingled with the struggles of human frailty. Aarif's death, though deeply personal to Amina, Adil, and Yasmin, seemed an echo of the broader tragedies that Ayodhya itself bore within its very soil.

The years leading up to the late twentieth century saw Ayodhya caught in a maelstrom of shifting ideologies. The voices of secular harmony, which had once kept the town's delicate balance intact, were drowned out by cries for historical redress. The ground beneath the Babri Masjid became less sacred, more political—a place that would decide the course of history for millions.

In the streets, debates bubbled up in *chai* stalls, courtyards, and temples. Stories were told, retold, and refashioned to suit agendas, each version claiming ownership of the town's essence. Amina, Adil, and Yasmin found themselves increasingly aware of the noise, though they never wished to be entangled in it. Aarif's absence had left a chasm that no debate or ideology could fill. Yet, as life in Ayodhya began to change around them, they could not escape the pull of its transformations.

In the evenings, Amina would walk slowly along the Sarayu, her silence growing deeper with each step. The river, ancient and unhurried, seemed to bear witness to everything Ayodhya had suffered and survived. Sitting by its edge, she would close her eyes and imagine Aarif beside her—his presence conjured in whispers, sent adrift on the breeze, carried out over the water.

When the setting sun bathed the river in molten gold, she would see small gatherings lighting earthen lamps, their soft chants mingling with the steady murmur of the current. Amina watched from a distance, her heart gripped by a quiet ache, a sense of being apart. She longed for a time before the fault lines grew so deep. Aarif's laughter had once blurred them. His love had made her believe faith could be stitched together. And in choosing that love, she had walked away from her own family forever.

Sometimes, she wandered to the ghats at *Ram Ki Paidi*, where pilgrims bathed in the sacred waters, faces lifted in reverence. She watched them not with judgment, but with a complicated tenderness—her own beliefs now a weave of rupture and resolve, shaped by her deliberate act of love across the great divide.

Her days began to revolve around the Sarayu. Each morning she arrived with a small basket of flowers cradled in her arms. She would sit at the edge, dipping her feet into the cool water, watching life unfold around her, fishermen casting their nets with practiced grace, birds circling overhead. The river took it all and gave nothing back, mirroring the sky with quiet indifference.

Sometimes she imagined Aarif beside her—not just as the young man with dreams in his eyes, but also as a boy, carefree, his laughter ringing out like the children's around her. In those moments, the river felt like a bridge

—linking what was and what remained, holding space for memory in its eternal, unbroken flow.

The Sarayu had its own stories, older than Ayodhya itself. It was said that the river had been born from the tears of the gods, a sacred thread connecting the heavens to the earth. Its waters were believed to purify the soul, washing away the sins of those who bathed in it. Yet, for all its spiritual significance, the Sarayu remained unassuming, a quiet presence in a town that often took its constancy for granted.

Amina had always been a quiet woman. She had spoken only when necessary, and she had always chosen her words carefully, as if they carried the weight of unseen consequences. But after that fateful day, her voice simply ceased to exist. She did not cry, scream, or even whisper. The world outside continued its relentless march. And Amina retreated into an inner silence that seemed as eternal as the Sarayu River flowing quietly past Ayodhya. Amina's retreat into silence was as unremarkable as the dropping of a leaf into the Sarayu. There was no declaration, no dramatic outburst, only the gradual dimming of her voice until it was no longer present. Her daughter, Yasmin, noticed it first.

"*Ammi*, do you want some tea?" Yasmin had asked one evening, holding out a cup.

Amina had looked at her, her dark eyes filled with a sadness that words could never articulate, and simply shook her head. Yasmin frowned but said nothing. Days turned into weeks, and Amina's silence became an unspoken reality. When neighbors came to visit, they whispered among themselves, casting worried glances at the woman who now communicated only with gestures. Adil did not coax her out of it. He never asked Amina why she had become silent, why her lips were always pressed together as though they were guarding a sacred truth.

"She needs time," Adil told his daughter, Yasmin, though his own voice wavered with uncertainty.

But time passed, and Amina's silence deepened, becoming a defining part of her existence. It was as though she had given up on language itself, choosing instead to let her presence speak for her. The Sarayu River, flowing gently along the edges of Ayodhya, seemed to mirror Amina's silence. For centuries, the river had watched the town's dramas unfold on its banks—births and deaths, prayers and battles, triumphs and tragedies. It had witnessed the rise of Ayodhya as a sacred city, the ebb and flow of empires, and the uncertain lives of its people. The Sarayu carried within its waters the history of Lord Rama, whose story was etched into every corner of Ayodhya. It had been the site where his devotees performed rituals, where pilgrims cleansed their sins, and where children played in its shallows. Yet the river itself never spoke. It flowed on, indifferent to the chaos and reverence it inspired. Watching the river's surface ripple under the setting sun, Amina would feel a strange kinship with it, a connection that went beyond words. The Sarayu's silence was one of enduring wisdom. It had seen everything, and yet judged nothing. Amina found solace in its quiet companionship, as though the river understood her grief in a way no one else could. Her silence was of course, rooted in loss. Aarif, her only son, had been taken from her in a senseless act of violence, his death a cruel consequence of the escalating tensions in Ayodhya. Aarif had been her light, her reason to endure the struggles of life. His absence left a void so vast that even her own voice seemed inadequate to fill it. The violence that claimed Aarif's life, became a symbol of everything

Amina could no longer reconcile. She could not understand the hatred that had turned her town into a battlefield, nor could she find words to express the depth of her pain. Silence, she realized, was her only refuge.

In many ways, Amina's silence mirrored the history of the Sarayu River. Like the river, she had borne witness to the unfolding drama of human existence, acts of love, sacrifice, and betrayal. The Sarayu had seen Ayodhya thrive as a center of devotion and then crumble under the weight of division. It had absorbed the tears of pilgrims and the blood of the fallen, yet it continued to flow, untouched by the turmoil on its banks. Amina, too, had absorbed the joys and sorrows of her life. Like the Sarayu, she carried her burdens silently, finding strength in her ability to endure. But her son's unexpected death had broken something within her, leaving her adrift in a sea of memories. Amina's silence did not go completely unnoticed. In the tightly knit Muslim community of Ayodhya, her withdrawal was sometimes a subject of whispered conversation. Some saw her silence as a form of protest, a refusal to engage with a world that had betrayed her. Others viewed it as a sign of madness, a retreat into a private world of grief.

Yasmin, now almost a young woman, often found herself defending her mother. "She's not mad," she would say firmly. "She's just... processing." But even Yasmin struggled to understand the depth of Amina's silence. As she grew older, she began to see it not as a weakness but as a form of coping mechanism. Her mother's silence seemed a kind of testament to the unspoken truths that words could never capture. The river's eternal flow reminded her that life, too, was a cycle of beginnings and endings. Just as the Sarayu continued its journey, so too would she, even if her path was now marked by silence.

As the years passed, Amina's silence became her identity. People in Ayodhya began to see her as a symbol of quiet strength.

"*Aap theek hain*, Amina Bai?" women would ask in the course of brief visits.

Amina would smile and nod, her eyes reflecting a peace that words could never convey. In her later years, Amina's walks to the Sarayu became shorter, her steps slower. Yet she continued to visit the river, her silent companion through life's trials. They say a river always remembers. The Sarayu River continued its journey, carrying Amina's story along with countless others. It has flowed silently, a witness to the timeless drama of Ayodhya, its waters silently reflecting the lives of those who have lived and died on its banks. Amina's silence, much like the river itself, became a part of Ayodhya's lore —a reminder that there is strength in enduring, in flowing forward, quietly and steadfastly, through the currents of life.

8

Adil Khan, my maternal grandfather, had never imagined himself a political activist, let alone one who would become a vocal advocate for the rights of Muslims in India. For most of his life, he had preferred a quieter path—working as a school teacher, raising a family, and engaging in thoughtful discussions about history and philosophy. Politics, in his view, was a messy business, filled with opportunism and deceit. But the senseless death of his son Aarif in one of those terrible seasons of communal unrest and violence that scarred the late decades of the twentieth century, was a turning point—a rupture so profound that it altered the course of his life.

The loss of Aarif was like a storm that swept through Adil's existence, leaving behind nothing but destruction and an unrelenting void. Grief, rage, and guilt intertwined in his heart, creating a restlessness that would not let him remain silent. Adil, however, found no solace in memories. Aarif had been caught in the crossfire of communal riots that erupted over a minor dispute. The memory of his son's lifeless body, his bright eyes closed forever, haunted Adil every waking moment. It was as though Aarif's death had torn away the veil that had allowed him to ignore the rising tide of communal tensions in Ayodhya. He threw himself into activism, channeling his grief into a relentless pursuit of justice. But even as he fought for change, he knew that nothing could fill the void Aarif had left. His son was gone, a bright light extinguished in the darkness of hatred and violence. And though Adil's world had been shattered, he resolved to keep fighting, if only to ensure that Aarif's death would not be in vain.

Adil's sorrow had quickly transformed into anger— anger at the mob that had taken Aarif's life, at the authorities who had failed to maintain order, and at himself for his earlier apathy. For years, he had told himself that the divisions between Hindus and Muslims in Ayodhya were an unfortunate but manageable reality, something that could be weathered through mutual respect and dialogue. But Aarif's death shattered this belief, forcing him to confront the depth of the animosity that had taken root in his town.

In the weeks following Aarif's death, Adil began attending community meetings organized by local Muslim leaders. At first, he simply listened, his grief too raw to allow him to speak. The meetings were filled with stories of injustice—homes burned, businesses destroyed, lives lost—all with the tacit complicity of a system that seemed indifferent to their plight. Adil found himself drawn to these gatherings, not only for the sense of solidarity they offered but also because they provided an outlet for the anger simmering within him.

One evening, an elderly cleric, Maulana Rahmatullah addressed the group. "We have remained silent for too long," the Maulana said, his voice trembling with emotion. "They want us to be invisible, to erase our history and our presence in this land. But we are part of India, just as much as they are. It is time we stand up for our rights, not with violence, but with strength and unity."

The Maulana's words struck a chord with Adil. He realized that his silence would achieve nothing, that his grief needed to be transformed into action. Slowly, he began to speak at the meetings, sharing his own experiences and ideas. His background as a teacher gave him a natural ability to articulate complex thoughts in a way that resonated with others. For Adil, the political awakening in Ayodhya was a call to action. But it was his grief for Aarif that had transformed into a quiet determination to protect the values he held dear. He started attending community meetings, where like-minded individuals gathered to discuss ways to preserve harmony in the town. These meetings, often held in small, unassuming homes or under the shade of *neem* trees, had once brought together Hindus and Muslims who had believed in coexistence. Before long, Adil became one of the most prominent voices in Ayodhya's Muslim community, advocating for justice and equal rights. In the years following Aarif's death, Adil had become a man consumed by anger and purpose. He spent hours reading news reports, analyzing political speeches, and attending community meetings. He joined rallies and began speaking out against the growing marginalization of Muslims. The once-quiet teacher had transformed into a fiery orator, drawing crowds as he spoke passionately about justice, equality, and the need for Muslim political representation. Adil spoke sparingly but with conviction, quoting verses from the Quran and recounting stories of the Prophet Muhammad's compassion. His words resonated with many, but he also faced resistance. The growing polarization in Ayodhya meant that even the simplest acts of unity were viewed with suspicion.

One evening, Adil came home to find Yasmin reading a book on Ayodhya's history. He sat beside her, and they talked late into the night. Yasmin asked him about the Babri Masjid, about why it had become such a contentious issue. Adil, choosing his words carefully, explained the layers of history, politics, and emotion that had shaped the conflict.

"But *abbu*," the young Yasmin asked, her voice hesitant, "do you think Aarif would have cared about all this?"

Adil paused, looking at his daughter with a mixture of pride and sorrow. "Aarif cared about people, Yasmin. Not walls, not stones. He would have wanted us to do the same."

As Adil plunged deeper into activism, the distance between him and Amina grew. Amina, devastated by Aarif's death, had retreated into a world of silence and introspection. She found no solace in Adil's fiery speeches or his growing involvement in political movements. Yasmin Khan, my mother, found herself adrift as she stepped hesitantly into the fragile dawn of her youth. In the quiet chaos of their fractured household, she did not know whom to lean on. Her father's relentless plunge into political activism felt, to her tender and questioning mind, less like a crusade for justice and more like a calculated retreat—a desperate effort to submerge his anguish in the noise of rallies and speeches. It seemed as though he had chosen to escape the aching silence of their shared sorrow rather than confront the unfillable void that Aarif's absence had carved into their lives.

"Why can't you just stay with us, *abbu*?" young Yasmin asked one evening, her voice trembling with suppressed emotion. "Isn't it enough that we've lost

Aarif? Do you have to lose yourself too? Do we have to lose you as well?"

Her father, Adil struggled to respond. He understood his daughter's pain, but he could not bring himself to abandon the cause that had given him a sense of purpose. "Yasmin," he said softly, "I'm doing this for Aarif, for all of us. We can't let his death be in vain. We have to fight for a better future."

But Yasmin could not see the future Adil envisioned. Her world had narrowed to the confines of their home, to the memories of Aarif that she clung to like a lifeline. Adil's growing absence—physically, emotionally, and spiritually—felt like another loss, one she could neither understand nor accept. Her mother's lapse into complete silence, she understood, was another route to channel their pain without addressing the void that Aarif's absence had left in their lives.

Over time, the chasm within their home became insurmountable. Adil began spending more nights away from home, staying in the homes of fellow activists or attending late-night meetings. Amina, who had once been his anchor, now seemed like a distant figure, her silence a reproach that he could not bear. Eventually, Adil made the painful decision to move out, renting a small place near the local mosque where he could focus on his work without the weight of Amina's silence or her implied disapproval. But the separation was hardest on Yasmin, well into the turbulent waters of her teenage years, and who found herself caught in the crosscurrents of loss and uncertainty. She loved both her parents deeply and could not understand why they had drifted apart. For a time, Yasmin visited her father in his rented place, bringing him home-cooked meals and news from the family. But the strain in their relationship was evident. Adil, consumed by his activism, had little time to offer her, and Yasmin resented his absence.

"Why can't you just come home, *abbu*?" she asked him often, her eyes brimming with tears. "Ammi needs you. I need you."

Adil took her hands in his and tried to explain. "Yasmin, what I'm doing is important. It's not just for us, but for our entire community. I know it's hard to understand, but someday you will."

But Yasmin, my mother, could not see the larger picture that Adil was so committed to. To her, his activism felt like a betrayal, a choice that prioritized strangers over his own family. The rift between them grew, leaving Yasmin feeling caught between two worlds. Gradually, the visits grew infrequent and then stopped altogether.

As the 1980s progressed, the divisions between Hindus and Muslims in Ayodhya had become more pronounced. The Ram Janmabhoomi movement, which sought to build a temple on the site of the Babri Masjid, gained momentum, fueled by an inexplicable mix of religious fervor and political opportunism. Processions and rallies, often accompanied by inflammatory rhetoric, became a common sight in the town. The Babri Masjid, once a symbol of coexistence, now stood at the center of a bitter dispute that threatened to tear Ayodhya apart.

Adil found himself at the forefront of the resistance, organizing protests and speaking out against the rising tide of communalism. He worked tirelessly to build alliances with progressive Hindu leaders who shared his vision of a pluralistic India. But the atmosphere in Ayodhya grew increasingly volatile, and Adil's activism made him a target. He received threats, his name appeared on lists of "troublemakers," and his movements were closely monitored by the authorities.

Despite the dangers, Adil refused to back down. "If we give in to fear," he told his fellow activists, "we've already lost. Our fight is not just for ourselves but for the soul of this country."

Adil's unwavering commitment to his cause came at a steep personal cost. His relationship with his now silent wife, Amina, already strained, disintegrated entirely. They communicated only through Yasmin, who acted as a reluctant intermediary. Adil missed the warmth of his home, the simple pleasures of family life, but he could not abandon the path he had chosen. Amina, meanwhile, withdrew further into her shell. Her silence, once a quiet protest against the violence that had taken Aarif, became a fortress that kept the world at bay. She rarely spoke of Adil, even to Yasmin, and refused to discuss the growing turmoil in Ayodhya. For Amina, the world outside their home had become a place of irreparable loss, a battlefield where love and reason had no place.

For Adil, the changes in Ayodhya were both personal and political. The town he had known and loved was slipping away, replaced by a place that felt foreign and hostile. It was a place of heartbreak. In spite of his growing despair, he remained determined to fight for the values that he had believed in—a commitment to justice and equality. Adil found himself deeply drawn into the chaos and the fray. His political activism, driven by the pain of Aarif's death, aligned him with those who sought to protect the rights of Muslims in the face of growing hostility. But this alignment had come at a huge cost, further alienating him from his family and deepening the rift with Amina.

As the Babri Masjid dispute escalated in the late 1980s, Ayodhya became a powder keg of religious tension. The political landscape in India was undergoing a seismic shift, with communalism becoming a potent tool for electoral gain. Adil's warnings about the dangers of polarization fell on deaf ears, drowned out by the clamor of slogans and the beating of drums.

The events leading up to the demolition of the Babri Masjid in 1992 were a culmination of years of division and hatred. For Adil, it was a bitter validation of everything he had fought against. The relentless demands of activism, combined with the personal losses he had endured, had of course, taken a toll on him. In the years that followed, Adil's work would be remembered as a legacy to the power of resistance. His speeches, his writings, and his tireless efforts to bridge divides left an indelible mark on those who knew him. But the cost of his activism was one he carried with him to the end of his days—a cost measured in the distance between him and his family, in the silences that lingered long after the battles were over.

For Amina and Yasmin, Adil's absence became a part of their story, a reminder of the complexities of love, loss, and the choices that define a life. And for Ayodhya, their fractured family became a microcosm of a town torn apart by history, its wounds carried silently within their lives. The Ayodhya of Adil's youth was not the Ayodhya of the 1980s. The town had become a battleground of ideologies. The rhetoric of religious nationalism had grown louder, and whispers about reclaiming Ram Janmabhoomi had turned into fiery slogans. For Adil, who had seen the town's Hindu-Muslim camaraderie crumble into mistrust, it was a disheartening transformation. All these years, he had kept his head down, preferring not to engage in the growing political unrest. But everything had already changed for Adil, my grandfather, the day Aarif was killed. There was a looming storm both inside and outside.

As Ayodhya inched closer to December 1992, tensions

reached a boiling point. The town, once defined by its quiet rhythms, was now charged with an energy that felt both exhilarating and dangerous. Processions filled the streets, their chants echoing through the alleys. The rhetoric of leaders on both sides grew sharper, their words slicing through the fragile fabric of Ayodhya's community life. Everyone in town grew increasingly worried. Everyone noticed how even mundane interactions in the bazaar carried an undercurrent of hostility. Shopkeepers, who once exchanged pleasantries regardless of faith, now hesitated, their words guarded. Everyone felt the weight of these changes acutely, and their memory of a changing town was tied to a more genteel Ayodhya that seemed to be slipping away. The Ayodhya of the 1980s bore little resemblance to the town that Adil had once called home in his youth. Where there had been a delicate harmony, a sense of shared space and purpose between Hindus and Muslims, there now lingered a palpable tension. It was a town teetering on the edge of something ominous, a battleground of ideologies where political ambitions mingled with religious fervor, reshaping the landscape and the hearts of its people.

The Ram Janmabhoomi movement, once a distant murmur, had become a thunderous roar. Slogans like "*Jai Shri Ram*" reverberated through the streets, each chant carrying the weight of an ideological storm that threatened to drown out the quieter voices of coexistence. Ayodhya's skyline began to change, not through the construction of buildings, but through the presence of banners, flags, and graffiti scrawled on walls, declaring allegiance to one cause or the other.

In the bazaars, the air felt different, heavy with unsaid things. The once-bustling market streets, where Hindu and Muslim shopkeepers had worked side by side for generations, were now marked by an invisible divide. Some shopkeepers openly displayed saffron flags or green banners, signaling their stance in the growing discord. Others avoided any show of affiliation, fearing repercussions in an increasingly polarized environment. The sweet shops, once a shared indulgence where Hindus and Muslims exchanged pleasantries over *laddoos* and *jalebis*, now stood like contested spaces. They had become uneasy relics, their sugary warmth curdled by suspicion, their counters echoing a silence that hadn't always been there. Even the shared delight of savoring guavas with chili salt on winter afternoons seemed tainted by the weight of suspicion in a town so deeply redefined.

Physical changes mirrored the emotional and ideological shifts. The town's infrastructure began to reflect the growing tensions. The Babri Masjid, with its three aging domes, had always been a landmark, a quiet testament to centuries of history. But in the 1980s, it became a symbol of contention, its very existence questioned and challenged. Security tightened around it; police pickets and barricades became a regular feature, further highlighting its contested nature.

Adil Khan could see these changes every day as he walked the streets. The alleys that had once echoed with the laughter of children now carried the sound of rallies and protests. He noticed how young men from both communities gathered in separate groups, their discussions growing more impassioned and their gaze more distrustful. The political rhetoric of the time had seeped into their lives, shaping their identities in ways that Adil found deeply unsettling.

The rising tide of changes was not confined to public spaces. The changes permeated households and personal relationships. Families, once bound by years of friendship and mutual respect, began to distance themselves from one another. Invitations to weddings or festive gatherings became fewer, and conversations turned cautious. The shared language of camaraderie was replaced by guarded exchanges. Adil recalled the Ram Leela performances of his youth, where both Hindus and Muslims had come together to enact and watch the epic tale of Ramayana. In those days, the roles of Rama, Sita, and Ravan were often played by actors of either faith, chosen for their talent rather than their religious identity. By the 1980s, such events had become fraught with political undertones, the casting itself a potential flashpoint. Even mundane interactions carried an undercurrent of unease. When Adil visited the *chaiwala* at the corner of the street, he noticed how conversations had shifted from light-hearted gossip to veiled remarks about "them" and "us." The tea, though still steaming and fragrant, seemed to carry a bitter aftertaste. For Adil, these transformations and its emotional toll were a constant source of pain. Aarif's death had already carved a deep wound in his heart, and the changing face of Ayodhya only deepened it. He often found himself lost in thought, wondering how a town that had once been a mosaic of shared histories and cultures had come to this.

Amidst this turmoil, the Sarayu River flowed as it always had, a silent observer to Ayodhya's changing fortunes. Its waters carried the memories of countless generations, bearing witness to both the town's moments of unity and its darkest hours. In the 1980s, the river seemed to reflect the town's mood, its surface often turbulent, its once-serene banks now dotted with gatherings that spoke not of peace, but of division. Pilgrims still came to the Sarayu to cleanse their sins, their chants mingling with the cries of hawkers selling marigold garlands and incense. But even this sacred ritual seemed to carry a new tension. Some looked over their shoulders as they prayed, wary of the charged atmosphere that had seeped into every corner of the town.

As the 1980s progressed, Ayodhya became a focal point for national politics. Leaders from both Hindu and Muslim communities descended upon the town, their speeches igniting passions and the politics of fear. The Ram Janmabhoomi movement gained momentum, with processions and demonstrations becoming a regular feature. The Babri Masjid became a symbol, not just of a contested site, but of a larger battle for identity and power. The daily rhythms of life of Ayodhya's residents was marked by a growing sense of caution. Parents worried about their children's safety, urging them to return home before sunset. Shops closed earlier, and the once-vibrant evening gatherings at the *paan* stalls grew smaller. The air, once filled with the sounds of laughter and casual conversation, now carried the weight of slogans and debates. Even festivals, which had once been occasions for communal joy, became sources of anxiety. The overlapping celebrations of Ram Navami and Eid, which had once been a testament to Ayodhya's shared heritage, now required careful coordination to prevent clashes. The streets, adorned with lights and decorations, seemed to mask the underlying tension rather than celebrate unity. As the decade neared its end, the atmosphere in Ayodhya grew even more charged. The town's identity, once rooted in its shared history, was being rewritten by forces that sought to divide rather than unite. The Babri Masjid stood at the center of this storm, its domes a constant reminder of the simmering conflict. Ayodhya in the 1980s was a town at a crossroads, its past and future locked in a struggle that would ultimately define its identity.

On December 6, 1992, the day of my birth, the morning began like any other. But the air was thick with anticipation. News had spread that a large rally was planned near the Babri Masjid. Everyone in Ayodhya stayed home, their hearts heavy with dread. The distant sound of slogans grew louder as the day progressed, until it was impossible to ignore. On December 6, 1992, Ayodhya woke to a dawn that felt eerily ordinary, despite the tension simmering beneath the surface. The town's rhythms unfolded as usual—the distant temple bells chimed at first light, the *muezzin*'s call floated softly from mosques, and the Sarayu River flowed as silently as ever, watching the unfolding human drama. Yet, an unspoken heaviness hung in the air. Everyone in Ayodhya knew that the day would not pass like any other. The streets, normally bustling with *chai* vendors, shopkeepers, and children playing, were deserted. Doors and windows were shut, not because of the winter chill, but because of the pervasive fear that had been building for months.

The previous day had seen thousands of *kar sevaks*, Hindu volunteers, pour into Ayodhya, their arrival marked by fervent chants of "*Jai Shri Ram*" echoing through the alleys and temples. Their faces, flushed with religious fervor, betrayed the intensity of their mission. Many locals, regardless of their faith, stayed indoors, avoiding eye contact with the processions that snaked through the streets. Whispers of what might happen tomorrow were exchanged in hushed tones, as though even speaking of the possibilities might bring calamity closer.

By mid-morning on December 6, the heart of Ayodhya, near the Ram Janmabhoomi-Babri Masjid complex, was a hive of activity. Tens of thousands of *kar sevaks* had gathered, their numbers swelling by the hour. Makeshift stages had been erected, where leaders of the Ram Janmabhoomi movement took turns addressing the crowd. Their speeches oscillated between fiery invocations of devotion to Lord Rama and condemnations of the Babri Masjid, which they called a "blemish" on the sacred birthplace of Ram. The rhetoric was incendiary, and the crowd responded with thunderous chants, their voices rising like a tidal wave.

For those who ventured closer to the site, the atmosphere was both electrifying and ominous. The *kar sevaks*, many of them young men wielding *trishuls* and saffron flags, seemed intoxicated with a collective energy. Some climbed trees or the roofs of nearby buildings with their tridents, to get a better view of the mosque, while others pressed against the barricades set up by the authorities. Police officers stood in uneasy clusters, their numbers dwarfed by the overwhelming crowd. They were armed but hesitant, caught between conflicting orders from their superiors and the surging sea of *kar sevaks*.

At around noon, the first breach occurred. A group of *kar sevaks*, spurred on by cries of "*Ram Lalla hum aaye hain, mandir yahin banayenge!*" ('We have come for Lord Rama, we will build the temple here!'), broke through the barricades and rushed toward the Babri Masjid. Their advance was chaotic but purposeful, driven by a mix of religious zeal and mob psychology. The police, initially paralyzed by indecision, attempted to push them back but were quickly overwhelmed. The thin line of resistance crumbled, and the *kar sevaks* surged forward, their ranks swelling with each passing moment.

The first blows to the mosque's structure were dealt with crude tools—iron rods, pickaxes, and hammers. The sound of stone being struck reverberated through the air, mingling with the chants and cries of the crowd. Within minutes, the *kar sevaks* had scaled the domes of the Babri Masjid, their saffron flags fluttering triumphantly against the blue sky. The sight was both surreal and devastating, a moment that seemed to collapse centuries of history into a single, violent act.

Inside their homes, Ayodhya's residents listened in stunned silence as the distant noise grew louder. For the Muslim families, each crash of stone felt like a blow to their collective soul. Many gathered in prayer, their whispered verses seeking solace and protection. The Hindu families were divided in their emotions. Some were jubilant, believing they were witnessing the reclaiming of a sacred site, while others were deeply uneasy, fearing the repercussions of such an act.

As the afternoon wore on, the Babri Masjid's domes began to collapse, one after the other. Clouds of dust rose into the sky, visible from miles away. The crowd roared with each fall, their chants reaching a fever pitch. The *kar sevaks* worked tirelessly, as though driven by an unstoppable force, dismantling a structure that had stood for over four centuries. The mosque was reduced to rubble by late afternoon, its ruins a stark testament to the destructive power of ideology.

News of the demolition spread like wildfire, reaching every corner of Ayodhya and beyond. The reactions were immediate and polarizing. While some celebrated with impromptu processions and firecrackers, others mourned quietly, their grief too profound for words. The authorities, caught off guard by the speed and intensity of the events, scrambled to contain the situation. But it was too late. The fragile peace of Ayodhya had been shattered, and the town was spiraling into chaos.

By evening, the violence that had been simmering beneath the surface, erupted. Groups of *kar sevaks*, emboldened by their victory, roamed the streets, targeting Muslim homes and businesses. Fires broke out in several parts of town, their flames illuminating the night sky. The wails of those who had lost everything mixed with the sound of sirens as the police and fire services struggled to respond. In some neighborhoods, Hindu and Muslim residents who had lived side by side for generations found themselves turning against each other, their shared history eclipsed by the shadow of communal hatred.

Amidst the chaos, the Sarayu River flowed on, its waters reflecting the flickering flames of a town in turmoil. It had witnessed centuries of human drama on its banks, from the rise and fall of kingdoms to the quiet moments of devotion and daily life. But this night was different. The river seemed to mourn silently, its currents carrying the weight of a shattered town. For those who survived the day, December 6, 1992, would forever be etched in their memories as a turning point—a day when Ayodhya, and perhaps India itself, crossed a threshold from which there was no return. The town's landscape, both physical and emotional, had been irreversibly altered. The Babri Masjid was gone, and with it, a piece of Ayodhya's complex history. In its place lay a void, filled with rubble, ash, and unanswered questions about identity, faith, and the price of reclaiming the past.

By evening, the news reached them: the Babri Masjid had been demolished. The streets of Ayodhya erupted in chaos, the fragile peace shattered beyond repair. Fires burned in the distance, and the sound of sirens pierced the night. Many clutched their prayer beads, their hands trembling. Parents held their young children close, whispering prayers in both Hindi and Arabic. Many did not sleep that night, their home filled with the weight of a tragedy that felt both personal and universal.

In the weeks that followed, Ayodhya became a different town, its future unwritten and then rewritten. The scars of December 6, 1992, the day of my birth, were visible everywhere, not just in the rubble of the Babri

Masjid but in the eyes of its people. They struggled to make sense of their place in this fractured world. Ayodhya's story, much like their own, was far from over. It remained a place of contradictions, a town where sorrow and fortitude coexisted, where history and memory intertwined in ways both painful and profound.

And in its broken heart, I was born. My first breath coincided with the gasp of a nation torn open. In a strange, almost mythic symmetry, my life began just as something centuries old came to an end. That night, as Ayodhya burned and mourned, I entered the world—unaware that my story would be forever entangled with the ashes of that day. I was born into a sky split by smoke and memory, into a city learning to live with its ruins. From my first cry, I carried the echo of that fracture. Some say birth is a beginning, but mine felt more like an inheritance—of grief, of division, and of a story that was never only mine to tell.

9

"Ayodhya is not just a city," my paternal grandfather, Shyam Trivedi, once said, leaning on his cane as he watched the setting sun bathe the Sarayu in gold. "It is a heartbeat, a memory, a presence, a right." I used to believe him.

When I was a child, I would sit at his feet, watching his lawyer's hands trace invisible maps of the city as he recounted the trial, the arguments, the moment when the verdict tipped in favor of the Ram temple. "We are restoring history," he said, "not erasing it." As I grew older, though, I began to wonder whose history we were restoring and at what cost. I stood in the courtyard of our ancestral home, the air heavy with the smell of marigolds and sandalwood. This house had witnessed generations of scholars, priests, advocates come together—all bound by a shared purpose: to uphold the sanctity of Ayodhya as the birthplace of Lord Rama. It was a house of stories, but my story had always felt like an anomaly, a thread fraying at the edges of the cloth.

"Your grandfather fought for something greater than

himself," my father, Ramesh Trivedi, said that morning over breakfast. His voice was calm, calculated, the voice of a man who had learned to wield power without raising it. "That is the legacy you inherit, Saanvi."

I didn't respond. Legacy was a heavy word, and I wasn't sure it was mine to carry.

The Trivedi mansion was a world unto itself, a labyrinth of sandstone and marble that bore the weight of centuries. To call it a house would have been a disservice to its grandeur. It was an edifice, a monument to my family's pervasive and lasting influence over Ayodhya. Standing on the banks of the Sarayu, its high walls framed by sprawling gardens, the mansion exuded permanence, as if it were as inseparable from the city as the ghats themselves.

The central courtyard, the heart of the mansion, was always alive with movement. Brass lamps lined its perimeter, their flames flickering in harmony with the breeze. In one corner, my paternal grandmother, Sumitra Trivedi, would preside over the morning rituals, her voice steady as she chanted mantras that seemed to rise and mingle with the cries of peacocks in the garden. She was a woman of formidable presence, her face etched with lines that seemed less the marks of age and more a testament to her unyielding will.

It was in this courtyard that my grandfather, Shyam Trivedi, had built his legacy. The walls bore framed photographs of him standing beside other prominent figures of his time—judges, politicians, spiritual leaders— all men who had shaped the course of Ayodhya's history in their own way. Beneath each photograph was a brass plate engraved with a date and a brief description: *Supreme Court verdict. Shyam Trivedi leads the legal team for the Ram Mandir.* These plates gleamed like medals, each one a reminder of the battles fought and won.

As a child, I was both awed and intimidated by the mansion's grandeur. Its corridors seemed endless, their cool stone floors resonating with the soft click of my shoes as I wandered from room to room. There was the library, a cavernous room lined with mahogany shelves that stretched from floor to ceiling, filled with leather-bound volumes on law, history, and philosophy. My grandfather often retreated there in the evening, his silhouette framed by the warm light of a reading lamp. He would sit at his desk, poring over old manuscripts and court documents, his glasses perched precariously on the bridge of his nose. The air in the library smelled of old paper and sandalwood, a smell I associated with his wisdom.

The mansion's dining hall was another world entirely. A long teakwood table dominated the room, its surface polished to a mirror-like sheen. Meals were elaborate affairs, with dishes served in silver platters and bowls. My grandfather would sit at one head of the table, and my father, Ramesh Trivedi, at the other head of the table, their presence commanding even in silence. They were men of precision, their words measured, their actions deliberate and calculated. I often felt like a spectator at these meals, my plate untouched as I listened to the conversations around me. They spoke of politics and religion, of court rulings and community gatherings, their voices charged with conviction. I envied their certainty, their sense of purpose.

Tucked in the eastern wing of the mansion was the *puja ghar*, the prayer room. It was my grandmother's sanctuary, a space filled with the fragrance of incense and the soft glow of flickering oil lamps. Idols of Rama, Sita, and Hanuman stood on a marble platform adorned with marigolds and *tulsi* leaves. Their serene expressions seemed to watch over the family, offering silent blessings.

Time seemed to stand still in the prayer room, a sanctum whose walls were adorned with intricate frescoes depicting scenes from the Ramayana—Sita's abduction, Hanuman's flight, Rama's triumphant return to Ayodhya. An ornate silver idol of Lord Rama stood at the center, flanked by smaller idols of Sita and Lakshmana. Every morning, my grandmother would sit cross-legged on the floor, her saree draped over her head, as she chanted hymns in a voice that seemed to carry centuries of devotion. My grandmother often brought me here, teaching me the verses of the *Ramcharitmanas*. Her voice would rise and fall in a melodic rhythm, her eyes closed in devotion. I tried to mimic her, but the words felt foreign in my mouth, their weight too much for me to bear. I never felt the same connection to the deities as she did. For her, the prayer room was a bridge to the divine; for me, it was a room of questions.

"Why do we only pray to Rama and Sita?" I asked her once, my voice tentative.

She looked at me, her gaze soft but firm. "Because they are the soul of Ayodhya, Saanvi. Rama is not just a god; he is *Maryada Purushottam*, the ideal man, the ideal king. To follow his path is to uphold *dharma*."

Her answer felt rehearsed, a line she had repeated countless times over the years. But it left me unsatisfied. In a house so deeply tied to the narrative of Ayodhya, I couldn't help but wonder if devotion was a choice or an inheritance.

The prayer room also held a small, locked cabinet. My grandmother referred to it as the *gupt dhan*, the hidden treasure. Once, when I was about ten, I asked her what was inside.

"Sacred relics," she said with a smile. "They belong to the family's history. You will understand their importance when you're older."

I never found out what the cabinet contained, but its presence lingered in my mind like a secret waiting to be uncovered.

Where the mansion bore the weight of the Trivedi legacy, the garden bloomed with the luxury it afforded. The garden, my favorite part of the mansion, was also my escape, a place where I could breathe without the weight of expectation pressing down on me. The landscape unfolded in quiet order, trimmed lawns interspersed with marigold clusters, jasmine creeping along low fences, and bursts of color from scattered flower beds. A few *neem* trees rose with unassuming grace, while an old banyan stood apart, its wide canopy casting a dense, deliberate shadow across the ground. A stone pathway wound its way through the garden, leading to a small gazebo overlooking the Sarayu. This was my sanctuary, a place where I could escape the weight of my family's expectations. I would sit in the gazebo for hours, mentally sketching the river and the temples that lined its banks. It was here that I began to ponder on and even question the legacy I was born into, the stories my family told and the ones they chose to omit. My grandfather would sometimes join me there. Leaning on his cane and fixing his gaze on the horizon, he would ask me, his voice soft: "Do you know why this house was built here?" I would shake my head.

"This land," he said, gesturing with his cane, "was once a field of *tulsi* plants, sacred to Lord Rama. My father bought it from a Brahmin family who could no longer maintain it. He believed it was our duty to preserve its sanctity."

"Preserve or claim?" I dared to ask him once before I could stop myself.

He turned to me, his eyes narrowing. "There is no difference," he said. "To preserve something is to claim it as your own, to take responsibility for its future."

His words stayed with me long after he had left. They echoed in my mind as I walked through the mansion's corridors, as I watched the servants dust the photographs on the walls, as I listened to my grandfather and my father's measured words at the dining table. I do not know why, but I would sometimes see the mansion not as a home but as a monument, a fortress built to guard a legacy that was both a source of pride and a burden.

The centerpiece of the garden was a stone fountain shaped like a lotus, its petals carved with scenes from the *Ramayana*. My grandfather had commissioned it soon after the Babri masjid had come down on the day of my birth. For him, it was a symbol of triumph and faith. "This fountain represents the purity of Ayodhya," he said during its inauguration. But as I grew older, the fountain began to feel more like a monument to exclusion than purity. Near the edge of the garden was a small pond surrounded by jasmine bushes. This was a spot where the noise of the household couldn't reach me. Here, I could sit for hours reading, trying to make sense of the world I was growing up in. One afternoon, when I was not yet ten, I sat by the pond and overheard two gardeners talking. They were discussing the land dispute, their voices low but urgent.

"They say the mosque was torn down to build the temple," one of them said.

"And who gave them the right?" the other replied. "The mosque was part of Ayodhya too."

Their words stayed with me, a quiet rebellion against the narrative I had been raised to believe.

Our Trivedi mansion's library was a cavernous room filled with rows of dark wooden shelves that stretched to the ceiling. It smelled of old paper and sandalwood, a scent that was both comforting and oppressive. This was more my father's domain, a space where he prepared his speeches and strategized his political moves. The library was also where I first encountered the idea of Ayodhya as a contested space. Among the religious texts and legal journals were books and articles that presented conflicting views on the city's history. I remember pulling out a book titled *Ayodhya: A City Divided* and reading about the Babri Masjid for the first time.

I asked my father about it later, curious about his perspective.

"The mosque was a historical mistake," he said, his tone measured, his eyes distant as though sifting through centuries of grievances. "It was built on the ruins of a temple that belonged to us. Rebuilding the temple is not about destruction. It is about restoration."

I tilted my head, trying to match his intensity. "But what about the people who have worshipped there for generations? Don't their stories matter too? How do you weigh the sanctity of one faith over another?"

He sighed, and for a fleeting moment, I saw the weariness of a man torn between his convictions and the realities of his time. "Saanvi," he began, his voice gentler now, "history is written not in ink, but in blood and sweat. For centuries, the mosque stood, yes—but not without dispute. In the later decades, it had largely fallen into disuse. No one had worshipped there regularly in years. But that's not the heart of it. The mosque wasn't just constructed—it was imposed. It was an act of conquest masquerading as creation. A Mughal emperor sought to assert his dominance, and the destruction of a Hindu temple wasn't merely an act of aggression. It was a statement and a message. It was more than a symbolic gesture. To turn a site sacred to us into something alien to its origins—it wasn't just an insult. It was a wound. A wound carved deep into the soul of our civilization."

I hesitated. "But does rebuilding truly heal that

wound, or does it tear open another? What about those who have known the mosque as their sacred space, as their history? Are they not victims of the same conquest, just centuries later?"

He rubbed his temples, his expression softening as though grappling with the weight of my words. "You have your mother's way of seeing the other side," he said with a faint smile. "But understand this: for Hindus, this temple is not merely stone and mortar. It represents a deep sense of belonging, a place where divinity touched the earth. Losing it was more than losing a structure. It was losing a part of our collective identity."

He paused, choosing his next words carefully. "One may call it repurposing; I call it desecration. Imagine your home, the place you love most, taken from you and painted with symbols you cannot bear to see. You'd grieve, wouldn't you? That grief doesn't go away. It festers as it is passed down through generations. Rebuilding the temple is not just about reclaiming a structure; it's about righting a historical wrong. And Hindus, Saanvi, have felt wronged for far too long."

"But does justice always come at someone else's expense?" I pressed.

His eyes hardened for a moment before softening again. "Perhaps. But justice has its cost. History has its cost. And peace? Peace is the hardest cost of all."

I said nothing and kept my gaze down. He sighed, his expression softening. "Saanvi, history is written by those who fight for it. We fought, and we won. That is the reality. But good God, you are too young to be questioning like this! Hey Ram," he whispered, his voice barely audible as he turned away, leaving me with more questions than answers.

It was in the library that I began to see the cracks in my family's narrative. The books I read opened windows into perspectives that had been carefully excluded from our household's version of history. I felt I could see through the unseen burden. Living in our Trivedi mansion meant living under constant scrutiny. Every action, every word, was weighed against the expectations of the family and the legacy they had built. My father, Ramesh, bore this burden with quiet dignity, but I could see the strain in his eyes. One evening, as we sat in the garden, he opened up to me in a way he rarely did.

"I never wanted to be a politician," he said, staring at the setting sun. "I wanted to be a writer, to tell stories that could heal rather than divide. But this family... it demands loyalty above all else."

"Then why stay?" I asked, my voice barely above a whisper.

He smiled, a sad, wistful smile. "Because leaving would mean letting go of everything we've fought for. And because some battles are worth fighting, even when they leave scars."

In that moment, I saw my father not as the confident, unyielding man I had always known, but as a person caught between duty and desire.

I don't remember the journey from my mother's embrace to our Trivedi mansion, though I have heard it retold in hushed, fragmented voices over the years. I was barely a few months old, too young to understand that I was being taken away from the one person whose love knew no boundaries. They say it was my grandfather, Shyam Trivedi, who made the decision. He couldn't bear the thought of his only son, Ramesh, being entangled in what he called a "shameful misstep."

"The child deserves to grow up with the dignity of her rightful heritage," he had proclaimed, his lawyer's voice echoing with finality. "We will give her a life worthy of the Trivedi name. But that woman... she has no place here."

My mother, Yasmin, did not fight to keep me. I learned much later that she had pleaded with my father, holding me tightly as if her grip alone could keep us together. But my father, though unwavering in his love for her, had no choice. In a battle against the towering figure of Shyam Trivedi, even love seemed powerless. The night I was taken from my mother, Yasmin Khan, she didn't cry. Not in front of Ramesh who had stood there, his eyes filled with an apology that was too heavy to carry, his hands clenching and unclenching as though they wanted to hold me but dared not. Shyam Trivedi's voice had cut through the air like a cold blade, issuing commands to the men who came to take my child.

My mother stood in the doorway of her small home, clutching the frame to steady herself. Inside, her heart must have raged, but outwardly, she didn't make a sound. A Muslim woman, she had learned, could not afford to appear weak. Especially not in a city where the air still quivered with the echoes of the demolition, where the divide between 'us and 'them' had turned from a simmering tension to an open wound. When the door shut behind her, the silence descended like a suffocating blanket. She looked at the empty cradle, the blanket still rumpled where I, Saanvi had lain. The smells of my baby skin lingered in the room, mocking her. And then, finally, she sank to the floor and wept. But mourning was a luxury she couldn't afford. The world outside was not kind to Muslim women who dared to love outside of their faith.

Ayodhya was no longer the city she had grown up in. It had become a battlefield of identities, a space where being Muslim meant walking with your shoulders hunched, your eyes lowered, and your faith tucked away like a secret. After the Babri Masjid was demolished, everything changed. The city, which had once been a shared home, felt hostile and alien. The streets she was used to walking with confidence, felt like enemy territory. Conversations in the marketplace grew quieter, whispers and pointed looks trailing in each other's wake. Even the air seemed heavier, laden with mistrust and unspoken accusations. There was a fear that had settled in her bones, a fear that didn't leave even when she locked her doors at night. Muslims were no longer just individuals; they were symbols of a faith that many believed did not belong. And in a city like Ayodhya, where history was wielded as both sword and shield, symbols were dangerous things.

And so, one night, I was carried quietly into our Trivedi mansion, swaddled in soft cotton blankets, unaware of the storm my presence had already unleashed within its walls. My first night in the mansion was, I imagine, a strange collision of chaos and silence. My grandfather, Shyam Trivedi, likely paced the length of the grand hallway, his cane tapping against the marble floor, issuing instructions to the servants to prepare a nursery. My grandmother, Sumitra Trivedi, would have sat in the prayer room, lighting incense and murmuring prayers for my "purification." But my father... I like to think he stood by the door of the nursery, his gaze fixed on me as I lay in the cradle they had hastily arranged. Perhaps he whispered an apology to me, a promise to make up for what had been taken.

From what I've been told, my arrival was announced to the world as the birth of a Trivedi heir, the inconvenient truth of my mother carefully erased from the narrative. To the outside world, I was a child of tradition, not of rebellion. If my grandfather's decision to bring me into the mansion was an act of control, my father's refusal to remarry was his quiet rebellion. It was the only act of defiance he allowed himself, a way to honor the love he had for my mother without openly challenging his family.

"Ramesh," my grandmother would plead, her voice breaking as she tried to reason with him. "The girl needs a mother. You need a wife. What will people say if you remain alone like this?"

"I don't care what people say," my father would reply, his tone calm but unyielding. "Saanvi has a mother. She doesn't need another."

My grandfather was less patient. "This is not about love or loyalty," he would thunder, his lawyer's voice rising to fill the room. "It's about respectability. Do you think you're the first man to give up his wife? You owe it to this family to uphold its honor!"

But my father never wavered. No matter how much they cajoled, pleaded, or threatened, he remained steadfast in his decision. It was a quiet act of resistance, one that earned him the grudging respect of some and the bitter resentment of others.

As I grew older, I began to sense the undercurrents of tension that ran through the mansion. My grandparents loved me, of that I have no doubt. But there was always a part of them that saw me as a symbol of their son's defiance, a reminder of the Muslim woman they could never fully erase from his life. My grandmother, for all her devotion and gentleness, often struggled to hide her discomfort. She would braid my hair in the mornings, her hands working swiftly and skillfully, but her words would sometimes betray her true feelings. "You are a Trivedi," she would say, as if reminding both herself and me. "You must never forget that."

My grandfather was more direct. He had a way of looking at me that made me feel like I was being measured against an invisible scale, weighed for my worthiness.

"You are your father's daughter," he told me once, his tone sharp. "But you must also be this family's pride. Do you understand?"

I did not, not then. But as the years passed, I began to see what he meant.

Despite their efforts to sever the connection, my father insisted that I visit my mother every weekend. It was a compromise, one of the few concessions he managed to wrest from my grandfather. Every Saturday morning, he would take me to the small, modest house where my mother lived. Sometimes, I imagined those visits were my sanctuary, a time when I could shed the weight of the Trivedi name and simply be a daughter. And yet, I was equally happy and loved in the Trivedi mansion. My mother, Yasmin, never spoke ill of my father's family, though I knew she carried the scars of their actions. She would welcome me with open arms, her smile warm and unwavering, as if trying to make up for all the time we had lost.

"Tell me about your week," she would say, her eyes sparkling with curiosity.

I would recount the events of the mansion, the seeming grand dinners, the lessons in history and philosophy, the expectations that seemed to grow heavier with each passing year. She would listen intently, nodding and asking questions, but she never commented on the things I left unsaid. It wasn't until I was older that I began to understand the full extent of my Hindu father's sacrifice. He had given up the 'respectable and married life' status so that he could stay loyal to a love that his family refused to acknowledge.

My mother's isolation was profound. I, Saanvi was gone, taken to a house she could never enter. Though

Ramesh had promised her that she could see her baby every weekend, the distance between us was more than just physical. Like her own mother, Amina, she spent her days in silence, her hands busy with the routine tasks of survival: cooking, cleaning, waiting. But her thoughts were always with her baby. Was she eating well? Was she happy? Did she cry for me at night, or was she too young to remember me at all? The weekends were her lifeline. When Ramesh brought me, her baby Saanvi to her, it felt like a sliver of sunlight breaking through a stormy sky. She would hold me close, breathing in my baby smells, memorizing every detail of my tiny face. But even those moments were tinged with sorrow, for she knew they were fleeting. '*Ammi*,' I would say in my baby way, my voice like music to her ears. She tried to pack a week's worth of love into those few hours, to give me enough warmth to carry back to the cold walls of the Trivedi mansion.

But she could see the influence of my other world creeping in. I began to speak to her of my grandparents, of the rituals and stories they would share with me. It was as though a part of me was slipping away from her, being absorbed into a narrative she could never be part of. My mother, Yasmin, was not alone in her helplessness after my birth. The Muslim community in Ayodhya was reeling, grappling with a collective sense of betrayal and fear. The Babri Masjid had been more than just a place of worship; it had been a symbol of their history, their presence in this city. Its destruction felt like an erasure, a message that they did not belong. In the months following the demolition, there was a palpable shift in the air. Many families had left, seeking safety in cities where their faith would not make them targets. Those who stayed learned to keep their heads down, to avoid confrontation, to exist in the margins. There were whispers in the mosque, the hurried conversations about what to do, where to go. "We have to protect our children," women said to each other, their voices trembling. "They will grow up in a world where they are always made to feel less than others." My mother would often think of her Saanvi, growing up in the Trivedi mansion, surrounded by a world that would never fully accept me as my mother's daughter. The thought filled her with a mix of hope and despair. In the quiet moments, when the weight of everything felt too heavy to bear, she would turn to her faith. It was the one thing that could not be taken from her, the one anchor in a world that seemed intent on drifting away. She prayed for me, Saanvi, for my happiness and my safety. She prayed for Ramesh, for the strength to navigate the impossible path he had chosen. And she prayed for herself, for the courage to keep going, to hold onto hope even when it felt like a fragile thread. Her faith was not of the loud, demonstrative kind. It was a quiet, steady presence.

My father, Ramesh visited her on weekends, though never for long. He was always torn between two worlds: the demands of his own family and the promises he had made to my mother. He would sit at the small wooden table in her kitchen, his hands wrapped around a cup of tea, and listen as he told her about me, Saanvi.

"She's growing so quickly," my mother, Yasmin Khan would say, her voice filled with equal parts pride and sadness.

"She talks about you all the time," he would reply, his eyes softening. "She loves you, Yasmin."

"But does she know me?" she would ask, cuddling me. "Or am I just a part of her weekends, a visitor in her life?"

My father, Ramesh, had no answer. He was a man

caught in the crossfire of love and loyalty, and my mother didn't blame him for his silence.

One evening, as we sat in the library, I asked my father why he had never remarried.

"Because love is not something you can replace," he said simply. "Your mother and I may not be together, but that doesn't mean I can ever stop loving her."

"But doesn't it hurt?" I asked.

He smiled, a sad, wistful smile that I had come to recognize. "Of course it hurts. But some things are worth the pain."

My father's love for my mother was a quiet, steadfast force in a house filled with contradictions. It was a legacy that he passed on to me, a deeply humbling and early lesson to me that loyalty and love are not weaknesses, but strengths.

As I stand in the courtyard of our Trivedi mansion, watching the shadows lengthen and the evening light cast its golden glow, I realize that my story was not just about the choices others had made for me. It may be that I am also my Muslim mother's daughter. I can see through both sides somehow. Sometimes, our Trivedi mansion seemed to me a house full of contradictions, a place where faith and power, devotion and doubt, coexisted uneasily. It was a house that shaped me, even as I resisted its influence. Don't get me wrong. I loved my grandparents and I love my father deeply. The Hindu part of me has its own conscience and its own consciousness. And yet, as I often stand in the courtyard and watch the sky turn shades of orange and pink, I know that my story is not just my own. It is tied to this house, to the people who had come before me, and to the city that has defined their lives. But it was also a story of choice—a choice to accept or to reject the legacy I had inherited. And as I look at the mansion's towering facade, its windows glowing with the light of countless evenings, I know that my journey is just beginning.

Of course, I was the silent arrival on December 6, 1992. I was my father and my mother's legacy of love and defiance. Of course, I carried the unspoken truth within me. Of course, I had to grow up in the shadow of tension as a progeny of my Hindu father and my Muslim mother's silent and inexplicable rebellion. For me, Ayodhya is not just any city. It is a city where time itself seems to bend, where the past is always present. In the narrow streets and ancient walls, you can feel the weight of centuries—of empires that rose and fell, of temples and mosques that once stood side by side, and of the blood that was spilled over these sacred lands. In school, our history lessons taught us about Ayodhya's prominence in the Hindu *Ramayana*, about Lord Rama's birth and his place in the heart of the Hindu faith. But outside the classroom, there were other stories: of Babur, the Mughal emperor who built the Babri Masjid. Of the violence that erupted when that mosque was torn down on the day of my birth. Of the years of court battles that followed, as Hindus and Muslims fought for ownership of the land. It was as though this city, which should have been a symbol of faith, had instead become a battlefield.

But for me, Ayodhya is neither just the birthplace of Rama nor just a city of mosques and temples. It is the place where my parents had met, where their love had defied the borders drawn by religion. It is the place where I had learned that faith, while powerful, can also be divisive. And it is the place where I now stand, asking myself whether I can carry both legacies, or whether one would always have to eclipse the other. The Sarayu still flows, silent and steady, indifferent to our wars and our worship, bearing witness to centuries of faith and fracture. Its waters have carried both ash and prayer, both loss and longing. Somewhere between its sacred banks and the crumbling walls of memory, I search not just for answers, but for the courage to live with contradictions. Perhaps, Ayodhya will never offer a resolution. It can only offer a mirror. And in that reflection, I must learn to see not only what was broken, but what might still be mended.

10

My grandfather, Shyam Trivedi, had become the lion of Ayodhya. "*Shyam Babu ne faisla likh diya hai. Bas court ka mohar zaroori hai.*" ('Shyam Babu has already written the judgment; now only the court's seal is necessary.) This was the refrain spoken in hushed tones across Ayodhya, in tea stalls where debates raged endlessly, in temples where priests whispered their thanks to Lord Rama, and even in the homes of families who had lived through the town's darkest days. My grandfather, Shyam Trivedi, wasn't just a lawyer. He was a myth made flesh, a man whose determination had tipped the scales of history.

As a child, I had heard these stories countless times, each retelling more embellished than the last. My grandfather had become a hero not only to our family but also to the wider Hindu community in Ayodhya. He was among those credited with securing the Supreme Court verdict that ultimately paved the way for the construction of the Ram temple on the disputed site where the Babri Masjid once stood. To the Trivedis, this was the culmination of generations of devotion, scholarship, and sacrifice. And yet, beneath the layers of reverence, I have always sensed a shadow. It is a shadow that fell over the city itself on the day of my birth, dividing it into 'us' and 'them,' turning neighbors into strangers, and leaving scars that even the most pious prayers could not heal.

The early twenty first century was a time of transformation for Ayodhya. The city seemed to exist in two parallel realities: one of triumph and resurgence for Hindus, and another of loss and alienation for Muslims. The foresighted temple's construction would be heralded as a victory for one side and a symbol of defeat for the other. Ayodhya's streets bore witness to this duality. The Sarayu river which had once flowed through a city of shared festivals and interwoven lives, now seemed to divide more than unite. On its one bank, there were celebrations, processions, and a renewed sense of identity among the Hindu majority. On the other, silence reigned, broken only by the call to prayer or the quiet rustle of veils as Muslim women walked quickly through streets that no longer felt like theirs. The political history of this time was as fraught as the city itself. The Hindu nationalist party, riding on the wave of the Ram Janmabhoomi movement, had cemented its hold on the national imagination. Ayodhya was the crown jewel in its narrative—a symbol of India's cultural resurgence and the reclaiming of its 'Hindu pride.' But the scars of the 1992 demolition and the violence that followed were still fresh. Families had been torn apart, lives lost, and trust shattered. For many, the legal victory would feel hollow, a triumph that would be achieved at an unbearable cost.

In the Trivedi household, however, there was no room for doubt or dissent. My grandfather's role in the legal battle was a source of immense pride, a defining chapter in the family's history. Shyam Trivedi, with his booming voice, sharp intellect, and unshakeable conviction, was seen as among those who had restored Ayodhya's 'rightful legacy.' He would always be Shyam Trivedi, the lawyer, the myth and the legend.

"Your Dadaji didn't just argue a case," my father, Ramesh, often said. "He argued for *dharma* itself."

As I grow older, I have begun to understand the magnitude of what my grandfather had achieved. He had spent years poring over legal documents, studying historical records, and crafting arguments that would resonate not just in the courtroom but in the hearts of millions. He was relentless, a force of nature who believed he was fulfilling a divine mandate. Yet, his victory was not without its costs. I remember sitting with him in the living room of our ancestral mansion, a room filled with heavy teak furniture and the smell of sandalwood. He leaned on his cane, his once-powerful frame slightly stooped but his eyes still sharp.

"We will not just win a case, Saanvi," he said to me one evening, his voice tinged with both pride and weariness. "We will restore history. History is never simple. It always comes with a price."

The price was visible in the strained relationships between communities, in the exodus of Muslim families from Ayodhya, and in the lingering tension that hung over the city like a storm cloud. For every Hindu family that celebrated my grandfather's legacy, there was a Muslim family that mourned what had been lost. I have often wondered how my grandfather reconciled these realities. Did he ever think about the lives disrupted by his pursuit of justice? Did he see the faces of the displaced, the frightened, the grieving? Or was he so consumed by his mission that he could not—or would not—acknowledge its consequences?

In our household, these questions were never asked aloud. To challenge my grandfather's legacy was unthinkable, almost sacrilegious. The Trivedis were united in their belief that they had done what was right, what was necessary. And yet, I can never shake the feeling that there was more to the story, a complexity that was being smoothed over in the retelling. The legal battle over Ayodhya was as much about symbolism as it was about the law. My grandfather understood this better than anyone. He knew that the courtroom was not just a place to argue facts but a stage on which to perform, to present a narrative that would capture the imagination of the judges and the nation. He spoke of Lord Rama not as a figure of mythology but as a historical reality, a presence so deeply ingrained in the collective consciousness of Hindus that his birthplace was sacred beyond dispute. He argued that the temple was not just a structure but a symbol of India's cultural and spiritual identity.

"Faith needs no evidence," my grandfather, Shyam Trivedi, would often say. "But evidence, when it exists, vindicates faith." This mantra had shaped much of my family's legacy in Ayodhya, particularly during the long and contentious legal battle over the Ram Janmabhoomi site. For generations, Hindus had believed with unwavering conviction that a temple dedicated to Lord Rama once stood at his birthplace in Ayodhya, long before the Mughal emperor Babur allegedly demolished it to build the Babri Masjid. To the devout, this belief was not a matter of debate but a cornerstone of their spiritual identity. But in the cold, empirical world of the law courts, belief was not enough. Facts, evidence, and expert testimony were required to settle what had become one of the most divisive disputes in modern India. And so began the archaeological excavations that would attempt to unearth the past, literally, to endorse the Hindu belief that a temple had been lost and a heritage stolen from them.

For centuries, oral traditions and scriptures had

passed down the story of Ayodhya as the birthplace of Lord Rama. The Ramayana, revered as both literature and scripture, described the city as the capital of the Kosala kingdom, where Lord Rama was born and later ruled. According to popular Hindu belief, a grand temple once stood at the exact spot of his birth, its sanctity unmatched by any other place of worship. This belief persisted through generations, surviving the tumult of invasions, colonial rule, and the changing tides of history. Even as the Babri Masjid stood for nearly five centuries, the Hindu community maintained that the mosque was built on the ruins of their temple. The notion was not merely symbolic but deeply personal, a reflection of their spiritual loss and the injustice they believed had been inflicted upon their heritage. In the nineteenth and the early twentieth centuries, tensions had begun to simmer. Local Hindu and Muslim communities clashed over access to the site, each claiming it as their own. By the time the legal battle escalated in the late twentieth century, the question was no longer just about faith. It had become a quest to uncover the historical truth.

In 2003, when I was barely eleven years old, the Allahabad High Court ordered an archaeological survey of the disputed site to determine whether a Hindu temple had existed beneath the Babri Masjid. The purpose of this excavation was to determine whether there was evidence of a Hindu temple or structure beneath the mosque. This was a turning point in the legal battle, and my grandfather, Shyam Trivedi, was at the forefront of the effort to ensure the survey would validate what Hindus had long believed. The Archaeological Survey of India took on the monumental task, deploying a team of experts, engineers, and laborers to carefully excavate the site. The work was painstaking and meticulous, conducted under the watchful eyes of representatives from both the Hindu and Muslim sides, as well as court-appointed observers. As the layers of soil were removed, the past began to reveal itself—slowly, tantalizingly, and controversially. Beneath the foundations of the Babri Masjid, the ASI uncovered a series of structural remains that pointed to the existence of a large, non-Islamic building. Pillar bases, carved stones, and artifacts adorned with motifs associated with Hindu temple architecture emerged from the earth, sparking a wave of excitement among the Hindu community.

Our Trivedi household repeatedly emphasized to everyone that even the renowned Muslim scholar endorsed their belief and conviction. A Muslim archaeologist, Dr. Mohammed Akbar, was a renowned expert in ancient Indian architecture and had earned a reputation for his rigorous scholarship and impartiality. His inclusion in the ASI team was a deliberate effort to ensure the credibility of the excavation's findings and to address accusations of bias from the Muslim community. Mohammed Akbar's presence at the site became a symbol of the uneasy but necessary collaboration between faith and science. He approached his work with a quiet determination, his focus unwavering despite the intense scrutiny and political pressure that surrounded the excavation. "It is not about proving or disproving anyone's faith," he had said in an interview that was widely circulated at the time. "It is about uncovering the truth, whatever it may be." As the excavation progressed, he examined the artifacts and structural remains with a critical eye. His findings were clear: the layout of the structures, the style of the carvings, and the materials used were consistent with Hindu temple architecture from the tenth to the twelfth centuries CE. He had also noted the presence of inscriptions that referred to Lord

Vishnu, lending further credence to the claim that the site had once been a place of Hindu worship.

When he presented his conclusions, they were met with a mix of admiration and hostility. To the Hindu side, his findings were a validation of their long-held beliefs. To the Muslim side, they were a bitter pill to swallow, raising questions about the fairness of the legal and social narratives that had emerged from the dispute.

The ASI's final report, submitted to the court, stated that there was evidence of a "massive structure" beneath the Babri Masjid that had features consistent with Hindu temple architecture. There were pillar bases arranged in a manner characteristic of temple construction. The carvings on the recovered stones bore traditional Hindu motifs, including lotus flowers and other sacred symbols. Fragments of inscriptions referencing Hindu deities, including Lord Vishnu and Lord Rama, were also found. These inscriptions were dated to a period long before the construction of the Babri Masjid. Terracotta figurines, pottery shards, and other items found among relics were consistent with the material culture of a Hindu temple. There was even structural evidence. The alignment and dimensions of the recovered structures suggested that they were part of a large, rectangular building, most likely a temple. However, the findings still remain controversial, with differing interpretations among historians, archaeologists, and legal experts.

For the Hindu community, these findings were a moment of vindication. My grandfather, who had closely followed the excavation process, was elated. He saw the report as a triumph not just for his legal case but for the cultural and spiritual identity of Hindus across India. "This is not about politics," he said during a family gathering, his voice rising with conviction. "It is about reclaiming what is ours, about restoring the dignity of our heritage."

But the findings also deepened the rift between communities. To many Muslims, the report felt like a justification for the demolition of the Babri Masjid, a loss that had already left them feeling vulnerable and alienated. The tension in Ayodhya had grown thicker as a result, the divide between 'us' and 'them' more pronounced. Faith, history, and the weight of evidence have all been on the side of Hindus.

As I sat in our Trivedi mansion, listening to my grandfather recount the findings, I couldn't help but feel conflicted even as a young girl. The evidence was compelling, even undeniable, but it didn't erase the pain and division that the dispute had caused. For every Hindu who felt a sense of victory, there was a Muslim who felt a sense of loss.

"History is written in stone, Saanvi," my grandfather said, gesturing toward a carved pillar fragment that he had brought home from the site—a token of the excavation, he said. "This is proof of who we are, of where we come from."

But even now, as I stare at the stone, its intricate carvings catching the light, I wonder: Was it really that simple? Could history be reduced to stones and structures, to evidence and verdicts? Or was it something more fluid, more human—a human world of memories and stories, triumphs and tragedies, welded together by the lives of those who had lived it?

The excavation and its findings marked a turning point in the Ayodhya dispute, but they also underscored the complexities of reconciling faith with history, belief with evidence, and identity with coexistence. Ayodhya, once a symbol of unity and devotion, had become a microcosm of the challenges facing India itself—a nation grappling with its past, its present, and its future.

For my grandfather, the excavation was a vindication

of his life's work, a testament to the righteousness of his cause. For me, it was a reminder of the weight of legacy, the burden of history, and the responsibility of understanding both. Perhaps, the fissures and the divisions within a divided India were deepened as a result.

As I walk through the streets of Ayodhya, the air filled with the sounds of temple bells and the *muezzin*'s call to prayer, I feel the city's heartbeat—the rhythm my grandfather had spoken of. It is a current that carries both hope and heartache, a reminder that history, like faith, is never as simple as it seems.

My grandfather's opponents, of course, presented their own narratives, their own truths. They spoke of the Babri Masjid as a place of worship, a space that had stood for centuries as a testament to India's pluralistic heritage. They questioned the evidence, the assumptions, the intentions behind the movement to build the temple. But in the end, my grandfather's arguments prevailed. The Supreme Court's verdict, delivered after years of hearings and deliberations, was hailed as a historic moment for Hindus. For my grandfather, it would mark the culmination of a lifetime of work, a vindication of his beliefs and efforts.

In the Trivedi household, the ASI findings and as a result, my grandfather's victory, were celebrated with fervor. Our mansion was filled with visitors, well-wishers who came to pay their respects and offer their congratulations. The air was thick with the smell of incense and the sound of conch shells, a cacophony of celebration that seemed to drown out any dissenting voices. But beneath the surface, there were cracks. My father, Ramesh, who had inherited my grandfather's sense of duty, often seemed conflicted. He spoke of legacy and responsibility, but there was a weariness in his eyes, a hesitation that suggested he was not entirely at peace with the family's role in Ayodhya's history.

As for me, I had always felt like an outsider in my own home even though I was doted upon and cared and loved for like no one else. Somehow, the pride that my family took in my grandfather's achievements often felt suffocating, a weight that I couldn't carry. I wanted to believe in the righteousness of his cause, but I couldn't ignore the voices of those who had been silenced, the lives that had been uprooted. Is it because my mother is Muslim that I feel that way? Was I insincere by temperament? Growing up as the daughter of Yasmin Khan in the Trivedi household was like straddling two worlds that refused to meet. I had inherited my father's Hindu name, Saanvi, and with it, the expectations of belonging to a family revered in Ayodhya for their role in securing the Ram Janmabhoomi site. But my mother's presence in my life, quiet though it often was, tethered me to another story—one filled with vulnerability, alienation, and the undeniable shadow of injustice.

For as long as I can remember, I have felt the unease of knowing my mother was Muslim. It wasn't because I was ashamed of her. I love her with a ferocity I cannot always articulate. But I knew, even as a child, that her identity placed her on the 'wrong' side of the lines drawn in Ayodhya, lines that my grandfather and father had spent their lives defending. It wasn't her faith that made her 'wrong' in the eyes of the world around me. It was simply the fact that she existed as a reminder of a community that Ayodhya, and perhaps India at large, had chosen to marginalize. The irony was not lost on me: the very same faith that my family revered for its tolerance and inclusivity seemed to leave no room for her.

My mother's silences are the loudest part of her presence in my life. She rarely spoke about the Babri Masjid demolition, even though I knew it haunted her. She rarely shared her own stories of growing up as a Muslim girl in Ayodhya, even though I could sense they carried a weight I wasn't yet old enough to understand. Instead, she expressed herself in quieter ways—through the food she cooked for me when I visited her on weekends, the soft *ghazals* she hummed while cleaning, the way she pressed her hand against her heart whenever she heard the *azaan* in the distance. Her silence, however, could not shield me from the world's noise. At my boarding school in the hills, I heard the whispers—how Muslims were traitors, how they refused to integrate, how they were the reason for India's problems. At home, the whispers were subtler but no less insidious. My grandfather's remarks about "restoring Ayodhya to its rightful glory" often carried an unspoken subtext that excluded people like my mother. Even my father, who loved Yasmin deeply and remained loyal to her despite his parents' pleas to remarry, seemed to sidestep any conversation that might acknowledge her struggles.

I often wonder what it would be like if she ever dared to visit me at our Trivedi mansion. Would she feel the weight of the portraits lining the walls—generations of Trivedis, all Hindu, all resolute in their commitment to preserving Ayodhya's "Hindu-ness"? Would she notice the way the servants would avoid her gaze, as if her very presence was an act of defiance? Would she hear the whispers in the marketplace, the ones that would follow her like shadows if she dared to walk alone? Or had she learned, over the years, to tune it all out, in order to ease the burden of history?

Living in Ayodhya meant living with the constant reminder of history's wounds. The city was a melting pot of human stories, most of them told from the perspective of its Hindu majority. The Ramayana was not just a sacred text here; it was a living, breathing narrative that shaped every corner of the city. Temples stood at every turn, their bells ringing out a rhythm that seemed to echo the heartbeat of Ayodhya itself. But for Muslims, the city's history was a different kind of burden. The demolition of the Babri Masjid in the year of my birth had not only destroyed a structure but also fractured the fragile coexistence that had once defined Ayodhya. I had read about the riots that followed in textbooks, and seen the grainy black-and-white images of unrest and smoke rising from neighborhoods in Faizabad and even as far as Lucknow and Kanpur. But it wasn't until I began to understand my mother's silences that I grasped the true cost of those events. For people like my mother, the mosque's demolition wasn't just the loss of a place of worship; it was a reminder of how easily they could be erased from the narrative altogether. It was a statement, loud and clear, that their history, their faith, and their presence in Ayodhya were seen as expendable.

I often wondered if my grandfather, for all his legal victories, potential and real, ever thought about this. Did he ever consider that his fight for the Ram temple came at the expense of another community's sense of belonging? Or was he so convinced of the righteousness of his cause that he never saw it as a loss at all?

By the early twenty first century, Ayodhya was a city transformed. The plans for the construction of the Ram temple were well underway. It would be a towering structure that would dominate the skyline and the narrative of the city. Pilgrims would flock to Ayodhya in droves, their devotion fueling an economy that had long relied on religion. But for all its progress, the city remained divided. The scars of the past were still visible, not just in the physical landscape but in the relationships between its people. The promise of reconciliation seemed as distant as ever, a dream that had been overshadowed by the realities of identity and politics.

As I grew older, the fault lines within me grew louder, like tectonic shifts beneath an otherwise calm exterior. To the outside world, I was a Trivedi, a Hindu, a symbol of my family's legacy. But to myself, I was also Yasmin Khan's daughter, someone who could never fully reconcile the two halves of her heritage and the weight of her fractured identity. I remember one evening, shortly after I turned thirteen, when a Muslim classmate came to visit me at our Trivedi mansion. It was during Ramadan, and she had brought a box of dates for me, her quiet way of including me in her world. We sat together in our garden, away from the eyes of my grandparents and the servants.

"Do you ever feel out of place here in Ayodhya?" I asked her, the question tumbling out before I could stop it.

She looked at me with those deep, searching eyes of a true friend's, the ones that always seem to hold more questions than answers. "Do you?" she asked in return.

I didn't know how to respond. How could I tell anyone that I felt torn between two worlds, that I loved my mother, but resented the way her presence complicated my life? How could I tell my friend that I felt guilty for the privilege of living in a household that dismissed my Muslim friends or my mother as outsiders?

Instead, I foolishly asked my Muslim friend a question that had been burning in my mind for years. "Do you think they're wrong? The Hindus, I mean, for believing there was a temple here before the mosque."

She paused, her hands resting on her lap. "Belief isn't wrong, Saanvi," my wise friend said softly. "But belief that denies someone else's existence, belief that erases someone else—that's where the danger lies. That's where it turns dangerous."

Her words stayed with me. My conflict wasn't just about who I was, but about learning how stories collide—how faith, history, and humanity often pull in different directions. I realized then that my struggle wasn't just about my identity; it was about understanding the lines between faith, history, and humanity. It was about recognizing that the truth wasn't always black and white, that it was often buried in the gray spaces where stories overlapped and contradicted each other. The truth lay tangled in a braid of memory, myth, and omission, hard to untie without snapping a few strands.

As I entered my twenties, I began to see Ayodhya through my mother's eyes and through the eyes of my Muslim classmates. I noticed the subtle ways in which the city excluded its Muslim residents: the neighborhoods that were unofficially segregated, the schools that subtly discouraged Muslim enrollment, the casual jokes that dismissed their concerns as paranoia. I noticed how the few Muslim families who remained in Ayodhya lived in a constant state of unease, their lives shaped by the fear of being targeted.

I also began to see how this exclusion wasn't just the result of the demolition or the riots; it was woven into the fabric of the city itself. Ayodhya's narrative had always been dominated by the Ramayana, its temples, and its Hindu majority. For Muslims, there was no space in that narrative—no acknowledgment of their contributions to the city's culture, no recognition of their shared history.

Even my father, who loved my mother in his own quiet, steadfast way, seemed unable to bridge the gap. He spoke of harmony and coexistence in his political speeches, but at home, he rarely addressed the discomfort that simmered beneath the surface. It was as if he believed that loving Yasmin was enough, that his personal loyalty to her absolved him of the need to confront the larger issues at play.

But for me, loving my mother was not enough. I needed to understand her, to see the world as she did, to make sense of the injustices that she endured with such quiet dignity. I needed to find a way to reconcile my love for her with the legacy of my family—a legacy that had, in many ways, contributed to her alienation.

Over time, my feelings of unease and the weight of injustice turned into anger. I couldn't ignore the way Ayodhya's Muslims were treated as perpetual outsiders, their loyalty questioned, their faith dismissed. I couldn't ignore the hypocrisy of a city that prided itself on its spiritual heritage while turning a blind eye to the suffering of its own residents.

But my anger wasn't just directed at the city or its people; it was also directed at myself. I felt complicit in the injustice, simply by virtue of being a Trivedi. I felt guilty for the privileges I enjoyed, for the sense of belonging that my last name afforded me, for the way I could walk through Ayodhya without fear while my mother had to tread carefully, always aware of the eyes watching her. And yet, I couldn't fully abandon my family's legacy either. My paternal grandfather's and my own father's beliefs—they were a part of me, just as much as my mother's withdrawal into silence was. I was caught between two worlds, two histories, two truths, and I didn't know how to reconcile them.

In the end, my own inner turmoil and mental struggle is not just about Ayodhya or the Ram temple or the Babri Masjid. It is about the question of belonging—who gets to belong, and who decides? It is about the lines we draw between 'us' and 'them,' the stories we tell ourselves to justify those lines, and the lives that are caught in between.

For my mother, belonging was something she had long stopped expecting from Ayodhya. But for me, it was something I couldn't stop yearning for—not just for myself, but for her as well. I wanted a city where she could walk freely, where her faith didn't make her an outsider, where her silence didn't have to carry the weight of centuries of injustice. And yet, why do I feel so self-righteous? Would I not have experienced any inner turmoil had my mother not been Muslim?

And so, as I stood on the steps of the Sarayu one evening, watching the sun set over the city, I made a silent vow to myself. I would find a way to tell her story—not as a counter to my family's legacy, but as a part of it. Because Ayodhya wasn't just a city of temples and mosques; it was a city of people, of stories, of lives that refused to be erased. And her story, I realized, was just as much a part of Ayodhya as mine. I also thought about my paternal grandfather's legacy. To the world, he was a hero, a man who had fought for his faith and won. But to me, he was something more complicated: a man who had believed so deeply in his cause that he had been willing to overlook the consequences of his actions.

"History is never simple," he had said. And in Ayodhya, where every stone seemed to carry the weight of the past, that truth was impossible to escape. And yet, I ask myself again, why do I feel so self-righteous? Would I not have experienced any inner turmoil had my mother not been Muslim?

11

My maternal grandfather, Adil Khan, on the other hand, was a man shaped as much by loss as by conviction. For years, he had lived a quiet life as a schoolteacher in Ayodhya. He was the kind of teacher who took immense pride in his craft—an educator not just of young minds but of souls, believing that knowledge was a light powerful enough to dispel the darkness of ignorance and prejudice. His classroom, tucked away in a modest government school in Faizabad, on the outskirts of and just beyond the bustle of Ayodhya, was his sanctuary, a space where the religious divisions that marked the town seemed to blur, if only temporarily. Adil's teaching style had been distinctive, deeply rooted in stories and examples that transcended religious and cultural divides. Whether he had recited verses from Kabir, narrated tales of Emperor Akbar's court, or had spoken of scientific discoveries, he had always framed them as part of a shared human heritage. He had taught his students, both Hindu and Muslim, that their fates were interwoven. To him, every lesson had been an opportunity to sow seeds of understanding in the hope they would grow into a more harmonious future. As a schoolteacher, Adil had earned the respect of the community. His Hindu colleagues had admired his dedication, while his Muslim neighbors had always seen him as a voice of reason and stability.

But all that had changed in a single, brutal instant during the communal mob violence that took his teenaged son's life. The sight of Aarif's battered face haunted him for years. He had drifted away from his wife, Amina, who had herself never recovered from Aarif's death. Her grief had turned inward, festering until it became an unbearable silence that filled every corner of their home. Adil, too, was shattered, but his pain had manifested itself differently. He had been consumed by questions—questions that had no easy answers. Why had his son died? Was it because he was in the wrong place at the wrong time, or was it because he was a Muslim in a city where being Muslim had become a liability?

For months after Aarif's death, my maternal grandfather, Adil Khan, had tried to find solace in routine. He had found it difficult to return to his teaching job or pretend that life could go on. But every time he passed the narrow street where his son had been killed, he had felt the weight of his failure as a father. He had not been able to protect his child, and worse, he had no way to seek justice for him. The police had dismissed the case as a 'riot casualty,' and no arrests were ever made. His wife, Amina, unable to bear the weight of their shared grief, had retreated into a silence he could neither breach nor understand. Their once-companionable relationship had dissolved into a series of quiet, disjointed moments, their shared pain making every interaction feel like an unspoken accusation. Amina's breakdown and silence had subsequently, pushed Adil away from her and into the political fray of action. For years, Aarif's face cut through his mind like a blade. Adil tried to pour out his grief and frustration to the imam of his local mosque as well as several community elders. For some time, he allowed himself to express the anger that had been simmering beneath the surface.

"We cannot keep living like this," he said, his voice trembling with emotion. "We cannot keep letting them treat us like we don't belong here."

The elders nodded solemnly, but their responses were cautious. "We must be careful, Adil bhai," one of them said. "The situation is delicate. If we push too hard, it could make things worse."

But Adil was past the point of caution. The day of Aarif's death had marked the beginning of his transformation from a grieving father to a man determined to fight for his community.

My maternal grandfather, Adil Khan, started small as an activist. He joined a local advocacy group that provided legal assistance to families affected by the riots. He spent hours in cramped offices, sifting through police reports and filing petitions on behalf of victims who had no means to fight for justice on their own. It was painstaking work, but it gave him a sense of purpose.

Over time, Adil's voice grew louder. He began attending rallies and speaking at community gatherings, urging Muslims to stand up for their rights. His speeches were fiery and impassioned, but they were also deeply personal. He spoke not just as an activist, but as a father who had lost his son to the very hatred he was trying to combat.

"We are not asking for favors," he would say. "We are asking for dignity, for justice, for the right to live in this country without fear."

His words resonated with people, and soon, Adil

Khan became a prominent figure in the region. He was invited to speak at events in Lucknow, Delhi, and even in Hyderabad, where his message of Muslim solidarity struck a chord with audiences beyond Uttar Pradesh. Adil's rise as an activist coincided with a broader shift in India's political landscape. The end of the twentieth century and the beginning of a new century were marked by increasing polarization, as right-wing forces consolidated their power and the rhetoric of Hindutva became more mainstream. For Muslims, this meant navigating a world where their identity was increasingly seen as a threat.

Adil's activism took on a sharper edge during this period. He began to challenge not just local authorities but also national leaders, accusing them of turning a blind eye to the systemic discrimination faced by Muslims. His outspokenness earned him both admiration and enemies.

One of his most significant battles came when he organized a mass protest against the demolition of a historic Muslim neighborhood in Faizabad to make way for a new highway. The government claimed the project was necessary for development, but Adil saw it as yet another attempt to erase Muslim heritage from the region. The protest was a turning point for Adil. Thousands of people gathered under his leadership, and their peaceful demonstration forced the government to reconsider its plans. The victory was a rare moment of triumph for the Muslim community, and it solidified Adil's reputation as a fearless advocate for their rights. Adil's personal life, by now, scarred by tragedy and loss, was completely inconsequential to him. The death of his son, Aarif had not only shattered his family but also stripped his marriage of its fragile foundation. Adil found himself incapable of seeking solace or reconciliation. Instead, politics consumed him entirely. He threw himself into activism, working tirelessly to redress the injustices faced by Ayodhya's Muslim community. The debates over the Babri Masjid and the growing dominance of Hindutva politics in the city became both his battlefield and his obsession. Politics demanded every ounce of his energy, leaving little room for the personal grief that had lingered in the recesses of his heart.

Adil had become a solitary figure, consumed by a purpose larger than himself. He spent long nights poring over legal documents, attending meetings, and writing speeches that called for justice and unity. The quiet schoolteacher who once saw the classroom as his sanctuary had now become a public figure, his voice rising against the din of divisive politics. Yet, beneath the surface of his fiery activism lay a man deeply scarred, carrying the burden of a broken family and a city at odds with itself.

It was during the aftermath of the highway protest that Adil was approached by a group of young Muslim leaders who urged him to enter politics. At first, he was reluctant. He had always seen himself as an activist, someone who worked outside the political system to bring about social change. But the leaders made a compelling argument: if he truly wanted to make a difference, he needed to have a seat at the table where decisions were made.

In 2004, as I stood on the cusp of adolescence, my maternal grandfather, Adil Khan, announced his decision to run for office as an independent candidate from the Faizabad constituency. It was a bold move in a town shaped by political loyalties and steeped in religious divides. His campaign was unconventional, relying more on grassroots support than on traditional party machinery. He traveled from village to village, meeting with farmers, laborers, and small business owners, and listening to their grievances. His message was simple: he was there to fight for justice, not just for Muslims but for anyone who felt marginalized by the system. Adil's authenticity struck a chord with voters, and he won the election by a narrow margin. His victory was celebrated not just in Faizabad but across Uttar Pradesh, where it was seen as a rare and uncommon win for a Muslim leader in a state dominated by communal politics.

As a politician, Adil Khan remained true to his roots as an activist. He used his platform to advocate for policies that addressed the systemic inequalities faced by Muslims, from access to education and employment to protection against communal violence. He also worked to build bridges with other marginalized communities, including Dalits and tribal groups, recognizing that their struggles were interconnected. His tenure as 'a voice for the voiceless' was of course, not without its challenges. He faced constant pushback from right-wing politicians and even members of his own party, who accused him of being "too radical." He even received death threats, and he was accused, truthfully of course, of abandoning his own wife and daughter. Through it all, Adil remained steadfast, drawing strength from the memory of Aarif and the belief that his fight was not just for his son but for generations to come. Adil Khan's entry into politics was marked by a singular determination: to amplify the voice of the marginalized. But as he rose through the ranks, he found himself constantly at odds with powerful political adversaries whose interests were deeply entrenched in the communal divisions of Ayodhya and beyond. His political rivals were not just opponents in the legislative assembly or at election rallies; they represented an ideological worldview that sought to maintain the status quo of inequality and polarization.

Adil's first major rival was Mahesh Rathore, a seasoned politician and a staunch proponent of Hindutva. Rathore had been a key figure in mobilizing support for the Ram temple movement and was deeply entrenched in Ayodhya's political landscape. Where Adil spoke of justice and equality, Rathore framed his rhetoric around 'cultural restoration' and 'national pride.' Their debates often turned fiery, with Rathore accusing Adil Khan of 'appeasing Muslims' and Adil Khan countering with pointed critiques of Rathore's divisive politics.

At one rally, Rathore declared, "This land belongs to those who revere it, not to those who question its sanctity." Adil's response was swift and cutting. "Ayodhya belongs to all Indians," he retaliated, his voice echoing across the crowd. "If we start dividing the land based on faith, we will destroy the very fabric of this nation."

The exchange made headlines, further cementing their rivalry. While Rathore's words resonated with his own political base, Adil's courage in standing up to such rhetoric won him immense admiration, even among those who didn't share his faith. As Adil's popularity grew, so did the intensity of the attacks against him. Rathore and his allies in the right-wing ecosystem launched a smear campaign, accusing Adil of being a 'foreign sympathizer' and questioning his loyalty to India. They dredged up his involvement in protests, framing them as evidence of anti-national behavior. One of the most insidious tactics they employed was to spread rumors about his personal life. Adil's decision to separate from Amina after Aarif's death became fodder for malicious gossip, with rivals suggesting that he had abandoned his family for political gain. Though these allegations were baseless, they stung deeply, particularly because they hit at Adil's sense of honor and the values he held dear. Adil, however, refused to be silenced. At a press conference addressing the allegations, he stated, "My personal life is not up for debate. What is up for debate is whether we, as a nation, will allow hatred to dictate our future."

One of the most significant confrontations between Adil and his political rivals occurred during a heated assembly session on education reform. Adil had proposed a bill aimed at increasing access to education for marginalized communities, including Muslims and Dalits. The bill also sought to allocate funds for the preservation of minority cultural institutions, a move that Rathore and his allies fiercely opposed.

"This is nothing but an attempt to divide the nation further," Rathore thundered during the session. "Why should one community receive special privileges at the expense of others?"

Adil stood to respond, his calm demeanor contrasting with Rathore's bluster. "This is not about privilege," he said. "It's about correcting historical injustices. For decades, these communities have been denied access to opportunities that others take for granted. This bill is not about division. It is about inclusion."

The debate raged for hours, with both sides presenting their arguments with equal fervor. In the end, the bill narrowly passed, thanks to support from progressive members of the assembly. The victory was a significant milestone for Adil, but it also deepened the animosity between him and Rathore.

Another flashpoint in Adil's career was the Ayodhya Housing Project, a government initiative ostensibly aimed at urban development. The project involved the demolition of several predominantly Muslim neighborhoods to make way for commercial complexes and luxury apartments. Mahesh Rathore championed the project, framing it as a necessary step toward modernization. Adil, however, saw it as a thinly veiled attempt at erasing Muslim presence from Ayodhya's landscape. Adil organized a series of protests against the project, drawing attention to the plight of the displaced families. His efforts culminated in a public debate with Rathore, who accused him of 'blocking progress for the sake of politics.'

Adil's response was scathing. "Progress is not measured by the number of buildings we construct, but by the lives we improve. If this project goes forward, it will displace thousands of families who have lived here for generations. That is not progress. That is oppression."

The debate galvanized public opinion, forcing the government to halt the project temporarily. Though the fight was far from over, the episode highlighted Adil's ability to challenge powerful adversaries and mobilize support for his cause. Adil's confrontations with his political rivals were not without consequences. His staunch opposition to the Hindutva agenda made him a target for threats and intimidation. His office was vandalized on multiple occasions, and even Amina, his silent and silenced wife from whom he had been separated for years, had received letters of threat and harassment. At one point, a close aide of Adil's was attacked in broad daylight, a chilling reminder of the risks involved in standing up to powerful forces.

Despite these challenges, Adil remained undeterred. He often told his supporters, "If we give in to fear, we have already lost. The only way to win is to keep fighting, no matter the cost."

Amid the relentless conflict, there was one moment that stood out as an example of what could be achieved when differences were set aside. In the aftermath of torrential rains and consequent flooding that struck Ayodhya, both Adil and Rathore found themselves working together to coordinate relief efforts. The crisis brought out a different side of their rivalry, as they put aside their ideological differences to focus on the immediate needs of the people.

For a brief period, there was a sense of camaraderie between the two men. Adil later reflected on the experience, saying, "It was a reminder that, at the end of the day, we are all human. If only we could carry that spirit forward in everything we do." Adil's interactions with his political rivals were emblematic of the broader struggle for India's soul. His battles with figures like Rathore were not just about policy. They were about competing visions for the country's future. While his rivals sought to define India through the lens of religion and nationalism, Adil fought for an inclusive vision that embraced diversity and equality. These conflicts left an indelible mark on Adil Khan, shaping him into a leader who was as brave as he was compassionate. For me, his granddaughter, his legacy was a reminder that true strength lies not in overpowering others, but in standing firm for what is right, even in the face of overwhelming opposition.

For Adil Khan, politics was never just about governance or policy. It was about history. Ayodhya, with its tangled narratives of devotion, conquest, and identity, loomed large over every aspect of his life. His political career, shaped by his personal tragedies, was intricately connected to the city's past. His awareness of the clandestine placement of Lord Rama's idols inside the Babri Masjid in 1949, decades before he entered Indian politics, had left an indelible mark on his psyche. This event did become a watershed moment and had triggered legal and communal conflict. That fateful night had become a turning point for Ayodhya's native Muslims, setting the stage for years of communal strife. Adil Khan often invoked that incident in his speeches and writings, using it to reflect on the fragility of coexistence and the enduring manipulations of political power. "History is not just what happened," he once said in a fiery debate. "It is how we choose to remember it, and how we wield it as a weapon." Such pivotal moments in Ayodhya's tumultuous history had cast an unshakable shadow over Adil Khan's political consciousness. To him, this act symbolized the fragile veneer of trust between communities being breached, igniting a flame of indignation that shaped his resolve. The knowledge of this incident deepened his commitment to defending Muslim identity, since he saw it not just as an isolated event, but as a calculated erosion of coexistence, pushing him to challenge the forces rewriting Ayodhya's shared past.

The surreptitious placement of the idols on December 22, 1949, did not occur in a vacuum. The roots of this act had stretched back to the early 1920s, a period of rising communal tensions across India. The Khilafat movement and Gandhi's call for non-cooperation had brought Hindus and Muslims together briefly, but the alliance was tenuous. In Ayodhya, these broader national currents intersected with local grievances and religious fervor. During the 1920s, Hindu organizations like the Hindu Mahasabha began campaigning for greater access to religious sites they believed had been usurped during Mughal rule. The Babri Masjid, standing at what was claimed to be the birthplace of Lord Rama, had become a focal point of their efforts. Historical records showed that while the mosque had existed peacefully alongside Hindu shrines for centuries, the political climate of the twentieth century transformed it into a site of contention.

Adil often mentioned this era in his speeches, describing it as the point when Ayodhya's shared cultural heritage began to splinter. "For centuries," he would say, "Hindus and Muslims worshipped side by side in Ayodhya. They respected each other's faiths. But the 1920s saw the emergence of a dangerous ideology that sought to rewrite that history." A group of Hindu activists, inspired by rumors of divine visions and emboldened by growing nationalist sentiment, had placed idols of Lord Rama inside the Babri Masjid in December 1949. The act was a deliberate provocation, intended to establish the site as a Hindu temple and challenge its status as a mosque. When news of the idols spread, it had sent shockwaves across Ayodhya and beyond. For the Muslim community, it was a profound violation of their sacred space. For many Hindus, it was seen as a divine reclamation. The local administration, caught in the maelstrom, had decided to lock the mosque's gates, barring both communities from using it. But the damage had been done. The incident had deepened the communal divide, creating wounds that would fester for decades. Adil Khan, born in the shadow of this event, grew up hearing conflicting accounts of that night. His father would recount the despair of the Muslim community, forced to watch as their heritage was eroded piece by piece. "It wasn't just a mosque they took," his father would say. "It was our dignity." When he became an activist and later a politician in the early twenty first century, he saw it as his duty to address this unresolved trauma. But he also knew that doing so would mean confronting powerful forces that had built their identities around the narrative of Ayodhya as a Hindu city. As Adil's political career gained momentum, his rivals, particularly Mahesh Rathore, weaponized the story of 1949 to bolster their cause. They painted the placement of the idols as a sacred act of resistance, a moment of divine intervention that corrected centuries of injustice. Adil, in turn, framed it as a cynical manipulation of faith for political gain.

In one particularly charged debate, Rathore declared, "The night of 1949 was not a crime. It was a revelation. It was the moment when Lord Rama reclaimed what was rightfully his." Adil's response was sharp and unyielding. "Faith does not need manipulation to prove its strength. What happened in 1949 was not a revelation. It was a calculated act of provocation. And the cost of that act has been borne by generations who have lived in fear and division."

This debate crystallized the ideological battle between the two men: Rathore, representing a narrative of Hindu resurgence, and Adil, championing a vision of secular justice. Their exchanges became legendary in Ayodhya, drawing massive crowds and intense media coverage. Of course, the archaeological evidence, or lack thereof, supported the claim that a Ram temple had existed on the site of the Babri Masjid. In the 1970s and 1980s, the Archaeological Survey of India had conducted excavations in the area, uncovering remnants of what some experts interpreted as Hindu temple structures. The findings had become a rallying point for the Hindu nationalist movement. Adil, however, was skeptical of the politicization of archaeology. He often pointed out the selective interpretation of the evidence and the way it was used to inflame communal passions. "Archaeology should be about uncovering the truth," he argued in an interview. "But in Ayodhya, it has become a tool for justifying violence."

Interestingly, and I must repeat this, my maternal grandfather was well-aware that, one of the archaeologists involved in the Ayodhya excavations was a well-known Muslim scholar who had authenticated and affirmed the presence of temple-like structures beneath the mosque. This created a complex dynamic for Adil, who respected the Muslim scholar's integrity but questioned the broader implications of his findings. Adil reached out to the scholar, hoping to understand his perspective. Their conversation was a turning point for Adil, forcing him to grapple with the nuances of history and identity. "It is possible," the Muslim scholar told him, "to acknowledge the past without weaponizing it. But that requires wisdom and restraint, qualities that are often in short supply in politics."

Despite his opposition to the Hindutva agenda, Adil was not opposed to the idea of a Ram temple. What he objected to was the way the issue was being used to marginalize Muslims and deepen communal divides. In his speeches, he often proposed a vision of Ayodhya where the temple and the mosque could coexist as symbols of India's pluralism. This vision, however, was met with fierce resistance from his rivals, who accused him of undermining Hindu pride. Adil's attempts at reconciliation became a lightning rod for criticism, with both sides questioning his motives.

For Adil, the battle over Ayodhya was not just political—it was deeply personal. The memory of his son, Aarif, who had been killed in mob violence, loomed large over every decision he made. Aarif's death was a reminder of the human cost of communal conflict, a cost that Adil was determined to prevent others from paying. In his quieter moments, Adil would confide to a few colleagues about his hopes and fears. "I don't know if I will live to see it," he once told her. "But I dream of an Ayodhya where no child has to grow up fearing for their life because of their faith."

Adil's commitment to his political cause and his work had inspired a new generation of activists and leaders who wished to carry forward his message of justice and redress for Muslims. In the final years of his life, Adil often spoke about Aarif in his speeches, using his son's story as a reminder of what was at stake. "I lost my son to hate," he would say. "But I refuse to let hate win."

Adil Khan, my maternal grandfather has never made any attempt to meet Amina, my mother, Yasmin, or me ever. I stand at the edge of the balcony in the Trivedi mansion, looking out at the twilight settling over Ayodhya and ponder on my maternal grandfather, the grandfather I have met and seen only once. The Sarayu River shimmers in the distance, its waters carrying the weight of centuries, much like my thoughts. The stories of my maternal grandfather, Adil Khan, had always been fragments passed through whispers, news clippings, and my mother's reluctant mentions. He had been a shadow in my life, a name imbued with gravity but without form. Yet, despite his absence and the aching silence he left in my mother's life, I found myself inexplicably drawn to his legacy.

I had encountered him just once in my life. He had made no effort to reach out to me or to my mother after she left him, breaking ties in the aftermath of their shared loss. And yet, the more I learned about him, the more I saw him not as a neglectful figure but as a man who had submerged his personal sorrows in the larger tide of his people's struggles. He had transformed his grief into purpose, channeling his pain into a fierce fight for justice. How could I resent him when the weight of the world he carried seemed heavier than any familial bond?

There was a strength in his absence, I realized, a kind of defiant endurance. Adil Khan, the activist, the politician, the voice for a silenced community—he had become an almost mythical figure to me. His speeches, as reported in old newspapers I'd found, were fiery, filled with conviction, yet tempered with an intellect that seemed untouched by his personal tragedies. He had called for unity even as the world fractured around him. He had stood firm in his identity while navigating the storm of Ayodhya's shifting political landscape.

I wondered if he had ever thought of me, of my mother. Did we haunt him in quiet moments? Did he regret the distance, or had he convinced himself it was necessary, a sacrifice for the greater cause? These questions lingered like shadows I could never dispel. But the answers mattered less to me now than the realization that I owed a part of who I was to him. His defiance and his unyielding spirit, both coursed through me as much as the traditions of the Trivedi household. I was his blood as much as I was my father's, and perhaps my duality was my inheritance from both.

As I gaze at the horizon, I feel a strange kinship with this man I have never known. In his fight for his people, I see echoes of my own struggles to understand where I belong and who I am. He has drawn battle lines, yes, but he has also drawn a map for others to follow, a path of courage and conviction. And though he has never reached out a hand to guide me, I feel his presence now, as real and enduring as the river below. In his absence, he has given me something profound—a sense of purpose, a reminder that even in silence, legacies speak. For me, his maternal granddaughter, Adil Khan was more than a politician or an activist. In the face of unimaginable loss, it was possible to find purpose and to fight for a better world. I gaze and ponder deeper—on my maternal grandfather, the grandfather I have met and seen only once.

12

I t was a quiet evening in our Trivedi mansion. Shyam Trivedi, my paternal grandfather, sat in his usual spot on the verandah, the fading light casting long shadows across his weathered face. A messenger arrived with a letter addressed to him. It bore Adil Khan's signature, stark and deliberate, against the crisp white paper.

"Adil Khan wishes to meet me," Shyam Trivedi announced, his voice steady, betraying neither surprise nor emotion. He looked pointedly at me and at my father, Ramesh. The house felt like it was buzzing with curiosity and apprehension. Why now? What could these two giants, long poised on opposite sides of Ayodhya's fraught history, possibly have to say to each other? I observed my father, Ramesh, who seemed uneasy.

"What do you think he wants?" Ramesh asked.

"To talk," Shyam replied simply, though his tightened grip on the letter suggested he anticipated something far more complex.

For decades, my two grandfathers, Shyam Trivedi and Adil Khan, had been symbols of opposing ideologies— Shyam Trivedi, the staunch advocate of Hindu rights, and Adil Khan, the voice of Muslim resistance. Their meeting, or perhaps reconciliation, could potentially be a moment charged with significance for the people of Ayodhya. I was curious and asked if I could go with him. Shyam Trivedi, who adored me, his beloved granddaughter, couldn't possibly say no.

The sky over Ayodhya was heavy with monsoon clouds, their deep grays casting an almost theatrical gloom over the city. I, Saanvi, found myself musing intensely as I sat by the window of our Trivedi family mansion, my thoughts restless. The day had felt pregnant with a strange tension, as though the centuries of Ayodhya's layered history would culminate in this single, momentous meeting. The sound of the Sarayu River, flowing steadily beyond the horizon, seemed to reach my ears like a faint heartbeat. My paternal grandfather, Shyam Trivedi, had become uncharacteristically silent since breakfast. Known across the region as the man whose legal acumen helped cement Ayodhya's future as a Hindu pilgrimage center, Shyam Trivedi carried his triumphs with a pride that had become synonymous with his identity. He paced the room silently, with a slow, measured step, his cane tapping lightly against the floor.

On the other side of the city, Adil Khan prepared for the meeting with equal resolve. In a modest office lined with stacks of legal briefs and community petitions, he buttoned his faded kurta and gazed at his reflection in the mirror. His face bore the lines of age and struggle, each wrinkle a testament to the battles he had fought for his people. Today, he wasn't just a politician or an activist. He was a man confronting a counterpart who had, in many ways, been his shadow.

The meeting between these two men wasn't just a personal encounter. It was a reflection of Ayodhya's history—its beauty and its wounds, its faith and its fractures. My grandfather of course, chose a neutral venue for their meeting, a government guesthouse perched on the banks of the Sarayu River. I was aware of the oppressive quiet of the space as soon as I entered quietly with Shyam Trivedi. The guesthouse, ordinarily a sterile and unremarkable structure, seemed imbued with the weight of history on this day. The faint smell of jasmine wafted through the air, mingling with the earthy smell of the river nearby. The room where the two men were to meet was modest and austere—two simple wooden chairs facing each other across a sturdy table, a single fan whirring faintly above. The furniture seemed too fragile to bear the weight of the conversation about to unfold. To my mind, the room itself looked like a metaphor—bare walls, a single wooden table, two chairs placed across from each other, and an oppressive silence broken only by the occasional call of birds from the riverbank. On that day, the air itself seemed to carry the weight of unspoken words and unresolved histories.

My maternal grandfather, Adil Khan arrived first, without ceremony, his *sherwani* and *topi* unassuming but his gait determined. His face, though aged, carried an expression that was sharp and unyielding, a blend of quiet resolve and guarded intensity. He carried the weight of his community's wounds and his personal tragedies, though his sharp eyes revealed a mind that refuses to be intimidated. He entered the room with the air of a man used to confrontations but weary of them at the same time. His arrival was deliberately understated. He revealed his characteristic stoicism, carrying with him an aura of quiet strength. His eyes, dark and contemplative, surveyed the space as though mentally preparing for the battle of words to come.

Shyam Trivedi entered moments later, leaning on his cane, his movements deliberate and composed. Clad in a crisp, white *dhoti-kurta*, his gait was steady despite the support of his cane. His presence radiated an air of authority and calm self-assurance, shaped by decades of courtroom debates and ideological victories. He looked every bit the patriarch—stoic, measured, his presence commanding respect. He glanced at Adil with a faint nod, a gesture that acknowledged the weight of the moment without betraying any sentiment. The two men exchanged pleasantries, but their polite words were laced with barbs as much as with tension.

"It is an honor to meet you, Mr. Khan. I hear your speeches have a way of stirring hearts, though I wonder if they mend them as well," Shyam Trivedi greeted him.

"And your legal arguments, Mr. Trivedi, have a way of rewriting history. I suppose we both leave our mark on Ayodhya in our own ways," Adil Khan responded. The tension between them was palpable. Their opening exchange was one of uneasy politeness. Their words, though carefully chosen, seemed to bristle with implied challenges.

From my vantage point, I could hear snippets of their conversation, though much of it was lost. What I did hear, however, was enough to make my heart ache.

Shyam Trivedi's voice was firm but tinged with an old man's weariness. "So, this is where we meet again, Adil Khan. Not in a courtroom, not in the halls of power, but here, in a guesthouse by the Sarayu river. Fitting, don't you think?"

Adil Khan's response was quieter, almost reflective. "Fitting, perhaps. Or ironic. The Sarayu has seen centuries of Ayodhya's history, and yet, it flows on, indifferent to our battles and beliefs."

"It has been years, Mr. Khan. Yet, here we are, still talking about the same Ayodhya. It seems some battles never truly end," Shyam Trivedi spoke a bit haughtily, I thought. I was allowed only a glimpse of my maternal grandfather as he had walked in, but I was able to hear bits of their conversation as I waited and sat on a bench outside their meeting room. They were just two old men, sitting across from each other. Their postures were stiff, their faces shadowed, but there was something in the air between them—a tension, an intensity—that caught my attention. As I drew closer, the realization hit me again, almost with the force of a tidal wave. It was the two titans meeting. My grandfathers. Shyam Trivedi, the staunch defender of the Ram temple, and Adil Khan, the tireless advocate for Muslim rights.

I froze, half-hidden behind the gnarled shadows of the door, my heart pounding in my chest. I knew I should leave, that I was intruding on a moment not meant for me. But I couldn't tear myself away. This was history unfolding before my eyes—personal history, yes, but also something larger, something that transcended the boundaries of family and faith.

"Some battles, Mr. Trivedi, were never meant to be fought in the first place," Adil Khan responded quietly. They were cordial, yet their words seemed to carry the weight of decades of history, loss, and defiance.

Shyam Trivedi had been a young, ambitious lawyer since the 1970s, and had spent his entire life poring over historical texts and legal documents to build his case for the proposed Ram temple. He always flaunted his unwavering belief in his cause and his ability to inspire others with his rhetoric. To my young mind, though, it showed a somewhat tender vulnerability in him at the same time, especially when I had heard him talk about the growing communal tensions in Ayodhya and wondering to his son, Ramesh, whether his actions were fanning the flames. Adil Khan's past, on the other hand, was painted in shades of tragedy and resolve. His political consciousness was completely besmirched with the memory of the day he had lost his young son in a mob attack, a moment that became the turning point in his life. It was not grief alone but the realization of his community's vulnerability that had propelled him into activism and, later, into politics. Adil Khan was plagued by his inner conflict —his desire to protect his people while longing for a world where such protection was unnecessary.

"You speak of Ayodhya as if it belongs to only one faith. Do you not see that it is a shared heritage? The Babri Masjid was not just a mosque. It was a symbol of coexistence. What happened in 1949, and again in 1992, was not justice; it was theft, Mr. Trivedi. Theft of trust, of history." My maternal grandfather's voice came through the crack in the door.

"And what of Lord Rama? Was it not theft when his birthplace was usurped centuries ago? The Hindus of this nation have waited patiently for generations. Do we not have the right to reclaim what was ours?" My paternal grandfather retaliated. I noticed the way my paternal grandfather's hands trembled slightly as he spoke of Lord Rama, a rare crack in his otherwise unshakable persona.

The meeting had begun with polite formalities, but the conversation quickly shifted to the crux of their shared history. The meeting between the two grandfathers, Shyam Trivedi and Adil Khan, marked an inevitable collision of ideologies that had long dictated Ayodhya's destiny.

"Do you see, Mr. Trivedi, how the Babri Masjid was more than just stone and mortar to us?" Adil Khan's voice softened, a rare tremor breaking through. "It was a refuge, a memory of coexistence. You see a temple lost. We see a trust broken."

Shyam Trivedi leaned back in his chair, his hands

clasped around his cane. "And what of Lord Rama, Mr. Khan? Does his birthplace mean nothing to you? Is it not possible that our truths can coexist without invalidating one another?"

For all their differences, they found common ground in their love for Ayodhya. Both men, in their own ways, had dedicated their lives to the city, though their visions for its future were irreconcilably different. The conversation took on a philosophical tone as they discussed Ayodhya's future. Adil Khan spoke of the importance of coexistence, of building a city where Hindu and Muslim children could play side by side without inheriting the burdens of history. Shyam Trivedi, in his turn, spoke of faith as a foundation, of reclaiming not just land but a narrative. The conversation soon returned, inevitably, to the events of 1949, when idols of Lord Ram were placed inside the Babri Masjid under the cover of darkness. For Shyam Trivedi, this act was not a desecration but a reclamation—a moment when history corrected itself, however imperfectly. I had heard about the night of December 22, 1949, a night that had irrevocably altered the course of the city's destiny. Under the cover of darkness, idols of Lord Rama had been surreptitiously placed inside the Babri Masjid. It was an act that, depending on the perspective, was either a divine intervention or a deliberate provocation. The subsequent legal battle, which Shyam Trivedi had a hand in decades later, traced its roots to this night. The event set the stage for communal discord, as Hindus claimed the act was a restoration of their rightful heritage, while Muslims saw it as an affront to their sacred space.

Adil Khan had grown up hearing about this event, its implications etched into the collective memory of Ayodhya's Muslim community. The incident wasn't just a historical footnote; it was a raw, unhealed wound that informed his political ideology. I, Saanvi, heard their voices from the shadows, my heart pounding. For the first time, I saw not just two men, but two eras colliding, each stubbornly clinging to their truth, neither willing to let go.

"To you, it was an intrusion," Shyam Trivedi said, his voice steady. "To us, it was an awakening. The temple was always there, Adil Khan, even if hidden beneath layers of time and conquest. The idols merely brought it back into view."

Adil Khan leaned forward, his hands clasped tightly together. "And at what cost? Do you know what I was told about that night? The Muslims of Ayodhya woke up to a city they no longer recognized. Fear had crept into their hearts, Shyam Trivedi. Fear that their home was no longer theirs."

The bitterness in his tone was palpable, and for a moment, Shyam Trivedi seemed at a loss for words. He had spent his life defending the sanctity of the temple, but he had rarely paused to consider what it meant for those on the other side.

"The past, Mr. Trivedi, cannot be undone. But the present? That we still have the power to shape. I fear that if we do not learn to share Ayodhya, there will be no Ayodhya left to fight for."

"Ayodhya is not a matter of sharing, Mr. Khan. It is a matter of faith, of dharma. It is not something to be negotiated."

"You speak of victories, Mr. Trivedi, but victories at what cost? The night the idols were placed in the masjid, did anyone consider the cost to the soul of this city? Or was it always about the temple and the temple alone?" My maternal grandfather challenged my paternal grandfather.

"And what of the centuries before that night? Was

there no cost then, Mr. Khan, when a temple was demolished to make way for the Babri Masjid? The Hindus of Ayodhya bore that pain in silence for generations. We waited—for centuries, we waited," my paternal grandfather responded.

Their words were charged with emotion, yet neither man raised his voice. They were two figures who, despite their ideological chasm, shared an understanding of what it means to fight for a cause. The conversation took on a philosophical tone as they discussed Ayodhya's future. Adil Khan spoke of the importance of coexistence, of building a city where Hindu and Muslim children could play side by side without inheriting the burdens of history. Shyam Trivedi, in turn, spoke of faith as a foundation, of reclaiming not just land but a narrative. Their arguments soon extended beyond Ayodhya, and touched on themes of identity, belonging, and the politics of memory. Both men were eloquent, their words sharp but never descending into vitriol. Their discussions, to my young mind, revealed not only their ideological differences but also their shared desire for a future free from violence. I could sense the pain in my maternal grandfather's eyes when he had recalled the loss of his son, a pain that had fueled his resolve. I had almost felt like walking inside and hugging him at that juncture. From my vantage point as a silent listener and observer, I had witnessed not only the words spoken but the emotions that lingered beneath my two grandfathers' words. I could sense that their mutual respect was overshadowed by their ideological divides. Shyam Trivedi saw himself as a restorer of a sacred heritage, while Adil Khan viewed him as a symbol of Hindu dominance over Muslim grievances. I myself see them now not just as representatives of their communities, but as individuals shaped by their personal losses and convictions.

Through my perspective, I now see the human side of these two towering figures. I see now that both men, though worlds apart and with individual journeys, shared similar pasts marked by loss. I have begun to respect my paternal grandfather's relentless work on the temple case, his belief in Ayodhya's significance for Hindus, and the generational pride instilled in him by his ancestors. I do have my doubts of course, on whether his efforts have brought harmony or merely sharpened divisions. I do have my doubts about my maternal grandfather's cause as well, in spite of his valor and his internal struggle with balancing personal grief and public responsibility. Unbeknownst to either man, I, Saanvi heard their impassioned arguments and felt torn between their worlds—my maternal grandfather's pain and resilience, and my paternal grandfather's pride and conviction. Their conversations and the moment had become somewhat of a turning point in my understanding of Ayodhya's legacy. My changed perceptions may shape my future choices, who knows? For a moment, the two men simply looked at each other, their silence more powerful than any words. As the conversation resumed, they delved into the historical backdrop and context of the early twentieth century that had shaped their psyche. The story of Ayodhya, particularly the night in 1949 when idols of Lord Rama were placed inside the Babri Masjid, loomed over and kept returning to their discussion. For Shyam Trivedi, it had meant a moment of reclamation, the first step toward restoring what he believed was the rightful identity of Ayodhya. For Adil Khan, it was an act of provocation that had shattered the fragile fabric of communal coexistence. Both had been very young at the time, but the knowledge and recognition had galvanized the political awakening of Shyam Trivedi at least.

"Do you remember that night?" Adil Khan asked quietly, breaking the silence.

"I remember it well," Shyam replied. "Do you?"

Adil's eyes narrowed. "Not as a participant, if that's what you're implying. But I remember the fear it sowed in the hearts of my people."

The conversation grew heated as they addressed the broader implications of the incident and the subsequent legal battles.

"Do you truly believe Ayodhya belongs to one faith alone? That the dreams of one community should override the fears of another?" Adil Khan challenged Shyam Trivedi in this ideological crossfire.

"Ayodhya's history speaks for itself. It has always been the city of Ram. The temple was never just a structure; it was a symbol, an anchor. How could we, as Hindus, let that anchor be lost?" Shyam Trivedi responded.

Adil Khan leaned forward, his voice rising slightly. "And what of those who have lived here for generations, believing this city was theirs too? What of those whose mosques, homes, and lives were destroyed in the name of that anchor?"

As the debate intensified, both men drew on history to bolster their arguments. Shyam Trivedi spoke of the Archaeological Survey of India's findings, which unearthed evidence of a temple structure beneath the Babri Masjid. Adil Khan countered by questioning the selective reading of history, pointing out that the Mughal-era mosque had stood for over four centuries as a place of worship.

"The past cannot be erased, Mr. Trivedi," Adil said. "Nor can it be used as a weapon to bludgeon the present."

Shyam Trivedi responded with a calm but firm tone.

"The past is not a weapon, Mr. Khan. It is a foundation. Without it, we are rootless."

As the argument ebbed and flowed, the conversation turned personal. Adil, for the first time, spoke of the mob violence that had taken his son, Aarif's life, and how that tragedy had driven him to leave his family and immerse himself in activism.

"Do you know what it's like to lose a child, Mr. Trivedi?" he asked, his voice breaking. "To see the light go out in your wife's eyes and know that nothing—no mosque, no temple—will ever bring it back?"

Shyam Trivedi's expression softened. He nodded slightly, as if acknowledging that loss was the one language they both understood. Though he had not lost a child, he had lost friends, neighbors, and the sense of unity he once believed was possible.

I had quietly observed the meeting of the two titans, my two grandfathers. It was inevitable that I felt a surge of conflicting emotions. My maternal grandfather, whom I had never met before this day, stood before me as a giant figure of courage and of conviction. Yet he had never reached out to me or my mother, choosing instead to dedicate his life to a broader cause.

My paternal grandfather, by contrast, had been a constant presence in my life. He had always seemed to embody the pride and tradition of our Trivedi mansion. He had loved and adored me. Yet I could see now how his single-minded pursuit of Ayodhya's 'restoration' had come at a cost—not just to the Muslim community but to his own humanity.

The meeting would end without any resolution, of course. Both men, despite their differences, agreed on one point: Ayodhya's future cannot be built on bloodshed. They parted ways, each carrying the weight of their convictions. As Adil Khan walked out, he paused, looked back, and said, "The river doesn't choose sides, Mr. Trivedi. Perhaps we shouldn't either."

"Yes indeed," Shyam Trivedi retorted.

Their meeting had concluded with an unresolved tension. Neither man could concede to the other, yet their parting words hinted at a mutual recognition of the other's humanity.

"The river flows on, indifferent to our quarrels. Perhaps it is time we learn from it," Adil Khan said.

"Perhaps. But some truths are like the riverbank, Mr. Khan. They cannot be eroded." Shyam Trivedi could not help giving his parting shot.

As Adil Khan left the room, I, Saanvi had felt a profound sense of awe and sadness. I realized that despite their differences, both men were bound by their love for Ayodhya, a love that was both their strength and their tragedy. Ayodhya was no stranger to tension, even as it has been pregnant with history. It is a city that has lived in layers—layers of belief, sacrifice, and contradiction. Every corner, every brick has borne testimony to its fractured soul. The Sarayu river, its waters imbued with myth and memory, have flowed indifferently, having seen both coronations and bloodshed. The city has become an epicenter of faith and conflict, where every debate seemed larger than life, and every action echoed through the corridors of time. I, Saanvi, sensing that their meeting would be ending soon, felt like an outsider to my own story. My two grandfathers, Shyam Trivedi and Adil Khan, represented to my mind, not just two families, but two worldviews. And today, after decades of avoiding each other, they had finally decided to meet. The reasons for this meeting were as complex as the city itself: neither had extended an invitation, yet neither had refused. I had always thought of my two grandfathers as opposites, I reflected. But now I see they were two sides of the same coin—both shaped by their losses, both driven by a fierce loyalty to their causes, and both, in their own way, flawed. After the meeting had ended, neither man had changed the other's mind, but there was a mutual acknowledgment of the other's pain and determination.

Adil Khan extended his hand. "Perhaps, one day, Ayodhya will belong to all of us."

Shyam Trivedi hesitated before shaking it. "Perhaps. But until then, we will fight for what we believe is right." Their handshake was brief, their parting words even briefer, but the moment lingered, heavy with the unspoken. They were still adversaries, still bound by their opposing convictions, but there was a newfound respect in the air. They were no longer just a Hindu lawyer and a Muslim politician. They were two old men, carrying the weight of their choices and the legacies they would leave behind. By the time the sun dipped below the horizon, casting the Sarayu in hues of orange and gold, something had shifted between them.

As Adil Khan, my maternal grandfather walked away, I, Saanvi caught something in my paternal grandfather's eyes—a flicker of respect, or perhaps a recognition of his own reflection. The two men parted ways, their differences unresolved but their respect for each other evident. I believe I heard my paternal grandfather, Shyam Trivedi, mutter under his breath, "A formidable man, despite his flaws." As I, Saanvi, had heard bits of the meeting unfold, I was more struck by the similarities between the two men than their differences. Both were uncompromising in their beliefs, yet both carried the weight of loss —Shyam Trivedi, of a faith suppressed, and Adil Khan, of a family shattered. I had always seen them as opposites, I reflected. But in that room, I realized they were mirrors of each other. Two men shaped by history, both trying to hold onto their version of Ayodhya. I began to fathom and somewhat understand my awe for my maternal grandfather, Adil Khan. Though he had never reached out to me or to my mother nor ever to my grandmother, Amina, his convictions and his sacrifices were undeniable. He had fought for what he believed was right, even at the cost of personal relationships. In their own way, they were both right. And in their own way, they were both wrong. The meeting between my two grandfathers has in some ways, become a kind of pivotal moment in my journey. It has helped shape my understanding of my family's legacy and the history of Ayodhya itself.

For me, Saanvi, the meeting was not just a clash of ideologies but a reminder of the complexities that defined her family and her city. Ayodhya was both my inheritance and my burden, a place where the past refused to stay buried and the future remained uncertain.

Their words had been measured, their tones civil, but the weight of their shared history was palpable. They had spoken of Ayodhya, of the events of 1949 when the idols of Lord Ram were placed in the Babri Masjid, of the riots and court cases that had followed. They spoke of faith and fear, of identity and loss. And as they had spoken, I saw not two adversaries, but two men shaped by the same forces that had shaped this city—men who, despite their differences, were bound together by their love for Ayodhya and their determination to protect what they believed was right.

As I mused, a storm started raging within me. I had grown up hearing stories of both my grandfathers, stories that painted them as heroes and villains, saints and sinners. To my father, Shyam Trivedi was a paragon of virtue, a man who had fought tirelessly for the rights of Hindus and the sanctity of the Ram temple. To my mother, Adil Khan was a symbol of resilience even though he had betrayed and abandoned her and his wife.

He was a man who had dedicated his life to justice and equality for the Muslim community. But to me, they were enigmas even as my inner turmoil grew. Two men who had shaped my family's history, and yet remained distant figures in my life. Shyam Trivedi, with his sharp intellect and unwavering conviction, had not only shaped my parents' personal history but had also shaped the rhythms of my daily life. Though I lived with him, he remained a man of reserve—rarely speaking of his personal emotions, keeping the chambers of his heart tightly locked. Adil Khan, on the other hand, was a ghost —a man who had never attempted to meet me or my mother, and whose name was spoken in hushed tones in my father's home.

And yet, as I thought about them again, I felt a deep sense of awe. Here were two men who had lived through Ayodhya's darkest days, who had fought for their beliefs with every fiber of their being, and who had borne the weight of their convictions with dignity, even as it fractured their families. They were flawed, yes—stubborn, prideful, perhaps even blind to the pain they had caused. But they were also extraordinary, their lives inextricably linked to the fate of a city and a nation.

It was Shyam Trivedi who had extended his hand first —a gesture of respect, perhaps, or acknowledgment. Adil Khan had hesitated for a moment, and only then taken it. Their handshake was brief, their parting words even briefer, but the moment lingered, heavy with unspoken truths.

As they walked away in opposite directions, I felt a strange sense of peace. For all their differences, for all the pain and division their beliefs had caused, they had shared something profound in that moment—something that transcended politics and religion. And in that quiet, fleeting moment, I understood that they were not just titans of Ayodhya's history. They were human beings, with all the contradictions and complexities that entailed.

I stepped out from behind the back door of the guest house, and the cool breeze of the Sarayu washed over me. I didn't try to follow them, nor did I call out to my maternal grandfather to tell him who I was. Instead, I stood there, letting the moment settle within me. Ayodhya, with its scars and its sanctity, had always been a place of paradox. And so, too, were my grandfathers—both right and wrong, both heroes and villains, both deeply flawed and profoundly human.

In that moment, I felt closer to them than I ever had before. This was my moment of understanding. I don't know how long I stood there, hidden in the shadows of a banyan tree outside, pondering about them. Time seemed to stretch and blur, the sun sinking lower until the river was bathed in hues of gold and crimson. And then, as the *muezzin*'s call to prayer echoed faintly in the distance, I was tempted to leave. But I still sat there musing to myself.

As I sat in the aftermath of that fateful meeting, I found myself grappling with a profound realization: both my grandfathers were right, and yet, both were wrong. Shyam Trivedi, my paternal grandfather, had fought relentlessly to reclaim what he saw as the heritage of Ayodhya. To him, the proposed Ram temple was not just a structure but a symbol of identity, history, and pride. His dedication to the cause had earned him reverence, but it had also blinded him to the cost—the divisions it had sowed and the humanity it had overlooked. For all his wisdom and eloquence, he could not see that the past, if wielded too rigidly, becomes a chain rather than a guide.

On the other hand, Adil Khan, my maternal grandfather, had dedicated his life to ensuring justice for his people, to defending the rights of a community that had been rendered vulnerable. His convictions were born of loss and anger, but they also carried a sense of hope—hope that the future could be better than the past. Yet, in his pursuit of the collective, he had sacrificed the personal. He had turned away from his wife, Amina, and from my mother and me, choosing his cause over his family.

They were two men, bound by their pain and shaped by their beliefs, standing on opposite sides of the same fractured land. One sought to honor history, the other to protect the present. One looked backward, the other forward. And yet, neither seemed able to truly inhabit the present—a space where history and hope might coexist.

I realized then that their meeting was not about one persuading the other or proving a point. It was about acknowledgment. In their handshake, hesitant and fleeting though it was, I saw the possibility of a middle ground—not agreement, but understanding. Not victory, but peace.

Perhaps that is the true legacy of Ayodhya: a place where contradictions live side by side, where faith and reason, pride and pain, hope and fear, all find a home. It is a city that demands reconciliation, not just of its people but of their histories, their dreams, and their flaws.

And in that moment, as I watched them part ways, I felt the weight of my inheritance. I am the product of these two men, these two worlds. Their strengths and their shortcomings flow through me, as does their love for Ayodhya, however differently expressed. My task, I realize, is not to choose between them but to carry forward what is right in both while leaving behind what is wrong.

As the evening sun cast its golden light over the Sarayu, I made a silent vow: I would not let Ayodhya remain a battlefield. I would find a way to make it a bridge. The banyan tree over me, stood silent as ever, its roots entwined with the history of Ayodhya, bearing witness to yet another chapter in the city's long, tumultuous saga. A warm breeze moved through its hanging roots, brushing softly against my skin like an ancestral whisper, neither approving nor condemning, only remembering. Ayodhya did not forget. This soil bore imprints of every foot that had marched in devotion, defiance, or despair. The city was not merely a place on a map; it was a palimpsest of centuries, overwritten and re-inscribed, each generation both heir and trespasser. The river beside me, the Sarayu, shimmered with an unspoken wisdom. It had seen too many sacrifices, too many processions of grief disguised as pride. Yet it flowed on—cleansing, forgiving, unknowable. It seemed to have an innocence that could undo the weight of history. Did the river pause to separate a believer from a doubter?

I thought of Ramesh, my father, always trying to walk the tightrope between belief and compromise. And of Yasmin, my mother, who spoke rarely but lived with an honesty that unsettled every lie we were told. Their love had been a secret bridge, built in defiance of the very divisions that Ayodhya had come to symbolize. I carried their legacy now, not in slogans or manifestos, but in questions, in wounds, in aching hope. What if Ayodhya was seen not as a site of conquest, but of convergence? What if every prayer, no matter whom it was addressed to, was understood as a human reaching toward something greater than themselves? Their love had been inconvenient, complicated, real. It made me wonder if bridges were ever built for beauty, or only because we had run out of land.

A flock of birds burst suddenly into the sky, startled from the tree's upper branches. I looked up, watching their silhouettes scatter against the fading amber light. In their flight was something urgent yet free, a reminder that even in a place heavy with memory, renewal was still possible. The places of worship that rose across the skyline were not adversaries in stone; they were cries for meaning. I stood and brushed the dust from my hands. The banyan had offered shelter, the river, clarity. Ayodhya would not yield its truth easily. But I would keep returning, not just to uncover the past, but to imagine a future. One step at a time, over a bridge yet to be built. I stood, brushing the dust off my palms, unsure what I had just vowed or to whom. The banyan's roots clung to the earth like a warning: nothing here could be easily untangled. Ayodhya would not bend to my idealism. A bridge, I had said. But bridges can collapse too. I turned away from the river. The night was falling, and I had no map.

13

My father, Ramesh Trivedi, was a man of quiet habits, living at the intersection of history and myth in a city like no other. Ayodhya, ancient and eternal, cast its shadow over every aspect of his life. The city, celebrated as the birthplace of Lord Rama, hummed with a quiet reverence, its air thick with stories of the divine prince who walked its streets. For my father, this heritage was not just a backdrop but a living presence—a reminder of *dharma*'s eternal struggle and the delicate balance between faith and reason. This, perhaps, is what defined him most: a man of books and ideas, grappling with the weight of a city that seemed to breathe history with every gust of wind and ripple of the Sarayu river. He was the kind of person who would disappear into the pages of a book while the world around him roared with its incessant clamor. For as long as I could remember, his presence at our Trivedi mansion was like a steady undercurrent—neither demanding nor intrusive, yet always there, grounding us in an unspoken stability. It was a contrast to the grandeur of our home, with its towering columns, intricately carved doorways, and ancestral portraits gazing down at us with solemn, watchful eyes.

Alongside his secret marriage and hushed but lifelong commitment to my mother, Yasmin Khan, he had devoted himself entirely to his role as a lecturer at Ayodhya College. In his lectures, he had tried to bring history to life, weaving together facts and philosophies with a scholar's passion. He spoke not just of events, but of their ripples through time—how the stories of empires and revolutions shaped the small, everyday lives of people. Students revered him, not because he demanded it, but because his sincerity and intellect commanded respect.

His days followed a routine as unwavering as the tides. At dawn, he would sit on the verandah with his first cup of tea, gazing out at the manicured gardens my grandmother oversaw with an iron will. Then, after breakfast, he would cycle to the college, his kurta crisp and his bag slung over his shoulder. Evenings were spent in his study, a room that smelled of old wood and books, its walls lined with shelves overflowing with volumes on history, philosophy, and politics.

At the heart of his quiet existence was an unspoken pain. The apparently separate existence from Yasmin, though a decision made under the weight of familial and societal pressures, had left its mark on him. My grandparents, while deeply loving in their own way, had been staunchly opposed to their union. Yasmin's Muslim identity, they feared, was a threat to the purity of our Hindu lineage. Though I lived with my father and grandparents, I visited my mother, Yasmin, on weekends, a tenuous arrangement that felt like a bridge stretched too thin over turbulent waters.

Despite the walls that had been erected between them, my father and Yasmin shared an unbroken bond. Their love lingered in the silences, in the unspoken understanding that coursed through our fractured family. When he spoke of her—rare as those moments were—his voice would take on a softness that hinted at the depths of his loss.

It was this life of quiet intellectualism and suppressed sorrow that slowly began to unravel when politics came knocking at our door. Ayodhya, with its layers of history and its scars of division, was always simmering. The city's ancient alleys carried whispers of the divine, tales of Lord Rama's birth, and the cosmic dance of *dharma* and *adharma* that unfolded on its sacred soil. Here, every stone seemed to echo the footsteps of the exiled prince, who would one day return to reclaim his rightful place. The Sarayu River flowed gently through the heart of the city, its waters bearing witness to centuries of devotion and discord alike. This was no ordinary place—it was a living myth, a city where faith and history converged, their edges blurred by time and interpretation.

My father stood just shy of six feet, his bearing marked by a quiet authority shaped by years of public life. He carried himself with an ease that came not from arrogance, but from discipline, the kind drilled into him by both family values and political necessity. His frame was sturdy, neither lean nor heavy, suggesting a man who took care of himself without vanity. Time had begun to scatter threads of silver through his dense, dark hair, but his presence remained undiminished. There was energy in his step, purpose in his voice, and an enduring sharpness in his gaze. His square face, usually composed, would occasionally soften with a fleeting smile—rare, but unmistakable in the warmth of his deep-set eyes. His thick brows, often furrowed in thought, lent him a natural gravity. Those eyes, steady and searching, had watched the country shift and heave; they had learned not just to observe but to withstand. The lines etched around his eyes and mouth were not signs of wear, but of witness. They hinted at long years spent listening, debating, consoling—at moments when policy met real lives. His complexion was a warm, earthy brown, and he nearly always wore traditional Indian attire—starched kurta-pajamas, crisp and unadorned. He had been raised on the rhythms of Hindu scripture, its cadences shaping his sense of *dharma* long before he encountered its political dimensions.

But his was not a childhood sealed in sanctity. it was not just religious teachings that had influenced him. He came of age in a turbulent India, one caught between dreams of progress and the fractures of its past. The socio-political climate of late twentieth century India profoundly impacted his aspirations. During his formative years, India was undergoing significant changes. The country was grappling with economic challenges, and political instability was rampant. The economic strains of the 1980s, the volatility of coalition politics, the surging fervor of the Ram Janmabhoomi movement—all left their imprint. The Ram Janmabhoomi movement, which sought to construct a temple at the site believed to be the birthplace of Lord Rama, resonated deeply with my father and his parents and most others in the Hindu community. It became more than just a religious issue; it morphed into a powerful symbol of cultural identity and political assertion. For my father, witnessing the fervor surrounding this movement awakened a sense of purpose and a desire to take an active role in shaping his community's destiny. For him, the movement was never just about a temple. It symbolized a long-denied cultural self-assertion. It stirred in him a resolve, not to retreat into religion, but to step forward into leadership.

The turning point in my father's life came when he

was in his late twenties. As a lecturer at Ayodhya College, he had become increasingly aware of the socio-economic disparities faced by the people in his community. The small town struggled with inadequate infrastructure, limited access to education, and rampant unemployment. Inspired by the teachings of social reformers and the need for systemic change, he decided that he could no longer remain a passive observer.

One day, after a particularly enlightening discussion with his students about the responsibilities of citizens, my father felt a surge of conviction. He realized that education was a powerful tool for empowerment and that the political landscape was in dire need of leaders who understood the ground realities. With this epiphany, he began to engage more deeply with local issues, attending town meetings and listening to the concerns of his neighbors. And though my father had long stayed away from the political arena, the currents of change were impossible to ignore. The whispers began with small invitations —to community meetings, to discussions about local issues. At first, he attended out of courtesy, out of a sense of civic duty. But the more he engaged, the more he was drawn into the vortex.

His initial foray into politics was cautious, almost reluctant. He would return from these meetings pensive, his brows furrowed as if he were grappling with an internal debate. I remember one evening when he sat at the dinner table, unusually quiet even for him. My grandmother, ever perceptive, asked, "What's on your mind, Ramesh?"

He took a moment before replying. "It's the state of the city, Ma. The growing tensions, the mistrust... it's like watching a storm gather on the horizon."

"And you think you can stop the storm?" she asked, her tone laced with a mix of concern and skepticism.

He shook his head. "Not stop it. But maybe... maybe I can help guide us through it."

Those words marked the beginning of his transformation. The scholar who had spent his life studying history began to step into its making. As his involvement grew, so did the demands on his time. He was asked to speak at rallies, to lend his voice to causes that aligned with his principles. At first, it was about education reform, about preserving Ayodhya's cultural heritage. But soon, the lines between social issues and political ambitions began to blur. It wasn't long before the local political leaders took notice of him. They saw in him a man of integrity, someone who could lend credibility to their campaigns. When the offer came for him to contest in the municipal elections, he hesitated. I overheard the heated discussions that followed, the arguments between him and my grandparents. My grandfather, a staunch traditionalist, was vehemently opposed to the idea.

"Politics is a dirty game, Ramesh," he declared one evening, his voice echoing through the halls of the mansion. "It will ruin you. It will ruin us."

But my father's resolve was firm. "If we all avoid the dirt, papa, who will clean it?" he replied, his tone calm but resolute.

When he finally announced his candidacy, the reaction was a mix of shock and support. Some saw him as a messenger of hope, a man who could bridge the divides that plagued our city.

Others were skeptical, questioning his motives, his capability to navigate the treacherous waters of politics. Through it all, he remained steadfast, his eyes fixed on the horizon, on the vision of a better Ayodhya. For my mother as well, it was a time of confusion and worry. She saw and experienced the toll it took on him even though she was hardly with him—the sleepless nights, the strain in his voice as he rehearsed speeches, the shadows that darkened his eyes. She worried about the battles he would have to fight, the enemies he would make. And yet, there was also a sense of pride, of awe at his courage to step into the fray. Sensing my mother's love for my father, I knew she would have wished to accompany him to rallies, to meetings in crowded lanes and open fields, and to his whirlwind campaigns. She could have personally witnessed his transformation then, and watched as he spoke to people, as he listened to their stories, their grievances. His words were, my mother knew instinctively, not the fiery rhetoric of a seasoned politician, but the measured, earnest appeals of a man who truly cared. And perhaps that was why people began to believe in him, to place their hopes in him.

But with hope came expectations, and with expectations came scrutiny. As his popularity grew, so did the whispers about his past. His relationship with my mother, Yasmin Khan, long buried under layers of secrecy, began to surface. Questions were raised, not just about his personal life but about his loyalties, his identity. The fact that he had a Muslim wife/mistress/beloved became a weapon for his opponents, a way to sow doubt and division.

Through it all, he refused to be drawn into the mudslinging. "My life is an open book," he declared at a press conference when the questions became too pointed to ignore. "I have nothing to hide, and nothing to be ashamed of. My past or my present do not define me—my actions do."

Those words silenced the room, but the battle was far from over. The forces he was up against were relentless, their tactics ruthless. They stoked the fires of communal tension, using fear as their weapon. And in a city like

Ayodhya, where the scars of division ran deep, fear was a potent force.

Despite the challenges, he persevered. His campaign became a movement, one that brought together people from all walks of life. For many in Ayodhya, his message of unity struck a chord deeply intertwined with the city's mythological essence. Ayodhya, as the birthplace of Lord Rama, was more than just a geographical location; it was a symbol of *dharma*, steadfastness, and the pursuit of justice. In his speeches, my father often invoked the story of Lord Rama not as a tale confined to the past but as a guiding light for the present. He spoke of Rama's exile as a lesson in humility, his battles as a testament to perseverance, and his return as a promise of hope and restoration. "Ayodhya," he would say, "is not just our heritage; it is our responsibility to uphold the ideals it represents." These words resonated deeply, reminding the people of a legacy that transcended communal lines and political divides. I saw firsthand the power of his vision, the way he inspired others to look beyond their differences, to see the shared humanity that bound us all. It was a lesson I would carry with me for the rest of my life.

As the election day approached, the tension in our home was palpable. My grandparents, though still wary of his decision, had come to support him in their own way. My grandmother, who had once viewed politics with disdain, now organized prayer meetings for his success. My grandfather, though he remained silent, watched him with a mix of pride and worry.

And through it all, my father remained the same. The quiet scholar who had once spent his evenings lost in books now spent them in the company of people, their hopes and fears laid bare before him. Yet, in the rare moments of solitude, I saw glimpses of the man he had always been—thoughtful, introspective, carrying the weight of the world on his shoulders. In those moments, I wondered if he ever thought of bringing my mother, Yasmin, to her rightful home, or if he ever questioned the path he had chosen. But if he did, he never let it show. He was a man driven by a purpose greater than himself, a purpose that would shape not just his future, but mine as well.

The campaign trail was like a river swollen with monsoon rains—unpredictable, meandering, and occasionally violent. Ramesh Trivedi's quiet resolve clashed with the cacophony of Ayodhya's political stage, where words were weapons and ideals were currency. Yet he navigated this treacherous terrain with a rare blend of humility and determination, even as the forces around him grew darker.

The Trivedi mansion's large verandah became a nerve center of activity, buzzing with volunteers, supporters, and political operatives. Some came with genuine hope; others sought to latch onto what they perceived as a rising star. My father, Ramesh, listened to everyone with the same calm demeanor, his eyes scanning each face for sincerity. For him, this campaign wasn't about ambition, but about duty to Ayodhya, a city poised at the crossroads of its destiny. Amid this frenzy, I found myself drawn into his world in ways I hadn't anticipated. My role as a silent observer shifted to that of an active participant. I became his sounding board, his confidant, and, occasionally, his critic. It wasn't just familial loyalty that drove me; it was the belief that he could genuinely make a difference. Yet, even as I stood by him, I struggled with my own questions. Could one man's integrity withstand the storm of politics? And what would it cost him?

The answer began to take shape one sweltering afternoon at a rally in the heart of Ayodhya. The venue was a dusty field framed by ancient banyan trees whose gnarled roots seemed to mirror the tangled history of the city. The crowd was massive, a sea of faces shimmering in the heat. They had come to hear Ramesh speak, drawn not by promises of wealth or power but by the authenticity of his message.

As he stepped onto the makeshift stage, the murmurs subsided. Dressed in his usual white kurta-pajama, he looked like an anachronism in a world dominated by flashy suits and fiery slogans. Yet, there was a quiet charisma in his simplicity, an honesty that resonated with the people.

"Ayodhya," he began, his voice steady but tinged with emotion, "is not just a city. It is a living entity, a repository of faith, memory, and aspiration. But today, our beloved city stands divided, its soul scarred by mistrust and hatred. This is not the Ayodhya we inherited, and it cannot be the Ayodhya we leave for our children."

The crowd listened intently, their expressions a mixture of hope and skepticism. He spoke of unity, of the need to transcend communal divisions, and of the shared heritage that bound them together. He invoked the story of Lord Rama, not as a weapon to inflame passions but as a reminder of the virtues of compassion, sacrifice, and justice.

"Rama," he said, his voice rising, "taught us that *dharma* is not about dominance but about balance. It is about understanding, about putting others before oneself. If we truly revere him, let us honor his values, not just his name."

The applause was thunderous, but it was not universal. In the crowd, I spotted faces twisted with anger, their eyes hard and unforgiving. These were the ones who saw his message as a threat, who thrived on division and discord. Their whispers grew louder in the days that followed, their accusations more pointed.

It began subtly, with murmurs in the marketplace and insinuations in the local press. They questioned his "secular" stance, framing it as a betrayal of his Hindu identity. They dredged up his past, his marriage to Yasmin Khan, and wielded it like a cudgel.

"How can a man who married a Muslim claim to represent Ayodhya's Hindu majority?" one editorial sneered.

The smear campaign escalated, fueled by shadowy figures who remained just out of reach. Flyers appeared overnight, littering the streets with their venomous rhetoric. They depicted Ramesh as a traitor, a man who had "sold out" his religion for personal gain. The language was incendiary, designed to provoke outrage.

For the first time and in the course of my summer vacation, I saw my father falter. It was in the privacy of his study, late at night, when he thought no one was watching. He sat at his desk, the light casting long shadows across his face. In his hand was one of those hateful flyers, its words like wounds carved into his skin.

"Baba," I said softly, stepping into the room.

He looked up, startled, then quickly folded the paper and set it aside. "You should be asleep," he said, forcing a smile that didn't reach his eyes.

"So should you," I replied, sitting down across from him. "You can't let them get to you."

He sighed, running a hand through his graying hair. "It's not about me," he said. "It's about what this means for our city, for our people. If they succeed in turning us against each other, they've already won."

"Then don't let them succeed," I said, my voice firm. "You've always taught me that *dharma* is about standing up for what is right, even when it's hard. Especially when it's hard."

He smiled then, a real smile, and reached across the

desk to squeeze my hand. "You're right," he said. "We can't let fear dictate our actions. But it's not just my fight. It's ours."

The days that followed were a test of endurance and faith. My father's campaign adopted a new strategy, one that focused not on countering the attacks but on amplifying his message of unity. He reached out to long-neglected communities, listening with intent and responding with concrete solutions. He spoke at temples and mosques, in schools and bustling marketplaces, trying to stitch together a city frayed by years of silence and division. One moment stood out to me, a scene that remains etched in my memory. It was at a gathering in a small Muslim neighborhood on the outskirts of Ayodhya. The air was thick with tension, the residents wary of this Hindu politician who had come to speak to them. My father stood before them, his hands folded in a gesture of respect.

"I am not here to make promises I cannot keep," he began. "I am here to listen, to understand, and to work together to build a future where our children do not have to inherit our divisions."

A silence followed, heavy and uncertain. Then, an elderly man with a long white beard stepped forward. His voice, when he spoke, was steady but tinged with sadness.

"You speak of unity," he said. "But how can we believe you when the world outside sees us as enemies?"

My father met his gaze, unflinching. "I cannot change the past," he said. "But I can work to change the present. And together, we can shape a future where no one has to feel like an enemy in their own home."

The man studied him for a long moment, then nodded. "We will hold you to your word," he said.

It was a small victory, but it felt monumental. As he left the neighborhood, there was something in him that had not seen in months: hope flickering in my father's eyes.

But hope alone was not enough to shield him from the storm that was building. The whispers grew louder, the attacks more personal. One night, a brick was thrown through the window of our mansion, shattering the weathered glass window that had stood there for generations. On it was a note scrawled in red ink: "Traitor."

The incident shook us, but my father refused to back down. "If we give in to fear," he said, "we lose more than an election. We lose our humanity."

As election day approached, the city seemed to hold its breath. The air crackled with anticipation and anxiety. My father's campaign had gained momentum, drawing support from unexpected quarters. Yet the forces arrayed against him were formidable, their resources seemingly limitless.

It was election morning, and having just finished a school term, I accompanied him to the polling station, buoyed by the thrill of the moment. The streets were alive with activity, banners and posters plastered on every surface. People lined up to cast their votes, their faces a mixture of hope and determination. My father greeted them with folded hands, his presence a calming influence in the chaos.

The days dragged on, each hour feeling like an eternity. Time crawled by, each hour stretching endlessly. By Tuesday evening, the first results began to trickle in. We gathered in the Trivedi mansion's drawing room, the atmosphere tense and electric. My grandparents sat together, their expressions unreadable. My father paced the room, his face a mask of calm that I knew hid a storm of emotions.

When the final results were announced, the room erupted in a cacophony of emotions. My father had won by a narrow margin, a victory that felt as much a vindication as a challenge. The road ahead was uncertain, the obstacles daunting. But in that moment, as he stood before us with tears in his eyes and a smile on his lips, I knew one thing for certain: Ayodhya had chosen a man who would not just represent the town but also embody its ideals.

And so, the quiet scholar who had once lived in the shadows of history stepped into its light, carrying with him the hopes of a city yearning for unity. The journey was far from over, but it was a beginning—a chance to rewrite the story of Ayodhya, to heal its scars and honor its heritage. For my father, it was a call to *dharma*, and he answered it with all the courage and grace that defined him.

Even my mother, Yasmin Khan, who had long lived quietly on the periphery of his political world, shared in the joy of his victory. That evening, Ramesh went to see her. No words were exchanged, only a shared silence filled with pride. In that fleeting reunion, their happiness knew no bounds—a rare moment when politics bowed before something more personal and profound. When I saw them together, it felt as if time itself had softened. Her eyes, usually a bit downcast, glistened with pride. He looked lighter too, as though the burden of the campaign had lifted in her presence. For those brief moments, the years of living separate lives, of silence, melted away. Their happiness was quiet, unspoken, and complete—a reunion not of politics, but of hearts.

The election results may have brought its share of celebration, but the morning after was a stark reminder of the magnitude of the task ahead. Ayodhya woke to the promise of change, but also the entrenched realities of mistrust and despair. As the dawn broke over the city, the streets buzzed with murmurs of hope intermingled with skepticism. Victory had been achieved, but the true battle was only beginning.

The first order of business was to address the fractious elements within the political establishment itself. My father knew that his message of unity would falter if he couldn't rally the council behind him. He spent days meeting with his new team, men and women whose loyalties were as varied as their backgrounds. Some had supported him wholeheartedly; others had been part of opposing factions, but were now drawn to his leadership by the tide of public sentiment.

The council's first official meeting was a microcosm of Ayodhya's broader challenges. Voices rose in heated debate, old grievances resurfacing like wounds that refused to heal. Yet my father's presence acted as a balm, his steady demeanor diffusing tension and steering the discussion toward constructive outcomes. He emphasized the importance of addressing the immediate issues of poverty, education, and infrastructure without losing sight of the larger goal: fostering harmony.

"If we fail to work together," he told them, "it won't just be my failure or yours. It will be Ayodhya's loss. And that is something we cannot afford."

Outside the council chambers, my father's connection with the people deepened. He insisted on regular town hall meetings, where citizens shared their concerns without fear of reprisal. It was in these meetings that Ayodhya's story began to intertwine with its history.

One evening, after a particularly heated session where land disputes were the primary topic, my father asked me to walk with him by the Sarayu River. The air was cool, the river reflecting the stars like fragments of a forgotten past. It was here that Ayodhya's history felt most alive, throbbing beneath the surface.

"Do you know why Ayodhya was called the 'unconquerable city'?" my father asked as we strolled along the bank.

I shook my head, eager to hear him tell the tale.

"It wasn't just because of its walls or its warriors," he began. "It was because of its spirit—a spirit rooted in the ideals of Rama, who was not just a king but a symbol of dharma. This city was born from the union of faith and valor, from the belief that harmony is strength."

He paused, his gaze drifting across the water. "But that spirit has been eroded by centuries of conflict, by the mistrust that divides communities, by the blood that stains our soil. If we are to rebuild, we must first reclaim that spirit."

The following weeks were a whirlwind of activity. My father's administration launched initiatives aimed at bridging Ayodhya's divides. One such program focused on education, bringing children from different communities together in shared classrooms. The idea was simple but radical: that understanding begins with the young. In these schools, Hindu and Muslim children learned side by side, their laughter a testament to the potential for unity.

Another initiative revolved around restoring Ayodhya's physical heritage. The city's ancient temples and mosques, many of them neglected or damaged, became sites of joint restoration projects. Volunteers from all backgrounds worked together, their collective effort symbolizing the possibility of coexistence. It was not easy. There were moments of tension and of disagreements over historical interpretations. But the act of rebuilding itself fostered a tentative camaraderie.

Amidst these efforts, my father's resolve was tested by those who sought to undermine his vision. Opposition came not only from political rivals but also from extremist factions unwilling to relinquish their narratives of division. Threats were made, protests organized, and on one occasion, a rally descended into violence. Yet my father refused to waver.

"We must expect resistance," he told me one evening as we sat in his study. "Change is never easy. But the alternative is stagnation, and that's something Ayodhya can't afford."

As the months passed, signs of progress began to emerge. The schools saw growing enrollment, the restoration projects drew attention from across the country, and the town hall meetings became platforms for genuine dialogue. Still, the road ahead was far from smooth. Economic challenges loomed large, and the scars of past conflicts remained tender. It was during this period that I came to understand the weight my father carried. His days were consumed by meetings and decisions, his nights often spent poring over reports. Yet he never let the strain show in public. To the people of Ayodhya, he was a messenger of hope; to me, he was a reminder of the sacrifices leadership demands.

My father even envisioned a festival where Hindus and Muslims could celebrate side by side, their shared joy a powerful antidote to the divisions that had long plagued the city. The streets would be alive with color and music and the aroma of shared meals, and the festival would be a microcosm of a new Ayodhya. For some time and even as he savored in his new found political success, he was convinced that the wounds of the past were beginning to heal.

Yet even as Ayodhya took its first steps toward unity, my father knew the journey was far from over. The deeper challenges remained, of economic disparity, systemic corruption, and the lingering mistrust between communities. He often spoke of these issues with a sense of urgency, reminding his team that progress must be both visible and sustainable. One such challenge came in the form of a proposed industrial project. The plan promised jobs and infrastructure but also threatened to displace hundreds of families. The council was deeply divided, with heated arguments on both sides. My father listened to every perspective, his face a mask of calm as he weighed the options.

In the end, he made a decision that surprised many. The project would go ahead, but only after extensive measures were taken to ensure the displaced families were provided with adequate compensation and new housing. It was a compromise that satisfied no one completely, yet it underscored his commitment to balancing progress with compassion. As the year drew to a close, Ayodhya began to see the first tangible fruits of my father's leadership. The schools continued to thrive, the restored heritage sites attracted visitors and funds, and the industrial project, once a source of contention, began to generate employment. But more than these milestones, it was the city's changing spirit that stood out. There was a newfound willingness to engage, to listen, to find common ground. It wasn't universal, and it wasn't perfect, but it was a start. For the first time in decades, Ayodhya seemed to believe in the possibility of a shared future. On the anniversary of his election, my father addressed a crowd in the city square. His words were measured, his tone resolute.

"A year ago, we stood at the edge of a precipice," he began. "Today, we have taken our first steps away from it. But let us not mistake these steps for the journey's end. There is much work to be done, many challenges to overcome. Yet I believe—I believe in Ayodhya, in its people, in its spirit. Together, we can rebuild this city into the unconquerable place it once was."

The crowd erupted in applause, their faces a mixture

of hope and determination. As I stood beside him, I felt a swell of pride and a deep sense of responsibility. My father's journey was Ayodhya's journey, and its story was far from over.

One evening, I found him alone in his study, seated by the window where the light faded gently into dusk. He was holding an old photograph – of my mother, captured in a moment when her eyes gleamed with the optimism of a different, untouched time. He didn't notice me at first; his gaze was fixed, not just on the photo but on a life that should have been shared together. He had loved her fiercely, quietly, enduringly. Even in her absence, she inhabited our Trivedi mansion like a soft echo—her silence a presence that clung to the walls more firmly than her absence from our Trivedi mansion. "She would love to see this," he murmured at last, his voice brushed with both pride and a sorrow too intimate for words. "A city coming together, despite everything. But she... she now spends her time just writing." I said nothing. I simply stood there, letting the silence hold us both, letting him gather his fragile moment of reflection like a prayer he dared not speak aloud. In that quiet, I saw the weight he carried—the weight of history, of choices unspoken, of a love never extinguished. The photograph trembled slightly in his hand, as if even absence could not stay still. Outside, Ayodhya city murmured with distant life, but within that study, time had paused—for him, for her, for whatever might have been.

14

My mother, Yasmin Khan, lived her days in a cadence of chosen stillness, her life marked by long spells of solitude and the tender interludes of happy weekend visits from Ramesh Trivedi. While Ayodhya roared outside with its processions, polemics, politics, and ever-churning news cycles and debates, her small sunlit house remained untouched—a quiet outpost on a narrow lane where the days moved gently, like drifting petals. Yasmin had grown accustomed to silence—not the kind that settles after a storm, but the kind that is baked into old walls, shared glances, and half-lived lives. The house itself, with its peeling walls and iron-grilled windows, was unremarkable to the world. But for Yasmin, it was a sanctuary—its air often sweet with the smell of jasmine and marigold from potted plants she tended with the same care she gave her memories. It was in this cloistered quiet that she began to write poetry. At first, it was a way to fill the long silences, a form of release from emotions too layered for conversation. But over time, it became more than refuge—it became passion. Whether it was the alchemy of loss and longing, or an innate talent awakened late by circumstance, Yasmin's verses soon carried a voice she had never before allowed herself. On paper, she could be fierce, tender, unforgiving, brave. Her poems became the only space where she did not hesitate.

Poetry did not come to her all at once. It arrived as scribbled fragments on the margins of grocery lists, or lines murmured to herself between household chores—shy, almost embarrassed by their own existence. But with time, the act of writing became a quiet revolution. Perhaps it was a talent buried deep, dormant beneath years of compliance and routine, now blooming late, like a stubborn flower in dry soil. Or perhaps it was the world around her—so sharp in its judgments, so loud in its certainties—that drove her inward, until the only voice she could trust was her own, rising cautiously through ink. In verse, she was no longer someone's secret. She was someone becoming. In Ayodhya, stories passed through generations like heirlooms—stories about gods and wars, faith and betrayal. Yasmin had none to pass on. All she had were poems.

On most weekends, Ramesh came. His visits were brief, quiet, and coded in discretion. They didn't touch in public, rarely even indoors. He would sit on the jute mat near the window, and she would pour him tea in chipped white cups, each chip a small rebellion against perfection. Their love was real but refused to declare itself. It had learned the art of camouflage—like the dusk that entered her rooms without drawing attention. When he left, Yasmin never cried. She folded away her ache like one folds an old shawl—worn, warm, and fraying at the edges. She understood, more than he did, the price of visibility. Ayodhya's air bristled with accusation—against the impure, the ambiguous, the in-between. She lived in that in-between, and her poetry became the only language that allowed her to breathe without apology.

Poetry arrived as fragments at first—the shadow of a line while washing dishes, an image of ash and river while tying her hair. At times, it felt like a memory returning from another lifetime. Over time, the verses began to sharpen. They stopped asking for permission. They took risks. She once wrote:

> *The gods we build walls for, ask for no walls.*
> *They walk barefoot, like the poor.*

She hesitated before keeping the line. Not out of fear, but reverence—for the truth it carried and the risk it posed.

Yasmin wrote in Urdu, sometimes in Hindi, rarely in English. Language, for her, was a border she crossed with care. Her verses were never overtly political, but neither were they innocent. Beneath their softness ran a current of quiet resistance. In a city that demanded allegiance, she offered ambiguity. In a city of loud faith, she whispered doubt—not to destroy belief, but to humanize it. She did not attend congregational prayers and had stopped even venturing near a mosque, years ago. She prayed in her own way—lighting incense, reciting a line of Rumi, tying a red thread to a *neem* tree when someone fell ill. She had grown beyond the need to prove her devotion. If anything, Ayodhya had taught her that faith was best kept unspoken. Sometimes, when the air was heavy with slogans and drums from temple processions, Yasmin would close the windows and write. The city celebrated its gods with fire and spectacle. She preferred quieter gods—ones who lived in corners, who listened more than they spoke.

Ramesh understood some of this, but not all. He had

a public self, she a private one. In her presence, he softened. But she knew he returned to a world where her name could not be spoken, where history weighed too heavily on the tongue. She didn't resent him for it. Their love, after all, had never sought validation. Still, there were moments—late at night, when the street dogs quieted and the jasmine released its second breath—when she longed for a world less afraid of nuance. She sometimes imagined what her life might have been had she married him publicly, converted, shared his name. But the thought never lingered. In truth, she no longer wanted the life that had been denied to her. She had made something else—smaller, perhaps, but honest.

Her mornings began with a ritual as sacred as any prayer. She brewed a pot of *chai*, the aroma of cardamom and ginger filling her tiny kitchen, and carried her cup to the veranda where narrow shafts of sunlight would dare filter and sneak in somehow. The city's cacophony felt distant here, softened by the chirping of sparrows and the occasional rustle of leaves in the breeze. This was her time to reflect, to think of Ramesh, and to prepare herself for another day of patient waiting.

Yasmin's poetry soon became her lifeline, a thread that connected her to a world beyond the immediate realities of her existence. She wrote about love, not the fleeting kind romanticized in films, but the enduring, almost painful love that she felt for Ramesh. Her verses spoke of the bittersweetness of their shared moments, the way his laughter lingered in her mind long after he left, and the ache of knowing that their love existed in the shadows, hidden from the prying eyes of Ayodhya's conservative society.

She also wrote about the city itself, a character as alive and complex as any in her poems. Ayodhya, with its ancient temples and bustling ghats, was both a source of inspiration and a reminder of the chasm that divided her from Ramesh. She often imagined the city as a river—its waters carrying the weight of centuries of devotion and conflict, its currents strong enough to sweep people apart or bring them together. In one of her most poignant poems, she described Ayodhya as *"a land of many gods and one truth / where love, like shadows, seeks refuge in corners."*

Despite her poetry's depth and beauty, Yasmin never sought an audience beyond herself. Her words were not meant to be shared; they were her confessions, her solace, her rebellion. She kept her notebooks stacked neatly in a wooden trunk, their covers worn and their pages filled with the ink of countless sleepless nights. Occasionally, she would reread her older poems, tracing the arc of her emotions over the years and marveling at how much and how little had changed.

Weekends with Ramesh were the highlights of her life, the moments when her quiet existence burst into color. On Friday evenings, she would prepare for his arrival with a mix of anticipation and nervousness. She would cook his favorite dishes—simple yet flavorful meals of dal, rice, and spiced vegetables—and set the table with her best crockery. The jasmine flowers he tried to bring for her would find their way into a small vase at the center of the table, their fragrance mingling with the aroma of the food.

Ramesh would arrive late, his face weary from the week's battles in the political arena but his eyes lighting up as soon as he saw her. Their weekends were a world unto themselves, a fragile bubble of intimacy and joy. They spoke of everything and nothing, their conversations flowing effortlessly from politics to poetry, from dreams to fears. Yasmin often marveled at how Ramesh, who was so commanding and assertive in his public life, could be so tender and vulnerable in their private moments.

But their time together was always tinged with the knowledge that it was fleeting. On Sundays, as the afternoon sun would begin to wane, a sense of melancholy would settle over them. Ramesh would hold her close, his arms a shield against the inevitability of his departure. Yasmin never asked him to stay longer; she knew the constraints of his life, the responsibilities he bore as a politician and as a member of a deeply traditional Hindu family. She accepted their situation with a grace that belied the turmoil within her.

Her love for Ramesh was a paradox—a source of immense joy and profound sorrow. She cherished their weekends, yet each parting felt like a small death. Her poetry captured this duality, the way her heart soared and shattered in equal measure. In one of her verses, she wrote:

> *You come like the monsoon, brief and fierce*
> *Drenching my soul with your presence.*
> *But like the monsoon, you leave too soon,*
> *And I am left to gather the pieces of my*
> *drought-stricken heart.*

Despite the pain, Yasmin never regretted loving Ramesh. He was her muse, her anchor, her reason to hope. She knew their love was unconventional, even scandalous by Ayodhya's standards, but it was also real and undeniable. It gave her the strength to endure her solitude, to face the whispers and judgment that occasionally reached her ears. The city's politics often intruded into her thoughts, a stark contrast to the personal, almost sacred world she shared with Ramesh. Ayodhya was a city on the edge, its streets simmering with tensions that threatened to erupt at any moment. The disputes over religion, identity, and power seemed to mirror the struggles within her own life. She often wondered if their love would survive the city's chaos, if they would ever find a way to be together without fear or secrecy.

Ramesh, too, grappled with these questions, though he rarely voiced them. Yasmin could see the weight he carried, the burden of balancing his public duties with his private desires. She admired his ability to fight for what he believed in while protecting what they had. Yet, she also worried about the toll it took on him, the way his eyes sometimes betrayed a weariness that no amount of rest could cure.

As the years went by, their relationship deepened, even as the challenges grew. Yasmin found herself writing more about the future, about the possibilities and uncertainties that lay ahead. Her poetry became a chronicle of their journey, a testament to their love and the strength it required. She began to imagine a life where they could be together openly, where their weekends would no longer be stolen moments but part of a shared everyday existence. But even as she dreamed of such a life, Yasmin remained rooted in the present, in the reality of their situation. She knew that love was not always enough to overcome the barriers of society, tradition, and politics. Yet, she refused to let despair take hold. She chose to believe in the power of their connection, in the possibility of a future where their love would be recognized and celebrated.

Yasmin's poetry, her weekends with Ramesh, and her quiet life became her way of resisting the forces that sought to confine her. She knew her life was far from perfect, that her love for Ramesh was fraught with challenges, but she also knew it was real and worth fighting for. She was not a revolutionary in the conventional sense, but her existence, her love, and her art were acts of defiance against a world that tried to dictate how she should live and whom she should love. In her own way, she was carving out a space for herself, a space where she could be true to her heart and her soul. Her poetry was not well-known. Each morning, Yasmin rose with the sun, swept the courtyard, lit a lamp, and watered the single *tulsi* plant that grew defiantly in the cracked pot by her door. This, too, was a ritual. Not religious. Not political. Just human. And each night, she wrote. Sometimes in verse, sometimes just a line or two. Words gave her what no one else could—presence. Not as someone's secret, not as someone's shame. Just herself. Unadorned, unclaimed, and alive.

Yasmin's mother, Amina Khan's passing left a deep toll on my mother. The days that followed Amina Khan's death were a blur, each moment stretching on endlessly, each breath a struggle for Yasmin to take. The air, once thick with her mother's presence, now felt empty, as though the walls had absorbed Amina's warmth and love and now stood cold and indifferent. It had come so suddenly—her mother's illness, the way her energy seemed to drain from her as if life itself was quietly slipping away. Amina had been ill for some time, but she had always been a withdrawn woman wallowing in her silence that Yasmin had believed she would outlast anything, even the relentless passage of time. But that final day, the breath in Amina's chest had faltered. She had lingered for hours in that fragile state, as if waiting for something, for some unseen force to bring her back, but it was not to be.

Yasmin had been holding her mother's hand when she had let go, her fingers slipping from hers as Amina exhaled one last time, softly, almost imperceptibly, as if slipping into sleep, her exhale soft and near imperceptible. It was as though her mother had been waiting for the right moment—perhaps for Yasmin to be with her, perhaps for the silence to be perfect, to let go without a single word of resistance. Amina's death was not dramatic, not filled with the chaos of screaming or pleading, but a quiet surrender to the inevitable, the only kind of death that seemed worthy of the woman Yasmin had always known. Though Amina had been ailing for some time, Yasmin had always imagined her to be indestructible, a woman who had learned to inhabit silence so thoroughly that she seemed beyond the reach of death. Her withdrawal had not felt like decay, but endurance. Even the slow draining of her vitality hadn't prepared Yasmin for the final breath, that fragile moment when life gently recoiled and departed. Amina had not raged against her end. It was, Yasmin later thought, a death in keeping with her life—quiet, unceremonious, dignified.

The moment she had passed, Yasmin felt something in her chest tighten, a pang of unbearable loss, and then a deep hollowing. Her mother, who had been the source of everything—of silent love, silent wisdom, and a silent strength—was no longer there. Yasmin was left with an overwhelming emptiness, as though a great piece of her had been carved out, leaving behind only fragments of memories that felt too distant to grasp.

Yasmin stood by her mother's body, her fingers lightly tracing the edges of the embroidered shawl that Amina had worn so many times. The room was heavy with the silence that followed death, a silence that had settled over everything, thick and oppressive. Outside, the world went on, the birds chirping, the wind rustling the leaves, unaware of the great void that had opened in Yasmin's heart. Yet, what stood out starkly in the stillness of the room was not just the death of Amina—it was the absence of those who should have been there, those whose presence would have once been expected in such a moment. Yasmin looked at the door, half expecting to hear the familiar creak of the hinges, the sound of someone walking in. But no one came. Not her husband, Ramesh. Not her father, Adil Khan. And as time passed, not a single member of Amina's family or Adil Khan's side of the family either.

It was as though the world had conspired to rob her of the simple dignity of shared grief, as though her mother's death had been a thing too small for anyone else to acknowledge.

Yasmin's mind flickered to her childhood, to memories of family gatherings when her mother had been the center of it all—her laughter, her advice, her presence that had made everything feel anchored. Amina had held the threads of the family in her hands, weaving connections between people, holding grudges at bay, and smoothing over differences with the quiet wisdom of someone who understood that life was too short for petty disagreements. Yasmin's mother had been the glue that kept the fragile and frayed edges of family ties together. But no one came to mourn the woman who had once held them all together. It was not just absence. It was erasure. As if Amina's death were too inconsequential to mark. As if a woman who had once been Uma—who had given up her Hindu identity for love—no longer fit within the mythology of either family.

In the aftermath of Amina's death, no one came to comfort her, no one to lend a shoulder to cry on. Her father, Adil Khan, had not shown up. His absence was, in a way, expected. His relationship with Amina had never been one of warmth after their young son Aarif's death. Though they had once shared a life together, their union had ended long ago, tangled in silences that had stretched over the years. He had distanced himself from

Amina after their separation, choosing a different path, one that did not include her. Yasmin had grown accustomed to the fact that her father never visited her and his wife, Amina, though she never fully understood why. The absence of Adil Khan, my maternal grandfather, cut deep into my mother, Yasmin's psyche. Adil Khan had once been a towering figure in their lives, a man whose name was now spoken with reverence in political circles, whose opinions held weight even among those who didn't fully agree with him. He had been the patriarch of the family, and Amina had always been his legal wife. Yet, despite this status, Adil Khan did not show up. Yasmin had never been close to her father after her brother had been killed. They had grown apart over the years due to the quiet political and ideological rifts that had formed between their worlds. But still, she had expected him to be there. She had hoped for some sign of acknowledgement, some gesture of support in this moment of overwhelming loss. Instead, there was only silence, a silence that gnawed at her soul and left her feeling abandoned by the very roots of her heritage.

The grief that accompanied her mother, Amina's death was compounded by this isolation. Yasmin felt as though she were floating in an abyss, untethered from anything solid. She had always believed in the strength of family, in the idea that, no matter how far apart people might drift, death would always bring them back together. But this—this was different. Her mother had died, and no one had come to mourn her. No one had come to show their respect for the woman who had lived with such quiet dignity, surrounded by complete silence. Yasmin's heart ached with a pain she couldn't name, a sorrow so deep that it felt like a black hole inside her, swallowing everything in its path. She stood at the edge of the grave, her heart heavy with a mixture of grief and bitterness. She thought of her mother's life—how she had once been the one to offer understanding, to provide a safe haven for those who needed it. Yasmin could still hear her mother's voice, soft and comforting, telling her that family was everything. But in this moment, it felt as though her mother's death had revealed the truth—that family was only something people clung to when it suited them, when there was something to be gained, something to be shared. In the end, when it really mattered, when the one person who had held everything together was gone, there was only silence. Yasmin knew that Amina had given up her Hindu religion, and had once been Uma. The absence of any of her Hindu relatives had hurt Amina like a knife, though she was not there to feel its sharpness any more.

The silence at the funeral was deafening. When the time came to say goodbye, there was no one but Yasmin and a handful of elderly mourners to offer the final prayers, to perform the rituals that would send her mother's spirit on its journey. Her father Adil Khan's s absence was expected, but it felt like a betrayal. Had he forgotten that Amina was still his wife? Was she now a mere memory to be swept away, relegated to the background of a life that no longer mattered?

My father, Ramesh Trivedi arrived quietly at Amina Khan's funeral, his presence not unnoticed amid the few mourners. He had not been expected to attend. But in this moment, his presence, though understated, spoke volumes. Yasmin, numb from the overwhelming loss of her mother, caught a glimpse of him standing at the edge of the gathering, his expression somber, his hands folded in a quiet gesture of respect. There were no grand gestures, no attempts to console, no words that might have brought relief or closure. Ramesh did not approach Yasmin directly or make any attempts to draw attention to himself. Instead, he stood in the background, silently paying his respects in the way he knew best—through his presence, calm and unassuming. Yasmin noticed him there, standing alone under the tree, the weight of the weekends they had spent together lingering, an unspoken bond. Although they had lived separate lives for years, and though their lives had been marked by silences and gaps, there was something in his quiet arrival that stirred something deep within Yasmin. Amina Khan's death had not erased the fact that, in some ways, he would always be her closest companion, the father of her child, the man she had shared her life with. In the silence of her grief, she felt a strange comfort in his proximity, as though, despite everything, he still understood her loss in a way no one else could.

In the months that followed, Ramesh's visits became more frequent. Each time he came, it was as though he was testing the waters, unsure of how to navigate the delicate balance between obligation and emotional distance. He would come in the early evenings, quietly entering her home with a simple gesture—a cup of tea, a small gift, or just a silent offering of his company. Yasmin did not ask him why he had started to visit more often; she didn't need to. In some unspoken way, she knew it was his way of acknowledging his increasing absences that now loomed between them, his attempt to reach across the increasing gulf that had grown between them as his political life had become more intense .

Their conversations, though infrequent, were never heavy or laden with any unresolved emotions. Ramesh spoke in the same calm, measured tone he always had, offering no grand displays of emotion, but simply being there, a quiet presence in the wake of her mother's death. Yasmin found solace in these visits, though she couldn't fully understand them. In the quiet exchange of words and the shared silences, a subtle healing began to take place. Perhaps it was the loss of her mother, Amina, or perhaps it was the passage of time, but Ramesh's more frequent visits started to fill a void Yasmin hadn't realized was there. It was not the return of their love that was always there, but something softer—a mutual respect born of shared history and the understanding that life, in its strange way, had a way of bringing people back together.

As the days passed, Yasmin found herself retreating into herself, her emotions too raw and too complicated to express. She could not bring herself to speak to anyone, to explain the ache in her chest, the confusion in her mind. How could she explain to others the deep betrayal her mother, Amina must have felt? How could she explain the anger that simmered beneath her grief and her life-long silence, the frustration at being abandoned at such a fragile time? Her mother had given everything to her family, and in the end, she had been met with indifference. The isolation she had felt was not just emotional, but also physical. No one had cared for or understood the depth of her loss. No one had understood that her life long silence was not just the loss of a son, but also the loss of a world she had known, a world where family was a refuge, a constant. She had been left to navigate the sea of her emotions alone, with no one to anchor her.

After her mother's death, Yasmin too found herself questioning everything—her relationship with and her memories of her father, Adil Khan, and the very foundation of family. What did it mean to be part of a family if, when the time came, no one but Ramesh came to stand by her side? What did it mean to be loved if, in your most vulnerable moment, you were left to face it all alone? Amina's grief slowly morphed into Yasmin's grief and that became her silent companion, one that she could not escape. There were no comforting words, no arms to hold her as she cried. Her heart, once full of love and warmth, now felt cold, hardened by the betrayal of those who should have cared. Her father, Adil Khan, had chosen his distance and maybe, his pride. No one but Ramesh had chosen to be there for her, and in the process, Yasmin began to feel the weight of an inescapable loneliness, as though the ties that had bound her to her family were slowly unraveling, thread by thread. Yet in the midst of this silence, something else began to stir within Yasmin. As the days wore on and the world continued its march forward, she began to understand something crucial—that her mother's life, and by extension, her death, was not defined by the absence of others. Amina had never needed the approval or validation of anyone, least of all the family members who had turned their backs on her in the end. Amina's life had been full in her silence.

As Yasmin began to process the layers of her grief, she started to write more intensely. Her words became a way to reclaim her mother's memory, to make sense of the silence that had swallowed them both. She wrote of the betrayal, of the absence, but she also wrote of the strength that Amina's silence had embodied in life, the strength that Yasmin had inherited. And slowly, as her pen moved across the paper, Yasmin began to find her way back to herself, to a place where she could honor her mother's memory without relying on the empty gestures of those who had failed her. Her mother was gone, but the silent love Amina had passed on to her would never fade. The silence of her family's absence could not erase the truth: Amina had lived a life of purpose, and Yasmin would carry that purpose forward, with or without the support of the people who should have been there. The family that had once seemed like a fortress in her youth had proven to be fragile, but Yasmin, in the depths of her grief, had found the strength to stand alone. The small house, which had once upon a time, only echoed with the comfort of Amina's steady and silent presence, now seemed oppressive. The days felt interminable, as though she were moving through a thick fog, unable to find a way through it. Yasmin sought solace in the quietest of spaces. The world around her felt alien and loud, too full of life for her to bear. She found herself retreating to her mother's room, a sanctuary of soft colors and memories, the space where Amina had spent her final days. The bed still smelled faintly of Amina's skin smells, and the wooden shelves were lined with books that she had once dusted carefully, now left untouched. It was here that Yasmin let her tears flow freely. They came in torrents, as if her very soul was being torn open, the flood of emotions too vast to contain. In the midst of this weeping, something else stirred within her—a need to give shape to the grief, to record it in some way, to hold onto the essence of her mother. The act of writing became a compulsion, a necessity. Yasmin had been writing poetry, but never had her words been driven by such raw, urgent emotion. She began with simple lines, barely coherent, as though her fingers were racing to keep up with the flood of thoughts that rushed through her mind. She could no longer speak the words that needed to be said, so she wrote them instead. She wrote of Amina's unspoken wisdom that had guided Yasmin through her own life. She wrote of the moments they had shared—of the countless afternoons spent in companionable silence, of the times they had laughed together over trivial things, of the times Amina had held her in the stillness of the night, offering nothing but the warmth of her presence. Her poetry captured the weight of her sorrow, as if trying to etch the memory of her mother into the pages so that it would never fade. Each line Yasmin wrote was a piece of her heart laid bare on the page. There was no formality to it, no striving for perfection—just a raw, primal need to express what could not be contained. She wrote to honor her mother, to memorialize her, to create something tangible out of the intangible absence that now defined her world.

As the days passed, Yasmin's writing grew more structured, her thoughts taking shape, her grief coalescing into something she could hold onto. She wrote of the quiet beauty in her mother's life, how Amina had lived with a silent dignity that was never ostentatious but deeply rooted in the smallest acts of kindness. Yasmin began to write about the things they had shared, the rituals that now felt sacred in their absence. The quiet rituals of tea in the mornings, the long evenings spent reading, the silent prayers that Amina had said each night, words Yasmin had never understood fully but had always respected. One evening, as Yasmin sat in the stillness of the room, she wrote:

> *The silence now is louder than any voice,*
> *Each room echoes with memories we made,*
> *But your absence is not empty*
> *It is filled with the weight of love, a love that is endless,*
> *Even in death, I find you in every breath I take.*

Her grief began to take on a form of its own, something she could look at and understand. Her tears, though still frequent, were no longer simply expressions of sorrow; they became the ink with which she wrote about her mother. Every tear that fell was a verse in a larger poem about her silent and silenced mother. As Yasmin wrote, she understood that her mother would never truly be gone. Amina's life had been woven into every fiber of Yasmin's being, and though she had left this world, her influence would endure. Yasmin's poetry became an extension of her own grieving, a means of preserving Amina's spirit in a way that nothing else could. The more she wrote, the more she understood: her mother had not left her. She would live on in every word Yasmin penned, in every memory that whispered in the corners of her heart. In time, Yasmin came to realize that the depth of her loss was matched only by the depth of the love that had existed between them—a love that had never required words but had been spoken in every glance, every gesture, every moment of shared life. Writing those verses was the only way Yasmin knew how to honor that love, and it was in doing so that she found a way to live with the loss, not as an absence, but as a presence that would always be with her.

Over time though, the focus of Yasmin's poetry began to shift. Her pen, once consumed with her own emotions and her love for her mother or for Ramesh, turned outward, seeking new subjects and stories. She found herself drawn to the lives of Muslim women who had lived in Ayodhya across centuries. It began almost accidentally, with a line she wrote about silenced women who lived in the shadows of history: "*We carry the weight of the ages, / Our voices unheard, our stories untold. / Yet in the folds of our silence, / A thousand songs lie waiting to be sung.*" This verse led her to reflect on the lives of women who, like her, had lived in Ayodhya, navigating love, faith, and identity within the constraints of their times. She began to imagine the courtyards of Mughal-era homes, where women veiled their faces and their dreams, and the bustling bazaars where whispers of rebellion might have echoed behind intricate *jalis*. She wrote about the nameless women who prayed in seclusion, their faith both a source of strength and a symbol of the worlds they could not fully inhabit. Her poems gave voice to the inner lives of Muslim women, capturing their struggles and quiet victories across generations. She wrote about Zainab, a sixteenth century poet who penned couplets in the margins of her husband's ledgers, and about Noor, a young bride in 1857 who witnessed the first sparks of rebellion against the British. She imagined the grief of Ayesha, whose husband died in the riots of 1949, and the determination of Fatima, a schoolteacher in the 1980s who taught her daughters to dream beyond the walls of their home. Each poem was a window into a world Yasmin could only glimpse through the fragments of history and her own imagination.

Yet, as she wrote, she felt a kinship with these women, a sense of shared silence and defiance. She saw herself in their stories, in their courage to love and to hope despite the constraints imposed upon them. Her poetry also began to explore the intersections of faith and identity, the ways in which religion shaped and was shaped by the lives of these women. She wrote about the rituals that bound them to their communities and the moments of rebellion that set them apart. She celebrated their strength and questioned the systems that sought to confine them, her verses carrying a quiet yet powerful critique of the forces that sought to erase their individuality. As Yasmin delved deeper into these stories, her poetry became a bridge between the past and the present, a way of understanding her own place in the world. She saw Ayodhya not just as a city of temples and politics but as a living, breathing entity shaped by the lives of countless women like herself. She began to feel a sense of purpose, a belief that her words could give voice to the silenced, that her poetry could preserve the stories that history often forgot.

The shift in Yasmin's poetry did not go unnoticed.

Ramesh, who read her verses during their weekends together, was struck by the depth and breadth of her new work. He marveled at her ability to capture the essence of lives so different from her own, to breathe life into the shadows of history. Her poems, he told her, were not just beautiful but important, a poetic record of women's lives across time. For Yasmin, this shift in her poetry was both a revelation and a release. It allowed her to move beyond her own pain, to channel her emotions into something larger than herself. It gave her a sense of connection to the women who had come before her and the women who would follow, a belief that their stories mattered and deserved to be told. And so, Yasmin continued to write, her pen tracing the contours of Ayodhya's history and the lives of its women. Her words blossomed quietly yet profoundly, jasmine like.

15

I Saanvi Trivedi, on the other hand, grew up in the sprawling grandeur of the Trivedi Mansion, a structure as grand as it was steeped in contradictions. Situated in the heart of Ayodhya, the mansion was an intricate blend of opulent facades and hidden sorrows. My father, Ramesh Trivedi, a formidable politician by the time I had entered my teens, presided over it all with a stern yet loving demeanor after my paternal grandfather, Shyam Trivedi, died suddenly of a heart attack. Our Trivedi Mansion still rose with quiet authority, shaped by their ambitions, its white marble pillars, expansive courtyard, and rooms that stretched beyond the reach of my childhood gaze. It was both my fortress and my gilded cage.

From the moment I could understand, I knew that my family was different. My mother, Yasmin Khan, lived outside these walls, her presence more a whispered memory than a constant reality. I met her on weekends when I was home for the holidays, a rendezvous that my father facilitated with a strict sense of decorum. These meetings, fleeting yet filled with warmth, were held away from prying eyes. Yasmin lived in a modest house, her life worlds apart from the grandeur of the mansion. I always thought of her as a soft yet steadfast presence, in stark contrast to my father's gentle yet commanding presence. My father's decision to keep my mother out of the public eye was a reflection of the society we lived in. In Ayodhya, where religion and politics were intertwined, the revelation of my mother's Muslim identity could have threatened his career and the carefully constructed facade of our family. Thus, my childhood was marked by a delicate balancing act—living within the walls of a Hindu patriarch's house while secretly carrying the bloodline of two faiths.

The mansion was my playground and my prison, a world within itself. Its high walls shielded me from the outside world, but they also confined me to a life of strict expectations. The mornings began with the ringing of the temple bells, a ritual my father insisted on. I would sit cross-legged beside him as the priest chanted Sanskrit verses, my hands folded in prayer, though my thoughts often wandered. The afternoons were reserved for tutors, who drilled me in academics, etiquette, and the history of our family—a lineage that my father believed was unblemished until I came along.

Despite its grandeur, the mansion often felt empty. My father's political engagements kept him away for long hours, leaving me in the care of servants or my doting grandmother. My paternal grandfather was a part of my life, and yet too involved in his legal career. The staff, though dutiful, maintained a certain distance, aware of their place in the hierarchy. My companions would soon become my books, the stories of western women, brave heroines and mythical beings offering me a solace that the echoing halls could not.

On the weekends when I visited Yasmin, the world

transformed. She would greet me with open arms, her eyes lighting up with a joy that was absent in the mansion. Her house, though modest, was filled with warmth. The scent of cardamom tea and freshly baked *parathas* would waft through the air, and the walls were adorned with Islamic calligraphy that my grandfather, Adil Khan, had left behind. Here, I was not Saanvi Trivedi, the daughter of a politician, but simply her daughter. My mother, Yasmin's poems fascinated me. She never spoke ill of her own missing father, Adil Khan, though I sensed the silent pain of her separation. She would stroke my hair and say, "You are the bridge, Saanvi. Between two worlds, two hearts." These visits, however, were shrouded in secrecy. My father's instructions were clear: no word of my mother was to reach the public or even the extended family. It was a heavy burden for a child, to love in fragments and to carry the weight of adult decisions.

When I turned eleven, my father decided that it was time for me to leave the mansion. He believed that a boarding school in the Himalayas would provide me with the discipline and education befitting a Trivedi. The school, nestled amidst pine forests and snow-capped peaks, was a world away from the chaos of Ayodhya.

At first, I resented the decision. The journey to the school was long, and as the train chugged through the winding tracks, I clutched the edges of my seat, dreading the unfamiliar. The campus was beautiful, with stone buildings that looked like they had leapt out of an English novel. The air was crisp, carrying the scent of pine and promise. But it was not home. The initial days were lonely. The other children, with their carefree laughter and tight-knit friendships, seemed foreign to me. I was the girl from Ayodhya, from a socially prominent and powerful family. And yet, I carried an unspoken secret that made me different. Slowly, I found my footing. The school library became my sanctuary, its shelves offering an escape into worlds where I could be anyone but myself.

Life at the boarding school taught me a lot, including patience. I learned to wake up to the chill of the Himalayan mornings, to trek through trails for Botany lessons, and to find comfort in phone calls from my father and rare greeting cards from my mother. The distance from the Trivedi Mansion and Yasmin's home gave me a perspective I had never known. It was in those moments of solitude, sitting on a rock overlooking the valley, that I began to piece together my identity. I realized that I was not just the daughter of Ramesh Trivedi or Yasmin Khan. I was Saanvi Trivedi, a bridge between two worlds, carrying the legacies of two faiths, two families, and two dreams. The mountains, with their unwavering strength and quiet grace, became my metaphor. Like them, I would stand tall, weathering the storms and basking in the sunlight of understanding. Looking back, I see my childhood as a mosaic of contrasts. The opulence of the Trivedi Mansion and the modesty of Yasmin's home, the rituals of Hinduism and the wisdom of Islam, the confinement of expectations and the freedom of self-discovery—each piece shaped the person I am today. The journey from the gilded halls of Ayodhya to the serene heights of the Himalayas was not just a physical one but a spiritual odyssey.

My story is not just my own. It is a reflection of the many children caught between worlds, carrying the weight of their parents' choices while forging their own paths. It reveals the layered nature of identity and the persistent search for belonging. As I write these memories, I do so with a clear awareness of the duality that shaped my upbringing. It taught me to see the world through multiple lenses, to grapple with differences, and not to reject the contradictions that make life so profoundly human. And so, I remain, Saanvi Trivedi, a child of two hearts, two worlds, and infinite possibilities.

The boarding school in the Himalayas was my sanctuary—a world apart from the simmering tension and relentless scrutiny that my father, Ramesh Trivedi, faced in Ayodhya. Nestled among pine forests and shrouded in mist, the school's ancient stone buildings offered me refuge, their halls resonating with the sound of laughter and the sharp crack of discipline. Here, I could momentarily escape the visible weight of my family's legacy—the rituals, the expectations. But the serene surroundings only made me more aware of the unresolved tensions within me. For even in this idyllic setting, Ayodhya's shadow loomed—its history, its controversies, and its indelible mark on my family's life never far behind.

Ayodhya was more than a city to me. It was an idea, a conflict, a memory, woven into my very identity. It was where my father's voice carried over rally crowds, where whispers of secrets intertwined with the chants of pilgrims. Its legacy shaped me in ways I could not yet fully comprehend, demanding that I confront both its grandeur and its pain. My earliest recollections of it were fragmented yet vivid: the towering ghats along the Sarayu River, the ceaseless chants of pilgrims, and the ever-present tension that seemed to grip the air like a vice. Ayodhya was where my father had risen to prominence as a politician, his fiery speeches about cultural heritage and integrity earning him both admiration and enemies. It was also where his deepest secrets lay buried, like the layers of history beneath its soil.

In the Himalayas, however, I was Saanvi Trivedi—just another girl in a sea of plaid uniforms and carelessly tied shoelaces. My days blended into a rhythm of study and camaraderie, punctuated by fleeting moments of solitude that gave me space to question who I was outside the shadow of Ayodhya. The school's curriculum was rigorous, its ethos steeped in discipline and the pursuit of excellence. But for me, it was the library that held the greatest allure. Row upon row of dusty tomes beckoned me, their pages promising escape and discovery. I devoured books on philosophy, history, and mythology, often losing myself in tales of ancient civilizations and their rise and fall.

It was in the library that I first stumbled upon a collection of essays about Ayodhya. In a quiet corner surrounded by the thick smell of aged paper, I was drawn to the essays' vivid depictions of the city's layered past. They felt like an invitation—a way to untangle the threads of history that had bound my family and me to this enigmatic place. Written by historians, archaeologists, and poets, the essays painted a picture of a city that was at once ancient and ageless, a crucible of faiths and ideologies. I learned about its early days as Saket, a flourishing city in the ancient Kosala kingdom, and its evolution into a sacred site revered by Hindus, Jains, Buddhists—and later, by Muslims after the Babri Masjid was built there.

The essays spoke of the Ramayana's portrayal of Ayodhya as the birthplace of Lord Rama, an idealized kingdom where dharma and justice reigned supreme. The story of Ayodhya begins not with bricks or mortar but with whispers from an ancient past. Its origins are entwined with mythology and history, a cradle where faiths were born and empires flourished. Situated on the banks of the Sarayu River, Ayodhya is celebrated in the Ramayana as the birthplace of Lord Rama, the seventh incarnation of Vishnu, whose life and deeds continue to shape India's spiritual and cultural consciousness.

The name "Ayodhya" itself is poetic. Derived from Sanskrit, it means "A place that cannot be conquered," a city fortified not only by physical walls but also by divine blessings. Ancient texts describe it as a city of unparalleled beauty, adorned with golden palaces, lush gardens, and streets bustling with joy. The Ramayana paints Ayodhya as an idyllic kingdom ruled by King Dasharatha, whose lineage and legacy became synonymous with dharma, or righteousness.

Yet, Ayodhya's story does not belong solely to myth. Archaeological evidence and historical accounts reveal a city that has witnessed centuries of cultural exchanges, invasions, and transformations. During the Gupta dynasty, Ayodhya flourished as a center of learning and spirituality. Buddhist stupas and Jain temples adorned its landscape, making it a melting pot of religious ideas. Chinese travelers like Fa-Hien and Xuanzang wrote of its grandeur, documenting its prominence as a cultural hub.

The medieval period saw Ayodhya transform once more. The Mughal Empire, under Babur, left its mark on the city with the construction of the Babri Masjid. According to some historical and local accounts, the mosque was built atop a pre-existing Hindu temple, allegedly marking the birthplace of Lord Rama. This act, though rooted in the politics of the time, added another layer to Ayodhya's complex identity. The mosque stood as a symbol of Mughal architectural influence but also as a harbinger of discord, foreshadowing the communal tensions that would erupt centuries later.

For me, Ayodhya's history is more than a collection of dates and events. It is a living entity, its essence interwoven with the lives of its people. The Sarayu River, with its gentle flow, carries the stories of sages and saints who once meditated on its banks. The temples, both ancient and modern, resonate with prayers that span generations. The streets, though now crowded with pilgrims and tourists, still echo the footsteps of Rama, Sita, and Lakshmana.

But the narrative grew darker as it approached the present day. The construction of the Babri Masjid in 1528, the claims of a pre-existing Hindu temple at the site, and the bloody riots that erupted after its demolition in 1992 were all laid bare. The city's history was a layered story of coexistence and conflict, its threads fraying under the weight of political and religious ambitions. Reading about Ayodhya in the quiet solitude of the library, I felt an ache that was both personal and profound. This was my father's battleground, the arena where his integrity and identity were constantly tested.

Yet, Ayodhya was also where my mother, Yasmin Khan, had once dreamed of building a life with my father. Their love story had always been one of whispered promises and clandestine meetings, a bond forged in defiance of societal norms. My mother had believed in the possibility of a shared future, but Ayodhya had other plans. Its divisions had seeped into their relationship, forcing them apart and leaving me to straddle the chasm between their worlds.

In the boarding school, I often found myself grappling with questions of identity. Who was I, really? The daughter of a Hindu politician or the child of a Muslim woman who had been relegated to the margins of my life? The history of Ayodhya mirrored my own inner turmoil, its layers of faith and conflict reflecting the complexity of my existence.

It was during a history class that I decided to explore these questions more deeply. Our teacher, Mr. Bhattacharya, had assigned us a project on the cultural heritage of our hometowns. While my classmates chose topics like Jaipur's palaces or Varanasi's ghats, I chose

Ayodhya. It was a decision that surprised even me, for I had always tried to distance myself from the city and its burdens. But something within me yearned to understand it—and, by extension, myself.

My research took me beyond the library and into conversations with my father. During my visits home, I would sit in his study, surrounded by stacks of papers and the smell of ink, and the soft hum of his laptop resting on the desk. Occasionally, he would glance at it, perhaps to check an email or review a draft, but our conversations always took precedence. At first, he was reluctant to share, his politician's caution keeping him guarded. But as I persisted, aided by the growing accessibility of information and the occasional mention of facts I had found online, his defenses began to crumble.

"Ayodhya is not just a place, Saanvi," he told me one evening, his voice heavy with emotion. "It is an idea—a symbol of hope and conflict, unity and division. It is a reflection of who we are as a people."

He spoke of his early days in politics, of fiery debates and tireless campaigns. He spoke of the demolition of the Babri Masjid on the day of my birth, and the riots that followed, events that had left scars on the city and its people. He spoke of his own struggles to balance his personal beliefs with the expectations of his constituents. And, for the first time, he spoke of my mother—of their love and the sacrifices it had demanded.

"Your mother and I dreamed of a different Ayodhya," he said, his eyes glistening with unshed tears. "An Ayodhya where our love could thrive, where our differences would not matter. But dreams have a way of slipping through your fingers."

His words stayed with me as I delved deeper into Ayodhya's history. I learned about the archaeological excavations that had unearthed remnants of ancient structures beneath the Babri Masjid site, each discovery adding fuel to the contentious debate. I read about the court cases, the political machinations, and the efforts at reconciliation that had faltered time and again. Ayodhya was a microcosm of India itself, its history a mirror to the nation's triumphs and tragedies.

Back in school, my project began to take shape. I framed Ayodhya not just as a city, but as a metaphor for the complexities of identity and belonging. Drawing from both mythological accounts and contemporary struggles, I crafted a narrative that mirrored my own splintered sense of self, using Ayodhya as both a lens and a mirror. I juxtaposed its mythological significance with its contemporary realities, weaving in personal anecdotes and reflections. The project became a labor of love, a way of bridging the gap between my two worlds.

But it also stirred unrest. Some of my classmates questioned my choice of topic, their whispers tinged with suspicion. "Why Ayodhya?" they would ask. "Isn't that place too controversial?" Their skepticism mirrored the larger societal divisions that Ayodhya represented. Yet, their doubts only strengthened my resolve. If Ayodhya was controversial, it was because it mattered. And if it mattered, it deserved to be understood.

As I presented my project to the class, I felt a sense of clarity that had eluded me for years. Ayodhya was not just a battleground of ideologies; it was a place of dreams and despair, of faith and fragility. It was a place where my father's ambitions and my mother's hopes had collided, leaving me to pick up the pieces and forge my own path.

The presentation earned me both praise and criticism, but it also sparked dialogue. My classmates began to see Ayodhya not just as a headline, but as a human story. They asked questions, shared their own perspectives, and, for a brief moment, the walls of prejudice seemed to crumble. In the months that followed, I found myself returning to my own hometown Ayodhya more out of intellectual curiosity. I walked its streets, visited its temples and mosques, and listened to the stories of its people. I met priests who spoke of devotion and harmony, and activists who fought for justice and equality. I saw the city through their eyes, its layers unfolding like the pages of a book. It was during one of my visits to my mother that I stumbled upon an old photo album tucked away in her bedroom. Inside were photographs of my parents in Lucknow and Ayodhya, their smiles luminous with the promise of a future they once believed in. In one image, they stood hand in hand by the Sarayu River; in another, their faces shimmered with the gentle light of a thousand *diyas* by the ghats, caught in a moment of quiet joy. The images spoke of a love that had defied the odds, even if they had not lived together in the same house as husband and wife. Holding the album, I felt a surge of determination. Ayodhya's history was not just about division; it was also about the possibility of reconciliation. And if the city could hold on to its dreams despite its scars, so could I.

The boarding school in the Himalayas had given me the tools to question, to explore, and to understand. Ayodhya had given me the context to apply them. Together, they had shaped me into who I was: Saanvi Trivedi, a daughter of two worlds, a seeker of truth, and a believer in the power of stories to heal. As I prepared to graduate, I knew that my journey with Ayodhya was far from over. The city's history was still unfolding, its layers still revealing themselves. And in its story, I could also situate my own—a story of dual identity, of dual belonging, and the dual courage to bridge the divides within and around me.

"My path from high school to Oxford was shaped with

intention, though it grew from the unrest of my upbringing and the delicate fractures in my family's past. It was a carefully cultivated dream, though its roots were entangled with my tumultuous upbringing and the fragile threads of my family's history. I, Saanvi, had spent my teenage years ensconced in the misty isolation of a boarding school perched high in the Himalayas. This school, a world apart from the political intrigue of Ayodhya, seemed almost like a retreat ordained by destiny to prepare me for the storm that awaited me beyond its serene walls. It was there that my fascination with political history and journalism first began to bloom, as naturally as the rhododendrons that painted the hillsides every spring. It was there that the seeds of my cultural curiosity and psycho-history had been sown.

In the quiet corners of the school library, I had devoured books that others might have considered too dense or tedious for a young girl. From the monumental history of empires to the gritty narratives of resistance and revolution, each page whispered secrets of power and betrayal. My fascination, however, didn't end with the dusty pages of books. After school, I would retreat to my personal computer, its dial-up connection a gateway to a world of knowledge. There, I poured over online archives, news articles, and political essays, piecing together patterns and perspectives that books alone could not provide. The whir of the modem and the click of keys became as familiar as the rustle of pages, and my searches often led me to insights I could not find in print. I had an insatiable curiosity about the mechanisms that shaped nations, and my father's shadow loomed large over this fascination. His presence was a constant reminder that the history I was so passionate about wasn't confined to the past—it was being made every day, and he was a part of it.

Ramesh, my father, was no ordinary politician. He embodied contradictions—a staunch advocate for Hindu values, yet a man burdened by the ghosts of a love he could never forsake. The pieces of his concealed relationship with my mother, Yasmin—a Muslim woman whose presence in his life was a closely guarded secret—formed an unspoken narrative that became a prism through which I viewed the world: fragmented, intricate, complex, and frequently marked by hypocrisy. It compelled me to question everything I encountered, from the rhetoric of leaders to the fine print of history, seeking hidden truths beneath surface-level narratives. I began to unravel the layers of carefully constructed stories, noticing how they often veiled uncomfortable realities. My teachers at the boarding school frequently remarked on my ability to dissect issues with a sharp and unrelenting focus, observing how I could pick apart even the most carefully crafted arguments and uncover their contradictions. The debate society became my laboratory, where I tested ideas, honed my logic, and learned the art of persuasion. It was here, amidst fierce discussions and heated exchanges, that I discovered not just the power of words but the responsibility that came with them—how they could shape perceptions, alter decisions, and even sway hearts and minds.

The day the acceptance letter from Oxford arrived, it felt as though the universe had conspired to validate my aspirations. The pristine envelope bore the crest of the university, and its contents promised not just an education but an awakening. My chosen program, a dual focus on political history and investigative journalism, was renowned for its rigor. Oxford would demand everything I had to give and more. My father, despite his political acumen and his earlier life as an academic, seemed uneasy about my ambitions. "Why dig into the past like I too did?" he asked one evening, his voice laced with a quiet apprehension. "The present is what shapes us." I often wonder if he was truly cautioning me, or simply testing my resolve.

"The present is the past speaking," I countered, my tone firm. "We can't understand one without the other." Perhaps he saw too much of himself in me—the same stubbornness, the same thirst for truth. Though he didn't openly oppose my decision, his silence spoke volumes. My mother, Yasmin, however, was unreservedly support-ive. Her quiet strength had always been a source of solace for me. "Follow the path that calls to you, Saanvi," she said, her eyes shining with pride. "You have the courage to walk it." I missed them both deeply during the years I spent away, pursuing my college degree, though I made sure to visit my hometown during breaks.

Oxford was a revelation. Its ancient spires and cobble-stone streets seemed to come alive with the wisdom of generations. Yet, for all its ancient grandeur, it was the diversity of minds that captivated me the most. My peers hailed from every corner of the globe, each carrying stories and perspectives that enriched our collective understanding. I threw myself into my studies with a fervor that surprised even me. The lectures were electrify-ing, filled with debates that sparked like flint against steel. I often found myself lingering after class, engaging professors in discussions that veered into uncharted intellectual territories. Political history unfolded like a vast, intricate map, with every revolution, treaty, and war revealing patterns of human ambition and folly.

Journalism, on the other hand, was a different beast altogether. It demanded not just intellect but intuition and courage. My first assignment was to investigate the role of media in shaping narratives during the Arab Spring. Hours of research led me to a profound realization: journalism was both a mirror and a weapon. It reflected society's truths but also had the power to cut through lies and distortions. This duality fascinated me. Balancing my academic pursuits with my personal life was a delicate dance. Oxford's rigor left little room for introspection, yet the shadows of Ayodhya and my family's legacy followed me relentlessly. I often spent late nights writing in my journal, trying to make sense of my place in the world. Was I merely an observer, documenting the ebbs and flows of history? Or was I destined to be an active participant, shaping the very narratives I studied?

One of my professors, Dr Tandra Mukherjee, became an unlikely mentor. She was a formidable historian with a penchant for challenging conventional wisdom. During one of our conversations, she said, "Saanvi, the best historians are those who dare to question their own biases. The best journalists do the same." Her words resonated deeply, pushing me to scrutinize not just the world but also myself.

The turning point in my Oxford journey came during a seminar on post-colonial narratives. We were discussing the partition of India and its enduring impact when a classmate remarked, "It's fascinating how history can be both a unifier and a divider, depending on who writes it."

Those words struck a chord. I realized that my father's story and my mother's silence were part of a larger narrative—a narrative that needed to be told. That evening, I began outlining a series of articles that would explore the intersections of religion, politics, and identity in modern India. These pieces became my catharsis, a way to reconcile the disparate threads of my life. I had learned my first lesson about the power of stories.

My first article, published in the university's journal,

sparked a wave of discussions. Titled "The Forgotten Voices of Ayodhya," it delved into the lives of those often overshadowed by the grand narratives of history—the laborers, the artisans, the families displaced by political machinations. The response was overwhelming, with readers appreciating the nuanced perspective I brought to a deeply polarizing issue. Encouraged by this reception, I continued to write, each piece peeling back another layer of India's complex socio-political fabric. My articles caught the attention of a prominent British newspaper that offered me an internship. This opportunity became a crucible, sharpening my skills and exposing me to the harsh realities of investigative journalism.

As I neared the end of my time at Oxford, I often reflected on the journey that had brought me here. The girl who had once roamed the Himalayan slopes with a head full of questions had grown into a woman determined to seek answers, no matter how uncomfortable they may be.

Oxford has not just educated me; it has transformed me. It has taught me that history is not a static record but a living, breathing entity that demands constant interrogation. It has shown me that journalism, when wielded with integrity, can be a force for justice and change. And above all, it has affirmed my belief in the power of stories—stories that bridge divides, challenge perceptions, and illuminate truths. As I prepared to leave Oxford, I carried with me not just my undergraduate degree but also a new mission. My journey was far from over; in many ways, it was just beginning. The world is vast, and its stories are infinite. I was ready to listen, to question, and to tell those stories with the honesty and courage they deserve.

16

My paternal grandfather, Shyam Trivedi's death came without warning—sudden, like the crack of thunder on a clear day. For decades, he had been a towering presence in Ayodhya, respected and feared for his fierce commitment to justice. His name carried weight, murmured with admiration by the downtrodden and with dread by those who had faced his incisive legal mind. His courtroom presence was magnetic—precise, passionate, and utterly unrelenting. But even giants are mortal, and his passing left a silence that echoed across Ayodhya's corridors of power.

The day began much like any other for Shyam. The sprawling veranda of our ancestral home, the famed Trivedi mansion, was awash with the first golden rays of the sun. He sat at his usual spot, a teak chair overlooking the manicured garden, sipping his morning tea. The gentle aroma of freshly brewed Assam tea mingled with the faint smell of marigolds that bordered the path to the gate. Shyam's mornings were sacred rituals, moments of tranquility before he donned the mantle of a fierce litigator. He scanned the day's newspapers, his reading glasses perched on the bridge of his aquiline nose, taking in the latest political developments with a furrowed brow. To anyone observing him, there were no signs of the storm brewing within his chest.

By mid-morning, Shyam had dressed in his usual crisp white kurta-pajama, the fabric as immaculate as the reputation he had cultivated over decades. He was due to appear at a high-profile hearing that day, one that had drawn the city's attention for weeks. The case, steeped in communal tension and historical disputes, had demanded every ounce of Shyam's intellect and resolve. He had been preparing for weeks, meticulously combing through documents and rehearsing arguments that would leave his opponents scrambling. "Justice cannot wait," he had declared to his juniors the previous evening, his voice resonant with conviction. It would be his last such proclamation.

Around noon, as Shyam stood in the bustling lobby of the District Court, conversing with a journalist who had sought his opinion on the case, the first twinge of discomfort struck. It was a fleeting sensation, like a dull ache creeping across his chest, but Shyam dismissed it. He was, after all, a man who prided himself on both his mental and physical fortitude, a man who had stood unshaken in the face of countless adversities. He continued speaking, his words measured and authoritative, as though sheer willpower could banish the faint unease gnawing at him.

The second wave came minutes later, more insistent this time. A sharp, searing pain radiated from his chest to his left arm, leaving him momentarily breathless. Shyam's face betrayed a flicker of distress, and his hand instinctively reached for the polished mahogany railing beside him. The journalist, noticing the sudden change in his demeanor, asked if he was feeling unwell. Shyam's response was characteristically terse: "Just a moment's fatigue. Nothing more." But his voice lacked its usual steadiness, and a faint sheen of sweat had appeared on his forehead.

Those nearby began to notice. A junior lawyer, rushing to greet him, paused mid-step as he saw Shyam Trivedi clutching his chest, his breathing now labored. Within moments, concern turned to panic. Someone shouted for water; another rushed to fetch help. But Shyam, ever the stalwart, waved them off. "I'm fine," he insisted, his words laced with a stubborn defiance that was both his strength and his downfall.

Then came the collapse. It was as if the very foundation of Ayodhya's legal world had crumbled in an instant. Shyam Trivedi's knees buckled, and he fell to the marble floor of the courthouse lobby, the thud reverberating through the grand hall. Gasps echoed, and a flurry of activity ensued. People crowded around him, their voices a chaotic mix of alarm and urgency. Someone loosened his kurta, another propped his head up with a rolled coat. Yet, Shyam's eyes, once so piercing and alert, now struggled to stay open, his breath shallow and uneven.

An ambulance was called, its siren wailing through the narrow streets of Ayodhya as it raced to the courthouse. By the time the paramedics arrived, Shyam's pulse was faint. They worked swiftly, administering oxygen and attempting to stabilize him, but the signs were grim. The man who had commanded courtrooms with an unassailable presence now lay vulnerable, his life hanging by a fragile thread.

As the ambulance sped toward the hospital, the city seemed to hold its breath. Word of Shyam Trivedi's condition spread like wildfire, reaching homes, offices, and even tea stalls within minutes. The courtroom where he had been scheduled to argue his case fell silent, the proceedings paused as the weight of the news settled over everyone present. For Ayodhya, this was not just the potential loss of a lawyer; it was the possible end of an era.

Despite the paramedics' efforts, Shyam Trivedi's heart gave out before the ambulance could reach its destination. The doctors at the emergency ward pronounced him dead on arrival, citing a massive cardiac arrest. The news, when it broke, sent shockwaves through the city. People gathered outside the hospital, their faces etched with disbelief and grief. For many, Shyam Trivedi had been more than a legal luminary; he had been a symbol of integrity and Hindu cultural pride in a city often torn by religious strife.

The days that followed were marked by an outpouring of tributes. Crowds thronged his ancestral home, offering condolences to his family. Political leaders, community figures, and ordinary citizens came together, their differences set aside in a rare moment of unity, to mourn a man whose life had been devoted to justice. The air was thick with the smell of marigolds and incense, the mourners' voices blending into a somber hymn of loss. For my father, Ramesh Trivedi, and for his wife and my paternal grandmother, Sumitra Trivedi, the news of his death was a blow that reverberated deeply. They could not deny the profound impact he had had on their lives. I, Saanvi, was as inconsolable, grappling in another town in another country, with the sudden loss of a paternal grandfather whose approval I had always unconsciously sought.

In Ayodhya, Shyam Trivedi's absence was palpable. His office, once alive with the buzz of legal debates and the shuffle of case files, now stood eerily silent. The unfinished case he had been fighting became a symbol of his incomplete legacy, a stark reminder of the fragility of even the most enduring lives.

Shyam Trivedi's death in 2015 marked more than the end of a life—it marked the unraveling of a fragile balance in Ayodhya. For decades, his fierce advocacy had shaped the city's legal and moral compass. With his passing, Ayodhya lost not just a prominent lawyer but a conscience, an anchor amid its persistent turbulence. The rhythm of life in the city resumed, as it must, but a stillness lingered beneath the surface. The absence of his presence was not merely symbolic; it was deeply felt in the very texture of civic discourse.

That year, Ayodhya simmered with renewed tension. The Supreme Court had announced its decision to revisit the long-standing Ram Janmabhoomi-Babri Masjid dispute, reigniting old arguments and sharpening the city's divides. Familiar ideological lines were drawn again, but the environment felt more brittle, more combustible. The city stood once more in the glare of national scrutiny—its streets echoing with questions of faith, identity, and justice.

Shyam Trivedi had long stood at the intersection of these questions. His was not the voice of a zealot nor the rhetoric of a detached technocrat. He argued from the constitution, grounding every plea in the language of law and reason. His method was deliberate, even surgical. He sought not to soothe with platitudes but to provoke with principle. In a city too often hijacked by religious posturing, he remained committed to a jurisprudence that honored pluralism.

In the months preceding his death, Shyam was immersed in a legal case that epitomized Ayodhya's struggles. A small parcel of land, wedged uncomfortably close to the disputed site, was claimed by both a Hindu religious trust and a Muslim family. He had taken on the case without compensation, viewing it not merely as a legal dispute, but as a symbolic crossroads. It was a chance, however narrow, to find a way forward through the bramble of historical grievance and contemporary fear. His arguments combined legal precision with a deep moral intelligence. "Ayodhya is not merely geography," he had said during an early hearing. "It is memory, it is mythology, it is a contract we renew daily with one another." Those words, spoken with conviction, had earned him both admiration and enmity. As the city mourned his death, the vacuum left by Shyam's absence became glaringly evident. The case he had been fighting was thrown into disarray, with no lawyer able to match his depth of understanding or his ability to navigate the city's fraught dynamics. Ayodhya's streets, already simmering with tension, felt heavier in the wake of his passing. For many, Shyam had been a voice of reason, a bulwark against the tides of extremism that threatened to engulf the city.

The impact of his death was immediate and disruptive. The case faltered, stalled by a lack of legal leadership capable of bridging the divides Shyam had so deftly navigated. His absence became a silence that echoed through the city's courtrooms, temples, and mosques. His reputation had been a deterrent to political opportunists; without him, they grew bolder. Ayodhya's air felt denser, its political climate more volatile.

Tributes poured in—some sincere, others opportunistic. Protests were held in his memory, even as counter-rallies erupted, inflamed by the very forces he had tried to temper. Politicians began descending upon Ayodhya with statements wrapped in reverence but laced with strategy. The media circled like vultures, seeking spectacle rather than truth. Shyam's death had not only left the city vulnerable—it had made it desirable, ripe for ideological conquest.

For Ramesh Trivedi, my father, the historical weight of Ayodhya's struggles was a poignant backdrop to his own personal grief and loss of a father. He had always admired his father's dedication to his city, even as in some ways he had quietly feared him for his strained marriage with my mother, Yasmin. Now, however, as he walked the streets of Ayodhya, he saw the impact of his father's life and death etched into the faces of its people. In the heart of Ayodhya's bustling markets, whispers of Shyam's legacy grew louder with each passing day. Tea vendors recalled how Shyam would pause for a steaming glass of *chai* after grueling court sessions, often engaging them in conversation about the city's troubles. "He never talked down to us," one vendor, Ramdeen, remarked. "He treated us as equals. That's what made him special."

The younger generation, particularly those studying law or aspiring to public service, found inspiration in Shyam Trivedi's life. Students gathered in makeshift study groups, poring over his landmark cases and discussing his philosophy. Some of his protégés took to social media, sharing anecdotes of his humility and brilliance, their tributes cutting across Ayodhya's religious and political spectrum.

Young lawyers shared stories of his mentorship, of how he had inspired them to pursue justice with integrity. The city's temples and mosques, its bustling markets and quiet lanes, all seemed to carry traces of Shyam Trivedi's proud legacy. Yet, they also bore the weight of unresolved tensions, a reminder that his work had been far from complete. Ayodhya's future remained uncertain, its path forward fraught with challenges that would demand the same courage and clarity that Shyam had embodied.

But not everyone saw Shyam's death as a tragedy. For those who thrived on the city's divisions, his absence was an opportunity. Political operatives began to stir, their narratives crafted to exploit the vacuum left by Shyam. Rumors swirled, some suggesting conspiracies surrounding his death, while others sought to downplay his impact on Ayodhya's social fabric. The city's fragile peace felt like a taut string, ready to snap under the weight of competing agendas.

Among the most affected were the families Shyam Trivedi had defended in his pro bono cases. Many were left in limbo, their fates uncertain without his steadfast advocacy. One such family, the Ansaris, whose land dispute case had been championed by Shyam, now faced renewed threats and intimidation. Shyam Trivedi had been their shield, his reputation alone deterring those who sought to encroach upon their rights. With him gone, they felt exposed, vulnerable to forces that cared little for justice.

At home, the personal became inseparable from the political. "He didn't just argue cases," Ramesh confessed to his mother one night. "He carried the burden of this city's soul. Who carries it now?" Ramesh, seasoned now in his own political career, understood too well the stakes. The balance Ayodhya had tenuously maintained could collapse with a single careless provocation. His public statement that Shyam's death marked "the end of an era" was not a rhetorical flourish; it was an indictment of the vacuum left behind.

And that vacuum was quickly exploited. Shyam's detractors, both overt and hidden, began to fill the space he once occupied with rumors, half-truths, and revisionist narratives. Some questioned the circumstances of his death. Others minimized his legacy. The city's fragile peace, never more than provisional, trembled under the weight of these competing versions of the truth.

Among those most profoundly affected were the families Shyam had represented—cases he had taken not for gain, but from conviction. One of them, the Ansaris, now faced threats they had been shielded from during Shyam's lifetime. His mere association had protected them. In his absence, they were vulnerable—stripped of the only advocate who had treated their story as more than just a headline.

Even in New Delhi, his passing reverberated. Leaders across the aisle issued statements, some touched by genuine loss, others colored by political calculus. Shyam had challenged them all—on the floor of the courts, in committee meetings, in legal drafts scribbled over midnight tea. His departure shifted the terrain in subtle but consequential ways.

My maternal grandfather, Adil Khan, also acknowledged the weight of Shyam Trivedi's legacy. Though his own political career had been fraught with challenges, he had never doubted Shyam Trivedi's sincerity or his commitment to Ayodhya, more so after their meeting. Adil Khan was not one to let words flow carelessly, especially when speaking about a man as esteemed as Shyam Trivedi, my paternal grandfather. A politician now, of measured eloquence, Adil Khan carried a gravitas that matched the profound silence often surrounding Ayodhya's contested spaces. When Shyam Trivedi passed away suddenly in 2015, it left not just a void in the legal world but also in the collective conscience of a city that had been shaped by his unwavering commitment to justice and fairness.

The two men had met just once and engaged in a heated discussion where Ayodhya's political and cultural past and future had been fiercely debated within my hearing. I recall how Adil Khan, ever the pragmatist, had initially approached Shyam with skepticism, aware of his Hindu identity and the weight it carried in such discussions. But as the conversation had deepened, Adil found himself captivated by Shyam's intellect and clarity of thought. Shyam Trivedi, even as he navigated a society fraught with religious divisions, had always spoken the language of the Indian constitution, wielding it not as a tool for exclusion but as a bridge between fractured communities.

When news of Shyam's death reached Adil Khan, it brought a somber pause to his otherwise stoic demeanor. Despite their differences—cultural, ideological, and personal—Adil Khan had always admired Shyam's ability to transcend the petty prejudices that defined much of Ayodhya's politics. In an interview conducted shortly after Shyam's funeral, Adil's voice carried both sorrow and conviction as he said, "Ayodhya has lost one of its truest custodians. Shyam Trivedi was not merely a lawyer; he was a visionary who understood that justice is not just a matter of law but of conscience. His loss is not just personal for me or his family. It is a loss for the entire city."

Adil also made it a point to attend the memorial service organized by Shyam's colleagues at the Ayodhya Bar Association. It was unusual for him to be seen at such events, but he felt it was necessary to honor a man whose principles had shaped the very fabric of legal advocacy in Ayodhya. He stood quietly in the corner, listening as senior advocates recounted tales of Shyam's unmatched legal acumen, his fairness in adjudication, and his steadfast refusal to allow communal biases to influence his interpretation of justice. When Adil finally rose to speak, his words carried the solemnity of one statesman honoring another. "Shyam Trivedi," he said, "believed in the power of dialogue and reason. He reminded us that in a city like Ayodhya, where emotions often override rationale, we must strive harder to protect the ideals of equality and fairness. His work will remain a guiding light for generations to come."

Even in private, Adil often reflected on Shyam's legacy, sharing stories of the impact Shyam had on Ayodhya's legal and moral landscape. "Men like Shyam Trivedi," he said, "are rare, for they understand the difference between law and justice and yet manage to uphold both. His absence is a tragedy, but his life is a lesson. Let us honor Shyam Trivedi not by looking back with regret," he said, "but by moving forward with the courage and conviction that he exemplified."

As the year ended, Ayodhya remained poised between memory and possibility. It was a year when the simmering tensions of the past collided with the aspirations of a generation seeking reconciliation, a year that reminded its people of the fragility of peace and the strength it took to sustain it. And as the city moved forward, grappling with its past and its future, the memory of Shyam Trivedi lingered like a persistent echo, a reminder of what Ayodhya could aspire to become. Shyam's passing was more than a personal loss for our family. It became a symbol of an era that was fading, a reminder of the values that Ayodhya was in danger of leaving behind. As the city mourned the loss of one of its most respected legal minds, it also found itself at a crossroads, grappling with the forces of political change that threatened to reshape its identity. The political landscape of Ayodhya in 2015 was one of profound transformation. The rise of new political actors, fueled by aggressive nationalist rhetoric, was met with both fervent support and quiet apprehension. While some celebrated what they saw as a reassertion of Ayodhya's cultural heritage, others worried that this newfound energy came at the cost of the city's fragile communal harmony. The scars of past conflicts, though no longer fresh, remained etched into the collective memory of its people.

Shyam Trivedi's legacy did not promise easy solutions. What it offered instead was an ethic—a refusal to capitulate to rage, a commitment to dialogue over division. For many, Shyam Trivedi had been a stabilizing force, a man who believed that justice could serve as a bridge between divided communities. His death, sudden and untimely, felt like the loss of a moral compass at a time when Ayodhya needed it most. His death had created a breach, but also a blueprint. In Ayodhya's tea stalls and courtrooms, in its prayers and protests, his voice lingered—not as an echo of the past, but as a quiet provocation for the future.

17

The history of Ayodhya is one of contention and reconciliation, a heady mix of myths, politics, and faith. Within its sacred and scarred terrain lies the story of how the Hindu Party rose to power, a meteoric ascent rooted in the volatile intersection of religion and politics. Interwoven with this history is the journey of my father, Ramesh Trivedi, a man of profound convictions and private conflicts. As a politician, Ramesh Trivedi had spent a few years on the periphery of the national stage. But the winds of change brought by the Hindu Party's soul-stirring rise pushed my father to a pivotal cross-roads, altering the course of his life and the Trivedi family's destiny.

In the aftermath of India's independence from the British Raj in 1947, the political landscape had been dominated by the Congress Party, whose secular and socialist ideals had shaped the nascent nation. Yet, beneath the surface lay currents of discontent. Religious identities, though ostensibly subsumed under the secular framework, remained potent and deeply rooted. The Jana Party, the precursor to the Hindu Party, had emerged in the early nineteen fifties, advocating for the integration of Hindu values into the nation's ethos. However, it was not until the late nineteen eighties that the Hindu Party found its stride, riding the wave of the Ram Janmabhoomi movement. The political tides of Ayodhya from 2016 to 2022 surged and ebbed, their waves carving out narratives of faith and power that would shape not only the city but the nation. In those six years, Ayodhya was not merely a place. It became an idea, a battleground of ideologies and a vessel for aspirations both ancient and modern.

The awakening came in 2016, as the streets of Ayodhya seemed to hum with a renewed urgency. The Hindu Party, its grip on the nation tightening under new leadership, set its sights firmly on the Ram Mandir, reviving a call that had long simmered in the hearts of its followers. Local markets buzzed with whispers of impending change, *chai* stalls bristled with debate, and temples filled with a palpable sense of anticipation. The Hindu Party's promises, however, were not mere slogans. Legal proceedings gained an unexpected momentum, with the Supreme Court deciding to expedite the long-pending Ram Janmabhoomi-Babri Masjid case. For Ayodhya, this was the opening act in a drama that had yet to reveal its climax. 2017 brought a landslide victory for the Hindu Party in Uttar Pradesh, and with it came a saffron robed monk turned political leader who strode into the consciousness of the city with a vision as fiery as his rhetoric. His first year as the chief minister saw Ayodhya shine brighter, literally. On the night of the Hindu festival of Diwali, millions of *diyas* lit the banks of the Saryu River, their glow visible from miles away. For some, these celebrations were a reclamation of Ayodhya's spiritual legacy; for others, they were a calculated spectacle. But the divide between believers and skeptics did little to dim the fervor. *Deepotsav* was not just a festival. It was a proclamation of a government's intent to make Ayodhya the epicenter of its cultural narrative.

By 2018, the drumbeats of mobilization echoed through Ayodhya along with the gathering storm. Hindu organizations, emboldened by the rise of the Hindu Party, intensified their calls for action. The World Hindu Committee organized processions that wound through the city's narrow lanes, their chants filling the air. The presence of the Hindu Party loomed large over the horizons though, its cadres working tirelessly to unify Hindu sentiment. Amidst this, opposition leaders ventured into Ayodhya, their visits carefully chalked, plotted, and choreographed. Samajwadi and Bahujan leaders invoked promises of secularism and justice, hoping to hold their ground. The city, however, seemed to have chosen its axis, one that revolved around the Hindu temple.

In courtrooms, the special bench's hearings grew more frequent. Each session brought Ayodhya closer to resolution, but also closer to the brink.

The core demand of the movement was the construction of a Ram temple at the site of the Babri Masjid in Ayodhya, believed to be Lord Rama's birthplace. This demand, fueled by a potent mix of mythology, faith, and grievance, resonated deeply across the Hindi heartland. The Hindu Party, under older and revered leaders, had seized the moment, framing the issue as a struggle for cultural and national identity. The *rath yatra* in 1990 had been a watershed moment for many devout Hindus, galvanizing support and polarizing opinions.

The demolition of the Babri Masjid on December 6, 1992 and that had coincided with my birth, had marked both a triumph and a tragedy. For the Hindu Party, it had been a historic culmination of their mobilization efforts. But it had also plunged the nation into communal riots and some amount of soul-searching. The party's ideological moorings became inseparable from its political strategy, and the temple issue became a rallying cry that propelled them to power.

Ramesh Trivedi, my father, had always been a man of principles. Born into the powerful Trivedi family in Ayodhya, he had inherited a legacy of intellectual rigor and public service. As a young man, he had been captivated by Nehruvian socialism, believing in a vision of India where caste and creed would recede before the ideals of equality and progress. Yet, as he rose through the ranks of state politics, he had found himself increasingly disillusioned.

By the time my grandfather died of a heart attack in 2015, Ramesh Trivedi had become a prominent figure in the state legislature. He was known for his fiery speeches and his ability to connect with the grassroots. But his career somehow had seemed to stagnate. The Congress Party, to which he had devoted his early years, appeared out of touch with the aspirations of ordinary citizens. Regional parties were gaining ground, and identity politics was becoming the dominant narrative. It was against this backdrop that my father, Ramesh Trivedi, began to reassess his political allegiance.

The Hindu Party's rhetoric of 'Ram Rajya'—a utopia of justice and prosperity rooted in Hindu values—spoke loudly to Ramesh's cultural sensibilities. Yet, he remained skeptical. He had seen the devastation wrought by communal violence and was deeply wary of mixing religion with politics. "The line between mobilization and manipulation is thin," he often told his confidants. Still, the tide was unmistakable, and Ramesh faced mounting pressure to align himself with the Hindu Party.

The Hindu Party had undergone a transformation with the onset of the new millennium. The party, under moderate leadership, had successfully projected itself as a viable alternative to the Congress. However, the rise of new leaders who embodied ideas of decisiveness and development, redefined the party's trajectory. By 2014, their charisma and the promise of *'Achhe Din'* or good days had swept the Hindu party to a historic victory. The new leaders tapped into the aspirations of a burgeoning middle class, the frustrations of the unemployed, and the grievances of those who had felt marginalized by decades of secular politics. The party gradually consolidated its Hindutva agenda, framing it within the broader narrative of nationalism and development.

For Ramesh, the elections were a turning point. The Congress was in disarray, mired in corruption scandals and leadership crises. The Hindu Party's disciplined campaign and the vision of a resurgent India were impossible to ignore. His friends and his colleagues all urged Ramesh to make the leap. "This is the future," they argued. "You've always been a man of the people. The Hindu Party is where the people are now."

Yet, the decision was not simple. My father had always been a secularist at heart. He had always valued the pluralistic fabric of India and feared that the Hindu Party's majoritarian agenda could unravel it. Moreover, he had always carried the personal burden of his abiding love and his secret marriage to my mother, Yasmin Khan. Their relationship had been transformative, a reminder of the complexities and contradictions of identity. Ramesh Trivedi had kept his marital relationship and his fidelity to Yasmin, my mother, a secret for all these years, owing to societal pressures. Even as Ramesh had built his political career, he had often wondered what might have been. This personal history made his decision to join the Hindu Party fraught with inner conflict. Could he, in good conscience, support a party whose rhetoric sometimes alienated the very community Yasmin belonged to? In the end, pragmatism prevailed. Ramesh saw the Hindu Party as the only vehicle capable of bringing about meaningful change. He rationalized his choice by focusing on the party's developmental agenda. "If I am part of the system," he reasoned, "I can steer it towards inclusivity."

Ramesh's decision had profound implications for our family. My mother, Yasmin Khan, was somewhat dubious, but she mostly stayed silent. She had always admired my father's idealism and feared that his association with the Hindu Party would compromise his principles. "Power changes people," she had warned him in her soft and quiet manner. My own feelings as a newly minted Oxford graduate in 2016, were and will always stay divided. Some saw his move as a betrayal of our secular upbringing, while others viewed it as a strategic necessity.

As my father, Ramesh Trivedi rose through the Hindu Party's ranks, he became a vocal advocate for development and governance. Yet, he often found himself at odds with the party's hardliners. Behind closed doors, he lobbied for policies that would bridge divides rather than deepen them. But the pressures of party politics were relentless, and his compromises took a subtle toll on him.

Throughout this period, my hometown, Ayodhya remained a symbol and a battleground. The Supreme Court's verdict in 2019, which paved the way for the Ram temple's construction, was celebrated by the Hindu Party as the fulfillment of a decades-old promise. For Ramesh, the moment was bittersweet. He visited the site in Ayodhya, standing before the temple's foundations with a mixture of pride and ambivalence. "This is not just about bricks and mortar," he claimed.

"It's about healing old wounds and forging a shared future."

The Supreme Court's verdict in 2019 had marked the resolution of a long-standing dispute that had sparked intense political, social, and religious debates for decades. The judgment granted the disputed land to Hindus for the construction of the Ram temple while also providing an alternative piece of land for the Muslim community to build a mosque. The ruling was celebrated by the Hindu Party as the fulfillment of a decades-old promise made by the party and its iconic leaders. This event became a significant moment in Indian politics, where the convergence of faith, politics, and law intersected dramatically. The story of Ayodhya had turned irrevocably on November 9, 2019. The Supreme Court's verdict was as monumental as it was polarizing. The disputed land was awarded to the Hindu Party trust for the construction of a Ram temple under the administration of the Ram Janmabhoomi *Nyas*, while a separate site in Ayodhya was allocated for the construction of a mosque. Fireworks lit the sky as jubilant crowds thronged the streets. In homes, elders narrated tales of a battle fought over decades, a dream finally realized. For the Hindu Party, however, the verdict was nothing short of vindication. Ayodhya had become the crown jewel in their narrative of cultural revival, a symbol they would wield with unmatched fervor.

Ramesh Trivedi had always known the importance of timing in politics. His rise was never a matter of sheer ambition but an understanding of the psychology of the people, the issues that defined them, and the promises that had yet to be fulfilled. He had entered politics with the aim of reforming his community, of balancing tradition with progress. But as the years passed, Ramesh realized that politics in India was much more than policy and governance. It was about identity. It was about belief. And it was about understanding what people wanted, even if they couldn't articulate it fully.

The Ram Janmabhoomi dispute in Ayodhya had been a dormant volcano, occasionally simmering to the surface but never fully erupting. Yet, when the Supreme Court's verdict came in November 2019, it shook the entire nation. The decision, which handed over the disputed site to Hindus for the construction of the Ram temple, was both a victory and a challenge for Ramesh. The Hindu Party celebrated the verdict as the fulfillment of a long-held promise, and the headlines screamed that a dream had come true. For Ramesh, it wasn't just the political triumph of the party that mattered. It was how this verdict would reshape the landscape of Indian politics, and his career.

For decades, the Ayodhya issue had been the central rallying cry of the Hindu Party. From the demolition of the Babri Masjid in 1992 to the subsequent years of court battles and communal tensions, the Ram Janmabhoomi issue had remained unresolved, festering in the political bloodstream of the nation. Ramesh had watched from the sidelines, understanding the political capital to be gained from this issue, but also aware of the delicate balance that needed to be maintained. He had been a moderate figure in the early years of his career, often caught between the need for progressive policies and the demands of an electorate rooted deeply in religious sentiment. But the 2019 verdict marked a turning point, not just in the history of Ayodhya, but in Ramesh's own journey.

The Hindu Party's celebration of the verdict was not just about the temple itself. It was about the power of fulfilling a promise that had been made decades ago. The Ram temple had become more than a building—it was a symbol of cultural resurgence, of Hindu pride, and of reclaiming an identity that had been stifled for years. Ramesh knew that in this moment, he could either align himself with this momentum or risk being swept aside by the tide of religious fervor that was sweeping across the nation.

As he sat in his office, watching the jubilant celebrations on television, Ramesh reflected on the decades of political maneuvering that had brought him to this point. His own rise had been intricately tied to the shifting political climate in Uttar Pradesh. He had always positioned himself as a voice of reason in the midst of heated debates. But now, with the verdict, the ground had shifted beneath his feet.

His phone rang, and the voice on the other end was familiar. "Ramesh, this is it," said the Hindu Party leader, his tone eager. "This is the moment. People are waiting for leaders like you to step forward and lead them. You know where we stand. It's time for you to make your move."

Ramesh felt a wave of uncertainty wash over him. He had always considered himself a man of principle, someone who stood for the unity of the nation above all else. But as the crowds chanted, as the temple foundation was laid, and as the Hindu Party's agenda seemed to gain unstoppable momentum, Ramesh realized that there was no turning back. His political future would now be defined by how he navigated this crucial moment. The verdict was more than just a legal ruling. It was a political tool. It was a statement of identity, of power, and of belonging. And in the world of politics, it was a rare opportunity—one that Ramesh could not afford to ignore. The following months were filled with fevered discussions. Ramesh met with his closest allies, strategizing his next moves. He had always been careful not to alienate any community—Hindu, Muslim, or otherwise—but the voices from the party were clear. This was the moment to embrace the cultural symbolism of the Ram Mandir. His hesitation could be interpreted as weakness.

The Hindu Party's rhetoric was unrelenting. They spoke of a new India—one that was rising from the ashes of its past struggles. A temple was being built in Ayodhya, and with it, a new chapter of India's history was being written. Ramesh knew that he could not afford to be seen as an outsider to this narrative. The people wanted a leader who stood with them in their moment of triumph, who understood the significance of the Ram Mandir as more than just a structure, but as a symbol of a nation's renewal.

As the days passed, Ramesh's decision grew clearer. He would lend his full support to the construction of the temple, not just as a politician but as a symbol of the political winds that were blowing through the country. He would join the celebrations—not just as a follower but as a leader, as a man who had understood the psychology of the people. His words would resonate with those who felt that they had been waiting for this moment their entire lives. The temple would rise. The people would rejoice. And Ramesh Trivedi would rise along with them. He had made his choice, and with it, he had solidified his place in the annals of Indian politics. The journey of the Ram Mandir was now intricately tied to his own. The months following the Supreme Court's verdict were pivotal not only for the nation but for Ramesh Trivedi. He had always been a man of temperance, holding to his convictions with a quiet strength that had garnered him respect across party lines. But as the momentum of the Ram Mandir grew into an unstoppable force, Ramesh had to confront the reality of his own place within the political landscape. It wasn't simply about supporting the temple's construction. That, in itself, was a given. The real challenge was how he would align his identity with the shifting sands of Indian politics, particularly in a region like Uttar Pradesh, where the echoes of Ayodhya's past reverberated louder than anywhere else.

As Ramesh pondered the future, the realization dawned on him: the stakes were higher than ever. The Ram Mandir was no longer just a political issue; it had evolved into the very embodiment of the Hindu identity that so many people felt had been marginalized for decades. The temple, under the banner of the Hindu Party, had transformed into a sacred symbol of cultural revival. It was no longer just bricks and mortar—it was a manifestation of the collective desires of millions, a monumental promise fulfilled after years of struggle. The calls from the Hindu Party leadership continued, urging Ramesh to step forward. "This is your moment," they would say, "the country is waiting for leaders like you, men of vision, to steer this movement forward." Ramesh knew that his support, while important, came at a personal cost. He had always walked a fine line between maintaining his moderate stance and engaging with the deeper currents of religious and cultural sentiment that had defined the political terrain for decades. Now, the lines between Hindu identity and political ideology had blurred. His support of the Ram Mandir was not just a political choice; it was a tacit endorsement of the party's vision for a Hindu-first India. This was a vision that promised to redefine the future of the nation—and his role within it.

Ramesh spent sleepless nights weighing his options. His political allies had pushed him to publicly align with the Hindu Party, to speak of his support in unequivocal terms. But he was careful not to let himself be swept away by the tide. He had seen what had happened to other leaders who had become mere puppets of a narrative larger than themselves. He had seen how ambition could cloud judgment, how loyalty to a party could sometimes lead to personal compromises.

It was during this time that Ramesh began to reflect on his own upbringing. His father, Shyam Trivedi, the well-known lawyer, had always emphasized the importance of integrity. Ramesh's mother, my paternal grandmother, on the other hand, had been a devout woman. She had taught him that religion was not a matter of politics. It was a personal relationship with the divine, a private faith that was not to be thrust upon others. This tension between his parents' contrasting values—his father's pragmatism and his mother's spirituality—had shaped Ramesh in ways he had not fully understood until now.

The temple's foundation was being laid in Ayodhya, and the world watched. The chants of "Jai Shri Ram" echoed across the nation, and in many ways, Ramesh could feel the collective heartbeat of India. But with the chorus of celebrations came a quieter, more insistent question: How would Ramesh Trivedi respond?

As the Ram Mandir movement grew, Ramesh's rivals in the opposition sought to challenge his position. The Muslim community, in particular, voiced concerns about the fairness of the verdict. Yes, the celebrations were not universal. Ayodhya's Muslim residents watched with a mix of resignation and unease, their voices muted by a collective desire for peace. The city's triumph felt incomplete, its harmony fragile. Ramesh, with his growing instincts as a strategist, knew that a single misstep could alienate significant sections of the electorate. Yet, it was clear that staying silent was no longer an option.

He had spent years cultivating relationships with various communities. As a leader in his state, he had walked a delicate path, balancing the demands of his Hindu constituency with the need for inclusivity. Now, however, his silence on the Ram Mandir issue had become politically untenable. His decision would either cement his place as a prominent leader in the new political order or push him into obscurity.

Ramesh knew that speaking out in support of the temple was politically wise, but he could not ignore the fact that the temple had become a symbol of a larger narrative that many of his former colleagues in the opposition had long warned against. It was the story of a Hindu resurgence that, if left unchecked, could sow deep divisions in the social fabric of India. He remembered the long evenings his father had spent talking about unity, about the importance of keeping faith with every community in India. Those teachings were hard to reconcile with the fiery speeches of the Hindu Party leaders who were now calling for a new India, one in which Hindu pride would reign supreme.

In the weeks that followed, Ramesh took a cautious but deliberate step forward. He spoke publicly about the verdict, framing it not as a victory for one religion over another, but as a fulfillment of a historical promise. He acknowledged the pain that the Muslim community had endured through the years of uncertainty and division, but he emphasized that the temple's construction was a necessary step toward healing.

"History has its way of shaping us," Ramesh Trivedi said in his speech, "but it is the future that calls us to rise above our past. The Ram Mandir is not just about religion. It is about honoring the faith of millions of Hindus who have waited for decades to see this day. But let us also remember that India is a land of many faiths. And it is our responsibility as leaders to ensure that this moment brings us together, not divides us further."

His words, while carefully measured, struck a chord with many of his supporters. They saw in Ramesh a leader who could navigate the treacherous waters of Indian politics without losing his sense of identity. The Muslim community, too, found some comfort in his acknowledgment of their pain, though many felt that it was a small consolation.

As the temple's construction began, the symbolism of the moment became clearer to Ramesh. The political calculus of supporting the Ram Mandir was no longer just about staying relevant in a shifting political climate. It was about embracing his role in history. Ramesh Trivedi had always known that politics was a game of survival and opportunity. But now, with the temple rising in Ayodhya, he understood that he was not merely a player in the game. He was helping to write the next chapter of India's political narrative. The rise of the Ram Mandir marked the rise of Ramesh Trivedi as a politician who could unite the past and the future. And as the temple took shape, so did his legacy.

Ramesh knew that the temple alone could not resolve the deeper fractures within Indian society. Ramesh's speeches in parliament often emphasized the need for reconciliation, urging his colleagues to focus on education, healthcare, and job creation. *"Ram Rajya,* he argued, "means justice for all, not just a few."

As I reflect on my father's journey, I see a man caught between his ideals and his ambitions, his past and his present. Ramesh Trivedi's story is not just about one politician's choices but about the dilemmas faced by a nation at a crossroads. The rise and dominance of the Hindu Party have reshaped India in profound ways, bringing both progress and polarization. My father's decision to join the Hindu party was emblematic of the complexities of our times, where personal convictions and political realities often collide.

In the end, Ramesh remained steadfastly true to himself, a solitary bridge-builder standing firm amidst a world increasingly fragmented by walls—physical, ideological, and emotional. He was no stranger to the whispered fears in the shadows, the grudges held tight in crowded tea stalls, the fervent prayers for justice and identity that clashed as loudly as the morning conch shells. Ayodhya, with its tangled layers of faith, history, conflict, and fragile attempts at resolution, was more than just a backdrop; it was a living mirror of my father's internal landscape. Like the city, he carried the weight of centuries—of sacred memories and scars alike—and the heavy burden of expectations placed on him by a people desperate for answers but divided by suspicion and fear.

He did not seek to deny or erase the contradictions that defined both the city and himself. Instead, he learned to navigate the shifting tides of belief and doubt, hope and despair, conviction and compromise. In his heart, he believed that the true essence of India lay not in simplistic narratives or sweeping certainties, but in the courage to embrace complexity—to hold multiple truths without surrendering to the ease of reductionism.

As the temple rose, magnificent and unyielding against the skyline, Ramesh understood deeply that nation-building demanded far more than stone and mortar. The grandeur of monuments could never alone heal fractured souls or bridge centuries of distrust. It was in his quiet, often unseen efforts—inviting dialogue where silence threatened, pushing for policies that sought fairness in the midst of fierce inequality, refusing to paint dissenters as enemies—that he found his truest work. His quiet efforts to foster dialogue, his insistence on equitable policies, and his refusal to demonize dissent became his own small acts of resistance within a larger, relentless machine. These small acts of resistance, subtle yet stubborn, formed the backbone of his struggle against a relentless machine that thrived on polarization and spectacle.

My father's words, his silences, and the gestures between both remind me that unity is never born from uniformity. Rather, it arises from the brave, uneasy choice to hold together what seems irreconcilable—to acknowledge pain without succumbing to bitterness, to seek common ground even when it is fragile and elusive.

In moments when I permit myself to imagine a better future, I see his legacy not as a grand monument, but as a steady presence—subtle yet enduring—amid the encroaching divisions, a quiet light in the growing darkness. It stands as evidence that, even in an age of hardening boundaries and deepening mistrust, connections can still be forged. In the most polarized times, bridges can be built, walls can be crossed, and the future, though uncertain and fraught with challenges, still holds the possibility of understanding and coexistence.

The story of Ayodhya and the life of Ramesh Trivedi are inseparably linked—each echoing the other's complexity, contradictions, and pain. Together, they reveal a difficult truth: that reconciliation, however partial, fragile or unresolved, is not just a moral aspiration but a practical necessity for a nation as layered and diverse as India. It is neither swift nor easy. It is a slow, often painful process, yet it is a journey that carries the possibility of a future where difference is not a fault line but a foundation for shared identity. It asks for endurance, for empathy, and above all, for an acknowledgment that lasting peace does not erase difference, but is built through it—stone by stone, moment by moment.

18

I had just returned from Oxford when Ayodhya was in the grip of volatile change. The air was charged with a tense stillness, as if something irreversible had been set in motion. My homecoming felt uneasy, infused with a strange undercurrent—something vital had shifted, quietly but irrevocably. My return was marked by a tense energy, a charged atmosphere that seemed to hum with unspoken change. My father had sent his chauffeur to pick me up—a gesture that felt somewhat like an obligation than a welcome. I understood his changed circumstances, of course. The Lucknow airport was an odd contrast to my troubled mind—familiar Indian faces, bustling voices, and yet, nothing had felt the same. As we drove to Ayodhya, the clamor of the outside world jarred against the storm quietly gathering inside me. Everything seemed unchanged, yet nothing felt the same. As I stepped into the house, the weight of my father's political change hit me like a storm. My father was no longer just Ramesh Trivedi, the man who had quietly navigated his way through complex political waters. Now, he was a part of the Hindu Party, a party that had been a source of deep political division for years.

The house seemed unchanged, but everything about it felt foreign, unfamiliar, like a memory I couldn't quite grasp. It was like a place I knew only in fragments, as if remembered from a dream. My footsteps echoed in the silence that seemed to have replaced the once warm, welcoming hum of familial conversation. The fragrance of our cook's healthy food, once a comfort, now seemed distant, almost hollow in the space where tension lingered like an invisible fog. The next evening after my arrival, I found my father in his study, papers scattered across his desk, a worn copy of *The Ramayana* open beside him. He looked up as I entered, his expression one of mild surprise mixed with something else—a weariness, perhaps, or guilt. He had always been a quiet, thoughtful man who had navigated the back channels of power with measured restraint, someone who had managed to blend his love for politics with his commitment to family. But now, he seemed more distant, more absorbed in something that was larger than us. He was now part of the Hindu Party, a faction that had long deepened the country's political fault lines.

"Welcome back, Saanvi. You do not know how happy I am seeing you again." he said, his voice steady. But there was something in it I hadn't heard before—an almost defensive edge, almost rehearsed.

I paused at the door, taking in the man who had raised me, the man who had always prided himself on his pragmatic approach to life. But there was no mistaking it now: Ramesh Trivedi had made a choice. And it was a choice I wasn't sure I could understand, let alone accept.

"I wasn't expecting you home so soon, papa." I dared, as I walked toward the desk, feeling the weight of the room pressing in on me. "Was it for my sake? I know I may have to return to Oxford for a Master's."

"Perhaps. You know I would want you and your mother beside me all the time." He paused, looking at me for a moment, his expression unreadable. For a fleeting second, I thought I saw something soften in his eyes, but it was gone before I could make sense of it. He pushed his glasses up the bridge of his nose and leaned back in his chair, the silence hanging between us.

"Yes. And I hope your decision to join Oxford has been the right choice." he said after a beat, his voice steady, but something in it had shifted—a quiet resignation, like a man who had already made peace with the choices he had made. He didn't look at me directly, his gaze fixed somewhere beyond me, as though trying to make sense of his own reflection in the words he had just spoken. I could hear the effort in his voice, the way he tried to make small talk as though nothing had changed. But everything had changed. I wanted to shout it at him, to demand an explanation. But I stayed silent, swallowing the frustration that bubbled in my throat.

"Oxford has been fine," I replied curtly, my eyes scanning the papers on his desk, hoping to find something, anything, that could explain this shift in his allegiance. "But we need to talk, papa."

His eyes flickered for a moment, and he set down the pen he had been tapping absentmindedly. The weight of the unspoken between us was unbearable now. I knew I was heading for a confrontation, and it happened soon after, inexplicably.

"What is it, Saanvi?" His voice was calm, but I could sense the tension underneath, a quiet acknowledgment that the conversation we were about to have was one neither of us had been ready for.

"You've joined the Hindu Party," I said bluntly. "I can't pretend to ignore it, papa. What happened? How could you, after everything?"

The words hung in the air, charged with the history that defined us. My father, the man who had always talked about balance, about unity, now seemed to be on the other side of a political divide that felt insurmountable. How could he align himself with a party that, to me, represented the erosion of everything I believed in? The rise of the Hindu Party had sparked not just political polarization, but a cultural shift that tore at the fabric of the nation, dividing communities in ways I couldn't ignore.

He sighed deeply, leaning back in his chair, a weary smile on his lips. "I didn't expect this reaction from you, Saanvi. I thought you'd understand."

"Understand?" I repeated, incredulous. "How am I supposed to understand this, papa? How are we supposed to understand the rise of a party that divides, that singles out people, Muslims, people like my mother, *your* wife?"

My father's eyes grew cold, distant. "You're still too idealistic, Saanvi. You've been in Oxford too long, surrounded by ideas and theories. It's not the same here, not in the real world. Politics is not about ideals. It's about survival. It's about what this country needs right now. And right now, the country needs unity, a strong sense of cultural identity. The Hindu Party represents that. It's not just about religion, Saanvi. It's about restoring what was taken from us."

I was taken aback by his words. "What was taken from us?" I echoed, almost unable to believe I was hearing this. "Papa, we've never been in danger of losing anything. My whole life, I've seen you navigate this world by creating space for us, by finding balance. And now you've chosen a side. A side that treats people like my mother as second-class citizens."

His gaze hardened, and I could feel his frustration building. "You don't understand. You've been away for too long, living in a world that's detached from the reality of this country. You talk about balance, but balance doesn't exist when people don't have a place in this society. Hindus, after everything that has happened—after centuries of invasions, of foreign rulers, of seeing their temples destroyed, their culture undermined—finally have a voice. A party that stands for them, for their right to exist as Hindus without feeling like outsiders in their own land."

I stood there, stunned by his words. He had always been a pragmatist. But this? This was a justification of a politics I could not, would not, accept.

"I don't care what the Hindu Party represents," I said, my voice rising in frustration. "I care about what it's doing to us. To people like my mother, *your* wife. To people like me. We're not the enemy, dad. Just because they are Muslim, and I am part Muslim too, doesn't mean we do not belong here. We've been here for generations, and now we're supposed to just watch as our identity is stripped away in the name of some imagined 'Hindu unity'?"

"It wasn't for your sake, Saanvi. It was for mine. I've spent my whole life balancing between worlds, trying to make everyone comfortable. I thought I could keep that balance, but the truth is... the world around us is changing. And I had to choose a side. You might not like it, but I've chosen." My father, Ramesh Trivedi's words hit me harder than I expected. There was a raw honesty in them, a confession of sorts, but it stung. My father, who had always been the bridge between two worlds, now seemed to have burned that bridge, setting foot firmly on the other side. The weight of his decision pressed on me, suffocating the words I had prepared for this moment.

"I thought you'd understand, Saanvi," he added, his voice tinged with regret. "I know it's not easy. But this country—our family—needs someone who can stand firm. Your mother, you, I... we've lived in the shadows of this nation's identity for too long. It's time for us to step out, even if it means sacrificing some parts of ourselves."

My father's expression had hardened by now, and he stood up suddenly, his chair scraping against the floor. "You're too young to understand, Saanvi. You don't know what it's like to feel powerless, to have your culture erased, to have your identity questioned at every turn. The Hindu Party isn't perfect, but it's a party that stands up for what India truly is. It's about pride. It's about acknowledging what has been wrong for centuries."

I shook my head, the words spilling out before I could stop them. "You're wrong, papa. This isn't about pride. This is about hatred. This is about division. You've forgotten what it means to be inclusive, to be a bridge between communities, not a wall."

He looked at me with a mixture of sorrow and frustration, his eyes hardening. "Maybe you're the one who's forgotten. Maybe you've forgotten where you come from. Your mother, Saanvi, she's a Muslim. Don't pretend that this doesn't matter. Don't pretend that this history doesn't define us."

His words hit me like a slap, and I recoiled, shocked by the sudden change in his tone. "I haven't forgotten who I am, papa. But you've forgotten who we are."

Before he could respond, the door opened, and my aging grandmother, Sumitra Trivedi, stepped into the room, her presence like a cool breeze in the midst of a heated storm. She looked between us, her eyes full of sadness, but her voice was calm.

"Enough, both of you," she said, her voice cutting through the tension. "Saanvi, your father's made his decision. And Ramesh, you don't need to defend it. We both know the cost of all this. But the truth is, none of us will change each other's minds. Not today, not ever."

My father's face softened at her words, but the silence that followed was thick and oppressive. It was the silence of something lost, something that could never be recovered. I was keen to meet my mother by myself, but my father, Ramesh Trivedi, insisted on driving down with me on Friday evening. He had never been one to allow many things to unfold without his presence, especially when emotions were involved. The car ride was a quiet one, filled with the hum of the engine and the occasional rustle of papers he always seemed to have with him, even in moments like these. He was deeply absorbed in his thoughts, but I couldn't ignore the heavy silence between us.

The familiar landscape passed by outside the window, but nothing felt familiar inside the car. My thoughts were a whirlpool of confusion, frustration, and a strange sense of anticipation. Our Trivedi mansion, the place where I had spent so many years of my life, was already feeling like a distant memory. And now, I had to prepare for my mother's house where I had spent my weekends. The memory of my mother's soft laughter, the smell of her cooking, the comfort of knowing she was always there—it all felt both comforting as well as foreign now, after everything that had happened. When we reached the house, the weight of the moment settled in. The door swung open before I had a chance to knock, and there she was, standing in the doorway. My mother, Yasmin Khan, her features softened with age, but still as striking as I remembered. Her dark eyes were full of emotion, a quiet sorrow that seemed to seep through every glance.

She took one long look at me before walking over slowly, wrapping her arms around me in a hug that was both warm and tense.

"Welcome home, Saanvi," she whispered, her voice a soft murmur against my ear. I didn't know how to respond. Part of me wanted to tell her everything—about Oxford, about how I had changed, about how the world seemed to have shifted beneath my feet. But as I stood there in her arms, I realized that I didn't even know where to begin.

"I missed you so much, *ammi*," I said quietly, my voice breaking slightly. "One year seems too long. And coming home just once a year does not seem fair at all." My words felt like they had been caught in my throat for months, and now, with the distance between us suddenly gone, I wasn't sure how to let them out. I pulled away slightly, looking into her eyes. "I missed you more than I can explain."

Her face softened, but her eyes betrayed something else—a depth of sorrow that had grown since I'd been away.

"It's good to have you back, Saanvi," she said, stepping back to look at me properly, as though searching for something in my face, something that might explain why I had come back, why I was standing here now.

My father, who had been standing silently behind me, cleared his throat. "I'll leave you two to talk," he said, his voice measured. He didn't wait for a response but walked to the adjacent room, leaving me alone with my mother.

I watched him leave the room, my heart aching with a strange mix of anger and confusion. Part of me wanted to run after him and demand that he stay, to somehow force him to answer for the political path he had chosen. But something held me back. The interrupted argument we needed to resume, those long-overdue conversations, could not be forced. They would come in their own time, when the world around us had settled. And right then, I needed my mother. I needed her more than I cared to admit.

"*Ammi,* are you okay?" I finally asked, my voice barely above a whisper.

She didn't answer immediately. Instead, she took a step back and gestured toward the tiny living room, motioning for me to follow her. We both sat down on the couch, the quiet of the house pressing in on us like a heavy blanket.

"I'm fine, Saanvi," she replied, though the way she said it didn't convince me. "I... I've been thinking. A lot. About everything."

I nodded, unsure how to continue. There was so much I wanted to say, but I wasn't sure where to start.

"Papa," I began slowly, watching her face for any sign of reaction, "he's changed. He's joined the Hindu Party, *ammi.* I don't know what to make of it."

My mother's expression hardened for just a moment, a flicker of something I couldn't quite place crossing her face. But she quickly masked it, her eyes lowering to the floor. She sighed deeply, almost inaudibly.

"I know," she said, her voice low and quiet. "I know, Saanvi. Your father... he's been different lately."

I couldn't help but feel a pang of disbelief. How had she not confronted him about this? How had she been living with this silent pain?

"You've been living with this... this change?" I asked, my voice rising. "You've just let him join that party without even saying anything?"

My mother turned to me then, her gaze firm but filled with sadness. "What do you want me to say, Saanvi?" she asked, her voice suddenly sharper. "What could I possibly say that would change anything? Your father has made up his mind, and he's not the man he used to be. But this... this is his path. I can't stop him. I don't think he can even stop himself."

Her words hung in the air, heavy with unspoken history and the weight of what I presumed was her own resignation. I wanted to shout, to demand answers from her, but the sadness in her eyes stopped me. She wasn't just angry; she was defeated, as though she had given up on the hope of reconciliation long ago.

"I don't understand, *ammi*," I said softly, my heart heavy. "How could he do this? How could he support a party that divides us, that makes us feel like outsiders in our own country?"

She didn't respond immediately, instead looking out the window at the fading light of dusk. For a moment, the only sound in the room was the soft rustling of leaves in the wind outside.

"When you were young, Saanvi," she said quietly, her voice almost a whisper, "your father and I would sometimes, only sometimes, talk about the future. We used to talk about what India could be, about the way we wanted to raise you—free of hate, free of the divisions that have always plagued this country. But things have changed. We've all changed."

I shook my head. "But *ammi*, mother, you... " I began, but she held up a hand, signaling me to stop.

"I don't know what to say, Saanvi," she replied, her voice low. "I don't know how to make you understand. I was born a Muslim in a world where my identity was already shaped by history, by religion, by politics. And now, I see my daughter fighting for a cause that was never mine. I see my husband embracing a party that is taking us further from the values I believed in." Her voice faltered, and she looked down at her hands, the sorrow evident in every line on her face.

"We've fought so hard to make a life here, even if you believe it is a fake life, a secret marriage. And now, it feels like everything is slipping away."

And I had assumed that Yasmin, my Muslim mother, had withdrawn into an unbearable silence. I was not prepared for this. Ramesh Trivedi, my father, walked in again. My voice broke through the quiet, a mixture of anger and disbelief.

"Yes, papa has betrayed you again, *ammi*," I whispered.

"Saanvi, please," my father said softly, his face weary, "it's not as simple as you think."

"No, it's that simple, isn't it?" I, Saanvi, retorted, pacing the living room, my thoughts clashing like a storm. "You, of all people—joining the Hindu Party? After everything we've been through? Everything *we've* been through?" My voice cracked as I turned to face him, the accusation heavy in the air.

Ramesh looked at me with quiet sadness, his hands clasped in front of him. "I didn't join the Hindu Party to abandon you or your mother, Saanvi."

"You didn't abandon us?" I laughed bitterly, my tone sharp, as I strode closer to him. "Then tell me, papa, how *are* you planning to explain this? To me? To my mother, your wife who you have never acknowledged to the world as your wife, your Yasmin?"

My mother, Yasmin was by now, sitting in the corner of the room, a silent observer, her gaze distant as she stared out of the window. The sorrow in her eyes was palpable, and yet, she said nothing. Her silence was louder than any words.

"Saanvi," Ramesh began, his voice quieter now, more controlled, "we're at a crossroads. The country needs to change. The people need leadership. The Hindu Party offers that. They speak for the Hindus."

My heart pounded. "Oh, they speak for the Hindus," I repeated, my words dripping with irony. "What about Muslims, papa? What about *ammi*, my mother? What about the fact that every day, Muslims like her and even hyphenated, half Muslims like me, are reminded that we're not part of this vision of India you're suddenly so eager to embrace?"

The words left my mouth with an unrestrained venom, my fists clenched. Ramesh stood up and walked toward me, his voice rising now, not in anger, but in frustration.

"I understand, Saanvi, I do," he said, his voice carrying the weight of an entire history. "But can you not see that the Ram Janmabhoomi movement is a question of identity? It's not about religion, it's about reclaiming something that was lost, something that was taken from us centuries ago."

I, Saanvi, blinked, disbelief flashing in my eyes. "What are you saying? That because a Hindu temple was destroyed centuries ago, it justifies what's happening now? The bloodshed, the hatred, the polarizing of our nation?"

Ramesh's voice grew quieter, almost as if he was struggling to keep his emotions under control. "It's about history, Saanvi. A history that is larger than us. And you cannot deny that the Babri Masjid was built over something that should not have been there in the first place."

I felt a flush of heat rise to my face. "You're telling me that Muslims should just accept the destruction of the Babri Masjid because it was built over a temple? That's your excuse for what's happening now?"

Ramesh shook his head, exhaling sharply. "You misunderstand. I'm not saying destruction is justified. I'm saying that the trauma of Hindus during those centuries—of having our temples destroyed, our culture erased—has to be acknowledged. We can't keep ignoring history."

I, Saanvi, recall staring at my father in stunned silence for a long moment. The words that had once held so much weight, that had once bridged the gap between them, now seemed hollow.

"But you're erasing my mother's history, my history," I said softly, my voice filled with grief. "You think that the Ram temple is a victory for you, but all I see is the deepening divide between us. Between *us*."

Ramesh's face tightened. He knew I was right, but he had come to believe that the future of India was intertwined with the rise of the Hindu Party, that his own political survival—perhaps even his legacy—depended on it. His eyes softened, and for a moment, he saw a glimpse of the man he had once been—a man who cared deeply for his family, who knew the weight of his choices.

But that man was fading. At least, in my blurry vision.

My mother, Yasmin had been sitting there, in the silence that had become her refuge. She had always been the calm one, the peacekeeper. But now, her silence felt like a weight too heavy to bear. She had heard every word, but she hadn't spoken a single one.

Finally, I turned to my mother, her voice now tinged with desperation.

"*Ammi?*" I asked gently, walking over to her. "What do you think?"

Yasmin's gaze never left the window, the soft glow of the setting sun reflecting in her eyes. There was a depth to her silence now, something far more painful than anger.

"*Ammi*, please," I repeated, my voice cracking. "Say something. Anything. I need you."

"I understand why you're angry, Saanvi," she said, her

eyes lifting to meet her daughter's. "I see how the rise of the Hindu Party, the building of the Ram Mandir, feels like an attack on everything we've built—everything that's been hard-earned. The very idea that our faith, our identity, could be diminished in the eyes of the state... it cuts deep. I get it. But, you must also understand the other side. The pain that my own husband, your father, feels. And the pain of millions of Hindus who have suffered, who have watched as their culture and temples were erased by invaders, who have watched as the very land they revere has been denied to them."

I watched my mother, the woman who had been both my shield and my refuge. It pained me to hear those words, to hear the underlying resignation in Yasmin's voice. She had been the one to bridge the gap between two worlds, balancing the love of her Hindu husband with the complexities of her Muslim identity. Yet now, the foundation seemed to be crumbling, and Yasmin's words rang with the agony of having to face what she had long suppressed. My mother, Yasmin, feeling the weight of her daughter's gaze, continued, her voice softer now but with a clarity that startled me.

I frowned, my thoughts tumbling like a cascade of conflicting emotions. I wanted to reject my mother's words, to hold onto the belief that there could be no justification for hurting an entire community just because of historical wrongs. But Yasmin's words carried an authenticity that I couldn't dismiss.

My mother sighed, a breath full of untold histories, of wars fought and lost, of the constant tug-of-war between loyalty to her own religion and a desire for peace.

"Do you think that when the Babri Masjid was built, it wasn't a statement? Not just an architectural one, but a statement of power, of conquest? Yes, Muslims had been and have been oppressed for years. Yes, we had been at the receiving end of years of brutality, but I cannot deny that the Hindus felt a similar sorrow when they saw their sacred spaces torn down. And what followed—the destruction of the Babri Masjid—was not just an act of reclaiming a temple, but an act of reclaiming dignity, of rectifying centuries of wrongs they had lived with. It became a symbol of resistance, and when that temple was brought down, they didn't just feel like they had lost a piece of history. They lost their sense of self, of belonging. A temple, a place of worship, it was not just stone; it was part of their spirit, their very identity."

Yasmin paused for a moment, as if considering the depth of her own words. Her gaze moved to the window, where the fading light of the evening poured through, casting long shadows on the walls. Her eyes softened as she spoke again, her voice quieter now, more reflective.

"I've lived in this country long enough to know the complexities of these wounds. I've seen the Hindus, who may never have touched a temple, carry a sense of collective hurt in their hearts—hurts from their ancestors, hurts from a history they have been taught, hurts that were never addressed, and were never healed. And then, when the Babri Masjid was destroyed, when the Ram Mandir became the battleground, it was as if someone had finally acknowledged their pain."

My eyes flashed with frustration. I opened my mouth to speak. But Yasmin raised her hand gently, signaling for her to listen.

"Don't misunderstand me," she continued. "I'm not justifying the violence, the hatred, or the discrimination that followed. I'm not excusing the atrocities committed in the name of religion or politics. But I am telling you, Saanvi, that there are layers to this. There are reasons why people take the positions they do. It's not just about power or politics—it's about healing, or the failure to heal, about finding a way to belong in a country that has forced its people to pick sides for centuries."

I, Saanvi, sank onto my mother's fading couch, my hands trembling slightly, the weight of my mother's words sinking deep into her heart. I had never expected to hear such an explanation from Yasmin, the woman who had always been my unwavering rock. My mother, Yasmin's ability to empathize with the Hindus' plight—her willingness to see beyond her own pain—was a revelation that shook me to my core. I had spent so much of my young life in some kind of false righteous anger, in a world where the Muslim identity had been stripped of its dignity by the very forces my mother was now speaking of. My father also watched the drama unfold in stunned silence.

Yasmin sat beside me, her eyes full of both wisdom and sorrow. "I've seen this country torn apart by violence, by hatred, and by fear. I've watched how Muslims and Hindus, who share so much—so many customs, traditions, even language—have been pitted against each other for reasons that stretch far beyond any one person's understanding. The Babri Masjid, the Ram Mandir... it's not just about religion. It's about power. But it's also about loss. And until both sides can truly understand that loss—without seeing the other's pain as an obstacle to their own -they will never find peace."

I, Saanvi, was silent for a long while, my mind reeling. I thought about my father's shift in politics, his newfound embrace of a party that I, stepping down from the august portals of Oxford University with its mighty intellectual aura, viewed as divisive and dangerous. But now, hearing my mother's words, I began to see something I hadn't before—a glimmer of understanding, even empathy, for the pain that had driven so many Hindus toward the Hindu Party.

"I know it's hard, Saanvi," Yasmin whispered, her voice barely audible. "But sometimes, we have to step outside our own wounds and try to see the other side. It doesn't make what's happening right. But it might help us understand why people do what they do."

As I looked at my mother, my heart filled with a strange mix of gratitude and grief. I didn't agree with everything my mother had said, but I could feel the weight of her words, the heartache beneath them. My mother was right in a way. This was a war of emotions, not just politics. And the Ram Mandir, for all its symbolism, was only a small part of a much larger struggle.

The struggle for identity, for belonging, for recognition. And maybe, just maybe, the first step toward healing was acknowledging that both sides had wounds—wounds that could not be ignored, wounds that needed to be addressed if India was ever going to find a way forward.

I stood there, stunned. The weight of my mother's words settled into my chest like a stone. I had expected anger, maybe even betrayal. But what I saw now was something deeper—an acceptance that there was no going back, no undoing the choices that had been made. I had somehow assumed that the Ram temple was a symbol for my father, Ramesh, for the Hindu Party, and to my Muslim mother, Yasmin, it was a symbol of everything that had been lost.

I wanted to scream, to shake my father and my mother into action. But as I stood there in the silence, I realized that no words would change what had already happened. The divisions had been set, the lines drawn.

But perhaps, just perhaps, this was the moment where I could carve out my own path. The one that didn't require choosing between them. The one that didn't demand surrendering my identity for the sake of political allegiance.

But in that moment, with the weight of history pressing down on them all, I, Saanvi, felt a deep loneliness. My heart was pungent with a very complex mix of emotions.

19

As my father navigated the tumultuous waters of politics in Ayodhya, he found himself becoming more than just a figurehead. He had aspired to become a voice for the unheard, but he ended up becoming a voice for the overheard. Each day brought fresh challenges that tested his resolve. The political landscape was a battleground, filled with rival factions and competing ideologies. He had to learn quickly how to strike a balance between being firm and flexible. His message needed to resonate with diverse audiences, yet he remained anchored to his core beliefs. It was a delicate dance, one that required not only political acumen but also an innate understanding of human nature.

During this time, my father's speeches became increasingly impassioned, infused with a sense of urgency that stirred the hearts of many. He spoke of the rich cultural heritage of Ayodhya, urging people to come together to celebrate their shared history rather than allowing their differences to drive them apart. In his eyes, Ayodhya was not merely a place of worship; it was a community replete with stories, dreams, and hopes for harmony. He often recounted tales from the Ramayana, drawing parallels between the struggles faced by its characters and those encountered in contemporary life. These narratives, deeply rooted in the collective consciousness of the people, served as both a reminder of their heritage and a rallying cry for unity.

Yet, behind the charisma and the speeches lay a man grappling with personal turmoil. My father's nights were often sleepless, his mind racing with thoughts of his long years of marriage to a Muslim woman, the weight of expectations, and the fear of letting down those who believed in him. There were moments when he felt utterly alone, standing on the precipice of a career that offered so much promise but demanded equally high sacrifices. He wrestled with guilt—guilt for his wife, my mother, and for the love that had begun to slip through his fingers like sand.

In the months that followed, his connection with the people of Ayodhya deepened, but it came at a cost. The demands of political life were relentless; the endless rallies, the networking, the strategizing—it was a whirlwind that left little room for introspection. On more than one occasion, I had witnessed him return home late at night, his face etched with exhaustion, a mere shadow of the man who had once filled our home with laughter and warmth. My mother, ever supportive, bore the strain of his absences. Their conversations risked devolving into silence, each unwilling to articulate the pain lingering between them. The cracks became evident. On weekends, when he did return, their shared moments felt fleeting, a ghost of the warmth that once filled our home.

And now, my father lived alone. Our Trivedi mansion no longer bore the weight of grandeur—it merely carried echoes. It no longer stood in pride—it endured. Its arches still curved with elegance, and the columns still wore their ancestral carvings like forgotten medals. But the walls no longer breathed. They rose like questions, once witness to a secular past, now nervously watching a city gripped by certitudes. The stone courtyard had heard too many discourses: about Hindu scriptures, about elections, about whose god claimed which acre. The estate, once alive with politics and prayers, had grown silent, a brooding giant that remembered too much. My paternal grandparents, the last custodians of its spirit, had passed on, leaving behind an aching void that no wealth or history could fill. When they passed, they took the house's spirit with them. Their absence had transformed the house into a silent witness to my father's struggles and my own pursuit of a life far removed from the complexities of Ayodhya. Now, its silence mirrored my father's. And mine—a life half-chosen, half-fled—from the layered labyrinth of Ayodhya.

When I had left for Oxford, it was with the quiet understanding that our Trivedi mansion would possibly remain empty, its chandeliers unlit and its rooms devoid of human presence. The decision to study abroad could be described as much an escape as it was an ambition. I carried with me the weight of my family's expectations and the unresolved tensions that simmered within our home. The mansion, with its echoing hallway and vacant courtyard, became a stark metaphor for the loneliness that had crept into our lives. It was a place where memories lingered, but where no new ones were being made. With the passing of my grandparents, the silence that fell wasn't just domestic. It was ideological. The house grew stiller as the city outside grew louder. Now, the mansion seemed both relic and resistance, watching my father's retreat and my own exile from its haunted threshold. We were two kinds of orphans—he of history, I of home.

In the years that followed, my father's political career

took center stage. The mansion, once a bustling hub of activity, became a repository of relics and forgotten heirlooms. And yet, the loyal and long standing staff made sure that not a trace of dust would ever settle on the antique furniture or cobwebs adorn the corners of rooms that would see sunlight every single day. The garden remained a striking exception to the mansion's desolation. It was always meticulously tended by the now old gardener, who continued to prune the hedges with precision and nurture the wholesome blooms that spilled over the pathways. The care given to the garden seemed almost defiant, a reminder that not all beauty within the estate had succumbed to neglect.

Despite the emptiness of the mansion, my father could not bring himself to make it a home once more. The reasons were as complex as the man himself. He had married my mother against the wishes of both their families, defying societal norms and enduring years of scrutiny. Their union, though rooted in love, had been a source of endless controversy. My mother, a Muslim woman in a predominantly Hindu community, had faced prejudice and judgment that my father could neither shield her from nor fully understand. Their marriage was always and unquestionably, a tale of their undying and unremitting love for each other. But it could also be interpreted as a reminder of the divisions that plagued our society.

My father's political aspirations added another layer of complexity. As a rising figure in Ayodhya's political landscape, he had to navigate the treacherous waters of public perception. Bringing my mother to live with him in the mansion would have been a bold statement, one that he feared might alienate his supporters and jeopardize his career. The Trivedi mansion, with all its grandeur, became a symbol of what he could not have: a life where personal happiness and professional ambition coexisted without conflict.

Instead, my father chose to live alone in the mansion, his days consumed by politics and his nights haunted by memories of what could have been. He would often retreat to the study, a room that had also been my grandfather's sanctuary. There, amidst stacks of books and faded photographs, he would pour over documents and draft speeches that sought to unite a divided community. The irony was not lost on him; he, who spoke so eloquently of unity and harmony, could not reconcile the divisions within his own life.

During my visits home, the emptiness of the Trivedi mansion was almost unbearable. The air felt heavy with unspoken words and unresolved tensions. My father and I would sit in the living room, our conversations polite but distant. He would ask about my studies, my friends, and my academic life at Oxford, but the questions felt perfunctory, as though he was trying to fill the silence rather than genuinely seeking to connect. In turn, I struggled to find the right words to bridge the gap between us. Our relationship, once warm and affectionate, had become a casualty of the choices we had made, choices that had taken us down paths that seemed to diverge further with each passing year.

On one particular visit, I asked my father pointblank why he did not bring my mother to live with him in the mansion. His response was measured, almost rehearsed. He spoke of the challenges of his political career, the demands of his constituency, and the importance of maintaining a certain image. But beneath his carefully chosen words, I sensed a deep-seated fear, the fear of what might happen if he dared to defy the expectations of those around him. It was a fear that had shaped his life and, by extension, mine. The Trivedi mansion, in its emptiness, became a mirror reflecting the sacrifices my father had made. It stood as a testament to the complexities of his existence, a life caught between duty and desire, between the public and the private. For me, it was a constant reminder of the cost of ambition and the weight of legacy. As I walked through its silent rooms, I could almost hear the whispers of the past, urging me to confront the truths that we had long sought to ignore.

Over time, I came to see the mansion not just as a physical space, but as a symbol of our family's struggles and stubbornness. It was a place where history and memory converged, where the past and present coexisted in uneasy harmony. And though it remained empty, it was never truly abandoned. It held within its walls the tales of those who had come before us and the promise of what might yet be. In its silence, it spoke volumes, reminding me that even in the absence of life, there is always the possibility of renewal. Ramesh Trivedi's rise to politics was not merely a calculated ascent; it was a journey shaped by the soil of Ayodhya, by its sacred air and the relentless tide of its history. The city of temples, chants, and memories of past grandeur seemed to demand a voice that could weave together its fractured aspirations. That voice, unexpectedly, became his.

In the early days of his political career, Ramesh Trivedi's name had resonated with the people like the deep toll of a temple bell, strong, unyielding, and full of respect for tradition. He was a man who spoke not in grandiose speeches but in measured, deliberate words, each one heavy with meaning. Ayodhya's heart beat with its temples, and Ramesh, in his early campaigns, had an almost intuitive understanding of this. His public meetings were often held in the shadow of ancient shrines, where he invoked the stories of Ram, Sita, and Hanuman not as mythological relics but as living parables, guiding the city's path forward.

My father, Ramesh was no ordinary politician. He did not simply rely on rhetoric; he immersed himself in the life of Ayodhya's people. He walked through its narrow lanes, often barefoot, as a gesture of humility and connection. There was a peculiar charisma to his presence, not flashy but deeply magnetic, as though he carried a piece of Ayodhya's ancient essence within him. His visits to farmers in the outskirts were marked not by pomp but by genuine curiosity and empathy. He spoke to them about crop failures, rising debts, and the quiet erosion of their dignity. He listened more than he talked, an oddity in the world of politics.

But Ramesh was not just the people's man; he was also a man of strategy. He understood that Ayodhya's destiny was tied not only to its spiritual legacy but also to its economic survival. Early in his tenure, he spearheaded an ambitious riverfront redevelopment project. On paper, it was a move to bolster tourism, but in execution, it was an act of cultural reclamation. The ghats were restored with an almost devotional precision, the labyrinthine by lanes leading to them cleared of years of neglect. He commissioned local artisans to create murals depicting episodes from the Ramayana, weaving Ayodhya's narrative into its very streets. The project provided employment, reviving the city's faltering artisan community, and brought Ayodhya a newfound pride.

Yet, Ramesh's vision for Ayodhya extended beyond the tangible. He championed education as the cornerstone of the city's resurgence. Recognizing the tension between tradition and modernity, he initiated the establishment of schools that integrated the study of ancient texts with contemporary sciences. "Ayodhya," he often said, "must not be a relic preserved in amber. It must breathe, evolve, and lead." His education policies were a testament to this belief, with classrooms echoing with verses from the Vedas alongside lessons in computer programming.

However, Ramesh's tenure was not without its shadows. The communal fault lines of Ayodhya, fragile and often exploited by those in power, posed an ever-present challenge. Deep down, he still carried his secular convictions, and so he walked a tightrope. He was painfully aware that any misstep could ignite a blaze. His response was to engage in quiet, almost invisible diplomacy. He reached out to religious leaders across the spectrum, inviting them to private dialogues. These meetings were never publicized, for Ramesh believed that true reconciliation did not require applause. He spoke candidly about fears and hopes, urging these leaders to find common ground in Ayodhya's shared heritage.

The unspoken tension between my father and myself, and my confrontation with him, the man I had always revered as my father, had indeed left an indelible mark on his psyche, even though my mother had defended him at the time. Given the fragile equilibrium of our household, it was not just a disagreement; it was more a reckoning. I had expressed my unabashed outrage about his joining the Hindu party, a move that had seemed to my mind at least, antithetical to the principles of fairness and inclusivity he had once espoused. Inevitably, after that confrontation, the shadows of Ayodhya's minarets and temple domes had seemed to loom larger for him, a metaphor for the divisive politics that had by now enveloped his life.

Ramesh, to his credit, did not shy away from my words. He had listened, his face a mask of stoicism, though his eyes had betrayed a storm within. Days and months had passed in silence, a deep chasm growing between us as I had left for England. I knew though, that the weight of my words, or perhaps the burden of his conscience, would make him rethink.

My father did begin to act. The first signs were subtle. Ramesh started attending community meetings, not the orchestrated rallies of the party but small, intimate gatherings in Ayodhya's mixed neighborhoods. He sat with Muslim elders under the shade of banyan trees and shared cups of *chai* with Hindu priests at bustling tea stalls. These interactions were not political maneuvers; they were genuine efforts to understand the grievances and hopes of both communities. One particular meeting stood out. It was held in a modest *madrasa* on the outskirts of Ayodhya. The room was sparse, with low wooden benches and the faint scent of ink and paper lingering in the air. Ramesh's presence was met with wary eyes and folded arms. Yet, he spoke with humility, acknowledging the distrust that his association with the Hindu party had engendered. He assured the attendees that he was there to listen, not to impose.

"I've come to understand," he began, "that the soul of Ayodhya cannot belong to one group alone. It's like a river that nourishes all who live by its banks. If we dam it for one side, we starve the other." His words were met with silence at first, but as the discussion unfolded, the room warmed up to his sincerity of purpose.

To navigate the ever-shifting landscape of state politics, my father forged alliances with grassroots organizations and local leaders who shared his vision for a more equitable society. He championed social justice initiatives and tirelessly advocated for the rights of marginalized communities. His ability to voice the concerns of the underprivileged earned him not only respect but also growing recognition beyond his immediate circle.

As his political involvement deepened, he came to

understand that passion alone would not suffice—leadership required mastery of the political machinery. He began attending workshops on governance and public policy, immersing himself in the intricate mechanics of legislative systems. This hunger for knowledge shaped his strategies and lent his leadership a quiet sophistication. His message of inclusivity resonated widely, especially after several successful initiatives—improving local schools, launching health awareness campaigns—that directly impacted people's lives.

What set him apart was his hands-on approach. He was often seen walking dusty by lanes, stopping to speak with residents, listening without judgment, taking notes. This genuine engagement endeared him to the public, and his grassroots support swelled.

The political climate was shifting. Regional parties, promising to prioritize local needs, were rising. My father's vision aligned with the aspirations of these times. He recognized that the youth were key to meaningful reform. He began organizing forums where young people could speak freely, debate, question, and participate. His outreach not only bolstered his campaign but also sparked a new generation of politically aware citizens.

The defining moment came when he decided to run again—this time for a more critical office. The campaign was intense: door-to-door canvassing, town hall meetings, and fiery debates. He poured his soul into it. Late nights were spent writing speeches, honing his message, revising strategies with his core team. Every handshake, every open-air address was a chance to share his vision of a better Ayodhya.

As the election drew near, tensions rose. Rivals attacked his record, questioned his loyalty, tried to sully his integrity. But my father stood firm, speaking with conviction about a future where Ayodhya, he promised, would "reclaim the spirit of *Ram Rajya*—a land of justice, compassion, and harmony." His words, anchored in heritage and hope, drew crowds. But beneath the surface, I could see the strain. I knew that there were cracks beneath that confident exterior.

Ramesh's vision began taking shape in tangible ways. One of his first acts was to restore a crumbling community center, once a beacon of cultural exchange. Securing funds from both Hindu and Muslim philanthropists, he had it rebuilt as a center for interfaith dialogue, art exhibitions, and skill-building workshops. The inaugural event—a poetry recital of verses from the Bhagavad Gita and the Quran, read in tandem—was symbolic, stirring, and controversial.

Not everyone in his party was pleased. "Ramesh ji, you're making us look weak," one senior leader sneered in a closed-door meeting. "You can't lead by trying to please both sides. You're becoming like that eggplant— neither here nor there."

The insult landed, but Ramesh's response was steady: "If being an eggplant means bridging divides, then so be it. I'd rather be mocked for seeking peace than praised for stoking hate."

His resolve was tested when a riot broke out in a nearby district. A rumor of temple desecration sparked fury. Ramesh acted swiftly, organizing a peace march with a Hindu priest on one side and a Muslim cleric on the other. He walked the city's most volatile streets holding a saffron flag in one hand, a green flag in the other. That image, captured by a local photographer, made headlines—becoming a symbol of hope to many and a provocation to others.

Behind closed doors, he wrestled with the weight of his position. Hardliners in his party accused him of alienating their core base. "You're soft," they warned. "You're losing the pulse of the real voter."

But Ramesh refused to budge. "Leadership," he insisted, "isn't about echoing what people want to hear. It's about doing what they'll someday be proud of."

In a rare moment of vulnerability, he wrote to me: "Do you remember when you asked why I joined the Hindu party? I thought I could steer it toward inclusivity from within. But steering isn't enough. Sometimes, you have to change the course of the entire ship."

He pushed forward. He drafted and championed legislation to protect religious minorities from forced displacement during redevelopment projects. Another bill proposed preserving sites of shared cultural and religious value—temples and mosques alike. Despite fierce opposition, Ramesh's moral clarity and eloquence swayed enough legislators to secure passage. But the cost was steep. Former allies turned cold. Invitations to party meetings dwindled. Applause for his speeches became more polite than passionate.

Still, he persevered. "The measure of a leader," he often said, "isn't how many follow you—it's how many you inspire to lead."

His boldest act came during a volatile time. After a divisive political rally stirred communal anxieties, Ramesh made an unannounced visit to a local mosque. It was not a political calculation—it was personal. Standing before a skeptical crowd, his voice steady yet intimate, he said, "Ayodhya is not mine or yours. It belongs to the ages—to every soul that ever found peace here." His words didn't erase the tension, but they carved a pause in which reflection could breathe.

Few knew that beneath the public idealism lay a personal torment. His long-secret relationship with Yasmin—my mother—had always remained in the shadows. Their love, concealed from the world, gave him a painful understanding of what it meant to straddle lines of belonging and exile. That hidden truth informed his politics. When he advocated for interfaith festivals or for preserving a sixteenth century mosque alongside a temple, he was not merely enacting policy. He was seeking to heal the torn map of his own heart. He was not just acting as a politician but as a man seeking to reconcile the warring parts of himself.

Under Ramesh's leadership, Ayodhya didn't become a utopia, but it became a city striving for equilibrium. The riverfront thrived with pilgrims and visitors, schools evolved into spaces of integrative learning, and though unrest still simmered, there was a steady undercurrent of hope.

The turning point in his rise to the national stage came during a major election—ironically, at a time when families were turning inward to celebrate and bond. While others lit lamps, he stood before a rural crowd, about to deliver a speech that could alter his career. The occasion was symbolic—it reminded him of what he had sacrificed at home. My mother, ever patient, had waited for him through long weekends with silent strength, her absence in his life deepening even as his public presence expanded.

It was during this time that key party leaders urged him to step up, to take on a more central role. Initially hesitant, unsure whether he could stretch further into the consuming world of politics, he ultimately accepted—driven by both duty and the conviction that he could do more.

As a central minister, Ramesh articulated a vision rooted in *sewa*—selfless service. Drawing on his years as a teacher, he focused on education and youth empowerment. He also championed infrastructure reform, recognizing that Ayodhya, revered across faiths, was ill-prepared for the growing number of pilgrims. He advocated for better roads, healthcare, and sanitation, always anchoring his proposals in lived stories—of women walking miles for clean water, of children studying by kerosene light.

But success brought greater scrutiny. The national landscape was even more divided, and established figures in Delhi viewed him with suspicion. They launched smear campaigns, discredited his work, spun false narratives. Yet he endured. He let his actions speak. He read policy tomes late into the night, built coalitions across party lines, and cultivated a reputation for pragmatism grounded in compassion.

He was invited to international forums, where he spoke not only of Ayodhya, but of the moral dimensions of governance. His speeches intertwined the local and the universal—each anecdote a window into a larger truth. What drew people in wasn't charisma alone—it was the quiet force of a man who had lived his convictions, and suffered for them.

As the decade advanced, the atmosphere in Ayodhya grew volatile, thick with the rhetoric of political leaders who wielded religion like a sword—appealing to faith, stoking division. The delicate mosaic of Hindu-Muslim coexistence had cracked under the strain of ideological warfare. Sacred sites, once revered as symbols of shared heritage, were reimagined as trophies in a rising battle for dominance. In the din of fervent slogans and orchestrated spectacles, the voices of local scholars, activists, and ordinary citizens—those who had long championed unity—faded into the background.

My father, a seasoned politician, stood precariously at the intersection of tradition and expediency. He had long worn his secularism like a second skin—firm, deliberate, and unshakable. But as the communal temperature rose, so did the demands from within his own party: louder declarations, clearer alignments, unmistakable displays of Hindu nationalism. Each of his decisions seemed to send ripples through Ayodhya—triggering outrage, admiration, suspicion, or all at once. The tension was palpable, simmering in tea-stall debates and whispered exchanges between neighbors. The general elections loomed, not merely as a democratic rite, but as a reckoning. Old wounds were being reopened, old grudges reawakened, and history itself was being weaponized for political gain.

Caught in the eye of this storm, my father grappled not only with the politics of the moment but with the integrity of his own identity. Could he remain a champion of harmony, or would the relentless pressures of power compel him to compromise? His public career—and perhaps the fate of Ayodhya—hung in the balance.

He would often retreat to his study in the evenings, long after the rallies ended, after the shouting died down. There, beneath a dim lamp, he'd sit with an untouched glass of water and a small framed photograph of my mother. I could visualize him in those moments—his gaze heavy with reflection, burdened not just by the fear of losing an election, but by the deeper dread of betraying a vision of Ayodhya that lived in his memory, or perhaps only in his longing.

The attacks grew more vicious. Anonymous leaflets accused him of betrayal—of favoritism, of hiding secrets from his past. Most were fabrications, but in the hands of those who shaped public sentiment, they were potent. His advisors urged retaliation, a matching counteroffensive. But he refused.

"If I stoop to their level," he told them, "I become them."

Then came the scandal. The night before his final rally, a trusted aide arrived at the Trivedi mansion, visibly shaken. A new accusation was being prepared: a fabricated affair, a story crafted to smear him, to taint his moral core. For a brief moment, I saw the fire dim in his eyes. He dismissed the messenger quietly, and turned to the few confidants still standing beside him.

"If I don't win this with truth," he said, voice steady, "then I don't deserve to win at all."

The next day, at the last rally of his campaign, he stood before the crowd without flourish or fanfare. No elaborate slogans. No promises. Just a plain kurta, tousled hair, and a presence stripped down to its essence.

"I have no manifesto to offer you today," he began, voice low but unwavering. "Ayodhya has already changed too much. It is not a platform for ambition. It is a living memory—of joy, of pain, of coexistence. We dishonor it when we try to possess it."

There was silence. Not the silence of indifference, but the stillness of people unsure whether they were hearing a politician—or a father speaking to his children. He continued, speaking not of policy, but of belonging. Of responsibility.

"I know promises have become the currency of politics. But integrity cannot be purchased with words. Each pledge made is a weight on the conscience. I cannot trade in empty coins."

The speech ended without cheers. It ended with stillness. With thought. And perhaps that was enough.

The fallout came swiftly. Party leaders grew distant. Strategy meetings happened without him. The invitations dried up. Some of his oldest allies faded into silence, their loyalty buckling under the weight of political convenience. But Ramesh remained unshaken.

"The mark of a true leader," he often told me, "is not how many follow, but how many are inspired to lead."

Something in our relationship began to shift. The long-held grievances between us softened. One evening, as he sat on the verandah watching the sun dip beyond the river and facetimed me, he said quietly, "You were right to challenge me. It's your generation's job to hold us accountable."

I said nothing, but I missed him. I missed *ammi.* And yet, I could see the contours of the man he was becoming —not perfect, not unscarred, but real.

Some called him an eggplant—neither fully aligned with his party nor wholly embraced by its opposition. But it was in that liminal space, in that in-between, that he found something rare: the freedom to be himself. His journey wasn't clean. It wasn't linear. But it was true.

And that, above all, taught me something enduring: that courage is not the absence of fear or contradiction— but the insistence on moving forward despite them.

For that, I am proud to call him my father.

Yes, the walls speak, not in words, but in textures. Under the afternoon sun, their surfaces feel uneven, as if history itself had left its fingerprints. On one side, the stone is warm, almost golden, its pores steeped in the faint scent of turmeric ground in countless kitchens, marigold garlands brushed against it during festivals, and the acrid sweetness of lamp oil that once burned for days without pause. On the other, the stone is cooler, shadowed, holding in its grain the memory of attar and rosewater sprinkled before prayer, the musky undertone of prayer rugs stored for generations, the faint echo of sandalwood smoke rising from a courtyard brazier. The smells do not mingle. They hover in separate currents, stubbornly themselves, as if each feared dilution by the other. Between them, a thin seam runs along the wall, no more than a line to the eye, but to the touch it feels like a border. In that seam, the air is strangely still, carrying neither turmeric nor rosewater, as though even the wind refuses to mediate between them. If you press your ear to the wall, there is no voice, no whisper—only the silence of centuries watching processions pass in both directions. It is a silence that knows the weight of drums and the rhythm of the *azaan*, yet refuses to declare which it remembers more fondly.

20

Even as my father got embroiled in his political career, the foundations for the Ram temple were being laid both physically and metaphorically during this turbulent chapter of Ayodhya's history. It was a period marked by fervent devotion, political maneuvering, and the collision of deeply entrenched ideologies. For my father, Ramesh, the temple's construction represented not just a symbol of faith but also a complex challenge that further entangled his political ambitions and personal dilemmas. While the movement gained momentum, he found himself drawn into its orbit, grappling with its deep implications for his career. In the years leading up to this point, the Ram Janmabhoomi movement had become a national phenomenon. Processions were held, speeches made, and the air in Ayodhya seemed charged with purpose and tension. My father, though initially skeptical of aligning himself with a cause that threatened to divide as much as it united, was acutely aware of its political power. His initial role in local governance had gradually evolved into a more prominent position in state politics and eventually led to a place in the central cabinet now. And with that ascent came the inevitable pressures to take a stand on the temple issue.

On the ground, the site where the temple was to rise became a focal point of activity. Laborers worked tirelessly under the scorching sun, clearing debris and digging trenches. Local leaders and religious figures visited frequently, overseeing the progress and holding rituals to sanctify the land. The chants of "Jai Shri Ram" echoed through the streets, blending with the sounds of hammers striking stone and the hum of activity at the construction site.

My father's involvement began with a simple speech, one meant to acknowledge the aspirations of the community without fully committing to the cause. Yet, as the movement's fervor grew, so did the expectations placed upon him. He was invited to meetings with influential leaders who saw the temple as more than a religious endeavor. To them, it was a statement of identity, a reclaiming of history. For Ramesh, these meetings were both an opportunity and a minefield. He knew that his support could solidify his standing among his constituency, but he also feared the potential fallout, the way such alignment could deepen the fractures within the community. He somehow watched these developments with a mixture of sadness and foreboding. Deep down, he had always believed in the power of education and dialogue to bridge divides. As the weeks passed, the construction site became a microcosm of the larger forces at play. Volunteers arrived from across the country, their enthusiasm infectious but also unnerving. There was a sense of inevitability about the temple, as if its completion was not just a possibility but a destiny. Yet, beneath the surface, tensions simmered. Disputes arose over land ownership, the allocation of resources, and the involvement of important political figures. My father found himself mediating these conflicts, his role as a politician and a community leader becoming increasingly intertwined. My mother, Yasmin, observed all of this with her characteristic quietude in her home. She rarely spoke about the temple or my father's political engagements, but her eyes often betrayed her worry. My mother said nothing because as I suspect, her silence was a statement in itself. For her, unity and identity were not abstractions to be debated or leveraged; they were lived experiences, the threads that had bound her life with my father's despite their spatial difference. She did not somehow feel that the temple, with all its symbolic weight, was driving a wedge between communities and within our family as well. And this still surprises me to this day.

As the temple rose, so too did the fault lines in our lives. The earth beneath Ayodhya was shifting, and with it, our future. My father became further entangled in the political and spiritual symbolism of the temple, while my mother retreated into a space of memory, of poetry, of private reflection. And I, caught between them, suspended between two worlds, began to realize that the story of Ayodhya was never just about gods and governance, nor about faith or politics. It was a tale of the heart—unsettled, yearning, split by contradictions it didn't know how to reconcile.

One evening, as the city lulled into its uneasy post-rally silence, another chapter began—not on the street, but within our story. The news came abruptly, carried by the thin, trembling wire of a late-night phone call. My maternal grandfather, Adil Khan, had died. He had passed alone in his deteriorating house, unnoticed by anyone until a neighbor, alarmed by the silence, went to check. By then, it was too late. The house, dim and disordered, held only the echoes of a man who had quietly receded from life. In his final years, Adil Khan had all but vanished from the public stage. Once a man of fiery speeches and impassioned ideals, he had withdrawn into the quietude of his fading years, disillusioned by the compromises and betrayals of the political arena. His once-commanding voice had grown silent, his presence in public affairs diminished like the light of a dying candle. The world, too, seemed to turn away, leaving him to the company of the cracked walls of his home, and the echoes of a life that had drifted into obscurity.

My father, Ramesh, received the news in silence, his face a mask of calm as he absorbed the gravity of it. He did not ask questions, nor did he hesitate. "We'll go," he said simply, his tone leaving no room for argument. That single sentence carried a weight heavier than it appeared. When he showed up at my mother's door to tell her, Yasmin was visibly stunned. Here was a Hindu man, a cabinet minister tied irrevocably to the temple's public image, standing at her threshold to acknowledge the death of a Muslim man estranged from his daughter and the world. And yet, in her eyes, there was no judgment— only a quiet understanding. Ramesh had chosen the right thing. Not for politics. For decency. For a man whose public persona had always been so deeply entwined with his Hindu identity, this choice felt almost radical. Yet, she understood. It wasn't just duty that propelled him, but something deeper, something unspoken. "We'll go." Ramesh had the good sense and the wisdom to go to her, to break the news to her.

Yasmin looked at him with a mixture of gratitude and apprehension, and then looked down, as if trying hard to recall the face of the father who had abandoned her a long time ago. It had been years since she had seen her father. Their relationship had been broken forever after his son's death and his decision to fight for the Muslim cause. He had no opinion about her choice to marry a Hindu, Ramesh, nor ever cared about her decision to stay on in the marriage without forfeiting her Muslim identity and embracing a life that defied the boundaries of tradition. Adil Khan had never forgiven the world, or perhaps himself, after the death of his son. That loss had unraveled him. He had merely withdrawn, taking his hurt and complexity with him into silence. But now, with the news of his death, grief overtook everything else. Yasmin nodded, and they prepared to leave together.

The journey to Adil Khan's home felt surreal, like a strange detour through time. Ayodhya was noisy, the temple's framework now clearly visible above rooftops, its soundscape filled with construction and chorus. Yet, amidst this building, a kind of destruction awaited us. A life had ended. A family had reached its final estrangement.. The streets of Ayodhya were alive with the noise of construction and the whispers of change. The rising Ram Temple loomed large, both physically and symbolically, casting its long shadow over the city. It seemed almost cruelly ironic that amidst this fervent act of building, there was an intimate act of undoing—a life that had ended, a family that had shattered beyond repair and reconciliation.

When they arrived at the house, it was as though time had slowed. The air was heavy with the smell of decay and dampness, the walls bearing the stains of neglect. Adil Khan's body lay on a simple cot, his face sunken, his frame frail and diminished. Yasmin stood motionless for a long moment, her gaze fixed on the man who had been her father and her anchor in her childhood. Slowly, she knelt beside him, her fingers trembling as they brushed against his cold hand. Whatever anger or resentment had lingered between them dissolved in that instant, replaced by a quiet, aching sorrow.

Yasmin's estranged father's house, small and unadorned, seemed to hold no memories of a life that once seemed full but now felt hollow. It was the kind of place where time seemed to slow, where every moment stretched out in quiet isolation. The walls of the house had never witnessed the slow crumbling of a family, once strong, now scattered. Adil Khan had deliberately erased everything from his life. Outside, the foundations of the Ram Temple were being laid, stone by stone, echoing through the city. Yet inside this house, her father, Adil Khan, an old man with little left, lay in a bed that had seen his decline. The noise of the temple's construction, so loud and all-encompassing outside, seemed distant within the thick walls of his solitude. In his final moments, there was no family by his side, no wife or daughter to hold his hand. The life he had built, had eroded under the weight of secrets and loss.

The room was dim, the air thick with the smells of illness. His once proud frame was now frail, the skin of his face sagging, his eyes clouded with the haze of death. His breathing had long been shallow, long interrupted by the occasional fit of coughing. He had heard the construction outside, but it had felt like the sounds of another world, one that would never include him. His dying thoughts, though, had returned him time and again to his past, to a life that had once been full of promise but had ultimately fallen apart. In his younger days, Adil Khan had been a man of purpose, and his sense of duty had carried him through life, even to the point of abandoning his wife and only daughter. He had once married Amina, a woman he had loved deeply, but whose quiet strength could not explain to herself why he had gone away from her life after the death of their son. He had inexplicably left the woman who had once been his partner in both love and marriage and who had even converted to his faith. He had struggled with himself all his life after leaving them, unable to reconcile with the part of him that had kept so much hidden—his complex Muslim identity, his loyalty, and the complexities of his own beliefs.

Adil Khan's relationship with his daughter had always been one of quiet distance. He had never been a man who knew how to bridge the gaps between the generations, between a father who had lived through religious strife and loss, and a daughter who was caught in a world that never seemed to understand him. As he was dying, he had wondered what kind of legacy he would leave behind. His life has been a series of unresolved contradictions—his loyalty to a country that no longer felt like home, his love for a woman who was long gone and whom he had left to fend for herself amid the weight of her own secrets, and his isolation, both self-imposed and circumstantial.

The growing contrasts within Ayodhya cast a heavy shadow. Outside, the city roared with ambition, each stone of the temple proclaiming its dominance. Inside that forgotten house, silence enveloped a man whose story had been reduced to whispers. The house bore no signs of warmth or memory. It had become a vault of erasure. The few items that remained hinted at a man who had removed all traces of his past.

Outside, the chanting continued—stones being placed, blessings offered. The sounds of the Ram Temple's construction outside were deafening—the steady rhythm of hammering, the shouts of workers, and the constant thrum of machinery. Ayodhya, once a place of quiet coexistence, now reverberated with the noise of something monumental being built. He was alone, truly alone, as the temple rose and the world outside moved forward. As the Ram Temple was built, my maternal grandfather, Adil Khan's death became a kind of symbol of the end of an era—a time when Ayodhya was not a battleground for religious identity, but a place where people of different faiths lived side by side. His life, marked by contradictions and secrets, was now a memory, and the world outside continued to change. The temple rose, but for those who remembered Adil Khan, it would stand as a monument not just to religious pride, but to the loss of a way of life that can never be reclaimed. In his death, Adil Khan was forgotten by almost all but the stones of Ayodhya, the walls that once spoke of peace, now silent in the face of the temple's construction. The city continued to evolve, but the memory of this quiet man, alone in his final moments, did not linger in the hearts of those who knew him—no longer able to speak, but still a reminder of the fragility of peace in a world that had forgotten how to build it.

The construction of the Ram Temple stood in stark contrast to the quiet of Adil Khan's room. Each hammer strike echoed the promise of a future built on faith, while Adil Khan's body weakened in a room that held no such certainty. The temple was not just a physical structure. It was a symbol, a statement of a city reshaped by the forces of religion and politics. For the dying and suffering Adil Khan, it had been a reminder of everything he had lost, a representation of a place he had once called home, but which had stopped feeling like his own a long time ago.

The sounds of the workers outside had blurred into the sounds of his memories—memories of a time when Ayodhya was not defined by religious division, but by the quiet dignity of its people, a time when temples and mosques stood side by side without question. Adil Khan had always believed that the walls of this city could speak of unity, of peace. Now, as the Ram Temple rose, those walls spoke only of separation.

As Adil Khan had lain dying, alone, he had vividly and uncannily, recalled the Babri Masjid—once a symbol of the coexistence of Hindus and Muslims in Ayodhya. He had walked by it many times in his youth, never imagining it would one day become a flashpoint in a battle for religious supremacy. And now, with the construction of the Ram Temple, he had felt as if the city was being irreversibly changed. The walls that once carried the whispers of shared lives now carried the weight of division. As his condition had worsened, Adil Khan had drifted in and out of consciousness. For many months before his death, he had spoken in broken sentences, his voice barely a whisper. Sometimes, he remembered the past with startling clarity—his early days in Ayodhya, before the world began to unravel. He remembered his daughter Yasmin, her smile, the way her presence once filled the space around him. He remembered the way his wife, Amina and he had spoken of their children, planning for a future together, believing in a life of peace. But then, those plans had felt like a cruel joke, as if they had never been real, after Arif died.

His dying thoughts returned to the Ram Temple, and he felt a deep sorrow. He wondered if the temple would bring the peace he had once dreamed of, or if it would only deepen the divide. The temple was being built in his lifetime, but he wondered if it would ever be completed in a way that honored the memory of a city that once knew only unity. He had lived to see the transformation of Ayodhya into something unrecognizable, but in his heart, he held onto the belief that this was not the Ayodhya he had once known—a city that had lived in the spirit of shared history, not in the shadow of division.

As the construction sounds outside had become more insistent, Adil Khan whispered to no one in particular: "Ayodhya was never just about temples or mosques. It was about the people. It was about the lives we shared. Now, even the stones will not speak the same language." Adil Khan's solitude was not just physical. The ghosts of his past made his solitude intensely emotional and spiritual. No one came to visit him. His daughter, raised as an alien from him but in the same town, did not even know of his condition. His wife whom he had left him many years ago, was gone too. And now, Adil Khan, a man who had once held his family together with the quiet strength of his convictions, was as alone at the end as he was when he had forsaken his family. The weight of his solitude felt almost unbearable. He thought of his dead wife, the woman who he had loved so intensely, the woman he had betrayed with his silence and his unexplained departure. Finally, as he lay dying, he had felt that he could never forgive himself for the way he had left her, for the way he had let their family fracture beyond repair. He thought of his granddaughter, Saanvi, whom he had never cared to meet and who was now far away, caught between two worlds. He knew she had grown up without him, raised by her paternal relatives, her Hindu identity perhaps solidified by a world that saw her as one of them. And in his final moments, Adil Khan wondered if she would ever understand the man he was, or if the distance between them, both physical and emotional, was too vast to bridge.

In his final and last moments, Adil Khan had clung to the fragments of his stray memories. He spoke to himself of the days before the political turmoil, when Ayodhya had been a place of quiet coexistence. He had remembered the evenings when he and Amina would sit together in silence, the air thick with the unspoken understanding of their shared love. Now he could no longer hold onto that memory. It slipped through his fingers like dust. His breath slowed, the weight of the world on his shoulders. The sounds of the construction outside became a distant echo as he whispered his final words: "Ayodhya, my city, my home. I leave it in pieces, just as I leave myself." With those words, Adil Khan died, his passing marking the end of an era, the end of a man who had once believed in the possibility of unity, but who now left the world behind, broken and fragmented.

The burial was a somber affair, attended by only a handful of people. The city's Muslim community had dwindled over the years, leaving few to mourn him. My father, Ramesh Trivedi, despite being an outsider in this space, insisted on helping with the preparations. He carried Adil Khan's body to the graveyard, his usually composed demeanor tinged with a solemn determination. It was a small, unassuming plot of land on the outskirts of the city, tucked away from the noise and chaos. The grave was dug by hand, the earth yielding reluctantly as if resisting the finality of the act.

Adil Khan's life had been marked by relentless hope and eventual despair. As a Muslim political leader in Ayodhya, his career had begun with fiery speeches about unity and coexistence. He had envisioned a city that could rise above its divisions, where people of all religions could live as equals. In the early days of his political career, he had been a force to reckon with, admired even by his detractors for his charisma and intellect. His party, once solely representing the marginalized Muslim community, had garnered considerable support across Ayodhya, a symbol of what seemed to be a new era of inclusivity. But politics in Ayodhya was a treacherous game, and the tides soon turned against him. The city's growing polarization eroded the very foundations of his vision. Riots erupted, fueled by opportunistic politicians who thrived on sowing discord. Adil Khan's pleas for peace had been drowned out by the cacophony of hatred, his voice reduced to an echo in the wilderness. The final blow had come when his own party began to distance itself from him. Once a champion of progressive ideals, Adil Khan found himself at odds with the party leadership, who had shifted their focus to more populist and divisive agendas. He resisted at first, delivering impassioned speeches in the state assembly, warning against the perils of abandoning their principles. But his warnings fell on deaf ears. Slowly, his influence waned, his presence in the political arena reduced to a shadow of his former self.

Adil Khan's disillusionment deepened when he realized that the very people he had fought for no longer stood by him. The Muslim community, beleaguered and fragmented, began to view him with skepticism. To some, he was too moderate, unwilling to adopt a more combative stance in the face of rising hostility. To others, he was a relic of a bygone era, his ideals deemed impractical in the harsh realities of modern Ayodhya. The alienation from his own community was a wound that never healed, a constant reminder of his failure to bridge the divide. In his later years, Adil Khan retreated from public life, his health deteriorating alongside his spirit. He spent his days in quiet solitude, surrounded by a few books and memories of a time when hope had not yet abandoned him. He would often sit by the window of his humble home, staring at the bustling streets of Ayodhya with a mix of longing and sorrow. The city he had loved so deeply seemed unrecognizable, its soul corroded by the very forces he had sought to combat.

When the end came, it was swift and unceremonious. News of his death did not even make a single headline, a stark contrast to the fanfare that had once accompanied his every move. At the burial ground, the absence of his political colleagues was glaring. Very few from his party attended, their absence a silent testimony to the erasure of his legacy. Those who did come remained on the periphery, unwilling to associate too closely with a man whose ideals had become inconvenient. His devotion to a political cause had devoured his personal life. And even though he had once been a man of passion and principle, he died not as a hero, but as a man estranged—from his country, his kin, his former self.

My father, Ramesh Trivedi, stood out in this sea of indifference. A Hindu politician, he could have been perceived as one of Adil Khan's fiercest rivals in the early days. But never once did Ramesh Trivedi strike any gesture of rivalry. At the graveyard, Ramesh took it upon himself to ensure that the burial was conducted with dignity. He coordinated with the few mourners who had gathered, his actions speaking louder than any eulogy ever could. As the final handful of earth was thrown over the grave, my father stood motionless, his head bowed in silent prayer. It was a moment of quiet defiance against the apathy that had come to define Ayodhya's politics. Ramesh spoke briefly of Adil Khan's unwavering commitment to his principles, even in the face of insurmountable odds. "He was a better man than most of us," my father said, his voice tinged with admiration.

As the prayers began, Yasmin stood slightly apart, her hands clasped tightly in front of her. She murmured the words of the Islamic burial rites softly, her voice breaking at times, but finding its rhythm again. Ramesh, unfamiliar with the rituals, remained respectfully silent, his presence alone speaking volumes. For a brief moment, they stood side by side—two people from different worlds, united in grief. It was as if the weight of their shared history, their secrets, and their sacrifices had been laid bare in the open air of that graveyard. When the earth was finally shoveled back into place, Yasmin knelt beside the grave, placing a small, withered rose on the fresh soil. She whispered something under her breath—a prayer, perhaps, or an apology. Ramesh placed a hand on her shoulder, a gesture of quiet support and solidarity. Neither spoke as they walked back to the car, the tension between them replaced by a fragile understanding.

The return to their separate homes in Ayodhya was marked by silence, each lost in their thoughts. For my father, it was perhaps a moment of reckoning. It was a realization of how deeply the personal and political could intertwine, how the boundaries of faith and identity could blur in the face of loss. For my mother, it was a moment of closure, bittersweet and incomplete, but closure nonetheless.

The city moved on quickly, as it always does, the memory of Adil Khan fading into obscurity. But for the few who had witnessed his journey from hope to despair, his story remained etched in their hearts as they saw how the bridge had crumbled. There had been no glimmer in sight. I too found myself reflecting on my maternal grandfather's, Adil Khan's life, sitting in my college library at Oxford. He was a man who had borne the heavy cost of his ideals. The tragic death of his young son had profoundly altered him, driving him to abandon his wife and daughter, leaving behind a shattered family. Yet, even in his brokenness, he had dared to work for the Muslim community, envisioning a better Ayodhya in a world deeply divided and resistant to change, a vision pursued against overwhelming odds.

On their way back from the funeral, and as my parents passed the construction site of the Ram Temple, the sound of hammering and chanting filled the air once more. It was a stark reminder of the world they were returning to—a world driven by ambition and division. Yet, in the quiet confines of the car, there was a sense of something almost sacred, a fleeting moment of unity amidst the chaos. The sounds of the Ram Temple's construction punctuated their thoughts—the steady rhythm of hammering, the shouts of workers, and the constant thrum of machinery reverberating through Ayodhya. It was a city in flux, torn between its ancient soul and the monumental changes shaping its future. As my maternal grandfather left the stage, I wondered if his words had reached the hearts of those who had come to listen. I wondered if Ayodhya itself was listening. In the end, both Ayodhya and my late grandfather, Adil Khan, seemed to echo the same truth—that what is built and what is lost are forever entwined.

The day of the Ram Mandir's inauguration was an orchestration of grandeur on a scale Ayodhya had never seen before. From the moment the first rays of dawn kissed the gilded *kalash* atop the temple's *shikhara*, the city seemed to transform into a living, breathing monument of devotion and spectacle. The streets were carpeted with marigold and rose petals, their fragrance mingling with the crisp winter air, carrying whispers of prayers and the rustling anticipation of history in the making. Overhead, saffron flags fluttered like restless flames, their symbols of *Om* and the sacred bow of Lord Rama catching the early light in a dazzling array of gold and crimson.

The Prime Minister himself arrived in a specially outfitted helicopter, its descent a thunderous announcement that sent waves of excitement rippling through the massive crowd gathered on the temple grounds. It landed on a freshly constructed helipad not far from the Sarayu River, where priests clad in pristine white dhotis performed a symbolic aarti, invoking blessings for the day's historic events. The leader stepped out, flanked by a retinue of ministers, security personnel, and saffron-clad saints who seemed to blend seamlessly into the tableau of reverence and authority. His attire, simple yet deliberate, included a pale saffron kurta with a golden shawl draped across his shoulders, embodying the merging of political power with spiritual symbolism.

Behind him, a parade of political dignitaries followed, their faces glowing with the unmistakable sheen of carefully curated piety. Industrial magnates, Bollywood superstars, and spiritual leaders of every ilk had been flown in from across the country, their arrivals staggered to ensure the crowd's attention remained perpetually rapt. The film stars, their luminous personae magnified by the cameras that followed their every move, donned modest but elegant traditional outfits, signaling their allegiance to the moment's cultural gravitas. Some even carried silver trays of offerings of coconuts, marigolds, and incense sticks, and posed graciously and with élan before the waiting press. Their energy and enthusiasm, their stylish confidence and spirited demeanor, added an element of distinctive charm and flair to their gestures.

The temple complex, the heart of the day's celebration, stood resplendent against the winter sky. The Ram Mandir itself is a marvel of modern architecture steeped in ancient tradition, every inch of it a tribute to the mythic age it has sought to resurrect. Its central *shikhara* towers a hundred and sixty one feet high, situated high above the sanctum sanctorum or *garbhagriha*, and it encompasses a three-story structure supported by three hundred and ninety two intricately carved pillars. The design integrates elements from both Nagara and Dravidian architectural styles, reflecting a fusion of North and South Indian temple traditions. The temple's façade gleams with freshly polished *Makrana* marble and sandstone, its every arch and cornice painstakingly designed to evoke the splendor of *Vaikuntha* itself. The main sanctum houses a life-sized idol of Lord Ram as *Maryada Purushottam*, his face serene yet commanding, draped in silk robes embroidered with gold.

The consecration ceremony for the Ram Mandir was scheduled to take place on January 22, 2024, with preparations beginning a week or more earlier. The grand event had promised to feature a range of rituals, with the temple open for *darshan* and *aarti* ceremonies throughout the day. The temple courtyards, sprawling over several acres, were adorned with decorations befitting the occasion. The organizers had sent out approximately thousands of invitations to prominent dignitaries, key political figures and cultural icons. The spectacle promised to blend spiritual significance with cultural grandeur, showcasing the temple as a symbol of unity and devotion. Tens of thousands of devotees filled the space, their collective chants of "*Jai Shri Ram!*" rising in waves, a sound that reverberated across the land like the beating of an immense, unified heart. Rows of oil lamps lined every pathway, their tiny flames quivering in rhythm with the sea of saffron-clad worshippers who moved like rivers converging toward the sacred source. The day would be etched into the annals of India's history as the moment Ayodhya cemented itself as both a spiritual epicenter and a political statement.

The temple courtyard, sprawling over several acres, was a spectacle in its own right. The earth, freshly paved and swept clean of even the faintest trace of dust, reflected the amber glow of the mid-morning sun. Rows of saffron-clad volunteers moved in precise, rehearsed synchronicity, their arms laden with trays of marigolds, incense sticks, and oil lamps. Each flower petal and flickering flame seemed to whisper an invocation to Lord

Rama, beseeching his blessings on a land that had endured centuries of tumult and yearning. From the perimeter of the courtyard, the rhythmic chanting of *"Jai Shri Ram!"* rose in waves, cresting and falling like a devotional tide. The air was thick with the mingling scents of sandalwood, ghee, and fresh garlands, their combined fragrance weaving a sensory tapestry that seemed to envelop every soul present. Around the central shrine, priests performed the *maha-aarti*, their voices carrying the ancient cadence of mantras that seemed to vibrate in harmony with the very stones of the temple. In one corner of the courtyard, a troupe of young boys, bare-chested and wearing traditional dhotis, performed an energetic reenactment of the *vanvaas*, Ram's exile into the wilderness. Their movements were sharp and purposeful, their expressions a blend of earnest devotion and theatrical flair. The audience, seated in neat rows under the shade of temporary awnings, erupted into spontaneous applause as the actors recreated the moment of Sita's abduction with a dramatic flourish. Above, the sun reached its zenith, casting the temple courtyard in a golden halo. The towering *shikhara* of the Ram Mandir gleamed like a divine beacon, its intricate carvings alive with light and shadow. At its base, the Prime Minister, flanked by spiritual leaders and political dignitaries, made his way to the sanctum sanctorum. Cameras captured every moment, their lenses framing his every gesture—the careful placing of the garland, the reverent touch of his forehead to the marble steps, the folded hands raised in prayer.

The crowd outside the temple complex was equally animated. Giant LED screens broadcast the proceedings to throngs of people who had traveled from across the country to witness history. Vendors wove through the masses, hawking miniature idols of Ram, saffron scarves embroidered with sacred verses, and pamphlets extolling the temple's significance. Somewhere, the distinct melody of a conch being blown pierced through the din, a sound so ancient and resonant it seemed to pause time itself. As the ceremony reached its crescendo, the entire courtyard erupted in a cacophony of bells, conches, and chants. A hundred thousand oil lamps were lit in unison, their flames flickering like tiny stars against the backdrop of the midday sky. It was as if the heavens themselves had descended to bear witness to this union of devotion and destiny. The spectacle was overwhelming, a sensory flood that left even the most stoic among the crowd visibly moved.

For me, Saanvi, returning from England and standing quietly at the far edge of the courtyard, the day unfolded like a threshold—where memory, myth, and the present blurred and quietly converged. I watched the Prime Minister address the nation from the temple steps, his words ringing out with the authority of someone who knew he was scripting more than policy. He was shaping identity. In the midst of all this grandeur, I remember my thoughts turning inward, to the spaces where the past lingered like a shadow. What of those who were not here? What of the unspoken histories buried beneath this temple's foundations? The golden afternoon light softened as the questions within me hardened. I saw myself standing on the edge of this sea of humanity. I watched the spectacle unfold with a mix of wonder and unease. I, Saanvi, born of two worlds yet tethered fully to neither, somehow felt the weight of my divided heritage as the event reached its crescendo. I could not but help wonder, pause, and ponder on the painstaking choreography of it all—the synchronized arrival of television crews, the perfectly timed *aarti* led by the country's most revered priests, the seemingly spontaneous yet carefully arranged release of white doves into the sky. Even the bells of the temple, newly cast and resonant, seemed to ring with a practiced precision.

The ceremony began with a recital of Vedic mantras by a group of a hundred and eight Brahmins seated in concentric circles around the ceremonial *havan kund*. The air was thick with the mingling scents of sandalwood, ghee, and camphor, their pungency underscored by the rhythmic drumming of *tabla* and the haunting strains of the *shehnai*. The Prime Minister, guided by the chief priest, stepped forward to place the ceremonial garland around the idol of Ram. Cameras clicked furiously as he bowed low before the deity, his hands folded in namaste. For that moment, he was no longer the architect of a political vision but a humble servant of faith, a devotee offering his obeisance to the timeless ideals of dharma and duty.

As the day unfolded, the celebrations spilled beyond the temple complex and into the city of Ayodhya itself. Temporary stages had been erected along the main thoroughfares, where performers reenacted episodes from the Ramayana with theatrical flair. A particularly dramatic retelling of the *Lanka Kanda* drew gasps from the audience, the flames of Ravana's burning palace mirrored by pyrotechnics that lit up the sky. Vendors sold everything from Ramayana comics to saffron-colored sweets shaped like bows and arrows. The city was awash in color and light, its narrow lanes transformed into rivers of gold as the evening approached.

Yet beneath the surface of this celebration, I could not help but feel an undercurrent of disquiet. As the Prime Minister addressed the crowd, his voice amplified across the sprawling grounds, I could catch phrases that rang with a peculiar duality. Words like "reclaiming heritage" and "resurgence of cultural pride" carried with them the echoes of a deeper narrative, one that spoke of divisions as much as of unity. My thoughts wandered to my mother, Yasmin, and to the long shadow cast by the Babri Masjid, whose absence lingered like a ghost in the landscape of my memory on the day I was born.

Of course, the new Ram Mandir itself stood at the heart of Ayodhya, a towering testament to faith and fervor, shimmering under the harsh sun with the ethereal glow of freshly quarried pink sandstone. Each slab seemed to echo a hymn, a silent chanting of names and hopes that had been etched into it over decades, perhaps centuries. The carved stone pillars, each spiraling upward like ascending prayers, bore intricate depictions of Lord Rama's journey—his childhood by the Sarayu River, his exile into the wilderness, his battles, his return, triumphant yet tempered. Every chisel mark was a story-teller; every floral motif, a whispered ode to the divine. As I walked through the temple's sprawling courtyards, my footsteps brushed against pale pink dust that seemed to float into the air. It felt as though time itself were disintegrating. The earth here was ancient, packed with myth and memory. I saw my father, Ramesh Trivedi, mingling with a deliberate sophistication, his shoulders squared and face calm but weary under the weight of leadership. The crowds swelled around him chanting, "*Jai Shri Ram!*" He stood tall and so handsome, yet cautious, his fingers curling tightly into the loose ends of a dhoti as if holding onto the edges of something bigger than himself—an identity, a history, a reckoning.

The newly built temple complex sprawled like a lotus in bloom before my eyes. Around the central shrine, concentric pathways led to smaller pavilions dedicated to other deities—Hanuman, Sita, Lakshman, and even Vibhushan, whose redemption earned him a smaller, tucked-away sanctum. Marble fountains murmured softly, their waters fragrant with marigold petals offered earlier in devotion. The layout was precise, its geometry inspired by Vedic principles. The courtyards formed mandalas, the spaces between them creating a labyrinth of meditation, perhaps reflection, though many walked briskly, their devotion tinged with impatience. Somehow, why did I get the feeling that my mixed heritage made me a stranger here, even though I had walked the streets of Ayodhya with my father as a child, when the foundation stone had first been laid. Back then, I do not think that there were any gleaming spires, nor the roars of saffron-clad crowds waving their flags aloft. There was only a barren stretch of land, marked by tension that hung like smoke. I do distinctly recall my father pulling my hand away from the broken glass shards that lined the pavement. "This is not the moment to touch history," he had said. I had not understood him then. I would not have been able to understand him even now, had he repeated his words to me now.

For the building of the temple came amidst a series of crisis. Back in 2020, as the pandemic had unfolded, Ayodhya had stood as a paradox. While the world reeled under the grip of a pandemic, the ancient city of Ayodhya surged forward with the construction of the Ram Mandir. August 5 marked a watershed moment, as the nation's leaders laid the temple's foundation stone. The ceremony had been steeped in ritual and was meant to be a spectacle of unity and strength, or so it was intended to appear. For the city's marginalized, however, the grandeur was a stark contrast to their personal struggles when lockdowns had paralyzed livelihoods, and hunger had gnawed at many families. Yet, few dared to question the priorities of a government that had made Ayodhya its centerpiece. And if 2020 was the year of foundations, 2021 was one marked by grandiose ambitions. Ayodhya's skyline had begun to change as cranes and scaffolding became fixtures. Plans to transform the city into a global tourist hub were unveiled with museums, circuits, and promenades that promised to blend mythology with modernity. The progress of course, came at a cost. Thousands of residents who had been displaced by these projects voiced their dissent, but their pleas were drowned out by the din of development. Ayodhya's streets, once the stage for communal discord, now bore witness to another kind of conflict: that between heritage and modernity. By 2022, Ayodhya was a city on the brink of metamorphosis. The temple's spires rose higher, their shadow a reminder of promises kept and debts owed. The government announced that the temple's inauguration would coincide with the next election cycle, a timing too precise to be coincidental. Ayodhya, once a city of saints and seekers, had become a symbol—of hope for some, of loss for others. As the nation looked to its future, Ayodhya seemed to mirror its dilemmas. Could faith and progress coexist? Could a city heal from the wounds of its past even as new fault lines emerged? In these years, Ayodhya's journey was not merely about bricks and mortar. It was about identity, individual and collective. It was about the weight of history and the pull of tomorrow. And as the spires of the temple gleamed in the morning sun, Ayodhya seemed to ask: what price is too high for redemption?

Now, the air was different. It throbbed with the hum of people—pilgrims, tourists, politicians, journalists, all gathered to witness this colossal reclamation of cultural pride. Beneath all the festive pride and veneer, I felt an ache. The golden *kalash* at the temple's apex glittered defiantly under the sun, but was it not also an unspoken warning? I imagined my mother, Yasmin Khan, peering out at this edifice from afar, her lips pursed, her silence a reflection of all the wounds Ayodhya carried like invisible scars. My mother, Yasmin Khan, who had once told me bedtime stories of courage when I had visited her on weekends, stories of Prophet Muhammad and his unshakeable belief in justice, might find no place for herself in this shimmering complex of Lord Rama's dominion. She had only defended my father's Hindu faith out of loyalty to him, I was convinced.

Even the temple's interiors were dazzling, perhaps too dazzling, I thought to myself. Gold and silver inlays sparkled on the walls, forming vines that climbed toward domed ceilings painted with celestial scenes. Murals told of Lord Rama's righteous rule, the stories overlapping in a cascade of ochres and vermilions. I could not help feeling overwhelmed, as though walking into the past, yet unable to escape the sharp edges of the present. My fingers traced the reliefs carved into one wall—of Lord Rama handing over the reins of his kingdom to his sons. What could my father's thoughts be at this juncture and if he saw me now, somewhat troubled? Would he still feel vindicated, a victorious Dharmaraj? Or would he mourn the loss of subtler truths, eclipsed by this grandiosity?

Even within the temple's dazzling interiors, the sight of Ram Lalla, the child Lord Rama, was a revelation that transcended grandeur. There he sat, no more than a foot tall, yet towering in divine presence, encased in a golden canopy encrusted with diamonds, emeralds, and rubies that shimmered like a celestial galaxy. His form was delicate, carved in a posture of childlike innocence, his right hand extended in a playful gesture, his left resting on his tiny knee. The soft glow of oil lamps and ghee *diyas* encircled him, their light reflecting off the golden ornaments and cascading like liquid fire onto the marble floor. His features were impossibly serene yet imbued with life, as though frozen in a moment of pure joy. His small, rounded face held a gentle smile, curved just enough to be mischievous, inviting the devotee to look closer, to feel closer. His almond-shaped eyes, inlaid with dark onyx and flecks of white, seemed to follow you wherever you moved, as though observing not your body but your very soul. His gaze pierced time, a child holding within him the weight of eternity—a king who had lived and ruled, but who now sat as an eternal child, untouched by the confines of chronology.

His skin, painted in the softest shade of sky blue, was tender yet luminous, a color that seemed alive with the essence of divine energy. The artisans had rendered his limbs with such care that one could almost see the faint outlines of veins on his tiny hands, as if life still pulsed through him. Around his neck rested a garland of fresh marigolds and *tulsi* leaves, their scent mingling with the smoky fragrance of camphor and sandalwood that hung in the air. The garland looked freshly woven, as though placed there just moments before, yet it bore the eternal freshness of an offering blessed by the gods themselves. The clothes adorning him were fit for royalty yet scaled to his diminutive size. A dhoti of golden silk clung to his small form, its edges embroidered with intricate patterns of flowers and swans. Over his shoulders was draped a scarlet shawl, edged with fine *zari* work that glittered like sunlight on water. Tiny anklets circled his feet, their delicate bells too silent to chime, as though out of reverence for the sanctity of the moment. A jeweled crown rested on his head, encrusted with emeralds the color of a monsoon forest, its peak reaching upward like a mountain aspiring to touch the heavens.

Behind Ram Lalla, the backdrop was a tapestry of cosmic splendor, a carved screen of marble depicting scenes from his life. There was the child Rama breaking Shiva's bow, the prince Rama in exile with Sita and

Lakshmana, the warrior Rama slaying Ravana with his celestial bow. These were not mere decorations, but narratives etched so vividly that they seemed to come alive in the flickering light. Above him, the domed ceiling bore a celestial mural of stars and constellations, painted in rich blues and silvers, as though the heavens themselves had bent low to protect him.

The air was thick with reverence, an almost tactile presence that seemed to press down on the senses. A low hum of chants filled the space, the rhythmic repetition of "*Jai Shri Ram*" resonating in the marble walls, as if the temple itself had joined the devotees in their praise. The sound was not loud but pervasive, a vibration that settled deep within, aligning heartbeats to its sacred cadence. Priests moved about with precision, their saffron robes swaying as they tended to the *aarti* trays, offering fire to the divine child. The flames danced in rhythmic harmony, as if they too were bowing in devotion.

And yet, amidst all this splendor, there was an unmistakable intimacy about Ram Lalla. The barriers between the divine and the devotee seemed to dissolve in his presence. Unlike other deities enshrined in grandeur, here was a god who invited tenderness. His smallness was not a limitation but an invitation to approach without fear. For a moment, the weight of the world outside seemed to fall away, replaced by an overwhelming sense of solace and warmth. The child in him reached out to the child in everyone, breaking down walls built by age, doubt, or despair. The sanctity of this connection was palpable, but it was also conflicted. As I stood before him, I could not help but feel the sharp edges of a deeper unease. What had brought me here? Was it faith, or was it duty? Did I seek the child Lord Rama for answers, or did I hope he would reflect my own uncertainties back at me, absolving me of the need to confront them? My thoughts wandered to my father, to his unshakable devotion to this temple and what it represented. Could he see me here now, standing in this space where he had poured so much of himself, not in silent reverence but in restless inquiry?

I found my fingers once again tracing the carved reliefs on the wall, moving over the figure of Lord Rama handing over his kingdom to his sons. The contrast was stark—there, the magnanimity of a king relinquishing power; here, the eternal child, untouched by the burdens of leadership, forever a symbol of innocence. What would my father say if he saw me troubled by this duality? Would he, like the priests, simply say, "It is all part of the *leela*, the divine play?" Or would he sense, as I did, the weight of history pressing down on this small figure, the paradox of a god who is at once a child and a king, a savior and a symbol? The silence in the sanctum was broken only by the faint jingling of a bell, signaling the next *aarti*. A priest approached, his hands cupping a small silver tray bearing a single diya, its flame steady despite the movement. He placed it before Ram Lalla, the light casting flickering shadows across the child god's form. For a brief moment, the room seemed to hold its breath, as though waiting for something unseen to manifest.

And then I understood. Ram Lalla was not simply an image or an idol; he was a presence, a mirror, a question. To some, he was the embodiment of faith, the eternal child who guarded Ayodhya. To others, he was a battleground, a symbol laden with the weight of politics and history. But to me, in that moment, he was both and neither. He was a paradox, innocent yet burdened, small yet immense, silent yet resonant. And in his gaze, I saw not answers but an invitation to confront the contradictions within myself. As I stepped back, allowing another devotee to approach, I felt the weight of his tiny form linger in my mind. He remained with me, not as a resolution but as a reminder, that faith, like life, was as much about the questions it raised as the answers it offered.

Outside, a towering statue of Lord Rama in his warrior avatar loomed over the central plaza, holding his bow with an expression of divine resolve. The crowds surged around its base, some offering flowers, others snapping pictures. In the shadow of the statue, a small troupe of street performers enacted scenes from the Ramayana. The children laughed as Hanuman flew across the stage—a simple man dressed in a bright red dhoti and a makeshift tail. The elders nodded solemnly, murmuring blessings as Sita placed a garland around Ram's neck. My gaze wandered past them, beyond the temple walls, toward the narrow alleys of old Ayodhya. There, in the shadows of its crumbling haveli courtyards and the steeples of forgotten temples, were echoes of my own mother's world. I thought of the mosque that had stood here, the *azaan* that had once mingled with the temple bells. Had the builders of this new complex heard those echoes, too? Or had they drowned them out with the rhythmic pounding of hammers and the metallic clang of scaffolds collapsing?

Standing amidst the fervent celebrations marking the completion of the Ram temple in Ayodhya, I found myself caught in a whirlwind of emotions. The rhythmic chanting of bhajans, the sharp fragrance of marigolds, and the resonant drumbeats created an atmosphere charged with devotion and pride. I could sense the depth of feeling that emanated from the crowds—a collective heartbeat of a people reconnecting with their heritage. Yet, beneath it all, I felt a fissure in my own identity, a pull between the two halves of my upbringing. Of course, the Hindu part of me felt a certain amount of pride in the Ram temple. I knew I had to get beyond my unresolved feelings and delve deeper, beyond the surface of celebration and into the historical, cultural, even the spiritual ethos that defined their connection to it. I understand that the temple is more than just a structure of carved stones and gilded spires. It is the culmination of centuries of struggle, of hope, and an unyielding devotion to Lord Rama. To some, it is a symbol of reclamation, while to others, it signifies a return to a perceived golden age. And for someone like me, Saanvi, born of a Hindu father and a Muslim mother, it represents a space where the interplay of faiths, histories, and narratives becomes both intensely personal and profoundly universal.

I am aware that Lord Rama, the seventh avatar of Vishnu, is more than a deity to the millions of Hindus who revere him. He embodies *dharma*, righteousness, and the ideal of a perfect life. His story, told through the epic *Ramayana*, resonates across time as a moral guide, a source of comfort, and an affirmation of faith. For devout Hindus, the Ram temple is a tangible representation of these ideals, a sanctum that anchors their spiritual aspirations and cultural identity.

But why would the construction of this temple evoke such intense pride? The answer lies in the layers of meaning attached to the temple's history and the significance of Ayodhya itself. As a child, my father would narrate the *Ramayana* to me, his voice imbued with reverence as he recounted Lord Ram's journey. He spoke of Ayodhya not as a mere city but as a divine realm, a place blessed by Ram's presence. For Hindus, Ayodhya is not just geography; it is mythology made manifest. To build a grand temple here is to reaffirm that sacred connection. For my father, the Ram temple was always a dream deferred. He often lamented how political strife had clouded the sanctity of Ayodhya, turning it into a site of contention. "Saanvi," he would say, "Ram is not just for Hindus. He is a symbol for all humanity—of compassion, justice, and sacrifice. But his home has been a battleground for too long." Of course, I understood the depth and meaning of his words as I stood in the shadow of the newly completed temple, where the grandeur of the structure seemed to mirror the magnitude of the emotions it evoked.

But for someone like me, the pride associated with the Ram temple cannot be separated from the history of Ayodhya—a history that is as much about faith as it is about conflict. The Babri Masjid, which once stood on this very site just before I was born, had been a focal point of dispute for decades. My mother, a devout Muslim, had spoken to me sometimes of the mosque with a quiet sadness. To her, it was not just a place of worship but a repository of memories, a testament to the syncretic culture that had long defined India. Growing up, I had often found myself torn between these two narratives. On the one hand, there was the pride my father felt in his Hindu heritage, a pride he wore with quiet dignity. On the other, there was my mother's pain, a pain rooted in the sense of loss and erasure. The demolition of the Babri Masjid on the day I was born in 1992, was more than a physical act. It was an emotional and spiritual upheaval for many Muslims, my mother and my maternal grandparents included.

As I walked again through the sprawling complex of the new Ram temple, I began to see how the narrative had shifted over the years. For most Hindus, the temple is not just a triumph of faith but also a reclamation of identity. The temple is the culmination of a long struggle to assert their cultural and spiritual heritage. To dismiss this pride as mere triumphalism would be to ignore the depth of sentiment that underpins it. The temple itself is indeed, a marvel, a testament to the skill of artisans and the devotion of its builders. Intricate carvings depict scenes from the *Ramayana*, each telling a story of courage, love, and sacrifice. As I ran my fingers once again over the cool stone, I thought of the countless hands that had shaped it, imbuing it with their faith and artistry.

For Hindus, the temple's architecture is not merely aesthetic. It is symbolic. I respect that the towering *shikhara* or spire, reaches toward the heavens and signifies the soul's ascent toward the divine. I recognize that the sanctum sanctorum, where the idol of Ram Lalla is enshrined, is a space of profound spiritual energy. Standing there, the Hindu part of me can myself feel the weight of centuries—the hopes, prayers, and struggles of millions converging in this sacred space. As someone who straddles two faiths, I will always find myself grappling with the duality of this moment. I recognize that the pride of the Hindus celebrating the temple was palpable. Yet so was the pain of those who mourned what had been lost. Could these two emotions coexist, I wondered? Could the temple be a space of reconciliation, rather than division? My father has often spoken to me about India as a land of harmony, where different faiths can coexist like the notes of a *raga*, like voices in a sacred chorus. "Saanvi," he tells me, "our strength lies in our ability to embrace diversity, not erase it."

Standing in the Ram temple, I realized that this vision of harmony was not a given. It was a choice, one that each generation must consciously make. The pride that Hindus feel for the Ram temple is rooted in their sense of belonging and identity. For many, it is a source of spiritual solace and cultural affirmation. Yet, as I reflect on my own journey, I realize that understanding this pride does not mean endorsing exclusion. Rather, it means acknowledging the deep emotional and historical ties that bind people to this sacred space. I recognize now that in a world increasingly defined by polarization, the Ram temple stands as a reminder of both the power of faith and the fragility of coexistence. For someone like me, who carries the legacy of two faiths, it is a call to bridge divides, to seek common ground amidst the complexity of history.

As the sun set over Ayodhya, casting a golden glow on the temple's spires, I felt a sense of quiet resolve. Perhaps understanding begins with empathy, with the willingness to see the world through another's eyes. And in that understanding, there is the possibility of healing—not just for individuals, but for entire communities. Through the lens of my father's pride and my mother's pain, I found a deeper appreciation for the complexity of faith, identity, and belonging. The Ram temple is not just a monument; it is a mirror, reflecting the hopes, fears, and aspirations of a diverse and dynamic people. And in its shadow, I found my own place—not as a spectator, but as a participant in the ongoing story of Ayodhya, of India, and of humanity itself. I knew that in order to truly understand the pride Hindus feel for the Ram temple, I had to confront my own heritage—the interplay of Hindu and Muslim identities that have shaped me. My father's unwavering devotion to Ram was not diminished by my mother's Islamic faith. Rather, it was enriched by the dialogues and debates that my father unfolded to me in his home. As I stood in the temple's sanctum, I thought of the *Ramayana* as a story not just of a Hindu god but of universal truths, of duty, sacrifice, and love. These values transcended religion, resonating with the teachings of my mother's faith as well. Perhaps, in embracing this duality, I could find a way to reconcile the pride of one faith with the pain of another.

Understanding the pride associated with the Ram temple is not about choosing sides; it is about honoring the complexities of history, faith, and identity. It is about recognizing that pride and pain can coexist, that the echoes of the past need not be drowned out but can instead enrich the present. In the end, the Ram temple is more than a symbol of pride for Hindus; it embodies the unwavering force of faith and the indomitable will of the human spirit. Ultimately, it can even reflect the unyielding nature of the human soul. And for someone like me, it is a reminder that understanding is the first step toward healing, that empathy can bridge even the deepest divides.

As the chants of *Jai Shri Ram* echoed across the temple complex, I could feel a sense of peace—not the peace of resolution, but the peace of acceptance. In this sacred space, amidst the celebration and reflection, I found not just the pride of a community, but the essence of my own journey. I knew that I had been shaped by two worlds, each rich with their own rituals, philosophies, and unspoken truths. My father's Hinduism was a landscape of devotion and tradition, while my mother's Islam whispered a quieter, more introspective faith. In the spaces between, I wandered, not bound by one but exploring both, never pressured to choose by my parents, who, despite their differences, always nurtured my right to find my own path. But I suspect that my father's so-called freedom wasn't just a gift; his passion for his political career, his fear of rebelling against his own family, and God knows what other unspoken fears may have also played their part in giving me the space to explore. And perhaps this 'freedom' was less about liberality and more about his own careful maneuvering, avoiding the confrontation he feared.

In the evening, as the *aarti* began, the temple complex

became transformed into a magical wonderland. Hundreds of oil lamps were lit in symmetrical rows, their flames flickering like tiny fragments of the sun. The air grew thick with the smell of burning camphor and sandalwood, mingling with the faint sweetness of marigold garlands strung across the temple pillars. The rhythmic clang of bells reverberated through the complex, each chime a call to the divine, as though summoning the gods themselves to witness this moment. The chants rose, ancient and deep, carried by a wave of devotion that seemed to envelop the space. Voices of the priests, steady and resolute, merged with those of the gathered devotees, their tones raw with yearning and faith. I watched as the flames of the *aarti* lamps were raised high and swirled in deliberate arcs before the deity, their light illuminating the intricately carved reliefs of the temple walls. The murals of Ram and Sita's journey flickered in the golden glow, as though the stories themselves had come alive to bear witness.

For a moment, I let myself be swept away. I closed my eyes and imagined Ram and Sita, not as gods, but as people, broken, exiled, struggling for their place in the world. I saw Sita walking through the dense forests, her feet bruised, her spirit heavy with unspoken sorrow, yet her head held high with quiet dignity. I saw Ram, burdened not just by the weight of his exile but by the impossibility of his perfection, a man tasked with embodying ideals that seemed to leave no room for human frailty. They were not celestial figures in my mind's eye but two fragile souls, bound by love and fate, navigating a world that demanded more from them than they could give.

When I opened my eyes, the night was alive with light. The temple courtyard shimmered under the glow of countless *diyas*, their golden light spilling out onto the stone pathways and reflecting in the small pools of water that lined the outer sanctum. The trees surrounding the temple seemed to have absorbed some of the radiance, their leaves glinting softly in the breeze. But I still felt the shadows. They lingered at the edges, where the light could not reach, reminding me of what lay beneath the surface of this grandeur, a history fraught with division, a city haunted by its own stories.

I found myself drawn to one of the smaller shrines, tucked away in a corner of the complex. Here, the crowd was thinner, the air quieter. A single *diya* burned before a simple idol of Hanuman, his form unadorned yet powerful in its simplicity. I knelt before him, not to pray, but to think. My mind wandered back to my father, to the moments he had described the temple to me when I was a child. His voice, filled with reverence and conviction, had painted a picture of a place where heaven touched the earth, where the divine presence could be felt in every stone. And yet, standing here now, I could not help but wonder: Had he ever paused to question, as I did? Or had his faith been so absolute that doubt had no room to take root?

The chants from the main sanctum grew louder, their cadence rising in waves that seemed to pulse through the air. I stood and walked back toward the crowd, feeling the energy of the gathering as it reached its crescendo. The devotees around me had their hands folded, their faces uplifted, eyes glistening with tears. For them, this was not just a ritual; it was a communion, a bridge between the mortal and the divine. I envied their certainty, their ability to surrender so completely to something greater than themselves. The chants, ancient and deep, carried a wave of devotion that seemed to envelop the space. For a moment, I let myself be swept away. I closed my eyes and imagined Ram and Sita, not as gods, but as people—

broken, exiled, struggling for their place in the world. When I opened my eyes, the night was alive with light. I felt the shadows.

And yet—for me, the experience was still mixed, still different. As I watched the flickering flames and heard the echo of prayers, I felt a tug-of-war within myself. On the one hand, there was the undeniable beauty of the moment, the way it drew people together in shared faith and purpose. On the other hand, there was the weight of everything that had been built around it—the politics, the conflicts, the narratives that had turned this sacred space into a symbol of division as much as devotion.

The final moment of the *aarti* arrived. The priest lifted the large lamp, its many wicks blazing, and turned toward the crowd. He began to move, carrying the light to each devotee, who reached forward to touch the glow with their hands, bringing it to their foreheads in a gesture of reverence. When the flame reached me, I hesitated. The warmth of the light was almost too much, its brightness blinding. I extended my hands slowly, letting the glow wash over my skin. For a brief moment, I felt its heat, its purity, and I brought my hands to my forehead, not out of faith, but out of respect—for the place, for the moment, for the countless lives that had come here before me, searching for something greater than themselves.

As the *aarti* concluded, the crowd began to disperse, their voices softening to murmurs of conversation and whispered prayers. The bells fell silent, leaving behind a stillness that seemed almost sacred. I lingered for a while, watching as the priests extinguished the lamps one by one, their movements deliberate, almost tender. The temple, so alive and dynamic just moments ago, began to retreat into the quiet of the night, its light dimming but not disappearing.

I turned to leave, my footsteps echoing softly against the stone floor. The shadows still lingered, as they always would, but so did the light. And as I walked away, I carried both with me, knowing that neither could exist without the other.

22

As I grew older, that moment I had once witnessed between my parents refused to fade into the haze of childhood memory. It lingered, no longer just a child's bewildered curiosity, but a haunting echo of something deeper. The passion, the intimacy, the unspoken connection between my father and mother seemed to transcend everything that divided them—religion, family, and the weight of societal expectations. What I saw was not simply affection; it was a raw, unspoken knowing. A truth neither spoken nor explained, but powerful enough to lodge itself inside me like a secret I wasn't ready to understand. In those few seconds, their closeness said more than words ever could—and I have carried that wordless revelation ever since. Their eyes had met not with hesitation, but with a familiarity that was almost sacred. I hadn't known then what I was witnessing, only that it felt immense, like a truth too large for words. And yet, it spoke to me—in silence, in stillness. That fleeting connection etched itself into my consciousness like a secret waiting to be understood. What I saw that night stayed with me, like a silent revelation, a hidden truth about the world. In those fleeting moments, the physical connection between them spoke volumes about something that, for much of my early life, I had not truly grasped.

It was only later, in the quiet chambers of my mind, that the memory began to reshape itself into an image, a metaphor that captured the collision of worlds I had witnessed. It was almost as if a temple suckled at and gained access inside the body of a mosque, and the twain nearly destroyed each other in making love to each other. The scene unfurls in a jagged, almost visceral clash, where sacred walls groan and heave under the weight of their own collision. It is as if the temple, proud and ancient, stretches its towering, ornate spires toward the heavens, its stone a hymn of reverence to the gods, only to find its embrace around the mosque, which stands humble yet unyielding, its minarets like fingers tracing the sky in silent prayer. The mosque's delicate arches curve inward, yearning for the temple's embrace, while the temple's columns press back, defiant, yet tender.

The air thickens as their forms intertwine, the sacredness of each place suffused with an intensity that goes beyond adoration. The union is violent, a ferocious dance of symbols that seem to both preserve and desecrate the sanctity of what they represent. The temple's carvings, gods with distant eyes and figures of myth, are defaced by the touch of the mosque's arabesque calligraphy, delicate curves that stretch and warp under the weight of their clash. Their very essence is rewritten, redefined in a moment of destruction and creation. And the mosque itself gets demolished in the act. The mosque, once standing with quiet dignity, its minarets piercing the sky like the solemn fingers of a prayer, begins to tremble. The weight of the temple's embrace is not one of reverence, but of dominance, an insistent force that bends and cracks the very bones of the mosque. The stone of the temple grinds against the delicate alabaster of the mosque's walls, eroding them, the ornate calligraphy slowly being consumed, unraveling in the heat of their struggle.

The crescent at the top of the dome, once proud and gleaming, warps under the pressure, its curve twisting like a dying star. The arches, so meticulously crafted, tremble as though the very breath of faith itself is being squeezed out of them. The once intricate, fluid patterns of the mosque's arabesques now tear apart, shredded into jagged fragments, as the sacred geometry of its design collapses under the weight of its violent intimacy with the temple. With each groan of stone against stone, the minarets begin to crack, the call to prayer now a shattered echo as they topple, breaking off in jagged pieces that fall like forgotten prayers. The great dome itself splits open, its inner sanctum revealed as it falls, splintering like the last breath of a god being expelled into the void. The mosque, in its solemnity and grace, is undone. Its purity, now smothered under the suffocating, consuming power of the temple, disintegrates in the moment of their union.

The mosque, I am told, as it engulfed the temple, had transformed it into a forgotten relic—its beauty erased, its history buried beneath the weight of an inevitable destruction. The act of creation had once become one of erasure, as the mosque's delicate sanctity is now swallowed whole again, leaving nothing behind but the ruins of a once-proud structure, now just a husk in the shadow of the temple. The clash of faiths, once separate, now lies in ruins, a violent testament to the forces that shape and break worlds.

In this moment, they are both lover and destroyer, forging something entirely new in their struggle. It is as though the divine energy that once flowed unchallenged through their separate veins is now torn, twisted, and reassembled, leaving behind nothing pure or untouched. As their shadows merge and twist across the ground, what was once separate becomes one unholy whole—creation in its most terrible and beautiful form. They do not simply collide; they become the very substance of the destruction and rebirth that births new realms of belief. In this act, they suckle at each other's power, drawing from the depths of their existence, and in the act of making love, they become each other's undoing.

It was in this act, this primal confluence, that they drew from each other's power with a hunger that could not be denied. They suckled at the essence of one another's existence, consuming and being consumed, transforming in the process. In the act of making love, they became each other's undoing, not out of malice but out of an inevitability written in the fabric of their being. I was born of this violent union, of sacredness and profanation willingly locked in an endless cycle, devouring and reconstituting each other in an embrace as destructive as it was creative.

Theirs was a love that seemed to dissolve the edges of identity, blending belief and tradition until neither could stand untouched by the other. My father, Ramesh, had never found himself drawn to my mother's faith. She had always suppressed the voice that murmured her prayers like a melody woven from memories older than he could ever fathom. It was something else he saw in her. It was not just her beauty, though that was undeniable, but the unfamiliar cadence of her words, the gentle sway of her body, a rhythm that seemed older than time, that captivated him. It was the way her hands moved through the air, almost as it were in prayer, the soft, sacred light in her eyes, that stirred something deep within him. He was a man who had always sought clarity and strength in his own faith, but in her presence, he encountered something else: an ache for communion that transcended understanding, an unfamiliar sanctity that seemed to awaken parts of his soul he hadn't known existed. In her existence, he felt something sacred yet foreign, something that awakened a love beyond what he had known.

Yasmin, for her part, was no less entranced. She had grown up with the quiet dignity of her own traditions, the rituals and verses etched into her childhood as firmly as the patterns of henna she sometimes applied on her palms. Yet in Ramesh, she found a kind of devotion that spoke to her in a divine language, one she hadn't realized she would ever long to hear. She had never been moved by the serene rituals of his Hindu upbringing—the oil lamps flickering in the twilight, the *vedic* chants rising in rhythmic waves, the incense spiraling upward in delicate threads like prayers made tangible. She had never once reckoned with my father's devotions nor by the firelit festivals of her youth reimagined through his Hindu traditions. Growing up in Ayodhya and aware of her own mother's origins, his faith had always been both familiar and foreign, a mirror that reflected and refracted her own understanding of the divine. What moved her, perhaps, was not just his handsome looks, but also the quiet, unshakable certainty with which his eyes projected his love for her. From the moment they had met several decades ago in Lucknow, it was as though his being carried for her, a bridge of light between heaven and earth. There was a tenderness in the way he offered himself to her, not as a demand but as a quiet offering, a prayer, a luminous humility that seemed untouched by ego or by any fear. It was this quality, this almost childlike belief in something larger than himself, that drew her toward him. In his eyes, she glimpsed not just the gods of his tradition but a vulnerability that mirrored her own—a shared ache for something infinite, something eternal, that transcended the confines of their divided worlds. She had been moved, too, by the way he seemed to look upon her—not merely as a bearer of another faith but as someone sacred in her own right. Ramesh had a way of listening, of looking at her, that made her feel as though she was not a contradiction to be resolved but a hymn waiting to be sung. It was in this acceptance, in the way his silence held space for her unspoken prayers, that she found herself drawn to him, despite everything the world insisted should keep them apart.

But there was a cost to their love, as there is to any union that seeks to bridge such chasms. Their love was not merely a blending but a reshaping, a recalibration of their deepest selves, each losing a part to gain something more. In the act of loving each other, they carved out a new existence in the spaces where their respective faiths intersected, creating something unrecognizable and, perhaps, incomprehensible to the world around them. They stood on sacred ground altered by their love, a ground that neither temple nor mosque could fully contain, and they knew that each moment spent together was both a blessing and a risk. Each moment they shared was an act of defiance and devotion, a risk and a revelation. They were together in a sphere transformed by their love—a sacred space that defied definition, belonging to neither and yet embodying both. Their union, as beautiful as it was perilous, bore the weight of something far greater than themselves: the possibility that love might transcend, even as it transforms. In loving each other for decades, they had carved out a new way of life in the intersections of their traditions, creating something beyond social traditions and values, something that neither a temple nor a mosque could fully encompass.

In those moments, I imagine their love felt like a prayer, an offering, as though two ancient sanctuaries had unlocked a door to something neither fully understood. It was a quiet ritual of devotion that demanded they surrender pieces of themselves to the other, fragments of faith, and dreams, given and taken in equal measure. The temple in my father reached out to her with open arms, a place of deities and incense welcoming a stranger, an outsider. The mosque in my mother entered his life like a soft echo, its presence subtle yet unyielding, grounding their union with a solemn beauty, a stillness that felt eternal. And in that meeting, each offered a silent prayer that neither could voice aloud, a prayer for understanding, for unity, perhaps even for absolution.

Even as they loved, the temple within my father and the mosque within my mother shifted and transformed, each reshaped by the other's presence, creating something both tender and tragic. Each act of intimacy between them was an offering, a communion of spirits that moved beyond the constraints of language or tradition. And yet, in this act of union, there was a sense of inevitability, a knowledge that what they created together could not exist without exacting a toll. Each kiss, each whispered promise, was a reminder of the forces they had dared to defy, the identities they had dared to merge.

In the end, they were left with something indelible—a love that could not be erased, a sanctuary that was part temple, part mosque, a space of beauty and sacrifice. For my mother and father, the act of loving each other had been both a blessing and a curse, a paradox that could not be untangled. They became, in each other's arms, a testament to the possibility of union amidst division, to a truth that transcended creed and custom, even as it bore the scars of both.

It is this mystery—the merging of temple and mosque,

of two souls bound by love yet scarred by history, that lingered in their gaze, in the quiet spaces they shared, in the moments they spent, lost in each other. Their love was not meant to be understood, perhaps not even meant to be witnessed; it was a love meant to exist in whispers, in the delicate dance of light and shadow, a love that reshaped and scarred them in equal measure.

As I grew up, I had started recognizing that their love was not just a private affair; it was a statement about the boundaries that people often draw between themselves. My father, a Hindu man from a respected and powerful family, and my mother, a Muslim woman whose faith was rooted in her very being, had found a way to connect that went beyond the dogma and rituals that defined their religious identities. Their love—expressed in those quiet, tender moments—was proof that human beings were not meant to be divided by the constructs of religion, race, or culture. What they shared was pure, primal, and unencumbered by the labels that society had imposed on them.

In the world outside their bedroom, my parents were acutely aware of their differences. My father was a political man, and his career demanded that he maintain a strong, unyielding Hindu identity. His family, too, expected him to conform to traditions that held the separation of faiths as a given. Yasmin, on the other hand, had never wavered in her own commitment to her Muslim identity. The world outside them saw them as separate, as belonging to distinct, often conflicting worlds. Yet in the quiet of their shared space, these divisions melted away. There, in that moment of connection, they became something else entirely. They were simply two human beings, bound by something that transcended belief.

This was the first lesson I took from their relationship

—that religion, for all its power to shape lives and histories, is ultimately a human construct. It is a system of beliefs and rituals that serves to categorize and divide people, to place them into neat little boxes for easier understanding. But beneath those labels, beneath the walls of tradition, we are all the same. We share the same human desires, the same emotions, the same capacity for love and connection. My father and mother had found a way to bridge the artificial gap between them, a gap that the world had created. And in doing so, they showed me that no matter how much religion seeks to separate us, we are all connected by something far deeper by our shared humanity.

I think back to that night, to the way my parents moved together in quiet harmony. Their bodies entwined, yes, but it was more than that. It was the way they communicated without words, without the constraints of religion or family expectations. In that intimate space, they were free to be themselves—free to shed the identities that had been forced upon them by the world outside. They were not Hindu and Muslim, not political figures or religious representatives—they were simply Ramesh and Yasmin, two people who loved each other in a way that transcended everything else. That love was not defined by their faiths, by the weight of their cultural histories, or by the expectations of their families. It was raw, untainted by division.

As a child, I did not fully understand the significance of what I had witnessed. But as I grew older, the depth of their connection became clearer to me. The love between my parents wasn't about compromise or acceptance of differences. It was about a deep understanding that those differences did not matter. The human heart does not need to be divided by religion or nationality. What I saw between them was a quiet rebellion against the division that the world sought to impose. It was a rebellion of love, one that sought to tear down the walls between them, even if only in the privacy of their own space.

In the years that followed, I began to see more clearly how these divisions played out in the world around me. I saw the way people used religion as a weapon, as a tool to separate themselves from others. I saw the way families and communities were torn apart by the belief that their God, their way of life, was the only valid one. I watched as politics and power dynamics fueled hatred and mistrust, as people were forced into opposing camps based on something as arbitrary as the religion they happened to be born into. And yet, the love between my father and Yasmin remained and sustained itself, a quiet reminder that these divisions were not natural. They were human-made.

What I witnessed between them taught me that love does not recognize boundaries. Love is not confined by religious doctrine or the walls of tradition. In the intimacy of their shared moments, there was a profound truth: that the divisions we create between ourselves are often the result of fear, misunderstanding, and a lack of empathy. It is easy to look at someone from a different faith and see them as 'other,' to let differences become barriers that prevent us from connecting. But my parents' love taught me that these barriers are artificial. When we look beyond the labels—Hindu, Muslim, Christian, Jewish—we see the same faces, the same hearts, the same desires for peace, for connection, for understanding.

My father never spoke much about his relationship with Yasmin, especially not in the context of their religious differences. But the quiet way he loved her, the way he continued to seek her out despite the pressures of his political career and family expectations, spoke volumes.

It was an act of defiance against the divisions that society sought to impose. And it was this act of defiance that shaped my own understanding of the world. It was a lesson in empathy, in seeing the person before the label, in recognizing that we are all more alike than we are different.

As I grew older and began to navigate my own path in the world, I often found myself reflecting on the quiet love between my parents. I saw how human society constantly sought to divide people—through religion, race, politics—and how it created fear and hatred between groups that should have been united in their shared humanity. But every time I thought of Ramesh and Yasmin, of the way they loved each other despite the divisions between them, I felt a sense of peace. I knew, in my heart, that love—true, authentic love—has the power to transcend all of that. It has the power to break down the walls we build between ourselves, to dissolve the divisions that we cling to so tightly.

In the end, my father and mother taught me the most important lesson of all: that religion, race, nationality— all of these things are merely labels, systems of belief that humans have created to organize their lives. But underneath those labels, we are all the same. We all seek love, understanding, and connection. And when we let go of the divisions that religion often creates, we open ourselves up to the possibility of something far greater: unity. The love I witnessed between my parents, the quiet, rebellious love that transcended their faiths, has stayed with me throughout my life, a constant reminder that we are all bound together by something much deeper than the labels we place on each other.

And I do recognize that in the end, my father's story is not solely about his quest for political leadership. Instead, it is a testament to the complexity of human relationships, and to the profound impact of place on human identity. His journey through the intricate landscape of Ayodhya will remain etched in my memory, a vivid reminder of the sacrifices made and the dreams chased, even as the backdrop of our lives continues to shift and change. Through his experiences and his efforts, I have learned that the pursuit of greatness often comes at a huge human and an emotional cost. But that cost also has the power to inspire, heal, and unite a community longing for hope.

Even as I reflect on my father's legacy, I find myself drawn to the rivers that define this place, as if they carry answers to questions I have yet to fully form. My blood is both Ganga and Sarayu, and in this place where the rivers once met, I now search for the peace that eluded my ancestors. Perhaps in embracing both sides, I can become whole. I stand on the bank, watching the waters flow, each current whispering stories of long-forgotten lives, battles fought, and sacrifices made. The Ganga flows with a fierce, unrelenting purpose some sixty miles or more from where I am. It carries the wisdom from distant mountains. And the Sarayu moves in quiet dignity, her depths mirroring the strength of all those who held their ground here, against tides and time.

As the rivers' currents intertwine in my mind, I sense a deeper truth—that Ayodhya's story is not merely a tale of division or conflict, but of connections waiting to be rediscovered. In the silence of this moment, I realize that my blood, drawn from both these rivers, is neither divided nor conflicted but intertwined. The voices of my ancestors, those who spoke different languages and tongues, prayed to different gods, dreamed different dreams, all converge here, within me, asking for nothing but to be heard, honored, and at last, set free. Perhaps, by listening to each voice without judgment, I can find the peace they never knew. Perhaps, by embracing both rivers within me, I can finally become whole. My dual legacy, I realize now, can bring me inner peace only through my acceptance of my heritage.

I was born in Rama's city and raised with Allah's name on my tongue—a child shaped by two heritages that still hesitate to breathe the same air. Standing here in Ayodhya, a place where history trembles beneath our feet, I sometimes wonder: Can I carry both legacies, or must one always eclipse the other? In Ayodhya, where every stone remembers, I often ask myself: Must I choose one past over the other, or is it possible to live with both folded into my being? I close my eyes and the air hums—not with nostalgia, but with presence. Time presses close: saints, kings, rebels, lovers. Their voices hang in the trees, etched into thresholds and courtyards.

I am not whole in the usual sense. I am made of misfitting pieces—voices in different tongues, gestures from different homes, names that don't always sit comfortably side by side. As a child, I fell asleep to both Rama's journey and the music of the Quran. My mother, stirring a pot or folding my clothes, told me stories where *dharma* was an anchor. My father, after prayer, spoke softly of surrender, not as defeat but as clarity. Their hopes met in me—sometimes in harmony, sometimes in dissonance. And though I feared the weave might one day unravel, it never did. It held, even in silence.

Now, as an adult, I stand on the soil that carries both dreams and scars. How can one place hold so much? Ayodhya, the birthplace of a god, the place where a mosque once stood, a city where faith collided and left a wound that has never fully healed. I realize that my life, too, is a kind of Ayodhya—a land of contested memories, a home where belonging feels both undeniable and impossible. Perhaps I am not alone in this struggle.

Perhaps every person born to a land of layered histories must find a way to bridge the chasm between them. In this moment, or sometimes, I vow to be that bridge—not by erasing one half of myself to soothe the other, but by letting each side live freely within me. To hold the name of Rama and the name of Allah as two hands in prayer, not fists in battle.

This is my inheritance, my responsibility. To carry the weight of both worlds, not as a burden but as a testament. To be the child of two worlds and to stand in Ayodhya, whole, bridging the old and the new. Is it now my destiny to bind the fractures of time in a land where the past and future converge, bearing witness to what was, and what might yet be? What are these threads of understanding, I think and then, overthink?

EPILOGUE

The leaves in Oxford have a way of catching the light that makes the entire town seem like it is burning with muted gold. Each cobblestone beneath my feet feels older than time, yet oddly familiar, echoing the layered histories I carry within me. As I made my way to the Bodleian Library, the air carried the faint, crisp, but insistent smell of autumn—a quiet reminder that seasons, like people, never stay the same. This place, with its spires that seem to pierce through time itself, became my sanctuary after Ayodhya, a landscape of contradictions, lost loves, and my father's unrelenting pursuit of meaning through politics. Here, in this city of cloisters and silence, I sought refuge from Ayodhya. But Ayodhya is not a place one leaves behind. It haunts the marrow. It lives in the hesitation before a sentence, in the shadow between breaths. Even as I buried myself in the intellect of Oxford, the smoke of that ancient town, and of my father's impossible ideals, curled around me, refusing to dissipate. Even as I immersed myself in the rigors of my master's program, the echoes of home were never far away. Ayodhya lingers in my bones, in the spaces between my thoughts, wrapped around me like a shawl spun from another life.

I had returned to Oxford for further studies and for what I thought would be an escape—escape from the noise, the questions, the weight of inherited expectations. But Oxford with its ancient quiet, doesn't let you flee or escape. It turns you inward, pressing you into the unlit corridors of your own mind, the recesses where buried truths lie coiled and waiting. It was in one of those silent inner chambers that I began to understand—leaving Ayodhya had never been about running away. It was about carving out the space to breathe, to unbecome what the years and their relentless forces had shaped me into, and to begin, quietly, to shape myself anew.

I was midway through my thesis on the intersections of cultural memory and contested sacred spaces, a topic that both haunted and nourished me, when I met Ezra. It was in the most unremarkable of settings: a shared seminar on religious pluralism. But something in that room shifted when I noticed him. He didn't speak much. Instead, he listened—with an intensity that felt like gravity. There was a stillness to his attention, the kind that draws meaning out of silence. When we finally spoke, I understood: Ezra was one of those rare souls who listened not to reply, but to truly receive, as if your words mattered even before they were fully formed.

Ezra's background was as layered and paradoxical as the stories I had grown up with. His mother, Miriam, was a devout Christian who loved music with the same fervor she reserved for scripture; his father, David, a secular Jew, preferred Nietzsche to Nehemiah and enjoyed debating metaphysics over wine. "You'd think they'd be at war," he once said, half-laughing, "but really, they're two sides of the same coin—the edge just happens to be sharp." The line stayed with me. It struck me then how much his description reminded me of my parents, and echoed something deeper: the quiet ache of my own parents, Ramesh and Yasmin—two souls bound by love, yet slowly unbound by history, by the implacable weight of identity.

Ezra and I were different in ways that, on the surface, seemed irreconcilable. He moved through thought like a craftsman—measured, precise, sculpting meaning from silence. I lived in the scatter of ideas, the breathless leap from one notion to another, often speaking before I fully knew what I meant. He sought precision; I craved tangents, my thoughts leaping ahead of my words. But in that insurmountable tension, a strange music emerged. He taught me the elegance of pause, of choosing one's words like stones for a bridge. I showed him how to wander, how chaos could be a kind of map. We were not each other's refuge nor destination, but something far rarer—a shared motion, an ongoing unfolding. A journey without a final clause. Together, we were neither escape nor destination but the journey itself, a perpetual state of discovery.

Our interfaith selves were both mirror and prism—reflecting back our inheritances, refracting them into something new. Through Ezra, I began to understand faith not as a structure but as a texture: mutable, shimmering, a thing that can both root you and release you. He didn't profess belief in any singular doctrine, but he moved through the world with a quiet reverence—for ritual, for contradiction, for the mystery itself. That ambiguity both unsettled and steadied me.

"Do you believe in God?" I asked him once, as we sat by the river and watched moonlight fracture across the surface like a scripture written in ripples.

He thought for a moment, his gaze steady. "I believe in moments," he said finally. "In the way a melody can make you feel like you're touching something divine, or how a stranger's kindness can feel like grace. Maybe that's God, or maybe it's just us, trying to make sense of the chaos." His response both confounded and comforted me. It reminded me of my grandfather, Adil Khan, who had once told my mother, Yasmin, that God was not a being but a becoming. "God lives in the spaces between us," he had said, "in the moments when we choose love over fear." Sitting beside Ezra, I felt that space close, felt it brim with the quiet understanding that had eluded me for so long.

The deeper we wandered into each other's inner geographies, the more I began to excavate the buried architecture of my own. Ezra's questions—always feather-light in tone, yet scalpel-sharp in effect—always gentle, always incisive, compelled me to revisit the corners of my past I had sealed off like rooms filled with volatile air. I told him about Ayodhya—about the brittle holiness of a city stretched thin between devotion and devastation, about my father's steady ascent to a central cabinet post, and the Ram temple that stood like a paradox: both sanctuary and wound, both prayer and provocation. I told him about my mother—about Yasmin Khan's defiant quietude, her grace under erasure, the way she bore the fault lines of our family not as weaknesses, but as the seams that held us together in spite of everything.

And finally, I told him about myself—the girl who grew up straddling fault lines she didn't create, shaped by histories she hadn't chosen, learning early that belonging could be as sharp-edged as exile.

Ezra listened the way only he could—with presence so complete it softened the very air between us. When I finished, he didn't fill the silence with answers. Instead, he took my hand, looked at me with that unsettling clarity of his, and said:

"You're not caught, Saanvi. You're connected. And maybe that's heavier. Maybe it aches more. But it also means you carry the thread—and the thread matters."

His words lodged themselves somewhere deep within me, quietly rearranging the architecture of how I understood my own narrative. Where I had once traced only divisions, I began to see threads—fragile, tangled, but unbroken. The divisions no longer seemed absolute; they had become tensions within a larger weave. Ayodhya, with all its layered griefs and tangled mythologies, was no longer a place I needed to outrun. It was a palimpsest I had to learn to read—and eventually, to inhabit. I realized that Ayodhya, for all its complexities, was not something to be escaped but embraced, understood, carried forward.

Ezra and I completed our doctorates several years later—mine in History, his in Economics—each of us orbiting different disciplines, but tethered still by questions of memory, power, and belonging. By then, the world had shifted—subtly in places, violently in others. In Ayodhya, the Ram temple had been completed in 2024, its foundation poured from decades of longing, litigation, and blood. I had watched its rise from a distance—on breaks between semesters, through the fever of headlines—and witnessed the Ram Janmabhoomi temple when it was finally inaugurated. I could never quite capture the emotional sediment of the place myself, but through the photographs my father sent me, proud yet conflicted, I began to sense it.

In one image, the temple's spires pierced a cerulean sky, their intricate carvings standing like prayers etched into stone by hands both ancient and anonymous. In another, the streets swelled with people—some weeping, some shouting, all swept up in a moment that felt as much culmination as it did erasure. I studied those faces closely, looking for the city I once knew, and for the child I had once been—somewhere in the crowd, or perhaps just beyond it.

It was during one of these moments, as I showed Ezra the photos on my phone, that we began a conversation that would shape our future. The images were almost surreal, with the temple's intricate carvings bathed in golden light. "It's beautiful," he said, studying the images with the same quiet intensity I had first noticed in that seminar. "But it's also heavy, isn't it? Heavy with history."

I nodded, understanding exactly what he meant. The temple was a symbol of devotion, of identity, but it was also a reminder of the cost of such things, of the lives and loves sacrificed in their name. Yet, standing there with Ezra, I felt a sense of possibility, a belief that the weight of history did not have to anchor us but could instead ground us, give us the strength to move forward.

I smiled wanly, the weight of his words settling in my chest. "It's more than a temple," I said softly. "It's a symbol of so many things—faith, identity, division, fortitude. For my father, it was the pinnacle of his dreams, but for others, it's a reminder of what was lost."

Ezra looked at me then, his eyes filled with that quiet understanding I had come to cherish. "And for you?" he asked.

I hesitated, searching for the right words. "For me, it's a story," I said finally. "A story I'm still trying to understand."

Ezra reached for my hand, his touch grounding me. "Maybe that's the point," he said. "Maybe some stories aren't meant to be understood fully. Maybe they're meant to be lived with, to be carried."

As our time at Oxford drew to a close, Ezra and I began to speak in tentative outlines of what might come next. We were drawn to academia—not just for its rituals of scholarship, but for the space it offered to question, to listen, to shape and be reshaped by inquiry. By the time we graduated, our futures felt not prescribed, but tentatively plotted—like constellations we had traced together.

Ezra accepted a teaching position in Economics at a university in London; I followed soon after with a lectureship in History. Our fields differed, but the conversations between them—and between us—deepened. We imagined a life built not just on shared affection, but on shared restlessness: the desire to think harder, to understand better, to speak across the gaps most people tiptoe around.

At times, Ezra spoke of founding an interfaith initiative—one rooted less in doctrine than in listening, in the quiet work of nurturing dialogue in places where silence had become a shield. I understood the impulse. I, too, had lived with the weight of inherited fault lines. I began to see how our home, modest as it might be, could one day become a site for gathering—not as a platform, but as a threshold. A space where stories, braided from different worlds, could be offered without fear and received without interruption.

We didn't speak in declarations. We spoke in gestures, in the slow weaving of daily life, in the hope that our future could be porous and generous—untethered from the binaries that had once hemmed us in.

By 2028, Ezra and I were married in a small, interfaith ceremony surrounded by friends and family. It was a ceremony that blended the traditions of our families while remaining uniquely ours. My father, then a senior minister in the central cabinet, delivered a speech that was equal parts wit and tenderness, threading stories from my childhood with his cautious, hard-won blessings for our future. My mother's presence was quieter, more distilled, but no less profound. She held my hand as I walked down the aisle, her eyes brimming with the kind of pride no language can quite hold.

When my parents draped a garland around Ezra's neck, their hands trembled slightly, as if releasing something and accepting something all at once. Ezra's father, David, spoke next—his words somehow managing to disarm and disarm again, leaving the room laughing through its tears.

It was a day of unguarded joy, of long-held contradictions resting side by side in temporary peace. A day of connection. Of becoming—just as my paternal grandmother had once described: not as resolution, but as widening.

We travelled to Ayodhya one winter, and it was inevitable that Ezra would see the Ram temple. The air was thick as ever with devotion, but beneath it, something heavier lingered—the sediment of centuries, the weight of memory pressing down on the present. Ezra walked beside me, his presence calm, almost anchoring, as we moved through streets throbbing with both devotion and dissonance. I saw the temple not through my father's eyes, sharpened by politics and legacy, nor through my mother's, shaped by silence and endurance—but through my own, at last. It stood not just as a monument to faith, but as a mirror to the contradictions that shaped us: sacred and scarred, triumphant and troubled.

As we left the temple and walked toward the Sarayu River, the wind carried with it something almost imperceptible, a loosening. I felt a strange lightness, as if the burdens I had carried for so long were beginning to lift. Ayodhya, for all its scars, was still home. And for the first time, I felt at peace with that truth.

As the years passed, we found ourselves returning to these conversations, each one adding another layer to our understanding of faith, history, and the spaces between. Our interfaith identities became not just a mirror but a map, guiding us through the complexities of our shared and individual pasts.

Now, as I sit by the window of our flat, watching the rain blur the city into a watercolor of grays and greens, I think of Ayodhya. I think of my father, whose ambition was both his gift and his weakness. I think of my mother, whose patience and grace taught me the true meaning of strength. I think of Ezra, whose presence has become the still point in my ever-turning world. And I think of myself, of the girl who once felt caught and now feels connected.

Ayodhya is no longer just a place. It is a story, fragmented, filled with moments, a constellation of moments that remind me we are all shaped not only by where we come from, but by the spaces between us. And as I watch the rain fall, I understand now: those spaces are not absences but bridges—fragile, flawed, yet strong enough to carry us forward.

This is not an ending, but a threshold. A beginning threaded with histories and futures, mine and Ayodhya's, intertwined in ways I am still learning to name. It is my futurology, an epilogue of possibility, where the past breathes quietly into the present, and memory kindles the quiet fire that shapes what is yet to come.

Dr. Nishi Chawla

Nishi Chawla is an academic, a writer and a filmmaker. Nishi Chawla has published ten plays, two novels, and seven collections of poetry. She has also written and directed four award winning art house feature films. She has also co-edited two global anthologies of poetry published by Penguin Random House: ***"Greening the Earth"*** and ***"Singing in the Dark."***

Dr Nishi Chawla holds a doctorate in English from the George Washington University, Washington D.C., and her post-doctorate from the Johns Hopkins University, Baltimore, Maryland. After teaching for nearly twenty years as a tenured Professor of English at Delhi University, India, Nishi Chawla had migrated with her family to a suburb of Washington D.C. She has taught English Literature for forty years at the University level.

Nishi Chawla has recently completed her fourth feature film, *"The Peace Activists"* on Gandhi, MLK, and Thoreau. Three of her art house feature films are on Amazon Prime: **'TechNous,' 'The Strange Case of Normalcy,'** and **'Mixed Up'** are streaming on Amazon Prime, and **'The Peace Activists'** should also be on Prime at the end of 2024.

Dr Nishi Chawla's play, *'Kasturba versus Gandhi'* was staged in New York in an off Broadway production in June 2024. Her tenth play, *'The Mahatma versus Gurudev'* has been accepted to be staged in June 2025 again off Broadway, New York, making her one of the few Indian playwrights to ever have a play staged off Broadway.